W9-AAA-189

# ERUPTION

Praise for

# ERUPTION

"Adrienne Quintana delivers with a plot that erupts with action and keeps you guessing."

—C. J. HILL
Author of *Erasing Time*

"Quintana masterfully balances urgent mysteries with alarming answers as Eruption unfolds. Every twist will keep you rocketing through this intense thriller in a search for the truth."

—EMILY H. BATES
Author of *Demon's Heart*

"Quintana has an easy visual style that drops you right into the story and takes you for a suspenseful ride that uses the mystery of an uncertain future to build pressure until the entire story explodes. *Eruption* takes an unnerving look forward as the marvelous use of the technology we are familiar with today expands into a full-blown terror of the information age."

—RANDY LINDSAY
Author of *The Gathering: End's Beginning*

"Hooked me from the first scene and didn't let go until the mind-blowing end. Seriously awesome book."

—R. C. HANCOCK
Author of *An Uncommon Blue*

"In her premiere sci-fi offering, Adrienne Quintana delivers an action thriller with a unique angle on time manipulation. Exploding with clock-ticking suspense and high-technology intrigue, Eruption provides us a glimpse into the alternative shape of things to come that is both fascinating and compelling. Jace Vega is a new kind of heroine—fresh, smart, vulnerable, and unwittingly prepared from the cradle with a secret from the future that she alone can decipher. Jace's 'memories' are the key to a genuine race against time to deliver the world from a destiny of domination."

—STEPHEN J. STIRLING
Author of *Persona Non Grata* and *Shedding Light on the Dark Side*

# ADRIENNE QUINTANA

# ERUPTION

SWEETWATER
BOOKS

AN IMPRINT OF CEDAR FORT, INC.
SPRINGVILLE, UTAH

© 2015 Adrienne Quintana

All rights reserved.

No part of this book may be reproduced in any form whatsoever, whether by graphic, visual, electronic, film, microfilm, tape recording, or any other means, without prior written permission of the publisher, except in the case of brief passages embodied in critical reviews and articles.

This is a work of fiction. The characters, names, incidents, places, and dialogue are products of the author's imagination and are not to be construed as real. The opinions and views expressed herein belong solely to the author and do not necessarily represent the opinions or views of Cedar Fort, Inc. Permission for the use of sources, graphics, and photos is also solely the responsibility of the author.

ISBN 13: 978-1-4621-1536-5

Published by Sweetwater Books, an imprint of Cedar Fort, Inc.
2373 W. 700 S., Springville, UT 84663
Distributed by Cedar Fort, Inc., www.cedarfort.com

LIBRARY OF CONGRESS CATALOGING-IN-PUBLICATION DATA

Quintana, Adrienne, 1976- author.
Eruption / Adrienne Quintana.
    pages cm
Just after quiet Jace Vega becomes one of Omnibus's newest employees, a mysterious new technology falls into her hands that shows a future in which Omnibus gains absolute political and military power.
ISBN 978-1-4621-1536-5 (perfect : alk. paper)
[1. Time travel--Fiction. 2. Identity--Fiction. 3. Science fiction.] I. Title.
PZ7.1.Q59Er 2015
[Fic]--dc23
                                        2014032419

Cover design by Kristen Reeves
Cover design © 2015 by Lyle Mortimer
Edited and typeset by Melissa J. Caldwell

Printed in the United States of America

10  9  8  7  6  5  4  3  2  1

*For Phil, Jake, Marina, Vivienne, Eve, and especially Marnae.*
*You took every exciting step of this journey with me*
*and always believed it could happen.*

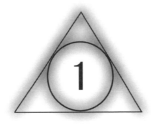

**I** gasped for air and my eyes popped open just before the alarm began buzzing. I reached up and silenced it immediately. Monday morning. Waking up was a relief. Familiarity, structure, routine: all survival techniques.

My hair was matted, and my eyes were moist. At the end of my bed, the sheets were twisted in a knot. After my heart and breathing slowed, I ran my fingers through my hair and then reached for a hair tie on the nightstand. My dream must have been intense, but I couldn't remember it. The more I tried, the heavier the fog became. It isn't abnormal for people to forget dreams, but it always bothered me—maybe because my memory was extraordinary otherwise.

Getting outside would push away my uneasiness. I slid into my running clothes almost noiselessly. Smoothing out my sheets, I tucked them in at the bottom, hospital corners. After a few sips of water, I connected my earbuds to my phone and slid it into an armband. I shut the front door softly, even though I knew my roommate was a heavy sleeper, and then tucked the key into my pocket.

The sounds from the city were soft in the distance. Living on the outer edge of St. Paul, I was closer to the cornfields in Wisconsin than the city skyline. Only a few blocks down the road, I would turn onto the creek path and away from any trace of noise and civilization. I missed the salty wind on Spanish Bay and the sand on the boardwalk, but Minnesota was growing on me. I waited until I was on the street to make a few lame attempts at stretching. I never held a stretch long enough to actually do any good. I only did it because my father said I should.

"If you want to be a runner, you need to train like one, mija," he always said. I smiled. *Mija*—I wasn't fluent in Spanish, but even when I was little I knew it meant I was Daddy's girl. I don't remember ever telling him that I wanted to be a runner; it had always been his plan for me. But I grew to like it until eventually it became part of me.

I took a deep breath and started my running playlist. I waited until the musical freight train passed and the guitar started on "Runnin' with the Devil." Each song on the list matched the cadence I wanted for warm-up, workout, and cooldown. I never deviated from the list. I pushed "start" on my run tracker and darted off into the dark. The run tracker was motivated more by habit than anything else. I was in Central Time. No one on the West Coast would "like" my run for several hours.

A hint of orange began to warm the horizon in the east. Cool air would soon become sticky and heavy. A few birds already chatted back and forth. A streetlight flicked off just as I passed it. I jumped. I still felt a little off, but I tried to ignore it. The darkness inside me would decrease gradually as the sun rose. Routine would make me feel normal.

I passed the middle-aged man in red shorts before reaching the creek path. He was a little faster than usual this morning—we normally crossed paths near the bridge. His wife must need him home by 7:30. Or maybe it was his turn to drive the carpool. He kept his eyes straight ahead until just before we passed each other. We both smiled and nodded. His wrinkles bounced up and down. He glanced at my legs before looking over at the trees on the left. *Fascinating trees. He can't get enough of the white spruce. Good man.*

"You Shook Me All Night Long" came on. I picked up my pace. The thick greenery cleared my head and let me breathe. Fifteen minutes passed with only my blood pumping to the beat of the music. When I reached the end of the trail at McKnight Road, I stopped and glanced at the Omnibus corporate building, which towered over the freeway in the distance. The quick construction of the corporate building reminded me of the company itself. I had never heard of Omnibus five years ago, and now it would be difficult to go anywhere without seeing someone using an Omnibus device. They had done a fine job of selling and promoting themselves to the public. Now that I worked for them, promoting Omnibus was my job.

The uncanny feeling that I had experienced this scene before made the hair on the back of my neck stand on end. Déjà vu. I turned away. I *had* seen all of this before—almost every day for over a month. The feeling would pass. It always did.

The sun streamed through the spaces between the trees in the park across the street and reflected off the pond. I was still tingling. Normally I would have turned right around and continued my run, but today I was going to take a picture instead—just after the red Chevy Camaro passed. I took my phone out of the armband. The noise of the car's engine purred toward me. I waited until it was gone before looking up to snap a few pictures of the pond. The weird feeling faded.

I slid my iPhone back into the plastic. It was probably time to consider switching to an Omnibus product. The company offered incentives for employees, but I resisted. I didn't want to adjust to a new one. I looked at my phone again to restart the music and saw my mom's face on the screen. It was dialing her number. I rushed to disconnect. I must have bumped the phone icon and her contact in my favorites. I couldn't make myself delete it, despite how much it hurt to look at it. I started running back down the path. She would never answer again when I called. I tried to focus on the path ahead of me, but my vision was blurred. I turned up my music, trying to drown out the thoughts.

*Maybe I should call a grief counselor.* I had considered talking to someone in Monterey, but I knew my father wouldn't approve. I should be strong enough to deal with things on my own.

Just before the next bend in the path, the emerging sunrays broke through the thick, leafy canopy behind me. Something reflected the light on the path ahead, temporarily blinding me as a shadow darted across the path. My hand flew up to my brow, but the flash had triggered an intense, stabbing headache. Skidding to a stop, I closed my eyes.

\* \* \*

*Dizzy. I'm on a swing. Patent leather Mary Janes appear and disappear as I pump my legs in front of me. A mountain smolders in the distance.*

*"Jace!" a woman's voice calls.*

\* \* \*

My eyes reopened as the pain subsided. Prickly goose bumps covered my body. I shook my head and my vision cleared. While I was trying to reorient myself, I saw the underbrush and tree branches to the left of the path whip violently back and forth. The rest of the trees around me were still. The shadow was gone. My heart raced, and I jerked my earbuds out. Skin tingling, I slowly moved toward where it had crossed. *Breathe. If it's a bear, stand still. If it's a mugger, run.* I clenched my fists.

As I got closer, I saw what had reflected the sun lying in the grass just off the path—a sleek black tablet. Someone had dropped it. What were they running from? My heart pounded.

"Hey, wait!" I yelled, looking toward the trees. I ran to the tablet and stood over it for a few seconds. I looked behind me before bending down to touch it. The faint noise of the cars on the freeway hummed in the distance, and the creek bubbled a few yards away, but I couldn't hear anything else. Whoever had dropped it was gone.

I picked it up. It was thin, lightweight, and more square-shaped than my iPad. A single button in the lower right corner glowed with a slowly flashing green *O*. The Omnibus logo—only the lines on the side of the *O* were thicker and the gradient made it look almost metallic when the green light wasn't illuminated. It was brand new. I imagined the panic that losing something like this would cause me. My heart pushed against my chest. *I can catch them.*

I tucked it under my arm and sprinted to the edge of the trees. Pushing through the underbrush and branches, I jumped over the creek. Whoever the tablet belonged to couldn't have gone far. The sidewalk was only a few yards up the hill. I negotiated the brush and avoided most of the mud until I broke through onto the empty neighborhood street.

"Hey!" I shouted again.

Nothing.

I looked right and left. No trace of life. The neighborhood was asleep.

I looked at my phone in the armband for the time. It said 7:15. My body tensed. I needed to get ready for work. Right was the only option. If I went the other direction, I would be late. Running full speed down the sidewalk, I kept my eyes as far ahead of me as possible, alert for any movement.

The tablet was throwing off my form. I couldn't swing my arms to keep up with my legs. After a few minutes of running at breakneck speed toward nothing, I slowed back to a steady jog. Anyone looking out of their window would think I had totally lost it. Maybe the tablet owner had gone the other way.

The stillness of the morning faded as the sun moved higher in the sky. Like a radio being turned up a notch at a time, the volume of the traffic increased as I ran toward the freeway. The street was empty. I was alone.

I made my way back to my townhouse, opening the door just as quietly as I had when leaving. Sheila's steady snoring drifted down the hallway. The Union Jack corner of the Australian flag that my roommate had pinned to her door hung limp in the half-open doorway. One of the tacks must have fallen out.

I set the tablet down and grabbed a hand towel to wipe away some of the sweat on my forehead. Out of the corner of my eye, I saw the flashing green light—much brighter in the darkness of my room. I walked to the window and opened the blinds. Pixie dust particles danced in the sunrays. Coming back to the bed, I lifted the tablet again. I looked it over, spinning it in my hands a few times. Should I turn it on? My stomach was suddenly full of butterflies. I didn't want to invade anyone's privacy.

I set it back down on my bed and unstrapped my armband, placing my phone next to the tablet before kicking off my shoes and socks and pulling off my sweaty T-shirt. 7:20. I needed to get into the shower. I watched the faint glow of the flashing light as I went into the bathroom and turned on the water. It always took a few seconds to warm up. I should at least turn the thing on to see if it worked.

I came back to the bed and picked up the tablet again. Ignoring the increasing flutters in my stomach, I pressed the glowing button. The screen lit up immediately, but instead of flat images appearing on the glass, the Omnibus logo was projected above the tablet forming a three-dimensional holographic image.

"Whoa!" I stepped away with trembling hands. It was hard enough to believe that Omnibus was developing this technology and even more surprising that it was already floating around in public.

I stood still, waiting for the symbol to disappear. Nothing happened. I touched several places on the glass screen. Nothing. If the button turned it on, it only seemed logical that it would turn it off too. After touching the glowing button several more times with no change, I finally gave up and went back to the shower. I didn't have time for this.

Not a good way to start the day. How was I going to return the tablet to its owner if I couldn't access any of the information on it? Maybe I should have just left it on the ground. Someone was bound to be looking for it and would probably retrace their steps when they realized it was missing.

My roommate from freshman year, Gina, had found a cell phone on campus a few years ago. The phone was expensive, but the battery had been dead. I had convinced her to turn it in at the security office in the old Union building where she had found it. Maybe I could turn the tablet in to Security at Omnibus. Someone there would know how to get past the startup screen. They could deal with finding the owner.

My routine was completely thrown off. I should already be blow drying. Annoying. I quickly washed and conditioned my hair and scrubbed myself down before turning off the water. I would have to let it dry naturally.

While I was still dripping on the bath mat, my phone began buzzing and flashing on the bed next to the tablet. It was unusual for me to get any phone calls here, but it was even stranger before 8:00 a.m. I dried my legs, threw the towel around me, and dashed to the phone. Just as I picked it up, the buzzing and flashing stopped and the missed call appeared on the screen. I didn't recognize the number—probably a telemarketer.

I carried my phone with me and went back to the bathroom, running a pick through my long hair. The phone flashed again. It was 7:35. I should have waited to listen to the message until I was in the car, but curiosity overcame me. I went back to the bedroom and set the phone down on my dresser. Putting it on speaker, I listened to the message while I opened my underwear drawer. The tablet was still projecting the Omnibus symbol above where it was sitting on my bed, but the light had dimmed slightly.

"Hello, this is Ramsey Dental Professionals calling to confirm an appointment for tomorrow, August 18, at 7:00 a.m. for Jace Vega."

"Voice recognition invalid," a clear, robotic female voice chimed. I jumped and dropped my bra on the floor. Whipping around, I covered myself with the towel again. The tablet screen was fully illuminated on the bed. The voice mail continued, instructing me to contact them if I needed to reschedule the appointment.

I put on my underwear before picking up the tablet again. The glowing light taunted me. Voice activated. That explained why touching it didn't do anything. I slid it inside my straw tote, still feeling like someone was watching me and laughing—but then, no one besides Sheila knew me well enough to get any pleasure out of the anxiety this little mystery was causing.

I finished getting dressed and ready in record time. Setting my purse on the seat next to me in the car, I saw the faint glow of the dimmed Omnibus logo through the holes in the straw. I tried to push aside my feelings of uneasiness. I hadn't done anything wrong. I was just trying to get this back to its owner.

I picked up my phone and tapped the number for the dentist's office. The appointment had been set two weeks ago after hunting around for a dentist that had extended business hours, but now I didn't want to keep it. It would interrupt my run. I couldn't miss my run. I would see if I could schedule a lunchtime appointment, even if it meant having a six-and-a-half month checkup.

The receptionist answered on the third ring and immediately put me on hold. The light changed. I was under the freeway overpass and almost to the Omnibus campus entrance when she finally came back on the line.

"Hello, this is Jace Vega," I began.

"Voice recognition validated," the tablet spoke clearly from my purse. My eyes shot down to the seat next to me. The phone fell out of my hands between the seat and the center console. Light flashed several times through the holes in my bag. I swerved over to the side of the road north of the overpass. I slowly took the tablet out of my bag. The company symbol had been replaced by three holographic icons: a hammer crossed over a pickax, a camera lens, and the Omnibus symbol intertwined with the letter J. *Why would it respond to my voice?* Every part of me tingled.

"Hello?" the receptionist's voice sounded annoyed. Reaching down to the floor, I felt for my phone. "Hello?" she said again. I found it. Fumbling, I looked back and forth between the two devices.

"Power down," I said instinctively. The tablet went dark. Watching the flashing green light for a second, I jumped when the receptionist spoke again,

"Can I help you?"

A car honked as it sped past me and turned into the Omnibus parking lot just a few yards ahead.

"I need to cancel my appointment," I said.

Speed walking toward the entrance of the building, I glanced at the time on my phone. Three minutes late. The last thing I needed was one more reason for my supervisor, Holly, to dislike me. My stomach knotted into a ball. The security guard was distracted as I emptied the electronics out of my purse before sending it through the X-ray machine. He glanced briefly at my security badge and then smiled at me. The bulky, blond-haired guard had been friendly since my first day. His thick Minnesota accent made his attempts at flirting almost comical.

"Boy, your hair sure is curly today, Ms. Vega," was a typical compliment. I wasn't sure that "thank you" was an appropriate response, but I couldn't think of anything else to say as I passed through the body scanner.

"It looks like you had a fun weekend," he said as I put my phone back in my purse. Mitch must have been one of the 134 likes I had gotten on the selfie taken with the Spoonbridge and Cherry in the background at the Minneapolis Sculpture Garden. The lighting at sunset was nice even without a filter, but Lo-Fi made the sky look unearthly.

"Hey, Mitch," I said, showing him the tablet as I pulled it out of the electronic scan basket. "Have you seen one of these before?"

I slipped the tablet into his hands, and he turned it over, inspecting it.

"Well, yeah. It looks like one of ours." He touched the Omnibus symbol. "Looks a little different, though. It's probably a prototype. Where did you get it?"

"Out on my run this morning. In the grass next to the path down by Battle Creek," I said. "Someone dropped it."

"Oh, that can't be good. I don't think prototypes are supposed to leave the campus. Someone is probably going to take some heat for this." I hadn't thought of that. Had someone stolen the tablet? Whoever had dropped it was running from something. I hoped no one would think I had been involved. They were bound to wonder how my voice was able to activate it. My palms began to sweat. "You should take it down to James Lansing. Have you met him yet? He's the project manager over tablet development."

James Lansing's face instantly popped into my head. I had seen his picture on a senior management flowchart. Take it to a manager. Product development. I had been hoping to hand it over to Mitch, but maybe it would be better to take it to James Lansing myself and explain what had happened.

Not wanting to tip Mitch off to one of my freak-show quirks, I downplayed my total facial recall. "I'll look him up. Thanks, Mitch."

"No problem." His cheeks turned red, and a dopey grin spread across his face. He was proud of himself. He looked just like Willard from the old *Footloose*. I turned and walked toward the elevators, feeling Mitch's eyes on me until I turned the corner. *He probably can't dance either.* I laughed to myself.

I stopped by my desk on the third floor, hung my purse, logged on to my computer, and checked my messages before looking for James Lansing's department on the building directory. I was just reaching for the tablet in my purse when Holly came by my desk in her flashy red heels and just slightly too-short skirt.

"Staff meeting in five minutes," she chimed. I pulled my hand away from my tote. The tablet business would have to wait for an hour. I grabbed a pad and pen and followed her to the conference room.

I admired Holly, but she intimidated me. Confident and powerful, she was still in her early thirties, tall, and slender. She wore her shiny golden hair tucked into a smooth ponytail or bun with strategic loose tendrils lapping at her jaw and the nape of her neck. Even though I always made sure to prioritize any work that she gave me, I got the vibe that she didn't like me. Her demeanor let me know that I had to prove myself with her, and rightly so. I was sure that she didn't appreciate the fact that she hadn't been involved in my hiring process.

Staff meetings were still uncomfortable for me. Aside from Holly's incredulous glances, I hated being the newbie. People didn't value my opinion yet. Even though I had the same job title as the six associates in the department, I was still a gofer for them while I learned the ropes. Occasionally they would let me help on a press release or have me review advertisements, but I mostly proofread brochures and web content. Today's meeting was especially tedious because a Human Resources representative was going over some changes in benefit packages. I wasn't even eligible for benefits yet.

I tried to stay focused, making a few notes about 401(k) plans and dental coverage, but my mind kept drifting back to my strange morning. I tapped my pen softly against my leg under the table. My weird out-of-body experience before I found the tablet puzzled me. We didn't have a swing set in Italy, and you couldn't see the mountain from the swing set at school.

I could feel Holly's eyes on me, but I didn't look at her. I wondered what she would say about the prototype in my purse. Maybe I should have shown it to her. I swallowed and tried to relax my shoulders. I brought my pen to the paper, trying to look like I was taking notes.

A familiar neck tingle started again. The HR guy was going to say something about sexual harassment training.

"Next month we are going to go over the sexual harassment section in the employee handbook. I'll send all of you the link so that you can review it beforehand," he said.

I closed my eyes. I really hoped that the forums on WebMD were right. Except for the people with epilepsy-related déjà vu, most people with chronic cases said it would decrease after 25. *Only a few more months.*

The meeting ended. I looked down at the doodle I had made: a rough sketch of the Omnibus logo with an interlaced J. I stared at it for a second, completely blank. After the fishbowl feeling passed, I realized I had drawn it. I slowly scribbled over it, glancing up at Holly, who was watching me out of the corner of her eye while she chatted with Jim Evans.

I gathered my notebook and hurried back to my desk. The tablet was safe inside my purse, just as I had left it. I watched the green light flash for a second. I put the strap over my shoulder. It was time to take it to James Lansing. I looked at the scribbled doodle on my notebook. What was behind the icon I had seen in my car? More holograms? I felt overwhelming curiosity. My stomach dropped. *What is wrong with you?* I thought. *It's not yours and it's none of your business. Get rid of it and get back to normal.*

I hurried to the empty elevator and punched the button for the first floor. For a second, I wondered what a normal person would do in these circumstances. Sheila probably would have looked at everything on it before even leaving the house and then called all of her friends to tell them about it. She didn't have much regard for people's property or privacy. I was doing the right thing.

The elevator stopped at the first floor and I stepped out. I tried to rehearse what I would say to James Lansing in my head, but my mind was blank. How was I going to explain the voice activation thing? I wondered if someone was going to be fired for this. Only a few people were in the security area near the entrance. I turned in the opposite direction, toward the east wing of the building. My heart pounded and I could feel the blood rushing to my head. *Breathe.*

Several conference rooms lined the long corridor that led to the product development area. My heels clicked against the flecked white-tile floor. I glanced into each empty room through the rectangular windows in the doors as I passed. The fishbowl feeling started and my head began to spin. I walked faster, hoping to reach the end of the hallway before the tunnel vision set in. I wasn't going to have a full-blown panic attack at work. I couldn't.

Near the end of the hallway I came to a door with no window. I could barely read the blurry silver plaque that said "maintenance" hanging to the left of the door. My arm tingled as I reached for the handle. I glanced behind me. The corridor was empty.

I pushed the door open and stepped inside. Closing it quickly, I stood with my back against it. *In through the nose on a three count, out through the mouth.* The dark calmed me slightly, but the shapes of the janitorial supplies slowly reappeared as my eyes adjusted to the blackness. Tingles and familiarity replaced panic. I looked up at the air conditioning ducts just before they began to rattle and hum, but the noise still made me jump. I let out a low breath and waited for the feeling to pass.

Maybe I couldn't handle things on my own. Was I really so close to a nervous breakdown that worrying about someone else getting fired could push me over the edge? *Pull yourself together and be rational.*

When my eyes adjusted to the dim light, I moved farther into the small room and away from the door. I lifted the tablet out of my bag and watched the light from the glowing button cast eerie shadows against the walls for a moment. Maybe it wasn't the other person that I was worried about at all. What if James Lansing didn't believe me? What if somehow I got fired for this?

Shortness of breath returned and I clutched the tablet against my chest. I wasn't being rational. What would my mom say? What would a normal person do? Maybe there was a different solution. What difference would it make if I turned it on again and looked for a familiar face on the camera? Or maybe I could find the name of who it was registered to in the settings. Maybe no one had to be fired. The thought was oddly soothing.

I set the tablet down on a box and pressed the glowing Omnibus button before I could change my mind. The Omnibus symbol filled the room with light.

"Jace Vega," I whispered.

"Voice recognition validated," the robotic voice chimed. I shivered. Where was the volume control? The three icons appeared. The details of the images were much more distinct in the darkness.

"Open settings," I said softly.

The icon with the hammer and pickax expanded as the other icons diminished in size. "Proceed with password," the voice demanded.

Password protected! *Why am I even doing this? Just turn it into James Lansing.* My shoulders tensed, and I almost powered the tablet down again, but I couldn't pull my eyes away from the camera icon. I might as well try to open it too. I was already in the closet of the future unemployed.

"Open camera," I said, my heart beating slowly and rhythmically in my ears.

The camera lens expanded, and the other two icons faded away. Two labeled file folders replaced them. One was titled Omnibus and the other was labeled Personal. I thought about which file to open.

The Personal file was more likely to have a selfie, but somehow the Omnibus file felt less intrusive.

"View Omnibus file," I finally said.

"Displaying full images in chronological slide show, beginning with most recent," the tablet's voice informed me. An image materialized and came into focus. I recognized the scene immediately—I had taken a very similar photo several years ago when my father had chartered a helicopter tour of the capital, but the National Mall was missing completely from this aerial image of Washington D.C. Two massive, hideous buildings stood between the Washington Monument and the Capitol Building. My heart raced as I scanned the image—a less-than-subtle Omnibus symbol had been placed near the top of the Washington Monument. I traced the shape of it in the air. The image gradually faded as I completed the O.

The new image was equally strange: the steps of the Capitol Building filled with hundreds of soldiers assembled at attention. Intimidating black uniforms with red triangular emblems on the left breast pocket. Reflective helmets and large black guns—something straight out of a bad sci-fi movie. I touched the tablet. For the first time, I had an inkling about the identity of the tablet's owner. It had to be a student. I had completed some strange projects like this in school. I could imagine one of my professors giving the assignment: "Show me how this product is the future. Show me how it will change the world."

These images were a strange way of showing it, but they did clearly get the message across that Omnibus was on the road to dominating America. My lips twitched as I smiled, wondering if my Photoshop skills would ever be this proficient. My shoulders dropped a little and the tension released, imagining this familiarity.

The second image began to fade away as two figures dressed in white appeared, standing arm in arm. The image became fully illuminated. I was staring into a three-dimensional mirror. My heart stopped and then began to race. My long, wavy chestnut hair hung loose over each of my shoulders, covering most of the top of the long white lab coat I wore. I took a step backward into a rope mop, almost tipping the yellow wringer bucket over.

*I'm losing it.* I closed my eyes tight for a few seconds, completely clearing my mind before opening them again. Still there. My stomach felt like it was in a vise grip. My eyes moved to the figure standing next to me. Corey Stein. Freshman English. His hair was shorter, and he was completely clean shaven, but it had to be him. With his thick, dark eyebrows framing his piercing blue eyes and angular features, he stood out. Even though he had lived in my apartment complex, just off the Stanford campus, I didn't really know him. I had seen him coming and going from an apartment on the other side of the pool from mine. I had always been curious about him, but we had never actually spoken. I had no idea that he was also working for Omnibus.

"Stop slide show," I said a little too loudly. I took three steps toward the hologram. How did hologram technology work? Could someone convert a conventional image of me into a hologram? But how was I in this image with someone I barely knew? And why did my voice activate it? My eyes were drawn to the emblem on the left pocket of Corey's lab coat. The triangular red patch on the pocket displayed the familiar O, identical to the flashing green logo on the tablet.

I pulled my phone out of my purse. 9:23. I needed to get back to my desk. "Power down," I frantically whispered. I needed to find Corey Stein.

I tried to convince myself that I looked normal and casual as I walked away from the maintenance closet, but my legs were moving too fast, and I couldn't slow them. I glanced at my tote, wishing I had brought one of my winter bags or a briefcase instead. How could I give the tablet to James Lansing now? He was going to turn it on and look at it. What would he think when he saw me in that third image? Would he think I had stolen it? Or worse, what if the Washington, DC, images weren't a project or a joke? I tried to calm myself. I knew I wasn't being rational.

Back at my desk, Holly had emailed several brochure mock-ups to proofread. I should have finished them right away, but I couldn't keep my mind from drifting back to the dark closet and the image of Corey Stein standing next to me.

Considering the fact that we had been neighbors at school for six years, I knew very little about him. His comments in our English class had been thoughtful and intelligent. My curiosity had been strangely piqued, but I didn't know the first thing about how to approach him and he'd never shown any interest in me. He even seemed to avoid eye contact. I wasn't sure if he was that way with everyone, or if it was just with me.

I opened a new tab on my browser and found the company's employee directory. I glanced up over my monitor before typing in his name. I waited impatiently for the results to load. The screen informed me that none of the names in the database matched. Did

I want to see similar names? I clicked yes. After scrolling down the page of unfamiliar names and faces, I was surprised and disappointed to find that Corey Stein was not an employee at Omnibus. How was I going to find him now?

*Focus.* I closed the tab and forced myself to concentrate on the brochures. The morning ticked away slowly. I shifted around the papers on my desk, trying unsuccessfully to focus on something else. At 11:15, I quit pretending to work, picked up my bag, and went to the cafeteria. I could barely wait to walk outside. The cafeteria was in the main corporate building. Omnibus had spared no expense on the interior of the brand-new facility. White walls and floors were accented by bright primary-colored furniture and abstract artwork. The décor was tasteful, clean, and simple.

Approaching the reception area, I heard Damien Trent's voice before I saw his distinctive figure leaning casually against the desk. He was engrossed in a flirty conversation with Amber, the attractive blonde receptionist. He looked too young to be a vice president. I suspected that as the son of the company founder, Victor Trent, Damien was merely a figurehead at Omnibus. After more than a month without running into him, I wasn't sure if he ever came in to the office. I was glad. He was exactly the type of guy I tried to avoid—the type who expected women to swoon if he even batted his eyes in their direction. Amber's loud laugh rang out.

I turned away. *Today of all days!* I had been hoping to avoid him altogether, but with a stolen prototype in my purse, today was especially unfortunate. The reception area was busy with people coming to and from the cafeteria. I debated whether to turn around or continue on. If I stayed near the outer edge of the room, I would avoid the reception desk, and Damien probably wouldn't notice me.

A group of six people came toward the desk, and I walked quickly around them, passing Damien just as they did. I was almost at the cafeteria entrance, thinking I was safe, when I heard him call out to me from behind.

"Jace, is that you?"

I spun around, trying to look surprised. "Damien!" My face burned and my heart pounded.

"How are you?" He sauntered toward me with one hand in his

pocket under his unbuttoned designer jacket. "Are you adjusting to life in Minnesota?"

"Yes, thank you," I replied a little too quickly. "I like it."

"Plenty of lutefisk and tater tot hot dish?" he joked.

"Plenty," I said, returning his smile. He took another step toward me—his proximity made me start to sweat.

"And how is your department?" he asked. "PR, isn't it?"

I nodded. "Great. Couldn't be better."

"Really?" He looked at me sideways through mischievous squinted eyes. "I was just talking to Amber about your department. She thinks I should check out some of the reports about a new employee who has been causing all kinds of trouble. You wouldn't know anything about that, would you?"

He flashed a full smile, revealing a pronounced dimple on his left cheek. Though it was obvious he was teasing me, the tablet seemed to double in weight on my shoulder. My heart wouldn't stop pounding in my ears. I took a step away from him, afraid he could hear it too.

"I'm still getting to know people, but I'll keep an eye out for troublemakers." He seemed pleased with my response.

"I have a board meeting in a few minutes, but I might stop by later this afternoon and see for myself." I tried to fake confidence as I met his smooth gaze. Damien's familiarity wasn't unexpected, considering our history, but I didn't remember anything about him. That didn't make me abnormal though. Kindergarten was a lifetime ago.

"Is that one of the hazards of your position," I asked, "keeping the new people in line?"

"Hazards, perks—it's a tough job, but someone has to do it." He stepped toward me again. He reached out and took the back of my arm, giving it a little squeeze. "I'm glad you're adjusting so well, Jace," he said, looking serious. "See you later."

I wondered if Damien was serious about stopping by the department. His obvious flirtation made me nervous, but part of me hoped he would. If the Washington, DC, images on the tablet had been an assignment or were part of an advertising campaign, Damien might know about it. It would be much easier to explain what had happened and hand off the tablet to him, since I already knew he liked me.

\* \* \*

As soon as I came back from lunch, I spent a few minutes tidying up my desk. I moved the small antique clock my mom had left me and a picture of my father in his Navy Whites to the opposite side of my computer and set my purse where they had been so that I could see it as I worked. I looked at the picture of my father for a few seconds. Admiral John Vega—handsome, but so stiff. I wished I had a picture of my parents together. Mom had softened him.

I feared that the warmth in our family had disappeared with the closing of her casket. Each shovelful of dirt pushed my already heavy emotions deeper and farther away from the surface. My father's face showed no sign of loss or pain at the funeral. He'd greeted people with ease, seeming to offer comfort and solace when he should have been receiving it. I had stood beside him, completely empty.

This job was a by-product of that day. Victor and Damien Trent had been among the sea of people. My father briefly introduced us, reminding me of my kindergarten connection with Damien.

"My wife and your mother were quite close," Victor informed me as he grasped my hands between his. They were like marble, cool and hard. I shivered. "Wasn't Jace your first girlfriend, Damien?"

"I spent hours trying to decide whether you would like the Spider-Man or Batman valentine best." Damien flashed his white smile, and I warmed slightly. "I still wonder if I would've had better results with Batman."

My father and Victor Trent had begun to discuss where their careers had taken them. Damien listened and smiled politely but kept his eyes mostly on me. "Jace graduated from Stanford last month *with distinction*," my father said, beaming. I lowered my eyes, but I glowed as he called me into the conversation.

Victor had touched my shoulder, congratulating me. "I believe we have an opening in our PR department right now, Jace. It sounds like you have the drive and determination of your father. We could use you at Omnibus." I felt a strange mix of flattery and foreboding. Was I ready to work in the real world?

I hadn't really considered accepting the position. I wasn't even sure it was a sincere offer, but my father spent the next few days sewing up the details. There was almost no decision to be made. My father's sales pitch let me know that any other offer I accepted would be less prestigious.

As afternoon turned into evening, I still hadn't seen any sign of Damien. I tried to deny my disappointment. I had only a half hour before I would leave. It was ridiculous to think that he didn't have more important things to do. I would have to look for answers about the tablet on my own. It was probably better. I couldn't imagine how I was going to ask him about it anyway.

I was just shutting my system down when I heard his voice. I jumped, sliding my chair back with an awkward, jerky motion. He was inside Holly's office. They were speaking just loudly enough for me to hear but not understand, and the conversation was peppered with bursts of pleasant laughter. They were well acquainted. Maybe he hadn't come to the department to see me at all. I tried to stop listening in.

I opened a drawer, took out a disposable sanitizing cloth, and began robotically wiping down my spotless workspace. I could hear the cadence of the conversation change as Damien moved to the door of her office. My heart raced a little, and I checked my reflection in the blank monitor. A curl in the front was trying to look frizzy, but I wound it around my finger and it sprang back looking pretty smooth. When I heard him coming, I gently placed my purse over my shoulder.

"Are you leaving already?" he asked.

"Damien!" I smiled. "Yeah, I'm done at five." He ran a hand through his thick, sandy blond hair. I was instantly sucked in by the disappointment in his eyes. They were a striking shade of blue—light, almost translucent in the center, but midnight blue around the edges.

"I forget that some people work human hours." He laughed. "Death by meeting this afternoon. I wanted to come over here earlier. Can I walk you to your car?"

Damien's boyish good looks were overwhelmingly attractive, but I knew I was playing with fire. Did I want to encourage him when I had no intention of dating him? Guys like him were typically looking for something I wasn't willing to give.

"That would be nice," I said, swallowing my uneasiness. I folded my arms across my body and pressed my bag against my side.

The elevator doors slid closed. "Do you remember when Carlos Schultz flew off the teeter-totter and had to get stitches?" he asked.

I shook my head. Damien began to reminisce about the

Department of Defense Dependent School in Sigonella, where our fathers had been stationed when we were in kindergarten. He seemed to have clear, detailed memories of our teacher and the other students in the class. I nodded and tried not to look blank, but some of my father's two-year-long deployment in Italy was almost a complete dark spot in my memory. It might not have seemed like a big deal to most people. A lot of people don't remember kindergarten, but it had always bothered me a little since my memories from the summer after kindergarten until my father was transferred were crystal clear—almost abnormally good.

Those memories involved sitting on a window seat in our living room, looking out at Mt. Etna in the distance. In my memories, it was constantly smoking and threatening to erupt. I was terrified of it and spent hours watching on high alert. My mom would try to coax me away with other activities, but my father seemed to encourage my paranoia by making evacuation plans with me while my mom wasn't around. I was his little soldier, always following his orders.

School must have been a nuisance to me at the time. It interrupted my watch detail. Herman the stuffed pig had to cover the shift from 0800 until I got back. I smiled thinking about it. Herman was probably packed up in a box of my things in my father's storage unit. I couldn't think about going through all of that stuff yet. My heart hurt just thinking about it.

We passed through the garden walkway that led from Building C to the large parking structure. Damien had finished telling a story about his role as the Third Little Pig in the end of the year play.

"Weren't you a flower?" he asked. I nodded but didn't say anything. If that was how he remembered it, it was as likely as anything.

The trees were thick and green and a slight breeze rustled through. I turned my head so that the breeze carried my hair away from my face for a second. Some might have found the humidity stifling, but I liked summer evenings in Minnesota. The abundance and proximity of the lakes in the area formed a protective barrier. You didn't hear of many forest fires here. I took a refreshing breath.

"How is your dad getting along without your mom?" Damien asked, bringing me back to reality with a stinging slap. My eyes fell to the ground and I pulled my shoulders back, quickly firing off my rehearsed response.

"They were married for twenty-seven years, so I know he misses her, but he's never been one to sit around talking about his emotions. He pushes forward—marches on."

"How about you?" he asked. "How are you coping?"

I paused for a second, my many coping methods flashing through my mind. "The change in scenery is helping," I finally said.

"Good." He smiled sympathetically. It was true. Nothing here reminded me of her. Being in her house with her things had opened a hole in my heart. My father must have felt the same way. He moved almost everything into a storage unit only a few weeks after the accident without even telling me. We were suffering the same loss, but we were suffering separately. I didn't know how to bring him into my hole, and he didn't want me in his.

The tablet bumped against my side as we walked. We only had a few minutes left before we reached my car. If I was going to ask him about it, I had to do it now.

"Can I ask you something?" I said, slowing down my pace.

"Of course," he replied without hesitation.

"How well do you know the people in my department?"

"I make it a point to know everyone," he said matter-of-factly. "Some better than others. Why do you ask?"

It rushed out. "I was just curious about some sketches that I came across that seemed to be part of an advertising campaign. They're a really unique approach, and I just wondered who they belong to." My heart stopped, but I tried to breathe normally.

"What were the sketches?"

I paused, collecting my thoughts. "One was a sketch of the National Mall in DC," I began. I proceeded to describe the first hologram with the Omnibus symbols and strange buildings. Damien looked puzzled. Then I told him about the Capitol Building and the Omnibus army with the laser tag–looking guns.

"Are you serious?" His burst of infectious laughter startled me. I tried to cover it, laughing with him.

I didn't realize how ridiculous it all sounded until I said it out loud.

"I haven't seen anything like that in our marketing meetings. Sounds like something Jim Evans might cook up. He's an old Navy buddy of my dad's. He's been with the company since the beginning.

I don't even think he has any background in marketing. I think my dad just owed him a favor." He looked at me and stopped walking. "Where did you see the sketches? I wish I had a copy."

"On the scanner behind my cube." My easy lie lit my face on fire. "I just wondered if they were real or a joke."

"I'm the voice of reason when it comes to branding. Nothing like that would make it past me. But I hope I get to see those soon so I can shoot them down." We laughed again. He looked completely at ease. He believed me. "It sounds like there really is a troublemaker in your department. I might need to come by tomorrow for a complete scanner inspection." He gave me his charming, full-dimpled grin. My legs became Jell-O.

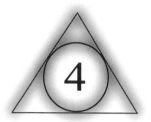

It only took a few seconds of separation for Damien's intoxicating effect to wear off. I immediately reprimanded myself. I hadn't gained any information from him. I had only lied. It was careless of me to say anything when I didn't understand what was happening. I pressed the accelerator, eager to be alone in my room where I could safely look at the rest of the images.

Sheila's boyfriend's Honda Fit was parked in front of our townhouse with two of the tires on the sidewalk. Disappointment seized me. I hoped they would leave soon. I sat with the engine running, trying to decide what to do, and pulled my bag onto my lap. I thought she usually worked Monday nights. I jerked the keys out of the ignition and marched up the path. Hopefully I wouldn't have to wait long to be alone.

I made plenty of noise with my key in the door and waited a few seconds before stepping inside, but my efforts were pointless. Sheila and Josh only came up for enough air to wave at me before continuing their sloppy display of affection on the couch. I kept my hand on the knob, averting my eyes.

*It's not a big deal*, I tried to tell myself. *Just walk past them. If they don't care, why should I?*

But I was frozen. "Hey, uh, I'm going to run to the store for a few things. Do you need anything?" I asked awkwardly.

Sheila didn't even look up, she just raised a hand, waved at me again, and then shooed me away with one quirky motion. I backed out the door quickly.

Back in my car, I drove aimlessly around the neighborhood. I had nowhere to go. I passed the park on McKnight. It was heavily wooded and covered two full city blocks. I pulled into the dog park south of Lower Afton Road. A walk would clear my head and give Sheila time to vacate the living room.

I took a quick look at the tablet and then nervously slid my purse under the driver's seat. I pressed the lock button twice before heading down the path. I passed a few people on their way back to the parking lot. Each had a dog and comfortable shoes.

After a short walk, I came out of the trees into a large open field with benches and exercise structures for the animals. Ten or twelve dogs of varying breeds were busy playing with balls and Frisbees. I sat down on the nearest bench and tried to disappear.

I glanced at my phone. 5:45 p.m. I tried to distract myself with social media. I hadn't posted any pictures since the weekend, but I had fifteen new notifications on my Instagram. I must have looked better than I thought with the Spoonbridge and Cherry. I didn't even know some of the people who had liked and commented on it. I was addicted, but I couldn't help it. I craved the validation that came from the likes and comments I got on my posts. It was almost like having real friends, only they were with me no matter where I went. There was also little danger of hurting or disappointing them, since everything I did was completely thought out and calculated. Controlled.

I pressed the camera icon on the lower panel of the application. The sun wouldn't set for over an hour, but the shadows of the trees were already elongated. I could probably get an interesting shot. Scenery shots were never as popular with my followers, but they made my profile look balanced.

I stood up and walked toward the edge of the dog run. Would it be weird if I posted a picture of someone else's dog? I crouched down and looked around at the choices. I would have to be closer for some of the smaller breeds to be visible, but I spotted a black Lab that stood out against the green background and glistening sun. I moved forward a few steps and crouched down again, catching the dog just as it jumped into the air to retrieve a Frisbee. I stood up and began scrolling through filters. After a moment, I glanced in the direction the Frisbee had been thrown as an afterthought.

The Lab had returned the Frisbee to a guy with a red bandana on his head and was running toward the trees again. I looked back down at my Instagram, but the butterflies in my stomach forced me to look a second time at the dog's owner as he was letting the Frisbee go. I recognized his heavy eyebrows right away. Corey Stein. As soon as the Frisbee left his hands, his gaze turned to me. Had he seen me taking a picture of his dog? I blushed and stumbled backward.

"Jace Vega?" He yelled from across the field. He had recognized me.

"Corey?" I called back, trying to keep calm. *In through the nose, out through the mouth.* I stood frozen, waiting for him to come to me.

Corey reached me in a few seconds and his Lab was just behind. We looked at each other awkwardly as the dog came directly to me and pushed his nose into my thigh. I placed my palms protectively between his nose and my leg, letting him sniff and lick me.

"Shane!" Corey called. "Come here, boy."

I watched as Shane obeyed. This wasn't normal. I had gone six years without having a conversation with my mysterious neighbor outside of class, and now here he was in Minnesota. My heart beat wildly.

"Stanford, right?" I said lamely.

"Yeah, I lived at Hawthorn," he answered with a smile.

"And English 101," I added.

The right side of his mouth curved upward and he raised his eyebrows. "I didn't think you would remember me."

I laughed, embarrassed. "What are you doing in Minnesota?"

He patted Shane's belly and took a step backward. "New job," he said.

My neck tingled.

"What about you?" he asked.

"I started in the PR department at Omnibus about a month ago."

He looked at Shane again. "Omnibus?" he asked, as if he wasn't sure he had heard me correctly.

"Yes. The campus is just across the freeway."

He made eye contact again. "I know," he said. "I work there too—product development."

"Oh wow!" I pretended to be surprised. "When did you start?"

"Today."

If Corey had just started at Omnibus, then the tablet couldn't be

26

his either. Could it? How would he explain the picture of us posed in the lab coats? My heart beat slowly in my ears.

Corey was watching me inquisitively.

"What number were you in at Hawthorn?" I changed the subject, trying to bring back normal.

"I was on the opposite side of the pool from you, in number 12." He looked away quickly, suddenly interested in the dogs behind us. "Go get it, boy," he told Shane, pulling the Frisbee into his side, ready to throw it.

"Who was your roommate?" I asked, not able to remember or associate anyone with him. Corey let go of the Frisbee as Shane ran out to fetch it.

He looked back at me slowly. "I lived alone."

Interesting. I didn't know anyone else who had lived alone at Hawthorn. Single students all had a roommate. *If I lived alone right now, I wouldn't be having this conversation*, I thought.

Shane came back with the Frisbee. "How do you like Omnibus? Has everything the recruiters promised you materialized?"

I smiled but felt a twinge of guilt. If recruiters had been interested in me, I wondered what they would have promised.

"So far, so good."

"I'm glad to hear it. I have to admit that I've been slightly dubious. You have to wonder when you look at the products."

"What do you mean?" The hair on the back of my neck stood on end.

"I've always had a hard time believing in fairy tales," he said, "If something seems too good to be true, it usually is."

I wondered why he was telling me this, and why he had taken the job if he was suspicious about the company. Maybe the job market had left him no choice.

I looked at my phone for the time. 6:03. I could probably go home now. I met Corey's eyes when I looked back up. He wore the same expression I had seen earlier in the image on the tablet. My eyes lost focus, and it felt like I was watching the scene from above. I took a breath through my nose and released it slowly through my mouth on a three count. *Déjà vu.*

Under the seat of my car, I had a tablet that had appeared on my path out of nowhere. It wasn't mine, but it had a picture of me that I had never posed for, with a man I had barely spoken to—and now I was standing in a dog park, without a dog, talking to him. *He's going to ask me if I'm okay*, I thought.

"Are you okay?" Corey asked. Was it my breathing technique or my long silence that had alerted him to my distress? I pulled my shoulders back.

"Can I ask you a weird question?" I said.

He straightened. "Uh, sure."

"Have you researched the products that Omnibus is developing?"

"A little," he said.

"Is Omnibus working on any tablets that project holograms?"

He reached up and straightened the bandana on his head. "Holograms?" he asked. "You mean the tablet projects the holograms?"

I nodded, cupping my palms together against my chest.

"You're not talking about an accessory that attaches to the tablet? A pyramid?"

I shook my head. "No. I'm talking about a three-dimensional hologram projected above the tablet."

"No," Corey said flatly. "Were you watching YouTube videos? Those are fabricated."

I didn't know what videos he was talking about, but by his tone of dismissal, it was obvious that he didn't think hologram technology had come far enough that Omnibus would be developing what I had described.

I realized that he was watching me process my thoughts. I couldn't read his expression. His lips parted, and his head tilted slightly, but his eyes stayed locked on mine. They were clear, concerned—honest.

*Show him*, a calm inner voice whispered. Maybe he would have a logical explanation for all of it. He might make it all rational and sensible. There had to be a simple answer to the question of where the tablet had come from and what I should do with it. And besides, we were both in that image. Corey would be in the same boat I was in if I gave it to James Lansing. I should at least see what he thought about it first.

"Have you had dinner?" I asked.

A broad, crooked smile spread across his face. He touched his bandana again and looked over his shoulder at Shane, who had dropped the Frisbee and was chasing another dog near the edge of the trees.

"Not yet. Have you?"

"Listen, this may seem a little strange, but I found something this morning that I want to show you. I think maybe you can help me." I realized almost instantly that there was nothing smooth about what I had said. My cheeks got hot, but I kept eye contact.

"Shane!" he called out, whistling three times. He looked at his watch. "I'm not really dressed to go out. But I live close. Do you want to meet somewhere after I shower and change? Thirty minutes?"

I hesitated. *He thinks this is a date.* Maybe I was making a mistake.

"Or you can come to my place and wait," he said, moving toward me.

"Okay," I heard myself say.

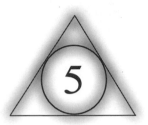

5

Corey lived in an apartment just across McKnight Road near the freeway. I parked in front of his 1970s-era, Tudor-inspired building. My townhouse was less than a mile away. I took the tablet out of my purse and sat looking at the blank screen and the flashing light while I waited for Corey and Shane to run home. I had offered to drive him, but he said that Shane didn't like riding in cars.

Corey sprinted full speed through the parking lot. He didn't stride in any sort of rhythm like most joggers or runners. He looked like he had learned his form from watching Shane. His upper body was loose and relaxed, his shoulders swiveling side to side as his arms hung with open hands near his waist. I half expected his tongue to poke out as he bent over with hands on his knees, recovering his breath.

I tucked the tablet back into my purse and silently followed him to his second-story apartment. The furniture was minimal. The small living room contained a faded red futon and overstuffed bean bag chair. A folding table was pushed up against the wall with two laptops set up next to each other. Two Chinese food takeout boxes were on the table with plastic utensils still sitting inside. I noted the unopened chopsticks.

"Make yourself at home," he called down the short hallway, already halfway through the door to his bedroom.

I set my purse down, then picked up his leftovers, and dropped them in the trash. The fridge was completely empty except for a gallon of milk and a few sodas. I helped myself to a Dr Pepper.

I looked around again, sipping my drink. Where were all of his boxes? Was this everything Corey had moved to Minnesota with? It all seemed very bare bones—especially for a guy who had lived alone at Hawthorne.

Whatever else the apartment was missing, Corey made up for it in books. On both sides of his small television, tall black bookshelves lined the wall from floor to ceiling. Aside from a few boring-looking physics textbooks, Corey seemed to be a fan of the classics. He had them alphabetized by author. I wasn't surprised by most of the titles, but having all seven volumes of *In Search of Lost Time* in French seemed a little excessive. His DVD collection was as minimalist as the rest of the apartment—just seasons one through four of *Through the Wormhole*. He was a nerd. I looked around the room again. I smiled. He must be a loner like me.

I was thumbing through a copy of *Paradise Lost* when Corey came out. He went straight to the kitchen and drank a big glass of water. I had momentarily forgotten the reason we had come to his apartment. I set down the book and moved over to where I had laid my purse. I lowered myself awkwardly onto the futon, wondering why anyone would ever buy one. Corey was obviously frugal.

I pulled out the tablet.

"Is that what you wanted to show me?" he said as he came around the corner from the kitchen. "The hologram projector?" he asked with a smirk. I wondered what he must be thinking about me.

"I didn't believe it either," I started, "but I don't pretend to be a technology expert." His smile faded as he sank down on to the futon next to me.

"Okay. Show me." I closed my eyes for a second, praying that we would see what I had seen earlier. I pressed the glowing button, and the Omnibus symbol materialized. I watched Corey's face. It didn't change. He paused before moving his hand slowly through the image.

"You said you found this?" he asked.

I nodded. "I was out for a run this morning. I found it just to the side of the path in the grass." I took a breath. "I meant to take it to James Lansing this morning, but I saw something on it that kind of freaked me out."

He stared quizzically at the tablet. "What did you see?"

I wanted him to see for himself, but what was he going to say when I showed him? I reached out and slid the tablet a little closer to me.

"Jace Vega," I said clearly.

"Voice recognition validated," the robotic voice spoke, and the three icons appeared.

"Nice," Corey said. "What did you look at?"

"I tried to open the tools first to see if I could find owner information, but it's password protected."

"Could you get into either of the others?" he asked after a brief pause.

"Open camera," I told the tablet. Corey watched as the three icons disappeared, replaced by the two file folders.

Corey looked at me, the right corner of his mouth turning upward again. I spoke the name of the Omnibus file exactly as I had earlier in the closet and waited for the tablet to begin the slide show.

Corey leaned toward the tablet when the aerial image of the National Mall appeared. I didn't say anything. I watched him discover the strange additions to the scene. The corner of his mouth dropped when he saw the Omnibus logo on the Washington Monument, and he silently raised his eyebrows. He searched the image methodically, stopping on the buildings where there should have been fountains and then on some of the vehicles on the streets.

"Can you zoom in?" he asked me.

I shrugged my shoulders. "Stop slide show," I commanded the tablet. "Zoom in."

A numbered grid appeared on the image. I looked at Corey, waiting for him to tell me what he wanted a closer look at. His eyes had moved from the image to me. He was studying my face intently. What was he thinking about me?

"Which section do you want enhanced?" My voice cracked a little. He looked away.

"Section 7. Try 20 percent."

I obeyed and the tablet responded immediately, magnifying a section that contained an intersection and several vehicles. The red sports car coming toward the camera was the most distinguishable. It looked like one of the concept cars I'd seen in a magazine in my father's bathroom.

"What made you decide to show this to me, Jace?" His blue eyes were clear and intense. "Why didn't you return it to James Lansing?"

*My gut told me not to.* I bit my cheek. I hoped he would understand after I showed him.

"Resume slide show," I said. The tablet brought back the first image. "Next image," I said with fake confidence.

Corey kept his eyes on me for a second before looking at the picture of the soldiers on the Capitol Building steps. I didn't give him much time to take it in.

"Zoom in," I said. When the grid appeared, I told the tablet to enhance one of the sections with soldiers near the camera. I enhanced the triangular emblem on the pocket of their uniforms. I watched Corey look at the Omnibus symbol.

"Who do you think this tablet belongs to?" Corey asked, his eyebrows knit together.

"I don't know. I was worried that someone in your department might be in trouble for taking a prototype off campus—then I looked at this image." I told the tablet to advance and watched Corey as the image of us in the lab coats appeared in the air. He was surprisingly impassive. He looked it up and down several times. No reaction.

A knock at Corey's door startled me. Without looking at me, he jumped up and ran to answer it. I suddenly felt like a deer in headlights. My heart raced as I pulled the tablet to my chest, hiding the image. It only took a few seconds for the smell of fresh pizza to drift into the room, filling my nose. My grip on the tablet relaxed. Corey came back with a large pizza box and dropped it on the floor in front of the futon, pulling out a piece immediately.

"Help yourself," he offered. Watching him eat a bite of pizza made my mouth water. When had he ordered this? He must have sensed that I wasn't interested in going out, that I just wanted his help with the tablet. Corey might be awkward, but he was perceptive. I tried again to think about who his friends had been at school. I couldn't picture him with anyone. He had been alone every time I'd seen him.

Moving down to the floor, I kicked my shoes aside and stretched my legs out. The pizza was an "everything but the kitchen sink" special. I loved a good combo, but I'd never ordered one with pineapple before. I reached for a piece, waiting for Corey to finish chewing a bite before pounding him with questions.

"I know I probably should have turned this in to James Lansing, but the pictures were so strange, and then seeing myself . . . I didn't know what to do. So, am I completely crazy?" I asked, immediately taking a bite and looking at the floor.

"I'm not qualified to diagnose you," Corey said dryly. I tried to smile, but after his casual reaction to the images, maybe I had over-reacted to what I had seen. "It does seem surreal. I can understand why you were freaked out."

*Surreal.* I looked up. This entire day was like a weird dream. I glanced back at Corey, who had started on another slice of pizza. The way he chewed was strange but oddly familiar. His nose moved up and down like a rabbit's. I had been right to be curious about him. He was anything but ordinary. He made me feel calm.

"How did they get the picture of the two of us?" I asked, touching the flashing green light. "We don't really even know each other."

He set down his pizza and reached for the tablet. "Tell it to power down," he said. I obeyed. The screen instantly went dark. He inspected it, turning it over and touching the thin sides of the screen. "There are no ports to charge it," he said.

I stopped chewing. I hadn't even thought of that. How long would it take for the green light to stop flashing? Would we have time to look at everything? Corey set it back down and resumed eating his pizza. I wished I could hear his thoughts.

"What does your dad do for a living, Jace?" he finally asked after a few uncomfortable moments of silence. I gave him a sideways glance. What did my father have to do with anything?

"He's a Navy man."

"My dad worked for the CIA. He was gone a lot," he continued. "We never knew where he was or what he was doing." He took another bite of pizza, choosing his words carefully.

"Most guys like my dad don't have families, but he sort of fell into his position when I was a few years old."

I nodded, encouraging him to continue.

"If you wanted to send a message to someone that no one else could understand, how would you do it?" he finally asked.

I hadn't really thought about it before. "I don't know. Maybe a different language or a secret code or something."

He finished his last bite of pizza. "Bring up that image of us again," he said. I pressed the button and navigated to the hologram. "Do you notice anything exceptional about this?" he asked.

Exceptional? Everything about the image and the tablet was out of the ordinary for me. I shrugged my shoulders.

"Look at our hands," he said.

My hands were hidden in the lab coat pockets. Corey had his right arm looped through my left arm, gripping it loosely just above the elbow. His left hand was partially tucked into his lab coat pocket. I hadn't noticed it before, but a silver chain encircled his hand, and a tarnished pocket watch hung just below the pocket. I had been so focused on our faces and the Omnibus symbols, I had completely missed this detail.

"What is it?" I asked.

"It was our code," Corey said, "That watch is a family heirloom that my father left me when he died. But when he was alive, it was his way of signaling me if something had gone wrong at work. If his cover had been blown, or we were in danger somehow, he would send that watch with someone to pick me up from school. I was supposed to go with them, no questions asked."

I felt like I was watching us from above. My neck tingled. I shook my head and rubbed my temples. Déjà vu again.

"Where do you think the picture came from?" I asked softly.

"Well, since we don't really know each other, I think we can rule out posing for it in the past."

My eyes became blurry.

"Photoshop?" I said, grasping for straws.

Corey sat silent. I forced my eyes to focus on the image again. Seamless. It was conceivable that someone at Omnibus could have created these images and orchestrated this whole thing—but why? Neither of us knew anyone well enough to be the target of a friendly joke, and even if we did, I didn't know anyone who would put the time and effort into something so elaborate.

Corey spoke the words as I thought them in exact synchronization. "I think we sent ourselves a message from the future."

"You think this is a message you sent yourself from the future?" The words sounded ridiculous as soon as they fell out of my mouth. I wanted to laugh, but I had a sinking feeling in my stomach.

"We sent ourselves," he corrected.

6

My heart raced, but the cloud that had been hanging over my mind suddenly lifted. I nodded slowly. As insane as it was, I believed him. "We have to look at everything," I said quietly.

"Can we see thumbnails of all of the images before we look at them?" he asked.

"Show all images," I tried.

"Specify file folder," the tablet responded.

"Omnibus file," I said. Ten thumbnails appeared.

"What about the other file?" he asked.

I opened the personal folder.

"Displaying images one through fifty of ninety-four," the tablet informed me. Everything from sporting events to holidays and vacations. I itched to open it and start at the beginning. Like the horoscopes in the newspaper, they begged to be studied first.

"We can ignore that file altogether," Corey said.

My heart sank. "How can you tell that without even looking at them?" His impatient, uninterested expression baffled me.

He raised his eyebrows. "Please don't tell me that you're one of those people who still enjoys a newsy Christmas letter from your friends."

I glanced at my phone. It had hundreds of pictures on it. "They might tell us more than you think."

"Well, we can safely assume that I wouldn't send us a message hidden in ninety-four images." His eyes gleamed mischievously. "But if you think you would send a message in the personal file, we can start with that beach picture." I scanned the thumbnails until I saw myself on a tropical shore, lounging in a swimsuit. Instant embarrassment. *My personal pictures. My future.* I guess I could understand Corey's lack of curiosity, but didn't he want to know if he was in any of them? I would look at them when I was alone.

"Open Omnibus file," I said. Corey gave a smug smile. My embarrassment pleased him, apparently. The Omnibus file reopened. I moved past the first familiar images quickly, still flustered. The fourth one was strangely serene. It captured the Lincoln Memorial prominently in the foreground with fireworks above and reflected on the water of the Potomac. Spectators stood on boats in the water, and more people lined a bridge. With their backs turned to the camera and tablet screens lit, many of the spectators on the bridge captured the fireworks display against the midnight blue sky. In the background, the other buildings and monuments were blurred. A flag with the Omnibus logo rose up above the spectator's heads, in perfect focus amid the exploding fireworks. Another smaller banner unfurled below the Omnibus flag. It read "Reclamation Day Celebration."

The image was taken by a professional photographer. It was brochure quality.

"What's Reclamation Day?" I wondered out loud. Not a single American flag was visible in the shot. I realized that the other two images hadn't had any either.

Corey shook his head. "I wonder if this is an advertisement. They're all using Omnibus tablets."

I advanced the image. The next was taken at a black tie banquet. Hundreds of people sat at round tables, all eyes and attention on the head table where a man stood at the podium. I gave the command to zoom and enhance that section.

"He looks almost the same as he did in Forbes last month." Corey recognized Damien as quickly as I did. He was right; Damien looked the same. I thought about my conversation with him earlier in the day. A small shiver ran down my spine. I shouldn't have told him about the images.

"This is inside the United Nations," Corey said. "Look at the emblem on the podium." I hadn't noticed the familiar blue and white globe framed by two olive branches. My eyes shifted from the modest-sized emblem to the enormous Omnibus banner behind Damien. "And look, Victor Trent is on deck to speak next." He was right. Victor's polished bald head, deeply wrinkled but distinguished face, and broad shoulders appeared just to the left of the podium.

"First the country, then the world, I guess," I said softly. The thought of Victor Trent moving into politics seemed natural. Even in just my short meeting with him at the funeral, I had felt his persuasive charisma. Corey didn't respond.

The next image was busy. It looked like a Stalin-era propaganda poster with bright blue and red artwork. The top right-hand corner showed the New York Stock Exchange in panic and confusion, everyone looking at or pointing to the blank screens. The top left-hand corner had angry protesters marching on the Capitol. In the middle, a black-shrouded figure labeled "Terrorist" smashed the word "Data" with an oversized sledge hammer. The foreground of the image was the semicircular table at the United Nations. Delegates applauded Victor Trent, who stood in the center of the opening of the semicircle with both arms raised as if he was signaling a touchdown. Large digital screens behind the podium said "Reclamation Treaty Signed."

Corey ran his hand across his forehead. He touched each corner of the image and scanned the center for several seconds before looking at me.

"Let's move on," he said, pressing his back against the futon.

I advanced the image, feeling growing despair with each passing minute. If the country's data was going to be attacked by terrorists, it must be on a large scale: enough to shut down the stock exchange, enough to bring protestors to Washington, demanding a solution. What else had led up to the country's need for Victor Trent and Omnibus to step in?

In the next image, top officials from all branches of the military surrounded a boardroom table with Victor Trent at the head. His ingratiating smile gave me the chills. Directly to Victor's left, my father sat—rigid in his crisp uniform. I gasped. My father was the Chief Naval Officer. I felt the veins on my jaw begin to pulse as I clamped it closed. How could he let something like this happen? His face was stern and unreadable. His hair was peppered with a little more gray, but otherwise he looked the same.

"Next image," I said, my heart beating out of control.

"What is it?" Corey responded to my reaction. "What did you see in that image?"

"Just someone I know." Horrified that my father might somehow be involved in this future for America, I wanted to escape in the next image, but the sinking in my stomach only grew. It was a close-up of Victor Trent sitting at a desk that looked suspiciously like the one in the Oval Office. A shiny silver nameplate on the desk was engraved: Victor Trent, Chief Interim Overseer. I swallowed hard, trying to keep the pizza down.

It was like my worst nightmare personified. The most terrifying dictators don't storm into power in an army coup; they slide into positions of power in the current government, taking advantage of a crisis. The Nazis didn't take Germany with military force. Hindenburg had appointed Hitler Chancellor.

"Someone you know?" Corey asked incredulously. "Do you hang out with the Joint Chiefs often?"

"The CNO in that last image is my father." My mind raced. How could my father let this happen? Had democracy crumbled completely? Why would the country need an Interim Overseer? It implied that he was just stepping in until things were back up and running, but letting go of the system—relinquishing power even for a short period of time—is a recipe for disaster.

Corey shifted in his seat and moved toward the tablet slightly. His eyes became charged. "Go back," he said. "Let's get a better look at the desk. We might find a date on something if we enhance it."

I brought the image of the conference room back. Aside from nameplates and powered down tablets, the dark wooden table was empty. The walls behind the table displayed digital times in red for ten different countries, five on either side of the un-illuminated flat screen televisions that hung in the center of the wall. I couldn't see anything that indicated a date, but the local time was 7:21.

Corey didn't seem to see anything for a moment either. I watched his clear blue eyes scan the image from top to bottom several times. He finally looked over at me.

"I wonder if any of these guys are current Chiefs of Staff. Zoom in on the nameplates. I'll Google them." I did as he asked.

"None of the current Chiefs have been in office longer than three years," Corey said, looking up from his phone. He compared each of the names we could see on the plates to the list he had pulled up. None of them matched.

Corey scratched his chin. "Ask the tablet to display the date," he said. It seemed so logical. I wondered why we hadn't thought of it sooner.

"Display date," I said. After acknowledging my command, an eight digit timestamp appeared in the bottom right-hand corner of the image. 01 01 22 07. "January 1, 2022?"

"Advance the image again," he said.

I brought the Oval Office image back. The timestamp at the bottom read 01 41 02 21.

"Obviously not," I said, disappointed.

"Don't worry," Corey comforted. "We'll figure it out."

"Corey, what are we supposed to do with this?" My father, holograms, pocket watches, Omnibus . . . it made my head pound. I wasn't sure I wanted to know any more—at least not tonight.

Corey seemed puzzled for a second. Then he smiled sympathetically. It had been a long day for both of us. I couldn't imagine what he must be thinking about Omnibus now. He moved from the far end of the futon right next to where I still sat on the floor.

"We only have a few images left to look at. Let's just get through them and you can go home and sleep. We can talk about what it all means tomorrow." He put his hand on my shoulder, and I instantly tensed up. I wasn't used to being touched. "Relax," he said. "You're wound tighter than a spring."

I took in a deep breath on a three count. "Next image," I spoke softly as I released the breath through my mouth. Corey began karate chopping my right shoulder. It was awkward and magical at the same time. I decided to ignore the awkward.

When I finally looked up at the image, three bright words stood out against a black background. The red Omnibus logo formed the "O" in each of the words—Order, Organization, and Opportunity. Below the words was written, "Omnibus, reclaiming and safeguarding our information. Equality for all."

Neither of us commented. Corey's hand was still on my shoulder, but I felt completely alone. I wondered how my father would feel about this future for America. Was it the country he devoted his whole life to protect? Judging by his role in the images, he might be instrumental in creating it. I couldn't believe that. I didn't wait or ask permission to move on.

The final image looked like it was straight out of a sci-fi utopian movie. Bright lights, green trees, happy workers, white clothes, shiny cars. Heaven on earth.

Corey was still chopping away at my neck and back. Every now and then he would stop and dig his thumbs into my shoulders. My mind felt heavy, trying to process what we had seen. I powered the tablet down. Corey didn't stop massaging, and I didn't ask him to for several minutes. I was exhausted.

"There was one other file on the main screen, wasn't there?" Corey asked. He set his phone on the couch next to him and moved away from me. I tensed, picturing the Omnibus symbol and intertwined J. *My initial.* What if I had somehow been involved in creating this new government? I turned the tablet back on.

Saying my name slowly, I brought up the three icons.

My body tingled, and my left arm ached. "Open J file," I said, trying to sound confident.

"Voice recognition validated," the tablet responded. "Proceed with password."

I was relieved. If the J file somehow implicated me, I wanted to be alone so I could figure out what to do. I turned my phone on for the first time since the park. 7:45. No new notifications, but I had a text from Sheila asking if I could stop at Byerly's to pick up some Nutella while I was out.

"What's next?" I asked. "What are we going to do with this?"

Corey was silent for a moment. "We haven't seen everything yet. The most important information is going to be in the password protected files."

I nodded slowly in agreement. "How are we going to figure out the password, and what are we going to do about the battery?" I asked.

"Leave it with me tonight," Corey said. "I'll see what I can find out about the battery. You work on figuring out the password. Make a list of all of the possibilities."

It was a logical plan, but I was hesitant to leave the tablet. I powered it down and watched the green light continue to flash slowly. Did I imagine it, or was it flashing slower than it had earlier in the day? I wanted to look at the other images, but what if the battery died?

"Until we know more, we should avoid communicating at work," he said. He picked up his phone and opened his contacts, then he entered my phone number and email address. I followed his lead, entering his personal and work numbers into my phone. I didn't like the idea of Corey having the tablet and then cutting off communication with me.

"How am I going to get the tablet back from you?" I asked.

Corey was silent and thoughtful. "Are you on Instagram?"

I nodded.

"My friend and I have a way of communicating through Instagram that's pretty difficult to track." He scratched three Instagram account names on a sticky note and handed it to me: *@bluegirl900, @staciberi90,* and *@stpaulvintage.* "Follow these and watch for messages. I'll let you know where to meet me tomorrow night."

I tucked the note in my purse. Corey's complicated plan seemed a little extreme. This information crisis could still be several years in the future. Did the images we had seen indicate imminent danger?

"And obviously we should keep this between us. You haven't told anyone else about the tablet, have you?"

I thought about the casual way I had carried it around the building that day. Corey watched my face.

"Have you?" he asked again.

I hesitated. "I showed it to Mitch, one of the security guards in building C." I thought about Damien too. He hadn't seen it, but I had described two of the images in detail. I didn't want to tell Corey.

"Well, we can't change that," he said, furrowing his brow, "but be careful going forward. I imagine that the powers that be at Omnibus would be very greedy to dissect this technology."

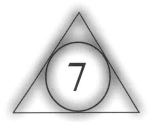

*I stand in a cool stream. Bold green mountains frame the meadow. I wade through the water to a large stone and sit on it. I drop my hands into the water, letting them move up and down with the current. I'm completely relaxed.*

*An ominous cloud hangs in the sky, moving much too rapidly. The sun is choked out. The water rises and rushes. I panic. I need to get back to the shore. Suddenly, I hear an explosion behind me. A billowing cloud of steam and ash pours out of the top of the mountain peak. The water turns to lava. I'm trapped on the rock.*

*Lightning flashes. My father appears on the bank of the stream. I call for help, but he just shakes his head, bitterly disappointed in me. He turns his back and walks away.*

*The cloud of volcanic ash surges toward me, leveling everything in its path. Over the deafening sound of falling trees and rocks crashing, I hear beeping. A series of short and long beeps grows gradually louder. Eventually, the pattern stops and the noise becomes steady, in rhythm with my heart.*

* * *

I slammed my hand down to silence the alarm. Adrenaline surged through me as I jumped out of bed. Remembering felt worse than just being left with the shadows of a dream. I didn't like it.

The events of the previous day replayed in my head. I tried to push away the ominous feeling that my vivid dream had left me, but my soul had been charred, just like the landscape in the dream.

But the sun would come glistening over the horizon in a few minutes, just as it had the day before. I got dressed to go running, just as I had the day before and the day before that. I would rely on my oldest friend again to rescue me from my distress: my routine.

The sky was pitch dark. Thick storm clouds hung low and heavy. The humidity was oppressive, but I continued down to the creek path regardless. I started my running playlist but reconsidered before pressing start on my run tracker. I was suddenly wary of publicizing my route to everyone in my social media world. My craving for their cheers could be repressed.

At the end of the trail on McKnight, I couldn't help looking for Corey's apartment building up the street. Was he awake yet? 6:45. I still had another hour before I left for work. My eyes continued further down the road to the Omnibus campus. I would never look at the company or its logo the same again. Corey's warnings to be cautious and quiet until we had a plan would make it difficult to feel normal at work. I wondered if he had grown up feeling like this with his father's job. Paranoia probably went with the territory.

My father's job made me feel abnormal growing up too. All of the other kids had a sense of home and community. The only permanent connection I had was to my parents—and now only my father.

As I sprinted back down the path, I couldn't stop my mind from returning to the funeral. Mom's beautiful, thick blonde hair billowed below her head on the satin pillow. Her face was sunken and drawn. No amount of makeup could re-create the glow she wore in life. I ached with physical pain, longing to call her. She would have reassured me about this entire situation. She would have listened calmly and then asked just the right questions to help me resolve the problem. She was my support.

I passed the spot on the path where I had found the tablet yesterday. I slowed for a moment to examine the area, half expecting to see a blue police box hidden in the trees. I saw nothing out of the ordinary. Rain began falling gently.

Part of me wanted to call my father as soon as he was awake on the West Coast, but the image of him turning his back on me from the dream seemed to encapsulate my fears. How would I even start a conversation like that with him? Time travel? He was going to think I was crazy. My father's intimidating, stern eyes had always made me uncomfortable when approaching him with anything that I wasn't sure was going to please him. I avoided his displeasure at all costs. Choices of friends, schooling, who I dated, and even this job had all been made with his approval in mind. On the other hand, his simple nod of acknowledgment of some accomplishment was like winning a gold medal for me. His praise made me overflow like a glass filled with too much carbonated soda. But it wasn't the same unconditional feeling my mom had given me.

I desperately wished I could call her now. She always helped me see things rationally.

I slowed my pace to a jog as I turned into my townhome complex. I would wait to call my father until I made more sense of everything.

* * *

I felt different walking into work that morning. I shook off my umbrella before going through security. Mitch quickly scanned my bag and sent me through the body scanner. He seemed distracted and didn't start a conversation.

My department buzzed with noise. I walked past Holly's office. Three of the associates stood inside, talking softly with deeply concerned faces. I tried to listen as I passed the half-open door but couldn't understand much of what was being said. I heard someone say, "Out of nowhere," and another voice said, "It makes no sense." Holly's calm, reassuring voice told everyone not to worry. No one noticed or acknowledged me as I sat at my desk and turned my computer on. I didn't have anyone I could ask what was going on.

I settled in and was working on proofreading a brochure when Jim Evans walked past my desk, carrying a cardboard box filled with personal effects, flanked by Mitch and another security guard. They were escorting him from the building. So that was what had initiated the department's negative vibe.

Panic. I couldn't help wondering if my lie about the drawings might have cost Jim his job. What if I was next? I had never been fired from a job before, but I knew I could never explain it to my father.

The minutes dragged on like hours. I read the same brochure several times without the words registering at all. None of my coworkers came by to chat that morning. I wondered if any of them had heard about the strange drawings that had gotten Jim fired. I felt exposed and guilty.

My ability to focus was still minimal in the afternoon, but I plowed through a lot of the busy work that Holly had given me. Thinking about what I had held back from Corey was giving me indigestion. I wished I had told him about my conversation with Damien. I wondered if he had been able to recharge the tablet battery. I felt increasingly desperate to see what was hidden in the J file. If the tablet was truly a message we had sent ourselves from the future, maybe the J file would contain specific instructions on what to do to stop the information crisis from happening.

In the late afternoon, I pulled out my phone and started making a list of all of the passwords I had ever used. It was extensive. As a teenager, I had read an article that recommended changing your password every three months. The article said that passwords should be easy to remember but hard to figure out, so I developed a system: I used the last names of my school teachers with the year I had been in their class—the first two digits before the name and the last two after. I had worked my way through grade school and high school teachers, and now I was on to college professors.

"How's your day?" I jerked my phone under the desk as I looked up into Damien's face. His crystal eyes looked right through me. My palms began to sweat almost immediately.

I pushed my phone under my leg and rolled my chair away from the desk until I was at a comfortable distance. I had a sinking feeling that nothing good would come out of a conversation with him. "It's been a little tense around here," I stammered.

Damien looked casual. "Office drama?" he asked as if he didn't have any idea what I was talking about.

"Just the natural panic that comes when a tenured employee suddenly gets fired."

"What?" he asked, looking sincerely confused. "Who got fired?"

"Oh, I thought you already knew. I saw security escorting Jim Evans out of the building this morning."

Damien didn't say anything. He looked over in the direction of Jim's office. He must have been able to see that Jim's nameplate was gone. He came around the corner of my cubicle and sat down slowly on my desk, his dimples gone.

"I know this must seem strange, but can I call you later?" He pulled his phone out of his pocket and opened his contacts, assuming that I could do nothing but give him my number. I paused for a second before realizing that there was nothing else I *could* do if I wanted him to think things were the same as yesterday. I gave him my information, and he quickly walked away from my desk.

8

**I waited** to look at the Instagram accounts Corey had given me to follow until I was alone in my car. @bluegirl900 looked familiar. Her profile said she was a Stanford student. I tapped on a close-up of her face. She was pretty but quirky looking. Her big brown eyes hid behind thick-rimmed glasses and jet black hair. In most of her pictures she was wearing homemade-looking crochet hats, long loose skirts, and layered T-shirts. Maybe she was the friend that Corey had been using these accounts to communicate with, but I was sure I had never seen them together. I couldn't place where I'd met her, but I knew her name was Megan right away. I didn't know her last name.

The second account was one of those habitual party girls. She had hundreds of pictures of herself in various stages of wasted. I could only imagine @staciberi90's relationship with her father. Maybe he had died or abandoned her. I couldn't fathom leaving the house dressed in her skintight sequined dresses and stilettos, let alone posting pictures of myself dancing around in them for the world to see. My father wouldn't have burned me at the stake for doing something like that. He would have just coldly explained the pitfalls of dressing like a prostitute and then punished me with his disappointment.

The final account was a St. Paul antique furniture store. I would have to tell Sheila about this one. Right away I noticed a picture of a set of vintage end tables that would complement the garage sale beaded lamps she had bought in Hudson a few weeks ago. She must have felt sorry for me that day sitting around the apartment, because she insisted that I go with her. I don't think she really liked being with me. I was more of a project to her.

"You've got to stop moping around, Jace," she had said. I liked the way my name rolled out of her mouth with her accent, even if she was criticizing me. "You're messing with my mojo. Just looking at you depresses me. When are you going to get out and meet people?" She had touched the beads on the lampshade and they tinkled against the metal. It was a mystery to me how a girl from Sydney had gone from not knowing a soul in the Twin Cities to having a network of friends in just a few short months. Sheila attracted strange people like moths to a light bulb. If I had a dollar for every ugly tattoo and body piercing I'd seen in our house, I could probably quit my job. "You wouldn't fit in with my friends, but I know plenty of stiff, conservative blokes who would fall all over themselves to show you a good time."

I had rolled my eyes and ignored her. She meant well, but her cutting comment had hit a little too close to home.

I looked back at my Instagram. @bluegirl900 hadn't posted any pictures yet today. I should have plenty of time to go home and eat dinner before setting out to meet Corey at his mystery location.

I had just changed into an old pair of dark-wash cutoffs and my favorite white T-shirt when my phone started buzzing. It was a Minnesota area code, but I didn't recognize the number. It was probably Damien. I waited for the fourth ring before picking up with a casual "hello?"

"Hi, Jace?" he asked, but he didn't wait for me to reply. "This is Damien. I just wanted to apologize for the awkward meeting at your desk today."

"Please, don't apologize, Mr. Trent," I replied. "It was perfectly understandable."

"Please don't call me Mr. Trent." He laughed. "We're the same age, and I wet my pants at your house once. I threw away the Princess Jasmine panties your mom sent me home in, so I still owe you a pair."

I couldn't help laughing, but I was glad he couldn't see my face. "I'm pretty sure the statute of limitations has run out on those. You don't owe me anything," I replied. I wondered what other embarrassing memories he had about kindergarten and cringed. Maybe it was better that I didn't remember.

"Listen," he said smoothly, "I want to take you out for dinner and drinks tonight. Are you free?"

I hesitated longer than I should have. Corey would be expecting me at seven, but I wanted to know if Jim Evans had been fired because of what I had said about the images. "I, uh . . . well, first I need to come clean and tell you that I don't remember anything about you or kindergarten, so I feel like you have an unfair advantage."

"I won't hold it against you," he assured me. "Can I pick you up at seven?"

I floundered. I imagined Jim being questioned about the drawings. Had he been fired because they thought the drawings were his idea, or because they thought he knew about the plan? Was there already a plan?

"How should I dress?" I asked. He sounded pleased as he gave me details on the casual Italian place he was planning to take me to. I promised to text him my address as soon as I hung up.

Corey wouldn't be happy about me ditching him. Before keeping my promise to Damien, I opened Instagram and scrolled down a few pictures in my feed until I found the picture just posted by @bluegirl900. A mushroom swing surrounded by a roller coaster with a Ferris wheel in the background—I recognized the amusement park inside the Mall of America, even before reading the caption. His secondhand CIA plan to meet almost twenty miles away would have worked perfectly if I weren't planning to ruin the whole thing. I only hoped he would be glad that I was trying to get more information. I imagined that he would do the same if presented with a similar opportunity.

I switched over to my texts and sent Damien my address.

Back on Instagram, I considered how to tell Corey before he drove across the city without breaking radio silence. It looked as if this was a legitimate account. Some of the pictures had been posted almost a year ago. I was guessing that @bluegirl900 was some kind of girlfriend who was letting him hack her account—she and Corey would make a cute hipster couple. Leaving a comment on the picture seemed to make sense.

"Sorry I missed you this time @bluegirl900! Hope your trip was amazing!" I glanced over it and then hit send. I threw the phone onto the bed and jumped into the shower. My thick hair took almost half an hour to blow dry. I needed to hurry.

After toweling off, I slipped into my go to eyelet black sundress. It was loose and comfortable but fit perfectly and accentuated all of the right places. The hemline was just above the knee, and the sleeves covered most of the shoulder. My father wouldn't have anything to say about this outfit, except maybe that the neckline plunged a bit too low.

My father was a religious man. The San José church was the heart Los Ojos, New Mexico, the tiny town where my father grew up. The stories he told about the nuns and their harsh punishments from his school years were meant to scare me, but I could feel his respect and gratitude for them. He credited their strict discipline for his success in life. If my mother hadn't been Protestant, I suspect he would have liked for me to become a nun.

After completely straightening my hair, I had a few minutes to admire my handiwork before Damien arrived. I was a pure mix of my parents. I had his olive skin and her ultra-feminine figure and face shape. Natural golden highlights contrasted my chestnut hair. The green eyes were uniquely mine—his were brown and hers were blue. I liked how I looked. I was the unifying blend of two cultures, and I belonged to both of them. I spritzed on a little perfume and dropped it into my handbag along with my lipstick. I checked my phone for messages before I dropped it into my bag too. I didn't have any new texts, but I noticed a strange email that I hadn't seen earlier in the day. It came from a Stanford student email address, but I didn't recognize the name. Jamie Peterson wrote:

> *Jace,*
>
> *It was so nice to see you yesterday. I hope we can hang out sometime soon. Here is a link to Angie's blog. Cute kids. Talk to you soon.*
>
> *Jamie*

It had to be from Corey. He included a link, which I clicked on immediately, wondering if it was some kind of clue or had a hidden message. It was a mommy blog, full of pictures of Angie and her blond-haired children. I couldn't find anything remotely like a hidden message, so I closed it. Calling or texting would have been so much simpler. I decided to suggest prepaid cell phones the next time we met to indulge his paranoia.

I checked myself in the mirror several more times, pacing back and forth. I pushed away my compulsion to take a selfie and post it. Corey and his fake accounts wouldn't appreciate the reason I was ditching them without a personal explanation.

As the minutes ticked away, my nerves started to kick in. *It's just a date.* I tried to calm myself. I had just sat down in front of the fan when I heard the doorbell. I snatched my keys and purse and took a deep breath before answering it.

Damien looked nice dressed down, much more our age in jeans and a polo shirt. His gaze gradually rose from the doormat to my eyes. "You look great," he said, his wide smile greeting me. I tried to swallow the butterflies as I stepped awkwardly out onto the porch and locked the door.

"You live alone?" he asked casually.

"No, but my roommate's a waitress. She works late most nights."

Damien's hand moved smoothly to the small of my back, sending a shiver up my spine. He guided me to the passenger's side of his black Tesla Model S, setting me gently inside like a newborn in a crib and closing my door without so much as a sound.

I ran my fingers over the leather seat while he buckled his seat belt. "Is this hybrid or electric?" I asked.

Damien smiled. It was the right question. Obviously an enthusiast, he started rattling off the specs and features on the car. From there, conversation never lulled. He asked me a lot of questions about Stanford and actually seemed like he cared about the answers. The drive wasn't long. He chose an old Italian place in downtown St. Paul. Cossetta's wasn't anything special to look at from the outside—a square, three-story brick building with green awnings. But the inside was quaint and charming. The smell of fresh garlic and basil made my mouth water as soon as we walked in. The ground floor housed a crowded deli and an Italian market. At the base of the stairs, a hostess took Damien's name and showed us to a quiet table on the third floor. Exposed brick walls, low lighting, and uneven hardwood floors created an Old World ambiance.

Damien gently guided me through the crowded tables with an occasional soft touch to my shoulder or elbow. I waited for the urge to run that usually came when a guy was too touchy-feely, but his touch wasn't unpleasant—the feeling never came. When we were seated at the table, he shifted his chair next to mine and began showing me his favorite menu selections. After determining that I liked seafood, he ordered a seafood salad appetizer.

"So what made you decide on PR?" he asked as soon as the waitress left our table.

"I think I decided a long time ago," I said, trying to remember whether my father had pushed me toward it or if it had been my idea. "I remember following the Bush–Kerry presidential debates with my father. I was in junior high. I was fascinated by the whole election process but especially by how the candidates seemed to have an answer to every question." I grinned a little. They had both seemed like my father. Damien leaned forward and squinted—like he wanted to see inside my smile. I dropped the corners of my mouth. "I joined speech and debate in high school and have been obsessed with speech writing ever since."

"Do you want to run for office?"

"I don't think so," I replied. "I prefer to make other people look good." I got embarrassed when he laughed. "What about you? What was your major?"

Damien looked over my shoulder and didn't answer right away. His eyes were distant. "I went straight into the Navy after high school, but then my father had other plans for me." I raised my eyebrows. He still wasn't looking at me. "Omnibus funds a few research projects at the PRISM Center at Purdue. I spent some time there observing the research last year, but I also took a really great pottery class and ballroom dancing. I have a hard time focusing on school with my other responsibilities."

The waitress brought our appetizer. My opinion about Damien's position at Omnibus was beginning to fade—it sounded like it was more important than I had given him credit for. I hadn't considered his education before. His tone struck a chord as he talked about his father's plans for him. My father's plans for me weren't always verbalized, but his expectations were omnipresent. Strange that Damien's father's agenda put education on the back burner. I savored the first few bites of squid, thinking about how different our lives were. Damien, at age twenty-five, was already fully entrenched in his career and future, while I was barely on the brink of mine. He had the experience that I lacked. I envied him a little.

Our main course came and Damien smoothly transitioned away from his father to lighter topics. Conversation flowed easily from books and movies to places we had traveled and the pitfalls of being Navy brats. Developing long-term relationships had always been difficult for me. I had many pleasant acquaintances around the world, but never anyone that I sent a birthday present to. Damien confessed needing a constant change of environment.

"I feel restless if I stay in an area longer than six months," he said.

I could relate. Scenery changes were a given, but I had a tendency to want to connect my past and present. Looking at pictures of the places I had lived and the people from my past on Instagram gave me an artificial feeling of roots, and my routine was the glue that held everything together. It was my home.

I touched my phone. A pang of guilt struck as I pictured Corey reading my Instagram comment surrounded by a bunch of kids in a giant shopping mall, while I enjoyed my Gamberi Florentine. I wondered if he had taken the tablet with him. I hoped he wouldn't be disappointed by my decision if I had something solid and helpful to share with him when we met again.

Damien was talking about his upcoming travel itinerary. I realized that his physical presence in Minnesota would be rare over the next few months. Disappointment and panic were immediate partners. Corey wasn't going to be impressed that I knew Damien's favorite college team. I set my fork down, unable to continue eating. Trying to formulate a question that would lead to the conversation I wanted to have made my stomach churn. I wanted to know if his father had political ambitions, but everything that I thought of to ask seemed obvious. I was afraid he would feel my motives.

"You're so quiet all of a sudden," Damien said, interrupting my internal argument right on cue.

I smiled and relaxed my shoulders. "Sorry, I can be the queen of awkward silence."

"Not awkward." He smiled. "I just wondered what you were thinking about."

My heart flipped over. *Change the subject.* "I guess awkward silence is better than awkward babbling."

"I can see you having a real problem with that." He laughed.

"Maybe not, but just one episode of uncontrolled rambling can leave emotional scars that take years to heal," I said, laughing uncomfortably.

"I'm not taking you home until you tell me about your one episode." His mock stern face was unexplainably more charming than his smile.

I blushed and hesitated before giving in. "First kiss," I said out loud. *Only kiss*, I thought, trying to suppress the blush brought on by the embarrassment of simply uttering the word. "I was nervous and completely inexperienced. I talked incessantly because my date was suddenly quiet, shifty eyed, and sweating." In high school, Ranger Carlson had been the only guy mature enough to try to cut through my walls. I cleared my throat. "We were sitting side by side looking at the stars, and, out of the blue, he leaned over and kissed my cheek. I was flustered and I panicked a little. Then I looked in his eyes and got completely embarrassed, so I turned away again. He must have gone in for the kill when we made eye contact, but I turned away too quickly, and he missed—kissing my cheek again."

"Amateur," Damien teased.

*Why did I tell him about that?* I shifted in my seat and mechanically pressed the button on my phone for the time. Just after ten.

Damien's laughter subsided and he smoothly followed my cue. "I hate to take you home," he said. "We were just making real progress, but I have a conference call at 5:00 a.m."

I lifted my purse strap off the back of my chair. "What a great evening." I smiled. "Thanks for forgiving my kindergarten amnesia. I can see now why we were such good friends." We stood up, and he slid both of our chairs back into the table.

I consciously let go of my tension, deciding that I wasn't going to try to manipulate the conversation to get information. The ride home was relaxed with periods of silence becoming more natural and comfortable. Damien delivered me to my doorstep as smoothly as he had picked me up. Our eyes met for a moment as I put my key into the lock. Sliding his hand over mine, he opened the door for me, and I dropped my hand to my side. His other arm wrapped around my waist, and he brushed my cheek lightly with his lips. Electricity. My mind went numb as the current passed through it.

"I want to see you again soon," he half whispered, kissing my cheek a second time meaningfully. I laughed nervously and nodded. "Call you tomorrow?"

"I'll be here," I replied, trying to sound casual while attempting to make my goose bumps retract. Too late. He had already seen them on my arm. My knees weakened.

The headlights of a car driving much too fast came around the corner. Damien shielded his eyes, and Sheila flew into the driveway, throwing her car door open and letting some screaming indie music come spilling out before she shut off the motor. I cringed.

"Finally!" she said. She slung her acid-green purse over her shoulder before sprinting up the walk. "Who is he?" she whispered as she pushed open the front door. Without waiting for a reply, she raised her hands up, saluting the moon and stars. "We thank you, O powerful Aphrodite, for sending Jace this fine-looking man to save us both from her prudish ways." She leapt across the threshold. "Amen. Carry on." The door slammed, and she was gone.

Blood surged to my head in a mixture of anger and embarrassment. Damien backed down the path a few steps with a huge smile spreading across his face. He was good enough to suppress his laugh.

"Tomorrow," he said.

9

*I* look *down at my shiny patent leather heels clicking against an even glossier floor. The sound of my footsteps echo as I pass by door after door. I feel thirsty and tired, but I keep moving. Each step expands the length of the corridor. My frustration mounts. I'm never going to get anywhere.*

*I walk faster. The clicking of my heels is unnerving. It's too loud. Not just one set of footsteps—a second, softer set mirrors mine. I tense. Should I look back, or should I run? I can't do either. My legs stop moving and slowly turn into wax, melting into the floor.*

\* \* \*

Gentle rain tapping on the roof shook me awake. *Two nights in a row.* Even if the dreams were weird, maybe remembering them was progress. I would look online later for an interpretation.

I lay in bed until my alarm went off, replaying my evening with Damien in my head. I hadn't really learned anything about Victor Trent or Omnibus, but I felt strangely satisfied. Damien held more than the answers about the future of the company; he had detailed memories of the year I was missing. I didn't want to rush things with him. I had to be careful if I was going to get all of the answers I was looking for.

By the time I left for my run, the sprinkling rain had turned to a downpour. Worried that the plastic case wouldn't be enough protection from the rain, I left my phone sitting on the dresser. Splashing through the puddles was exhilarating. The man in the red shorts wasn't out this morning. Maybe the thunder had scared him off. I was completely alone with my thoughts, so I didn't try to keep them off Damien. I closed my eyes for a second and remembered his lips on my cheek. He was impossibly easy to look at and be with. Confidence and charm poured out of him like a fountain.

I wondered how things would have progressed if I hadn't found the tablet. Would I have been so eager to let him in if I wasn't looking for information, or would I have pushed him away like anyone else I had ever been remotely attracted to? I hadn't ever searched it, but I could probably find a diagnosis for my relationship issues. Single people are supposed to be attracted to other single people. It's normal. It angered my roommates that I had droves of male social media followers who would still go out with me if I gave them any encouragement. But I wasn't playing hard to get—I wasn't playing at all.

An image of my father with his arms folded sternly across his chest flashed in my head. If it hadn't been for my father's introduction, and his connection with Damien's father, I knew I would have avoided him. I would have acted uninterested and ignored his calls. All but the most persistent guys had been kept at bay with similar treatment. Maybe it was different with Damien because it felt like my father already approved of him.

When I had almost reached the end of the path and McKnight, a tall runner came bounding over a hill with a dog at his heels. Corey and Shane. The romance of the pouring rain transformed into painful taps against my exposed skin and heaviness on my clothes. I didn't expect to have to explain myself to him until later. A surge of nervous energy shot through me as he approached.

"Hey! What happened last night?" he called when I was still several yards away.

I waited to answer until he was right in front of me. "Damien Trent invited me to dinner, and I thought it would make sense to get closer to him." I watched for his reaction, not sure what to expect.

"Damien Trent? Are you crazy?" he asked. "Turn around, and let's keep running." He grabbed my arm.

"What is your problem?" I snarled.

"Damien Trent *invited you to dinner*. That doesn't just happen, Jace."

"Okay," I admitted. "Our parents have known each other since we were in kindergarten. Our fathers were stationed together in Italy."

Corey stopped running and ran both hands over his soaked bandana. "You might have mentioned that," he said, taking a few steps away from me to the side of the trail. Shane followed him. "Does he know about the tablet?"

"No," I said softly. "But I did ask him about some of the images before I saw you at the park. I was just trying to make sense of this whole thing."

"So your plan is to date the dictator? Has it occurred to you that he might be dangerous, Jace? We don't know what he and his father have done—or will do—to get to the top."

I folded my dripping arms. I knew he was right. I was clearly on the edge of the unknown, but Damien had something I needed, and his role in the dictatorship wasn't completely clear to me. Speaking in front of the United Nations isn't a crime. Victor Trent had been the one sitting in the Oval Office. My father sat next to him with the Joint Chiefs. If Corey was accusing Damien just because of his relationship with his father, then he might as well be accusing me too. My father looked almost as guilty as Victor Trent in those images.

"I can't make solid judgments until I have all the facts," I concluded, "and Damien knows more about Omnibus than anyone. I can take care of myself."

Corey raised his eyebrows. "Well, while you've been getting comfortable with the boss, it might interest you to know that Omnibus is keeping tabs on you."

"What? How do you know? What do you know?"

"A friend of mine at Stanford set up that blog I sent to you yesterday afternoon. She's able to trace the IP of anyone who clicks on the link. I sent that link to your personal email, Jace. Megan shows it's been looked at by four separate computers at Omnibus."

Did Damien know about this? I obviously wasn't the only one with ulterior motives. Had Damien been trying to find out what else I might know about the company's plans? If so, he was a much more subtle and natural liar than I could ever be. My stomach sunk. Corey continued. "I'm not sure what they know, but they are very interested in you."

Why was Damien so easy to trust? I didn't want to admit that I had been sucked in because I was attracted to him. Just because he looked good on the surface didn't mean something else wasn't bubbling beneath.

I looked at Corey and then lowered my eyes. Humility hurts. "I'm sorry. I'm not used to all of this. I'll be more careful."

His expression softened. "Maybe your connection to Trent will be useful if you can stick to business. If you ask the right questions, you might be able to find out what we need to know with much less risk than if I tried to hack into their system."

The rain tapered off. I walked in a small circle. The darkness was disappearing, but the sun wasn't yet visible through the thick clouds.

"What do we need to know?" I asked.

"Anything would be helpful. What did you find out last night?"

"Not much," I admitted, "and Damien is only in town for three more days, and then he'll be traveling off and on for several months. I doubt he's going to tell me any company secrets in three days." We both considered it in silence for a moment.

"Did you have any luck with the battery?" I changed the subject.

"Not yet. I might need to take it apart."

Irrational fear gripped me. "No," I shouted before I could restrain myself, "don't do that!" *He can't take it apart*, I thought. What if he couldn't put it back together?

Corey's eyes narrowed and he touched his bandana again. My heart was racing. I needed to get control of myself. A small breeze rustled through the trees, and a few rays of sunlight broke through the clouds, warming up the path momentarily.

"Have you been thinking about the password?"

I nodded slowly. "I made a list, but I'm still not sure. I think it would be something obvious—something unmistakable, like your pocket watch."

His lips curled upward for a second. He seemed surprised and pleased with me.

"When do you think you'll hear from Trent again?"

"He said he would call me today."

"Good," he said. "Maybe you can start by finding out about his political affiliations. Do he and his dad support any specific candidates or platforms?"

It seemed like a logical place to start—but the thought of being so direct made me nervous.

"Corey, someone in my department was fired yesterday because of what I said about those images. I need to be careful. He's got to trust me," I said, wondering how I was going to keep my nerves in check.

"Somehow I don't think it will be hard for you to convince him," Corey muttered.

I ignored the insinuation. "When and where can we meet to try the passwords?"

"I can take care of that if you have your list."

"What do you mean you can take care of it?" I was confused. He didn't have the tablet with him. "You'll need my voice to activate the tablet and navigate it."

"I managed to get what I needed from you the other night," he said, pulling his phone out of his pocket and shaking it side to side. "It's just as responsive to a recording as it is to your actual voice. You can just say the passwords for me and I can try them later."

"You recorded me?" Anger instantly bubbled up inside. "Did you look at the other pictures—the personal ones?" This wasn't some snap decision to look at the personal pictures when I hadn't shown up last night. He must have planned to look at them alone all along.

He stepped backward, putting his arms out in front of him. "A few," he said casually. "I was more interested in getting into the settings or the J file. That's where I think we are going to find some answers."

Why had I let him keep it? His fake disinterest in the personal pictures and his casual attitude had lulled me into a false sense of security.

"I want it back, Corey. I want it back now."

"Calm down," he said, stepping toward me. "Be rational, Jace. You brought the tablet to me. I was just looking for answers."

"You lied to me. If you wanted to record me, you should have asked." What did I really know about Corey anyway? Only that we looked comfortable together in those lab coats. Maybe I had been wrong to trust him.

"I'm sorry." He hunched forward, almost as if he were tucking a tail between his legs. Reaching awkwardly for my arm, he tried to calm me. "This is my first time dealing with time travel and world takeovers. I'm obviously better with technology than with people. I shouldn't have done it."

I pulled my arm away from him. Was he really sorry? How could I judge his sincerity? How could I know what to do when I didn't know who I could trust? My eyes lost focus, and I bit my cheek hard to bring it back. It was easier not to trust anyone. I needed to take back control.

I cleared my throat. "Here's what's going to happen," I finally said, my voice low and trembling. "You are going to meet me at the Sunray Library after work. You're going to give me the tablet back, and then I can try the passwords."

Corey nodded. "What time?" The rain started up again and poured down his face and off the end of his nose.

"5:30," I said.

**M**ercifully, I had nothing to proofread that morning. I spent most of the day in Photoshop editing stock photos. I was able to manipulate the images while my mind was otherwise occupied. I wasted most of the morning reliving Corey's little deception. I hadn't been completely honest with him either, but somehow I had expected him to fully trust me. Why had he wanted to look at it alone?

I thought of the beach picture he had pointed out and his sly smile. What else had he seen in the personal images? My head swam in circular thoughts and unanswerable questions. Why did it bother me so much? My open profile on Instagram allowed innumerable strange men to look at images of my life at will. That didn't bother me at all. *But I know what those images are. I know how they portray me.* I had no control of what he had seen, and I didn't like it.

I pulled out my phone, compulsively checking my social media for notifications. Nothing. Instant emptiness and depression. It had been several days since I had posted anything. What did I expect? If I disappeared from social media, no one would miss me.

With late afternoon approaching, the sun appeared through a break in the clouds. I tried to stop tapping my feet and fidgeting with the pens on my desk. Soon I would be looking at the personal images on the tablet. Corey wasn't the only one who wanted answers. After I saw them, we would be on equal footing again.

I drove home to change before going to the library. My meeting spot was much closer than Corey was probably comfortable with. I could almost walk there from my townhouse. I parked on the driveway in front of the garage, only intending to be inside for a few minutes.

The neighbor's dog barked persistently as I walked up the path. The screen door had been left open partway. My hair stood on end. Sheila trusted people too easily, but she usually locked both doors. Maybe she had the evening off. I touched the doorknob before sliding the key into the lock. It twisted easily to the right. She hadn't locked the main door either. My hand trembled. I pushed it open slowly.

"Sheila?" I called.

No response. I surveyed the room before stepping inside. Maybe she was in the shower. Everything appeared normal on the main floor. Kitchen, living room, and dining room looked just as I had left them that morning. After listening to the dog bark for a few seconds, I came all the way inside and slammed the door, locking it immediately.

I took off my shoes on the mat and carried them to the kitchen, checking for the pile of mail that Sheila typically threw on the counter. I only saw the organized stack of grocery ads I had sorted the day before. My stomach tightened as I made my way up the stairs to my bedroom. Sheila's door hung open and I couldn't hear the shower running. I threw my shoes into my room and walked down the short hall to Sheila's.

"Sheila?"

The door produced a low creaking sound as I pushed it open. I flicked on the light. The room was in complete shambles. My heart jumped into my throat and stopped beating for a second before resuming wildly. All of her drawers had been emptied onto the floor, and the mattress and bedding had been thrown against the wall.

Blood surged to my extremities as I ran back to my own room, throwing my fist against the light switch. It was the same. Drawers and mattress—completely dismantled. Could they still be in the house? *Run.*

I grabbed my shoes off the floor and ran back down the stairs, leaving the lights on as I bounded for the front door. My hands slipped when I twisted the handle back and forth. It flung open, and I jerked it closed immediately behind me. Clicking the unlock button repeatedly on my keys, I dove inside the car, knocking my shoulder against the steering wheel.

Trying to catch my breath, I fumbled inside my purse for my phone.

My shaky hands finally connected with the power button. 5:20. Corey would be on his way to the library. I started the engine. Omnibus was watching my communication. I couldn't send him a message. I looked back at the townhouse. My pulse made visible flashes in my darkening tunnel vision. *Omnibus.*

*In through the nose on a three count. Out through the mouth.* I closed my eyes until my heart rate slowed. I thought about the undisturbed lower level of the house. Someone had been looking for the tablet. I turned the air conditioner on full blast, instantly feeling less claustrophobic as it pushed away the heat and humidity. I backed out of the driveway, and the car lurched away from the house.

I hit both red lights on the way to the library. I kept an eye on my rearview mirror. The only car behind me was a minivan with a middle-aged mom driving. She continued on straight when I turned on the side street that led to the library. I breathed a sigh of relief.

I clipped the curb with my right rear tire when I rounded the corner into the mostly empty library parking lot. I shivered, thinking about the photo I had Instagrammed the week before of the ivy climbing up the side of the square stone building. The caption I had composed about the quaint 1970s architecture transporting me to another era felt oddly prophetic. The building from the past now housed the images of my future—if Corey had come.

My temples throbbed. He had to be inside. I looked for a driver in each of the parked cars before leaving the safety of mine and then tried not to sprint around the side of the library to the sliding doors.

Only a few patrons wandered the isles. I attempted to act casual as I caught my breath and passed frantically up and down the rows of books looking for Corey. I spotted him sitting at a desk in a corner near a window. I froze, watching him before he saw me. He had a few books spread out in front of him, and blue sticky notes dotted the table and the wall behind it.

"Hey," I whispered when I stood directly behind him. I had to bite my cheek to keep from blurting out everything about the break-in.

"Hey," he answered without looking up from the book in front of him.

When he didn't pick up on my tension, I glanced over his shoulder to see what was so engrossing. "What is all of this?" I asked as I read some of the notes. A series of numbers and then a word on each paper. Victory. Key. Answer. Mountain.

"Give me a moment," he replied. "I'll show you. Do you think they have a conference room we can use?"

"I'll ask," I panted, jerking back toward the entrance and the checkout desk. Anyone else would have asked me what was wrong, but Corey seemed oblivious.

The mousy librarian pointed me to a door behind the children's section. I nodded to Corey. He gathered up his notes and books and followed me there. The room had a small window in the door and several long narrow windows lined the outer brick wall.

"They're looking for it," I said as soon as I closed the door. I tried to keep my voice slow and steady, but it shook. "Someone was in my townhouse today searching for it."

Corey's face turned white. "What happened?" He walked back toward the door where I was still standing.

"It was while I was gone to work." My voice cracked. "They didn't clean up after themselves."

Pupils dilating completely, Corey's eyes went cold. "Did anyone follow you here?"

I shrugged. "I don't think so."

He looked toward the windows. "I have to show you something." He dropped his arms to his sides and moved to the table. Opening a book, he spread out the blue sticky notes. I followed him, pulling a chair away from the table.

"What is this?" I asked breathlessly.

"Remember the timestamp on the bottom of the images?"

I nodded.

"I went back through each of the images and copied them down. It's one of the oldest, simplest codes out there. My dad and I sent messages back and forth this way when I could barely read and write."

I looked at the numbers on the top of his sticky notes. They looked completely random.

"How do you solve it?"

"You need a Bible," Corey said, reaching for his phone. "It's much easier now. Back in the day, I had to search through the actual book for the words. It was tedious." He opened up an online King James Version of the Bible.

Picking up the first sticky note with the numbers "19 35 03 07," he showed me how it worked. "The first two digits are the book." He went to the table of contents and counted down nineteen books. Psalms. He typed it into the search bar, followed by chapter 35 and verse 3. I held my breath while it loaded.

*Draw out also the spear, and stop the way against them that persecute me: say unto my soul, I am thy salvation.*

"The seventh word is *stop*," he said. "You see—simple."

I scanned the other words he had looked up. Each note was numbered in the upper left-hand corner. I began pulling them off of the book, placing them in order.

*stop victory find answer how inside fruitful meadow mountain key*

"My father and I tried to keep it simple and meaningful," Corey said, watching my face as I read the message over and over. He was silent for a few seconds. "Does it mean anything to you?" he finally asked.

I looked up at his clear searching eyes. He knew how to find and interpret the message, but he looked lost. *He doesn't know what it means.* My neck tingled. I did.

I saw myself moving the papers before I began doing it. Without speaking, I rearranged the notes into three separate rows. Picking up Corey's pen, I scratched out the last letter on victory.

*stop victor*
*find answer how inside fruitful meadow*
*mountain key*

I could feel Corey's excitement as he leaned toward the table. "Okay," he said, touching the words, "what are the fruitful meadow and the mountain?"

"Where's the tablet?" I whispered.

Corey reached inside his backpack and pulled it out. Relief surged through me like a drug when I saw the flashing Omnibus symbol. I took the tablet out of Corey's hands and held it for a moment before pressing the button.

"Open tools," I said as soon as the three icons appeared.

"Proceed with password," the voice prompted. Password. *In through the nose on a three count. Out through the mouth.* Password. My heart slowed and my head cleared.

A fluorescent light flickered above us. Looking at the ceiling, I pinched my eyes shut when the flashing caused a quick, intense head-ache in my temples.

\* \* \*

*I kneel in the window seat, face pressed against the glass, watching the smoldering mountain in the distance. Responsibility sits heavy on my little shoulders. During my watch, I sketch out hundreds of plans to put the fire out: garden hoses, bucket brigades, fire trucks, water towers, and even more creative kindergarten solutions like giant marshmallows. My father will systematically reject each of my plans, calmly explaining the inner workings of a volcano, but I continue drawing anyway. How can I make him understand?*

\* \* \*

The pain faded as soon as I opened my eyes. Clarity took its place.

"Etna," I whispered.

The tools menu opened silently. Corey raised his eyebrows. Shivers ran down my spine. *It really is mine.*

"The mountain?" Corey asked.

I nodded. "It's the key—the keyword, I suppose."

"What about fruitful meadow? Does that mean anything to you?"

"My father," I said, blinking away the mist in my eyes. "It's what *vega* means in Spanish—fruitful meadow."

"Then we need to talk to your father," Corey concluded.

My head pounded as I considered it. My father—old friend of Victor Trent, future member of Victor Trent's Joint Chiefs of Staff. My father had practically accepted this job for me and made all of the arrangements to move me here. He might have the answers about Victor Trent, but I needed to be sure my father would want to stop him before I told him about any of this. I swallowed hard.

"I don't think I'm ready to do that yet."

"Why not?" Corey wanted to know. "If he knows how to stop Victor . . . " His voice trailed off as his eyes bored into mine. I looked away.

He nodded like he understood. "The admiral intimidates his own daughter." He slid away from the table, looking at the tools menu that was projected above the tablet.

I looked down, trying to suppress the sting of his words. It was true. I was intimidated. I was afraid to find out that my father wasn't the man that I thought he was—afraid that his future actions might distance us even more than we already were from each other. I was afraid that I would be left completely alone.

"I just need more time. I need to know more before I ask him."

"Jace, time is something we might not have. Someone knows you have the tablet."

My mind began to spin. I thought about the casual way I had carried it around the building that first day. Omnibus was sure to have security tapes of me showing it to Mitch—tapes of me walking down that hallway—ducking into the maintenance closet. If someone wanted to know the truth about the tablet, all they had to do was ask Mitch. I thought about the lie I had told Damien about the images and how he had acted like he didn't know about Jim Evans being fired. But if the two events were related, then Damien had either told someone else what I had said, or he had decided to fire Jim himself. Why hadn't I pushed myself to pry for answers from him when I had had the chance?

I couldn't even begin to think about how we were going to stop Victor. My mind was consumed with the lie I had told Damien and the thought of losing my job. I looked at Corey. What had compelled me to lie to Damien and trust Corey with the truth? Damien was in a much more powerful position to stop Victor.

"We have to give it to him," I blurted out.

"What?" Corey asked. "Give what to who?"

"Corey, I told Damien about the first two images. I got Jim Evans fired. I showed the tablet to security. I carried it around the building. They have it all on the security tapes. Damien knows that I lied to him. If we want to keep our jobs, I think we have to give it to him."

Corey kept intense eye contact as he considered what I said. "Jace, if they're looking for it and firing people because of what you said about just the first two images, why do you think that showing them the rest of the images is going to save our jobs?"

He was right. The world seemed to be closing in around me. How could I save our jobs?

"What if we delete everything except the two images that I told him about?" I paced as the idea became clearer in my mind.

Corey looked from me down to the tablet.

"Everything?" he asked. "We haven't even looked at the J file yet."

I paced back toward the table a few steps and froze when a shadow passed by the windows on the front side of the building. I held my breath. Corey's eyes followed mine.

"Power down," I quickly spoke. The tablet instantly went dark.

A second, miniature shadow toddled into view. I let out a long breath. Looking at the J file here was too dangerous.

"Did you see anything in the personal images that would get us fired?" I asked in a hushed tone.

Corey didn't answer right away. He searched my face, trying to understand what I was thinking. "No," he finally replied, "but don't you still want to look at them?"

*Of course I still want to look at them*, I thought. I looked down at the floor. "What if we can get Damien on our side, or at least convince him that we are on his?"

Corey looked doubtful. "How are you going to do that?"

"Corey, we don't really know what role Damien is going to play in the takeover and the new government. What if he is just an innocent bystander like us? Maybe the information crisis is going to bring him to his knees just like the rest of the country. We don't know him yet. Maybe he can help us stop it."

Corey rolled his eyes. "Or maybe having the tablet will accelerate their plans." His voice was gruff. "Do you really want to do something that might give them more power, Jace?"

The thought made my shoulders tense. I didn't want to do anything that would give Omnibus more power, but they already knew about the tablet. They were looking for it. Eventually they were going to find it unless we were willing to run away and hide. We couldn't do that.

"How are we going to stop them, Corey? How are we even going to fight them? Timing can't be a coincidence here. We could have sent the tablet to ourselves at Stanford or even earlier, but why do you think we waited until now? The day you started at Omnibus, Corey. We need to keep our jobs. We need to seem like we aren't a threat." My voice was growing gradually louder. "I want to give the tablet to Damien. If we delete the Omnibus file, he won't have any more information than he already has. We can build trust with him and take suspicion off us until we can come up with a solid plan."

Corey's eyes shifted and he took a step away from me. "What about the J file?"

"He doesn't know that we have the password. Nobody does." A chill went through me.

"We should look at it and then delete it too."

I knew that the information in the J file was vital, but I was suddenly afraid to look at it. If my plan didn't work—if Damien was already entrenched in a plot to take over the country, then I would have to lie about the J file. My mouth was dry.

I looked into Corey's eyes. "I think we should wait," I said. "It will be less dangerous for both of us if we don't know what's in it."

"So you won't have to lie about it," he replied. His tone was almost mocking.

Without waiting for Corey's approval, I opened the Omnibus file. Corey sat in silence as I moved the first two images to the Personal folder.

"Do you have everything you need from the Omnibus file?" I asked.

"You're going to delete it?"

"Yes," I said, "If I just leave the DC images and personal images, I think I can convince Damien that the whole thing was a misunderstanding. I can tell him the truth about how I found it."

I sucked in a breath of air. "If anything goes wrong, I'll take the blame. They don't know anything about you or our connection. You'll be safe."

Corey nodded slowly. He didn't say anything right away. He paced away from the table with his arms behind his back.

"Okay," he said, turning back toward me. "Show it to him." It sounded like a command. "But show him the third image too. If you're going to tell him the truth, he might as well know about me too. Show him the pictures and see what he says."

Why would Corey want to take the fall with me? My neck tingled. Maybe he was afraid of being questioned about it. Maybe he was worried we had been seen together. I wished I had chosen a safer meeting place.

I nodded and reopened the Omnibus folder. I moved the image of us in the lab coats to the personal folder.

"Delete Omnibus folder," I said. The tablet verified and confirmed that I wanted to delete the content and file folder. The images and folder evaporated. My stomach tightened.

I went back to the tools menu.

"View history," I said. A small surge of anger resurfaced when I saw that Corey had accessed all of the files in the personal folder, not just "a few." My face was on fire, but I stopped myself from saying anything about it.

"Delete history," I said.

I took a deep breath and picked up my phone before I could talk myself out of it. Pulling up Damien's number with trembling fingers, I clicked on it. It started dialing before I decided exactly what I was going to say. He answered on the third ring.

"Jace, this is a pleasant surprise. I was planning to call you later."

"I need to talk to you, Damien. Do you have time to see me tonight?" I tried to hide that I was breathless.

"Are you okay?" It almost sounded like real concern in his voice. It was impossible for someone with my inexperience to say.

I forced myself to speak slowly. "Yes, I'm okay. I just have something really important that I need to talk to you about."

"Sure. Should I come over?"

"No," I said, a little too quickly. "Can we meet somewhere, or I can come to you?" Corey watched me intently.

"Of course. Why don't you come here?"

"Thank you." I felt relieved. "In about twenty minutes or so?"

"Sure, that's fine."

I hung up the phone and looked at Corey.

"Be careful, Jace," Corey said. "I think you have to assume that Trent is the big bad wolf."

"Don't worry. I will."

"I'll meet you in the cafeteria tomorrow at noon if we both still have jobs," he said.

Nodding, I gathered my things and walked away from the library. I programmed Damien's Summit Avenue address into my phone's GPS. It was time to see if my Stanford education was worth what I had paid for it. I was about to test every advertising theory I had ever learned—selling myself.

12

After passing downtown St. Paul, I exited the freeway on Lexington Parkway into an area built around the turn of the century. Well-kept historic mansions lined both sides of Summit Avenue. The homes sat far back and were surrounded by manicured yards. I hadn't ventured to this part of the city before, but Sheila had mentioned that her boyfriend's mom was an astrologer in the area.

Several joggers and cyclists passed by, enjoying the warm evening. I longed to be a jogger at that moment. A run would have brought my thoughts into focus. I jumped when the voice on my GPS informed me that we were approaching our destination. The gated, three-story brownstone home wasn't what I expected. With a new money megafortune, the Trents should have been living in a larger home in a newer part of town.

I parked and tried to empty my mind. I had gone through several scenarios, trying to plan what I would say. None of them made sense now. *In through the nose on a three count. Out through the mouth.*

I finally pushed the car door open and walked through the unlocked gate up the path. Damien answered the door himself just a few seconds after I rang the bell. He met my nervous gaze with a reassuring smile, silently motioning me inside. Wearing a fitted, untucked Purdue T-shirt, dark-wash blue jeans, and brown flip-flops, he looked perfectly at home and comfortable. I let his magnetic eyes pull me across the threshold, but my legs trembled.

Once I was inside the expansive, dark wood–paneled entry hall,

Damien softly touched the back of my arm, guiding me toward a small conversation room just to the left of the wide wooden staircase. He didn't ask any questions. He seemed to sense my nerves. I looked back at the entryway before leaving it. The hall was lined with ornately framed portraits. Navy men mostly. I couldn't help gawking a little.

"Your family?" I asked, hoping to sound normal.

Damien nodded. "Eight generations in the United States Navy." He pointed at the painting to our left. "Henry Drake was a blockade runner in the Revolution." The stern-looking captain had Damien's classic good looks and blond hair.

Damien smiled and continued through the doorway into the antique-filled parlor. He offered me a drink and looked disappointed when I asked for water. He probably thought a drink would relax me—but I knew I had to stay in control. He sat down next to me on a vintage floral sofa and set our drinks on coasters on the polished coffee table.

"So what's going on, Jace?" he finally asked. "You seem pretty tense."

I set my water down and inched away from him a little. "Damien, I have to tell you something."

He looked puzzled and amused, reaching his hand over to my knee. "What is it? It can't be much worse than forgetting what we meant to each other in kindergarten." I managed a laugh, but it wasn't very convincing. My mind had gone blank. I could only focus on his hand.

Fumbling with my purse, I pulled out the tablet and set it on the couch between us. He examined it for a second, running his finger over the Omnibus symbol in the corner. His smile disappeared. He moved his hand off my knee to pick it up. I let my breath out slowly. He lifted his gaze back to my eyes and smiled, silently waiting for an explanation.

"I found this on Battle Creek path Monday morning when I was out running. I tried to catch up with whoever dropped it, but they were gone."

Damien set the tablet down on the sofa and put his hand back on my knee. I jumped. "Relax," he said. "I'm not going to bite you."

I took another deep breath before continuing. "I had planned to bring it to work to see if someone was missing it, but I accidentally turned it on." I pressed the button for effect, sending the Omnibus hologram into the air and simultaneously pushing his hand off my knee.

Damien sat motionless. If he was surprised, I couldn't tell.

"Don't worry about it, Jace. Anyone would have been curious."

Surprised at his nonchalance, I took a little sip of my water. "I wish that were the whole story, but turning it on was only the beginning."

"Go on," he said.

"Well, first of all, I discovered that it's voice activated and it only responds to my voice." He moved forward on his seat. "And then I looked at some of the images on the camera and they were a bit confusing."

I opened the camera. Damien kept his eyes on the tablet. When the first image appeared, it took him a few seconds to realize what he was seeing. He looked first at the Washington Monument and the Capitol Building, and then his eyes moved to the buildings in between. His face lit up with recognition, realizing that this was the image that I had described to him, supposedly lying on the scanner in the office. I waited for disappointment or anger when he realized my dishonesty, but instead, his amusement seemed to amplify.

"Is the one with the soldiers and ray guns on here too?"

I nodded, showing it to him.

"Why did you make up the story about the scanner instead of just showing this to me right away?"

"I'm sorry about that," I said sincerely. "At first I thought it must belong to a student working on some strange advertising project, but I was just so confused after I looked at the next image."

I advanced to the image with Corey and the lab coats. Damien's jaw dropped. He moved forward on the couch and reached his hand into the hologram, penetrating the stark red Omnibus symbol on my white coat.

"What is this?" he asked.

I had finally shown him something unexpected. I held my breath. "Exactly what I wanted to know. I'm sure you can imagine how I felt when I saw this."

"Did you find it the same day that I walked you to the parking lot?"

"Yes," I said. "I was so confused about the whole thing. I wanted to try to figure out who would have created the Washington, DC, images and why they included one of me and Corey."

"And then dropped the thing right on a path where they knew you would find it."

"Exactly."

Damien looked from me back to the image.

The smile left his face. "Who's Corey?"

"Well, that's strange too. He just started working for you in product development. He went to school at Stanford and lived in my apartment complex there, but I barely knew him."

He hesitated before asking, "So why did you decide to come to me with this now?"

I took another drink of water. "I know this all seems crazy. I think this tablet belongs to me, but the technology belongs to Omnibus."

"Belongs to you?" He seemed intrigued more than questioning.

"It's full of pictures of me," I replied. "Pictures that I don't remember and I never posed for. It doesn't seem to be the result of photo editing."

Damien absorbed my words for almost a full minute. He stood up, walked to the window, pushed aside the lace curtain, and peered out. *What is he thinking? Does he believe me?*

"I wanted to show you before. But tonight I realized that I need your help. When I came home after work, my townhouse was turned upside down."

He stopped dead in his tracks. "Your place got broken into?"

"Yes, and they didn't take anything. I think that someone knows about this tablet and is looking for it."

He sat down again next to me, this time even closer. He brushed his arm against mine, and uncontrollable butterflies swarmed inside me.

"It's good that you came to me. Is there anything else on this besides the pictures?" he asked.

I navigated back to the startup screen. "The tools and this other file are password protected."

Damien pushed his hand through the Omnibus symbol with the intertwined J. He was lost in thought.

"Do you know what the password is?"

I shook my head, trying to keep my face from flushing.

"Can I look at the rest of the images?" he asked. This was exactly what I had hoped would happen. My heart picked up.

"I haven't seen them yet either."

"In three days?" Damien's eyes widened. "Why not?"

I hesitated. "I ran into Corey at the park on Monday night. It all just seemed so strange and coincidental. I showed him the tablet and he wanted to keep it and tinker with it overnight. It doesn't have any ports. He wanted to try to figure out how to charge it."

Damien examined it. "Hmm. It doesn't, does it?" The holograms hadn't surprised him, but this detail seemed to. After a moment, the concern left his face. "Well, let's have a look."

I hoped that Corey was right, that the personal images weren't incriminating. Realizing that I had no control over what we were going to find, I took a deep breath and advanced the image.

The first image was a scenery shot in the mountains with a lake in the foreground. Fall colors and the reflection on the lake created a beautiful composition. If I had been alone, I would have spent more time admiring it. A clever hashtag and the X-Pro II filter would easily get this image two hundred likes.

The next image had more to look at. Still picturing the mountains, the image featured the backpacks of five hikers. No faces were visible, but the mountain was in perfect focus. Two of the figures were female and three male. I studied it for a second and then looked at Damien for approval to move on.

"Can't tell much from this," he said.

"Next image," I said.

A blazing campfire at sunset. Five hikers surrounded it, but this time three females and only two males. Even in firelight, I recognized myself in the center of the image.

"You dress down nicely," Damien said. Khaki hiking shorts and a black tank top didn't look like I was trying to impress anyone, and my long hair was piled high in a messy bun. The picture could have been completely current. I didn't look any older. But the other people were all strangers. I didn't recognize anyone.

I moved on. This one was taken inside a classroom. Eight rows of uniform-clad students sat at simple long tables, blank tablets in front of them. They looked so young, probably kindergarten or first grade. The students posed with hands crossed on top of their desks, smiling for the camera. One little girl on the second row in the center stood out, looking oddly familiar. She had striking bright-blue eyes, dimples, tanned skin, and sandy blonde hair pulled back in a smooth ponytail. My stomach fluttered.

"Interesting," mused Damien. "Very minimalist."

I studied the image without responding. The classroom of the future looked too sterile for my taste.

I advanced to the next image. It was a selfie. Completely my style. The little girl stood with her face right next to mine. Blue eyes instead of green and lighter skin and hair, but she was a miniature me. My spine tingled.

"Oh, wow!" Damien exclaimed. "She looks just like you! Go back to the school picture. I think I saw her in the middle."

"Previous image," I squeaked.

He sat forward on the couch, pointing out the little girl. My mind and body froze. I couldn't register it. *My child?*

Advancing to the close-up again, I studied it.

"She's beautiful," I said, tracing her heart-shaped face. "She looks so much like my mom."

"So do you," Damien observed softly.

I didn't want to think about my mom now. I bit my cheek to keep my emotions in check. My eyes jumped back to the image. The little girl couldn't be mine. *I* was the little girl—I still needed a mom too much to be a mom.

Damien watched me shift my eyes and clear my throat, trying to compose myself enough to advance the image. He stood up and reached for my hand. "Have you had dinner? I could use a little break."

I shook my head and blinked. He didn't say anything else; he just led me out of the room and down the hall into a large, modern kitchen. My emotion eased with each step away from the tablet and its images.

He sat me on a stool behind a counter where I watched him begin to work. He was completely comfortable and knew his way around the kitchen. It only took him a few minutes to cook a ham-and-cheese omelet. I yawned just as the smell of the sautéed food reached my nose. My mouth watered.

When we were seated side by side at the counter, Damien finally spoke. "I wonder if we should really be looking at these pictures. I mean, they're clearly of your future. I don't understand how or why, but we don't want to do anything that will change her world." His concern for the little girl touched me and then placed a guilty load on my shoulders. I hadn't even considered how all of this might affect her. I had been too busy wallowing in self-pity.

My phone suddenly lit up and began buzzing. I turned it over and saw Sheila's name on the screen. How could I have left her with my mess to clean up? I hadn't even thought about what she was going to come home to. My face caught fire.

"Hello," I answered timidly. Sheila's words spilled out like steaming coffee. "Jace! Praise the mother you're alive! The door wasn't locked when I came home and the house was turned upside down." Her voice became muffled; she must have put her hand over the receiver. "It's okay, officers. She sounds fine." She uncovered it again. "Where are you?"

"I'll be home soon," I said looking at Damien.

"Yeah, I thought you'd finally snapped. Or that you'd been kidnapped. You should see this place! But you'd better pop some Valium first."

Damien could hear everything Sheila said. Was he wondering why I hadn't called the police? I was losing my grip on reality.

"I'll be home soon. Is there anything I need to do?"

"You'll probably have to file your own police report if anything's missing," she said, "That's the most irritating thing about this. It seems like my stuff's all here. What kind of idiot breaks in without taking something? I mean, really—anything! 'Don't have much to do tonight. I think I'll just pop by Sheila's place and try on every pair of her panties and then make a dung heap sculpture with them.' Who does that? The television is only like eight feet from the door. Make a ruddy effort, moron."

Damien listened with amusement as he gathered our dishes. I hung up as soon as I could.

"Roommate," I said.

He smiled.

"What do you think? Should we call it a night?" He hesitated and then added, "Or do you want to look at more pictures?"

It wasn't a real question for me. I wished I could trust Damien with the whole truth—Corey, the pocket watch, the code, and my father having the answers. We had to look at the images. The tablet had been dropped in my path for a reason. The personal pictures might not tell me what to do, but they were important enough to be included.

"I want to look at them."

He moved to the door without hesitation. I was relieved that his curiosity seemed to match mine. Hopefully, knowing about my future would help the little girl, not hurt her.

When we were seated next to each other on the sofa again, we resumed. We passed through several images of the little girl at the park on a playground, at an Easter egg hunt, at a dance recital, at a petting zoo. I was in many of them, interacting with her—holding her hand, touching her shoulder, pushing her on a swing, crouched down together looking at a ladybug on a leaf.

I noticed the simple emerald-cut diamond ring on my left ring finger in one of the images. Damien made eye contact just after I saw it. I blushed, staring at the carpet.

"How is her father always missing in these images?" Damien asked.

"He must be taking the pictures."

"But don't you think it's weird that there aren't any of him and the little girl?"

"Maybe he's shy or has some kind of deformity," I said. Damien threw his head back and laughed. My anxiety melted a little.

I became more engrossed as picture after picture passed, and I knew this wouldn't be the only time I would look at these. This future. The little girl. My life. It looked satisfying. My shoulders gradually let go of the tension they had been holding, and I found myself smiling.

About fifty images in, we came to three banquet pictures that seemed out of place. Taken in a ballroom, a large digital screen displayed the Omnibus symbol behind a modern white fiberglass podium. One of the images focused on the audience seated at elegant place settings around large round tables. In the second, the people stood, applauding. The third was a close-up of the podium, embellished with a large Omnibus symbol. The digital screen displayed the keynote speaker's name: Dr. Corey Stein. My heart pushed painfully against my ribs.

"Interesting," said Damien. I had momentarily forgotten his

presence in the room. What was he thinking about the images? That Corey Stein would be important to Omnibus someday? I couldn't stop skimming the image for clues about my relationship to him. If I assumed that I had taken these pictures, I could come to only one conclusion: *Corey Stein will be important to me someday.*

It was difficult to distinguish individuals in the sea of tables. After a moment, I focused on the crowded table closest to the camera.

"Look! I must be sitting right here. The chair is empty, and that looks like my name on the card." Without hesitating, I told the tablet to zoom and the numbered grid appeared. "Section 15, zoom 40 percent."

The section I had blown up was curious. The name card took center stage, but only half of it was even readable. The slightly blurry left side of the image was my first name, but the right side with the last name was completely obscured with a shadow.

"Strange lighting," Damien commented.

I nodded, still deep in my own thoughts. If I had been alone, I would have tried to enhance the image, but I didn't want to seem overly obsessed. I advanced the image when our silence became awkward.

Corey and Damien materialized. They shared the same stage and podium from the previous images, smiling and shaking hands like old friends. *Disturbing.* I watched Damien from the corner of my eyes. His expression didn't change, but I imagined he was making a mental note to call Corey into his office. *What will Dr. Corey Stein contribute to Omnibus?* I wondered.

As the last image faded, I powered down the tablet and picked up my phone. More than an hour had passed since dinner. I blinked hard, reviewing the evening: the little girl, swimming lessons, horseback riding, golf, amusement parks, hiking, camping. Nothing in the images revealed any dissatisfaction with Omnibus—or the identity of the child's father.

"That's it?" Damien sat back, his arms folded across his chest, deep in thought.

"What are we going to do with this?" I asked.

He waited, sitting forward and touching the corner of the tablet again, "It's yours, Jace. You found it, and it obviously belongs to you. It's your future, so what are you going to do with it?"

Clarity eluded me. The personal images and the Omnibus images sent directly conflicting messages. How would stopping Victor and Omnibus change my beautiful future? My stomach balled up.

Damien watched my face intently. I shifted in my seat. He didn't even begin to understand what it all meant. All he had seen were a couple of strange pictures of Washington, DC, and a prolific photo album.

"It's my tablet, but the technology belongs to Omnibus. I work for you, Damien." I watched for some kind of reaction, but his face didn't change. "Do you want to show your father?" I asked.

"No," he said calmly. "I don't think we should tell anyone else about this."

Astounding. Completely unexpected.

"What about whoever ransacked my apartment? It seems like someone else already knows about it." I watched his face closely for a reaction. If Omnibus had sent someone to find the tablet, had Damien been aware of it?

"Stay close to me, Jace, and I'll make sure you're protected." His promise sent a shiver down my spine. He was saying exactly what I had hoped he would. He was on my side, but staying close to him terrified me.

**I** awkwardly gathered my things.

"Are you going to be okay going home tonight?" he asked.

"I'll be fine." I couldn't get to the door fast enough.

"I would feel better if you stayed here until I can set up some security for you."

"Wouldn't that be a little awkward with your father?"

"My father?" He looked puzzled and then laughed. "My father's house is in Mendota Heights. It's a few miles south of here, but I doubt he's in town. He rarely is."

"I'd better get back to check on Sheila," I stammered. His eyes were bursting with amusement. He saw through my excuse before I finished giving it. Innocence was written all over my face, punctuated with flushed cheeks and a clumsy exit.

* * *

Sheila had already put her room back together and offered to help me when I got home.

"Where have you been, anyway?" she asked with a smirk.

I hesitated, folding my pants so that the crease was centered before stacking them in graduated color order from lightest to darkest.

"You've been with your life-sized Ken doll again, haven't you?" She laughed and elbowed me in the ribs. "Who is he?" She scooped up an armful of my camisoles and dropped them into the wrong drawer. "How did you meet him?"

"He's an old friend of the family." I tried to brush her off with my tone.

"You mean that you could have been seducing that fine piece of eye candy this whole time, and instead you've been at home eating your fiber and watching infomercials on the telly?"

I didn't answer, but a little smile slipped across my lips before I could extinguish it.

"By the way," she told me, "I ate the rest of that Kashi crap you buy. It was pretty good."

Later, I lay in bed. I was exhausted, but I couldn't turn my thoughts off. I finally reached for my phone and opened Instagram, hoping pictures of normal people would help me forget everything long enough to let me relax and fall asleep. My eyes drifted shut looking at a picture of a high school friend's new convertible.

* * *

*Soldiers. Swimming lessons. Banquets. Corey's face. Volcanic eruptions. Lava bubbles and spurts and rolls down a hill toward a hole in the ground. A shadowy figure shovels dirt into it, covering a coffin. My father's stern face. He turns and looks at me. I push him aside and dig the coffin out of the ground with my bare hands. Prying the lid off, I discover the little girl inside, posed with golden hair framing her face on a satin pillow. Just as I touch her hollow face, her eyes open and she gasps for air.*

* * *

Afraid to go back to sleep, I watched my alarm clock for almost twenty minutes before it finally went off. Everything that was happening to me seemed to be unraveling my already tattered psyche. Considering the events of the previous three days, my run was potentially ill advised, but I couldn't help myself. I needed a burst of adrenaline and a place to clear my head. I set out in the dark, looking over my shoulder several times as the wind moved through the trees. Images of the little girl haunted me. I felt a dull, empty ache for her. Whatever Corey and I planned to do to try to change Omnibus and the world was going to change her world too. I felt it. I had to consider it.

Hours later, I walked into the work cafeteria with some trepidation and spotted Corey at a table in the corner. He acted like he didn't see me. The cafeteria buzzed with coworkers' voices and utensils clinking. I dished up a plate at the salad bar and paid for it before joining Corey.

Slumped in his chair with his legs stretched out to the side of the table, he had posed himself to look casual. But his eyes were already asking for a full report of the evening before I sat down. He leaned forward with elbows on the table as I arranged my napkin and stirred my salad.

"What happened?" he asked as I was lifting a bite.

"It was better than I expected. I don't know how much Damien knew about the tablet before last night, but he seemed surprised by everything except the tablet itself." I paused. "Are you sure Omnibus isn't developing hologram technology?"

"Not here," he said, "but Megan discovered that Omnibus has a facility in India that's almost identical to this one. Who knows what they're working on there."

"We looked at all of the images together," I said. "I can see why you discounted it being a message. If the personal file has a purpose, it wasn't clear."

I held my breath, waiting for his approval. He didn't say anything, and his silence made me squirm.

"The little girl seems to be a central theme. What did you both make of her?" His eyes were almost accusing. I pictured her face in the casket from my dream. I bit my cheek to clear the image from my mind.

"Our life looks pretty idyllic," I said. "Whatever turmoil and chaos affects the rest of the world doesn't seem to impact me and my daughter." Verbally acknowledging my relationship to the little girl sent a chill through me.

He nodded. "Your husband must have an important role in the new governing body." His eyes flashed.

Why did he seem bitter that things had gone so well? His sarcasm was confusing and disturbing. I pushed another bite into my mouth before responding. *Corey's approval isn't any more important today than it was yesterday*, I tried to tell myself.

"Interesting that in almost one hundred images, we didn't manage to include one of the entire family together. It's almost like I didn't want myself to know who the father is."

"Did the two of you have any guesses?" he asked. I searched his clear eyes. Was I seeing anger? Jealousy?

"I have no way of knowing for sure," I said, brushing his insinuation aside. "If you're suggesting that I think it's Damien, you can calm down. We barely know each other, and I'm not some silly schoolgirl." His eyes didn't shift from mine.

"And you didn't see any resemblance in the little girl?"

I thought about it for a second—the blue eyes, the golden hair. Both would have seemed, to Corey, to come from another source than me. I should have just let him think whatever he wanted, but I felt compelled to ease his mind.

"Yes. She's the miniature of my mom: blue eyes, blonde hair, everything." My voice came out harsher than I had planned.

He broke eye contact, briefly embarrassed, before changing the subject. "How did he react to the Omnibus soldiers and DC images?"

I softened. "We didn't discuss it much. He only wondered why I had made up the story about finding the images on the scanner. I'm hoping he thinks that I believe Omnibus is going to have a really strong partnership with the government—sort of like Nike supplying uniforms and balls to a football team."

Corey grunted. I knew I was simplifying the situation. Damien wasn't stupid, and those images suggested more than a working relationship.

"And the J file?"

"He didn't question me when I told him that it was password protected."

"So what now?" he asked.

I paused. "Get as much information as possible? Look for a chink in their armor? Right now, the tablet is safe and so are our jobs. Damien acted like he didn't know anything about the break-in. He didn't want to show the tablet to his father. Damien promised to protect me. He has his security company watching my place."

"And what did he say about me?"

"Based on what we saw last night, I'd say he thinks you're going to be more valuable to him than I am."

He looked away. He knew I was right.

"So then, I don't see any reason to avoid seeing each other or hide our friendship," he said.

I nodded. I felt oddly happy to hear him call us friends.

"We should probably keep our meetings minimal and in public

places for a while until we're sure that he trusts you." What he said made sense, but I felt slightly deflated.

* * *

That afternoon, every time I closed my eyes, even to blink, I could see the flashing green light. My anticipation escalated as the end of the day approached. Sheila was working late. I could finally be alone to explore the tablet—with the password.

I closed the garage before I got out of my car and listened at the door before entering the house. Even with Damien's promise to protect me, I felt on edge.

The house was quiet. Everything was in its place. I closed the blinds downstairs and went to my bedroom. I locked my door and brought the tablet from the corner of the closet, where I had hidden it inside a box of my high school yearbooks.

My palms were sweaty. The real answers about the tablet—the reason for it being sent to me—would be in the J file. I was sure Corey wanted me to wait to look at the file until we were together, after we were sure that Damien trusted me, but I couldn't wait. I didn't want to. I didn't want to be influenced by or worried about his reaction. I wanted to know what was in it first.

Sitting down on the end of my bed, I looked at it before pressing the button. The light had dimmed significantly, and the dark pause between flashes was much longer. My heart dropped like a lead balloon.

I fumbled to press the button, taking a deep breath when the Omnibus symbol appeared. Whatever was hiding in the J file had better be concise.

"Jace Vega," I said quickly.

"Voice recognition validated," the voice soothed. The O with the interlaced J was the first of the three icons to appear. My hand trembled.

"Open J file," I spoke clearly.

"Proceed with password," the voice coaxed.

*In through the nose on a three count.* "Etna," I said. *Out through the mouth.*

The three icons faded and two file folders materialized. The hologram began to dim. My heart sounded like a tribal drum.

*No.* I looked at the flashing button. Even slower now, I pressed it.

The light turned red. *No, no, no!* I pressed it again and again, but the screen went dark.

I threw myself back on the bed and closed my eyes. Biting my cheek, I pushed away tears of anger and frustration. I was failing myself. *If I hadn't spent so much time looking at the personal images with Damien . . . If I had looked at the J file at the library with Corey . . .* Rolling over, I yanked my phone out of my pocket. 5:35. I opened my texts and composed one to Damien:

*I had an idea of what the password might be on the tablet. Was going to try it but the battery died.*

I changed my clothes and went downstairs. Flipping on the TV, I waited for Damien's reply. An old episode of *Iron Chef America* came on. I curled up on the couch and must have dozed off. Sheila's key in the lock woke me sometime later.

"What's up, buttercup?" she asked. Her burgundy hair was slicked up into a spiky ponytail. It was getting easier not to stare at her strange fashion creations, but tonight it was almost impossible. The red and purple plaid jumper might not have caught anyone's attention if she hadn't paired it with thigh-high patent leather combat boots. Tonight she was all punk, but Sheila was a fashion schizophrenic; tomorrow she might wear a vintage dress with her hair in pin curls. I had Instagrammed her outfits for my first two weeks in Minnesota but began to slack off when I realized that she made me look boring in comparison.

"What time is it?" I yawned.

"Just after 10:30. The last two hours have been torture," she complained. "I had two tables with parties of twelve. They all wanted separate checks. Don't even think about asking me for a diet Coke, 'cause I will pour it in your lap."

I reached for my phone as Sheila went on complaining about her night. Strange euphoria overcame me when I found a text waiting from Damien. I tried to rationalize that my senses were still in a dreamlike state, and I yawned again to try to convince myself.

*Have to go to Chicago tonight for an unexpected meeting. Be back Saturday afternoon. I think I know who can help with the battery. My security company is watching your house. Call if you need anything.*

I had expected him to put a higher priority on finding out what else was on the tablet. Did his sudden trip have anything to do with the tablet? My hands turned clammy.

Even my routine couldn't bring me out of the funk I was in the next morning. I looked at the lifeless tablet on my dresser. It felt like I was mourning another loss. It was an inanimate object. Self-disappointment tried to push away depression.

The day was drab and uneventful. I didn't make contact with Corey. I didn't want to tell him about the battery yet.

When evening came, I told myself that I wasn't disappointed that Damien hadn't called. For once, I wished that Sheila wasn't working. Doing something normal on a Friday night would have helped my mental state. I finally decided to take a walk over to the park on McKnight. Locking my front door, I looked around and wondered where Damien's security people were hiding themselves. None of the vehicles parked along the street had people in them.

Just as I was getting to the footpath that led to the park, my phone buzzed in my pocket. I fumbled a little for it, hungry to see Damien's name on the screen. I was surprised instead to see my father's name and number. Disappointment brought on guilt. He rarely called just to see how I was doing. Inside, I hoped that his intuition had told him to call, but I knew that line of thinking would only lead to disillusionment.

I cleared my throat before answering. I wasn't sure how much I should tell him about the week's activities, but I ached to blurt everything out and ask for his advice. It didn't matter anyway. My father hated talking on the phone. He got right to the point without even asking how I was doing.

"I'm going to be in the Twin Cities Monday and Tuesday next week, mija. I'd like to meet you for dinner on Monday and maybe come and see you on Tuesday if my meetings finish early enough."

I was surprised. What business brings a Navy Admiral to Minnesota? He traveled a lot with his job, but I thought it was usually scheduled months in advance. Would a normal daughter invite her father to stay with her? I brushed away the notion. I knew he wouldn't. I just told him that I would be excited to see him and would clear my schedule for Monday night.

"Great," he said. "I'll see you then." He ended the conversation. I spent the rest of my walk wondering how a dinner with my father would be without my mother there to soften the conversation and make it flow. I could count the number of times we had eaten together alone on one hand. When had it all changed? We had been so close when I was little.

I was back at home getting ready for bed when my phone finally buzzed with a text from Damien.

*I think I have the solution to the battery problem. Dinner at my place tomorrow night at 5?*

Without hesitating, I responded that I was free. Then my stomach tightened. I greedily anticipated his help with the battery, but then what? I had to make sure that I could look at the J file alone.

My phone buzzed a second time. It was Corey asking me to meet him in the park the next morning. I was relieved. I should probably talk things out with him before seeing Damien again.

That night, I tossed and turned. A colorful thunderstorm had blown in after sunset, filling my room with lightning flashes and shadows.

\* \* \*

*I walk into a crowded church. Faceless people dressed in black fill the pews and the center aisle. I can barely push my way past them. Finally breaking free, I walk toward the coffin at the front of the room. My mother's face is porcelain inside the satin-lined casket. I want to touch her—to try to wake her up. Tears roll down my face.*

*Light flashes. She's gone, replaced by the little girl's lifeless body. I should be equally distraught, but instead I'm just afraid.*

*The light flashes again. My mom's body in the coffin. My heart hurts. My cheek hurts. My palms hurt.*

*Light flashes. A cloud of volcanic ash spews out of the top of a pine-covered mountain. Two more flashes. City buildings on fire, burning to the ground.*

* * *

I woke up exhausted with a dull headache. I dressed quickly and sat for a moment scrolling through my Instagram feed, trying unsuccessfully to shake away the uneasy feeling my dream had left. Maybe being with Corey would help. I thought about Stanford. Hawthorne. Normalcy. I would give anything to go back.

Corey was playing at the park with Shane almost exactly as I had seen them on Monday, but today he threw a ball instead of a frisbee. My spine tingled. *Not déjà vu*, I told myself. *I really have seen this before.* He didn't stop what he was doing when he saw me. He waited for me to walk from the path to him on the far side of the field. When I reached him, he threw the ball one more time.

"How's life?" I finally asked.

"It's interesting," he replied. I waited for him to elaborate, but apparently he wanted me to fish.

"Anything specific?" I asked. I couldn't read his face.

"I have some news." His voice was barely audible. "Do you remember me mentioning Megan, my friend who was helping from Stanford?" I nodded and stepped toward him. "She's been digging around—finding things that completely corroborate what we saw on the tablet."

He paused to throw the ball again. "Omnibus has sizeable contracts with the Department of Defense."

I shrugged my shoulders. It wasn't unexpected.

"She stumbled onto something—they're storing massive amounts of product in state-of-the-art maximum security facilities in remote areas. Almost all of them offshore."

"Product?" I failed to see the significance.

"Think about it, Jace," Corey said, retrieving the ball from Shane's mouth and setting it down on the ground. "If Omnibus knows that this information crisis is coming—this terrorist attack— what if they're preparing to stage a rescue of the system? What if they're preparing to reclaim everyone's information, but on Omnibus devices, on the Omnibus network."

I was silent for a moment. "Don't you think that concluding Omnibus is going to cause the system crash is a bit premature? The images show Victor Trent coming to the rescue. They didn't clearly show who caused the crash." Corey paced toward the tree line.

"How did Megan get this information?" I continued to press. "I can't imagine that Omnibus just has the whole plan mapped out in a file somewhere for students to look up and write research papers on."

"No." He rolled his eyes. "But how do you explain Omnibus storing 800,000 smart phones in an underground warehouse in Zimbabwe?"

Why would they do that? Stockpiling devices didn't make any sense. My mind raced.

"She's on to something," he continued. "I trust Megan. She knows what she's doing. She's been careful to cover her tracks, but she contacted me yesterday to tell me that an Omnibus recruiter came into the computer lab looking for her and started asking a lot of questions. They knew exactly what she'd seen." Corey stepped in my direction. "She didn't tell them anything about us; she tried to cover for herself, but she's on edge now."

Shane came back with the ball. Corey scratched behind his ears for a second, then turned, and started walking toward the tree-lined path. I followed him silently.

"Jace, we need to come up with a solid plan."

I was at a complete loss. The boulder in my stomach didn't help. I felt keenly aware that I was playing this game at a disadvantage. I was a powerless pawn, and I didn't even understand the rules or the object of the game.

"What are you thinking?" I asked sincerely.

He pulled the ball from Shane's mouth and held it in both hands. "I think we should try to stop the information crash from happening."

I paused. "That would be good, but how?"

"Maybe if we take the tablet to the CIA or FBI . . ."

I immediately shook my head. Why would they believe us? They would take away the tablet. I was sure of that.

"Don't you think that if we had wanted the CIA or FBI to have

94

this information, we would have sent the tablet to them in the first place?"

He didn't answer right away. "You're right. We're going to have to stop them ourselves."

"How?"

"I think blowing up the storage facilities is a viable option," he said with a completely straight face.

I laughed awkwardly. His face didn't change. "You're joking, right?"

"Well, think about it. What other choices do we have? I could plant a virus and create chaos in their system, but that's going to get me caught. They're watching our every move electronically. They would expect that of me." My spine tingled. Based on what he had said about his friend, he was right. "We need to come up with something that doesn't lead them back to us. Use their own tactics. Make it like a terrorist attack. They wouldn't be looking for either one of us to strap a bomb to our chests and blow up a building."

"I think you should keep refining that plan," I said. "Maybe keep an open mind if something better comes along." I hoped that laughing at him would make him see how crazy he sounded, but he still looked determined and serious. "Corey, please don't tell me that you have a supply of explosives hanging around your apartment. I don't know the first thing about blowing something up, and I really hope you don't either." As soon as I said it, my stomach tightened. *Did he?*

"Should we try another of your big plans?" he asked sarcastically. "Maybe it could involve scheduling a picnic with Victor Trent, then baking a note inside his cherry pie asking him nicely to please *not* take over the world."

His words stabbed me in the chest. He thought I was completely ridiculous for trusting Damien. Why did I care so much? I didn't have to answer to him. Where was his sudden superiority complex coming from? He wasn't more educated, or smarter than me, and if he had been so opposed to my plan to take the tablet to Damien, why hadn't he been more vocal before I had done it?

When I didn't answer him back right away, Corey knew that he had hit a nerve. He let me steam in silence.

"I'm going to pursue this idea," he said. "Those propaganda images on the tablet try to paint Omnibus in a good light, but I'm not buying it. I don't want any part of what they are selling." I folded my arms across my chest, feeling a chill. "If you come across any information that will help me, I hope you won't keep it to yourself."

I took a step away. I didn't want to admit it, but his sudden contempt and bitterness toward me because of what had happened to Megan hurt. It wasn't my fault that the recruiters knew what she had been looking at, but it felt like he was blaming me. My heart tried to punch him repeatedly through my ribs.

"I'll tell you everything I know, you don't need to worry about that, but if you're going to light yourself like a Roman candle, I hope you're planning to Instagram it."

My passionate comeback didn't have the impact that I'd hoped for. Corey laughed nonchalantly.

"Come here, Shane!" he called. "Time to go, boy."

16

I tried not to think about my conversation with Corey, but it replayed in my mind while I was getting ready. Corey obviously didn't value my opinion or my friendship. I brushed mascara violently onto my lashes. He could continue to hunt for clues about how to blow up Omnibus with Megan. I would look to the tablet for answers.

The last time Damien had seen me, I had been a frizzy, wrinkled mess after the break-in. Tonight, I would be fresh. In a fitted pair of jeans and a loose white blouse, I looked nice, but not overdone. My curly hair was even and smooth after some quality time with my wand.

The nervous feeling in my stomach moved up and spread to my entire body by the time I reached Damien's front door. He didn't answer right away. I had just rung the bell a second time when he came. He took in my appearance, instantly showing his dimples. He reached for my hand and gently pulled me inside.

"You are a sight for sore eyes," he said as he led me to a family room adjacent to the kitchen. He had some pasta boiling on the stove and garlic bread toasting in the oven. My anxieties began to melt away.

"You're pretty handy in the kitchen," I said.

"I love to cook, but I don't get a chance to do it much with how often I travel." It seemed that his promise to protect me if I stayed close to him was going to be difficult to keep with his travel schedule. I picked up a carrot from the relish tray he had set out.

"How was Chicago?" I asked.

"Things went well." He walked over to the kitchen and pulled the bread out of the oven. "My friend thinks he knows what to do about the battery," he continued, "and he knows how to disassemble the tablet and remove the hard drive if we can't figure out the password on our own."

"What did he say about the battery?" I asked.

"He thinks it's recharged when the tablet comes into contact with an induction charging device we're developing. I wondered if that might be the case when you showed me that it didn't have any jacks or ports."

"What is it?" I asked "Do you have one?"

"It's very innovative. Omnibus actually began developing the technology to power pacemakers, but then they saw the potential of using it to power all of our devices." I walked over to where he was slicing the bread. "It's a chip that's able to harvest the electricity produced from the body's movement. It's encased in a silicon material that can be implanted anywhere in the body. To power a device, it would be implanted in the palm. It's just like using a charging mat for your Wii Remote, only you always have the charger with you."

I could picture what he was talking about, but the idea that it was real mystified me. "So, in order to see if it works with the tablet, you would need to test it with someone who has one of these chips implanted?"

"Yes," he responded, placing the sliced bread on an antique china tray.

"Does anyone in the area have one?" It was difficult to hide my excitement.

"We have thirty-five subjects testing them in the Atlanta area."

I had been hoping for an immediate solution to the problem. Damien finished dishing up the pasta and sauce and added some steamed vegetables to the side. He could hold his own on the Food Network. Everything looked picture perfect.

"Will you be going there anytime soon?" Masking the deflation I felt was difficult.

"I have a pretty tight travel schedule for next week, but I might have a solution that will fix the problem. Getting a charge in Atlanta would be a temporary fix—maybe a few days, and then we'd need a charge again." He pulled a clear thin strip out of his pocket. It was about the size of a dime. I could see the chip through the silicone. My body tingled.

"You want to put that in one of us?" My heart raced.

He looked into my eyes. "It's perfectly safe. I'm willing to do it, but it's your tablet, so it might make more sense for you to have the power source for it."

He set the chip on the table in front of me. I picked it up and flexed it several times. My brain was screaming that this was a terrible idea. I didn't want to have a piece of Omnibus permanently implanted in me. What if it was some kind of tracking device? But it would be an instant, permanent solution to the battery issue. I pictured the lifeless tablet sitting inside my purse. Omnibus was already watching my every move anyway. My slow breathing decelerated my heart.

"And you say that all it does is harness the electricity that my body produces?"

He lifted one corner of his mouth. "This generation is purely a power source, but we are developing a network that will provide customers a data signal almost anywhere in the world. The chip will eventually send and receive the data."

"Why?" My question escaped involuntarily. "I mean, why have the chip send and receive the signal instead of the device?"

I brought a bite of the mouthwatering pasta to my lips. Damien seemed to know how to make everything too appetizing to resist.

"The goal is to simplify upgrading. With the chip, customers will be able to change to the newest device without manually transferring their settings and contacts. The chip would instantly transfer that data from the cloud."

We ate in silence for a few minutes. My temples began to pulse. A green aura appeared in my right peripheral vision with each pulse.

"Who would implant it?" I set my fork down.

"We have a competent doctor right on Omnibus's campus who can implant the chip in just a few minutes." Damien's voice seemed to be coming from the other end of a long tunnel. "It would just be a local anesthetic and you can go to work the same day."

We both finished our dinner.

"I have something else I want you to consider, Jace," Damien said. He took our dishes to the sink and I followed him. "You're doing a great job in the PR department, but I don't like leaving you when I travel." I felt my face get hot. "Someone else knows about the tablet, and until we know who that is and what they want with it, I don't like leaving you alone." He turned off the faucet and began washing a plate in the bubble-filled sink. "My public relations liaison quit a few weeks ago, and I was thinking that you might be perfect for the job if you would consider it."

I backed away a little. Damien watched me out of the corner of his eye. "You would travel with me. You'd be in charge of writing my speeches and making me look good—right up your alley." *Stay close to me.* He wanted to keep his promise to protect me, but what if he wanted to do more than that? I felt like throwing up, but I would have constant direct access to Damien. With Corey's recent mood swings, I couldn't predict how he would feel about this.

I hesitated. "Can I have some time to think about it?"

"Of course." He nodded and then dried his hands on the dish towel. "But don't think about it too long, Jace," he said, touching my elbow. "I want you to come with me to New York next week. I have some important meetings and an appearance before a United Nations committee. I could use your help preparing for all of that."

My stomach tingled at his mention of the United Nations. If I traveled with Damien, I would know who he was meeting with and maybe even what his meetings were about. I knew I would say yes. How could I say no? But I needed to know what was in the J file before any of that. Without it, I would be flying blind.

Before the dishes were finished, I heard myself agree to have the chip implanted before Damien left for Baltimore on Monday morning.

MY decision left me so unsettled that I couldn't fall asleep. If only I could call my mom to talk to her about it. I opened my Instagram and forced myself to look at the pictures I had taken the week she had died. It was like pulling the scab away from a scrape: the alumni golf tournament I had helped organize, my pedicured toes inside a fountain, and a girls' night out at the theatre. If only I could replace the meaningless photos with pictures of one last trip to Monterey—cuddled up on the couch with my head on her shoulder, watching *Pretty in Pink* for the hundredth time. Maybe if I had been there she wouldn't have died.

I fell asleep with the lights on.

\* \* \*

*I feel the rumble of an explosion. I look all around for Corey. I can't see him, but I know he is somewhere close. He caused the explosion. The coffin appears in the darkness, but this time I won't open it. I already know what's inside. Fear seizes me. Instead I run—away from the coffin, away from the explosions.*

\* \* \*

Sometime in the night I got up and turned off the light. I slept much better after that.

I spent most of Sunday getting my townhouse ready for inspection in case my father decided he wanted to see it. He would expect to be able to bounce a quarter on my bedspread and see his reflection in my toaster.

My mind was swallowed up in the events of the previous week. I couldn't reconcile everything that had happened. How had the tablet been placed on my path? Who had put it there?

My father's unexpected visit seemed to be ominous timing. I still couldn't tell him about the tablet or the images on it, but I was ready to ask him some questions. I needed to understand his relationship with Victor Trent. I needed to know where his loyalties lay. Did my father believe the country's problems could still be solved by appealing to the Constitution, or would he be as enamored with Victor Trent as the rest of the country? I could never accuse him of what the images on the tablet seemed to indicate. I only hoped that there was some other explanation for my father sitting next to Victor Trent in those images.

Corey's partnership with Megan still confused and hurt me. I had gone out on a limb from the beginning to trust him, but for some reason he still didn't seem to trust me fully. Everything we had learned from the tablet suggested that we trusted each other implicitly in the future—we had used his code but my message. I had followed the plan almost exactly in taking the tablet to Damien, but Corey seemed so distant and bitter now. It bothered me that he was using Megan to help him come up with his own plans to stop Victor. Why did she have to be involved?

I hoped that Damien's chip would solve the battery problem. I was putting a lot of stock in what the J file would contain. I wanted it to spell out a plan. I wanted answers.

Sheila didn't have to work. She sat around watching her recorded soap operas all day while I cleaned. It wasn't until late afternoon that she came into my bathroom, where I was mindlessly scrubbing the grout in the shower with a toothbrush.

"Isn't this kind of excessive, even for you?" she chided.

I didn't laugh. My father's visit had triggered my obsessive thoughts and a cleaning frenzy. Corey's extreme plans to stop Victor and my complex relationship with Damien only fueled the flames.

"What's going on with you, Cinderella?"

I put the toothbrush down and pushed the hair off my forehead with the back of my arm. For once, Sheila looked genuinely concerned. I took a deep breath. "Nothing," I lied.

"C'mon," she pressed. "You've been at it all day. What's bothering you?"

I couldn't tell her what was really going on with me, but her small effort—the fact that she might care even a little, brought tears. I blinked them away, pretending my eyes were irritated by the fumes. I flipped on the exhaust fan, leaving my cleaning supplies on the bathroom counter.

"My dad's coming to town," I finally said. "We haven't talked much since my mom died. I guess I've just been thinking about it—wishing he would open up to me a bit."

Sheila nodded. "Maybe you have to open up to him a bit first," she said. "You're not exactly a walking emotional encyclopedia, and most men are even worse than you when it comes to talking about their feelings."

Her words struck a chord. Could I verbalize what I was feeling to my father, and if I did, how would he respond? Maybe talking about my mom would be a good place to start. Her death had infinitely widened the chasm between us. Could the dreams I had been having mean that I blamed myself for her death? The déjà vu had been so strong that day, but I had ignored it—telling myself that it would pass, just like it had thousands of times before. What if I had done something else? Even if I had just called her and talked to her about it, I might have delayed her enough that she wouldn't have been in the wrong place at the wrong time.

"Maybe you're right." I sighed, trying to stop the tears that were pushing against my lashes again.

"Of course I'm right." She punched my arm. "If you need them, I saved a few episodes of Doctor Phil for you that might come in handy. You could start with the one about how parents pass on obsessive-compulsive disorder."

I couldn't help laughing. I sat down in front of the television with Sheila. She pressed play on her episode of *The Young and the Restless*, and we silently watched for the rest of the evening.

* * *

The procedure was set for 7:00 a.m. I almost skipped my run because of my nerves, but I finally decided that it would help calm me down. Part of me wished I would run into Corey and Shane. I needed someone to talk me out of what I was about to do. But Corey's insensitive sarcasm would probably only further my resolve. I wanted to trust and confide in him, but the contempt and frustration I felt from him put me on the defensive. He was obviously important to my future, but he wasn't treating me like I was important to his.

I turned up "Thunderstruck" and finished my run alone—still unsure if I was doing the right thing.

\* \* \*

Damien stood waiting for me in front of building J. It was the building farthest from the main road. He looked confident and powerful in his suit. My eyes stayed on him a little too long. He could see that I was staring at him. I looked away and took a deep breath, waiting for my face to cool down before getting out of my car. I touched the lifeless tablet as I put my keys in my purse.

Inside the building, we passed through security and down a long corridor to a row of elevators. We entered one, and Damien pressed the button for the sixth floor.

"You look nervous," he said when the doors closed.

I smiled but stayed quiet, trying to hide the sweat on my palms. Damien reached out and held the back of my arm with a reassuring smile. His electric touch flipped my stomach upside down. I focused on my breathing. The elevator door opened to a clean, light blue and white furnished waiting room. Damien led me past the rows of chairs through a heavy door into a hall full of medical equipment. Guiding me inside an examination room, he sat me down on the table and then excused himself, promising to return quickly.

I looked around the room, trying to prevent the tunnel vision I felt coming on. It was just like any other doctor's office I had been in: a tall examination table against the wall, a desk with jars full of cotton swabs, gloves, and alcohol wipes. Posters about vaccination and various medical conditions lined the walls. I rubbed my hands gently on my cotton skirt. I wished that I was being put to sleep now. The thought of accidentally seeing my hand being cut open made me feel faint.

What would my father have told me if he was here? Probably "Visualize the outcome; whatever pain you feel will be worth it." I wasn't sure if that was the case this time. It had been true of my wisdom teeth and tonsils, but this wasn't solving a physical problem. Or maybe it was.

Damien came back with a short, gray-haired man in a white lab coat. He introduced himself and then immediately began listening to my heart and taking my blood pressure. Once he had charted all of my vitals, he opened a small drawer and pulled out a package of sterile surgical instruments. He arranged the instruments on a tray connected to the examination table.

Damien sat down in one of the chairs next to me. The doctor instructed me to lie back on the partially reclined table. I obeyed, trying to relax. He draped me with a paper sheet and asked me to place my hand on top of the drape. As I did, he retrieved a long syringe from another of the drawers. Needles were always the worst for me. I could feel my heart beating in my throat, and my chest heaved up and down dramatically. I tried to control it.

"You're going to be just fine." Damien stroked my arm with the back of his hand. "It will all be over in a few minutes."

It was all happening too fast. I wasn't sure that I wanted to do it anymore. *Stop the doctor before it's too late.* I looked up at the bright light above the table and tried to push away the throbbing headache that was starting in my temples.

\* \* \*

*I am on the swing. I hear it squeak when I move forward and groan when I pull my legs back. A little blue-eyed boy swings next to me. He goes forward when I go back. We both turn and look when a lady calls us for lunch. Her voice is sweet, but she is too far away to see her face.*

\* \* \*

Damien's blue eyes placed themselves between me and the bright light. "Ready?" he asked. I pinched my eyes closed and shook away the singular vision. Instead of putting on the brakes, I wetted my lips and nodded. The doctor injected the anesthetic into my left hand. The first jab was a little bit painful, but on the second and third, I only felt the pressure of the needle. I watched the doctor as he sterilized the surgical site with a brown solution. My hand felt enormous.

He opened the package that contained the chip, placing it on the table with the instruments. He waited for a few minutes and then began poking my hand to make sure it was numb. I couldn't feel any pain. I closed my eyes softly. I felt the pressure of the incision and retraction. The doctor quickly positioned the chip before closing the opening with two small stitches. I opened my eyes to watch him finish stitching me shut. He covered the area with a sterile pad, wrapped my hand in an ace bandage, and instructed me to avoid using it for the rest of the day.

Damien thanked the doctor and shook his hand. They walked outside the door for a moment, and then Damien returned alone.

"That's it," he said. "You did great." His praise warmed me.

I smiled and sat up. My head still throbbed, but I felt the tension slowly release. It was over. The chip was inside me. I would be able to look at the other file soon. Something rational could replace Corey's insane plan.

"What time do you leave today?" I asked.

"This afternoon. My plane leaves at five."

"How soon will this start harvesting electricity?"

"Right away, but you won't be producing much, since you will be taking it easy for the next twenty-four hours," he replied. "We'll be able to look at the J file when I get back."

I turned my palm over and stroked the bandage. I couldn't feel anything. Damien buttoned his suit coat and straightened his tie. He hadn't been kidding about how short and painless the procedure was. The anticipation had been worse than the actual event—like getting a flu shot.

"Listen, I've been thinking about your offer," I said, "and I'd be crazy not to take this opportunity."

He didn't repress his full dimpled smile. "You won't regret it," he vowed. "It will prepare you for your next job as the president's speech writer." He held his hand out to help me down from the table. I put my right hand into his and he wrapped his left arm around my waist, steadying me as I slid to my feet.

"I'll make all of the arrangements, and I'll notify your manager. Be ready to move into your new office on Wednesday." I lifted my eyebrows and smiled, waiting for him to let go of me. My heart pounded hard and I couldn't hide it. How was I going to keep my feelings under control spending every day with him?

"There are big things on the horizon for Omnibus," he said. He didn't loosen his hold. I looked at the door. Did he think this was typical boss and employee interaction? "I don't think we need the tablet to tell us that you are an important part of the future of this company."

My spine tingled as my legs melted. I couldn't peel my eyes away from his. For better or worse, my future was entangled with Omnibus's. The pounding in my chest became painful. *In through the nose on a three count. Out through the mouth.*

Damien continued to hold me there, silent with intense eye contact, waiting for me to move. If I came toward him, he would kiss me. He wanted to; I could tell. If I moved away, he would let me go. I held my breath and stood my ground. Finally, he slid his arm slowly across the small of my back. He squeezed my hand firmly before letting it go and walked to the open door.

18

My hand was slightly tender as feeling returned to it. I waited until I was safely at my desk to remove the ace bandage. I took off the gauze pad and covered the site with a regular Band-Aid. It was much less noticeable. I had no intention of explaining it to my father or Corey. If anyone asked, I would say that I had dropped a glass in the sink and cut myself.

The day passed quickly. As evening approached, my thoughts turned to my father. I was anxious to see him again, but I wanted it to go smoothly. He would be pleased to hear about my promotion, but I wondered what kinds of questions he would ask about it. Professionalism and decorum were top priorities for him. I didn't want him to think that I had earned the position based on anything other than my merits. With Damien's obvious interest in me, I couldn't fool myself. I wasn't the most qualified person for the job—there were others in my own department who deserved it more than I did.

Sheila was gone when I came home to get dressed and ready for dinner. I was a little disappointed since she had told me it was her day off. Maybe I was hoping for another pep talk before I left. I set my phone down on the kitchen counter and ran upstairs to change.

A few minutes later I heard pans and dishes clinking around. I hurried to finish and ran down to talk to Sheila before I had to leave. I wanted to find a nonpathetic way to tell her "thank you" for making me feel normal the night before.

My goodwill faded when I saw her by the counter, holding my phone. "Who's Corey?" she asked, scrolling through my texts.

I snatched it away from her.

"You're crushing my Mother Teresa image of you," she mocked. "Two-timing Brad Pitt?"

"He's just my friend. They're both just friends," I steamed.

She raised her eyebrows and puckered up her lips. "Do they know about each other?"

"I have to go," I grunted, pushing past her and out the door. I tried to tell myself that I didn't care, but Sheila's disregard for my privacy and her insensitivity hurt. Maybe I was just a joke to her.

I was meeting my father at his hotel in Minneapolis. It was my first time venturing into downtown, but I didn't take time to enjoy the scenery. The Marquette was right on Nicollet Mall. My father was waiting for me in the modern marble lobby. He sat in a chair against the wall farthest from the entry doors. Just behind him, striking blue lamps hung below the center on either side of a round, thick, black-framed mirror. I checked my reflection as I walked slowly toward my father. He looked up from his phone when I was standing directly in front of him. He finished typing the message he had been working on, then stood up, and greeted me.

"You look fit, mija," he remarked. "Still running, I hope?"

"I kept up an eight-minute-mile pace on my long run last week." I slid my right arm through his for an awkward one-armed hug. I didn't let go right away, running my finger over the golden eagle and rows of bars on his uniform. I drank in the feel and smell of his jacket.

"I made reservations for six o'clock at a Mexican place just around the corner. Have you eaten at Rosa's?" I smiled and shook my head. "A little walk will be good." He stepped away from me and started toward the hotel exit. I followed him, a few paces behind. My father was an attractive man. He didn't show many signs of aging, only a little bit of gray hair on his temples. His bronze skin was rugged but unwrinkled, except for the tiniest lines in the corners of his eyes. He held the door for me, and we walked arm in arm silently down the street toward the restaurant.

He glanced down at his watch as soon as he saw the sign for Rosa Mexicano. I didn't have to check mine to know that we would arrive exactly at six o'clock.

After we were seated, my father ordered a chile relleno. He was bound to be disappointed when it came served on a bed of brown rice with asparagus on the side. I laughed silently, but I didn't say anything, sure he had read the description too. I prepared myself to hear about how much better the food was back home.

He waited to ask me any questions until the waitress left the table.

"How's your job?" he wanted to know. I focused on telling him the more interesting sounding parts—instead of telling him that I mostly did proofreading and grunt work for the tenured associates.

"It may not be exactly what you want to do long term," he said, "but they're lucky to have you and your eye for detail. Nothing slips by you, mija." It sounded so much nicer than when Sheila called it OCD. Attention to detail was a passion we shared. His praise lit me up.

Our food came. His nose wrinkled as the server set the plate in front of him. He smiled graciously, but as soon as she left us his comment came.

"Is this what you are used to here, mija? No wonder you've gotten so skinny." I laughed as he cut into the cheese-filled pepper. We were quiet as we tasted our food. My shrimp tacos didn't resemble anything my gramita had ever made, so I was free to enjoy them without comparison.

Our conversational lull prompted me to ask about Victor. Why was it so difficult? It would only seem natural that I be curious about my new boss.

"I've been wondering," I finally said, "how did you meet Victor Trent?"

He smiled, looking up from his meal. "He was under my command in Sigonella," he said simply.

"How did you become friends?" I tucked my left hand under my leg, trying to keep it from fidgeting.

"Haven't I ever told you about Victor?" He wiped his mouth with his napkin. Then he took a slow drink. I tried not to look overly interested, but my anticipation was excruciating. "It was my first command, and Victor had just made lieutenant in the computer and telecommunications station." He took a bite of his rice. "He distinguished himself quickly."

"How?" I asked, impatient for him to continue.

"He always seemed to be in the right place at the right time." He paused for a second. "And he's very good with people. The seamen all respected and liked him."

I smiled. My father liked Victor because of his leadership abilities. My father was like me; he didn't have any real friends.

"He was with me during a three-day training exercise—it must have been in 1995 or early '96." He paused for a second, trying to recall the detail. "It would have been January of '96. It was just after Christmas."

I sat forward a little on my chair, holding my empty fork above my plate.

"It was a new training simulation program, and I hand-selected twelve men to participate. Victor was the communications officer on the mission." My father looked past me as several people at the table behind me erupted in loud laughter. "It was my first real opportunity to observe him for a long period of time. His people skills were second to none. No matter what the simulation threw at us, he was calm and prepared—and his confidence boosted the morale of the other men."

*Calm and prepared.* My father's assessment of Victor's merits was a bit discouraging. He obviously admired him. He paused long enough that I thought the story had ended. I took a bite of shrimp.

"Then, the last day of the exercise," he said, still looking behind me. "The final phase of the simulation—a dive retrieval of hazardous materials on a downed sub. Our equipment was in perfect order before the dive. It should have been routine, but something went wrong. My regulator hose ruptured just before we made our ascent." I held my breath, imagining my father without a regulator.

"How deep were you?"

"About ninety-two feet," he replied. He continued eating and I set my fork down.

"How long does it take to safely decompress from that depth?" I asked.

"About three minutes. I never would have made it without Victor."

"He helped you?" I whispered.

"He was the first of the men to exit the sub after me. I still think that something must have struck me and caused the rupture just as I came through the hatch. The loss of pressure pushed me away from the sub. Visibility wasn't good. Victor came after me. His clear thinking kept me alive." My father blinked, his face calm and emotionless.

"Were you conscious?"

"I was in and out," he answered. "Victor followed procedures—sharing his regulator and making thirty-second decompression stops every ten feet. I'm sure the other men would have done the same, but his presence of mind probably saved my life." I could hear the embarrassment in my father's tone. Did he blame himself for the accident?

He cleared his throat quickly. "I always told him that he had unlimited potential in the Navy, but he obviously had other plans."

I blushed at the mention of Victor's plans. It seemed that the Chief Interim Overseer had used crisis opportunities to his advantage in the past too.

"He hasn't completely abandoned his military roots," I said. "I think the company has contracts with the Department of Defense." I watched my father for a reaction.

"I imagine so" was his response. "Victor is developing a lot of important technology. If we aren't buying it, other countries will."

I didn't say anything. How could I ever tell my father about the tablet? Would he believe that the man who had saved his life was poising himself to overthrow the government?

"After the training exercise, your mother invited his family over for dinner. She and Victor's wife became instant friends."

I wanted to find out how close in touch they had stayed. "Did the Trents leave Sigonella first, or did we?"

"They did." My father looked into my eyes, pausing for a moment. "Victor was promoted a few months after the training mission. His new position allowed him to work directly under the highest ranking officers at the base." He took another drink. "He thrived. He knew everyone. Even though I wasn't directly over him anymore, his name always seemed to be coming up. He had incredible networking skills."

He was silent again for several more seconds. I looked up from my plate.

"He runs his company with the same *charisma*." I emphasized the last word. "All of the employees in my department are very loyal to him and his son."

"Damien?" My father squinted, looking at me sideways. "Have you seen much of him? Have you worked with him at all?"

"I ran into him last week," I said.

"What's your opinion of him?" he asked. I blushed.

"He takes after his father," I said, forcing my voice to lilt upward. "He's competent and confident, and his people skills inspire loyalty from his employees."

"It sounds like you like him." My father's face was stern, but then the corner of his mouth turned up. My discomfort intensified.

"Well, I seem to have made an impression on him already," I said. "He's offered me a position working for him directly."

My father didn't look especially surprised.

"A permanent position?" he asked.

"Yes," I said. "He wants me to be his PR liaison: coordinating his personal PR campaign, prepping him for meetings and speeches."

I looked down, waiting for a barrage of questions, but he sat silent. "I suppose you'll be traveling a lot with this promotion?" he asked after a moment.

I nodded. "He wants me to start next week. He has meetings in New York."

Again he was silent and stone-faced.

"I accepted the offer this morning," I said. He pushed the last spear of asparagus around his plate.

"It will look great on your résumé," he finally said.

I should have been relieved that my father approved, but instead I felt hollow. *My résumé.* Was that all I would ever be to him? What would my mom have said about the promotion? A headache started in my temples and my eyes lost focus.

Just then, our waitress came to the table with a dessert menu. My father ordered a slice of blackberry cake for us to share. His phone buzzed, and he excused himself from the table to answer the call. I breathed a sigh of relief. As soon as he stepped away, I took out my phone to check for messages. Sharp pain reminded me about my hand as the phone bumped against my stitches. I almost dropped it on the ground. I saw the flash on my phone of an incoming text. Dizziness. I pinched my eyes shut.

\* \* \*

*They put me in bed, but I can still hear them talking. I creep out of my room, walk down the hall to their closed door, and press my ear against it.*

*"This is just a phase, John. It will pass."* My mom's voice is calm and sweet.

*"She's not normal, Bridget. She needs help,"* he replies with finality.

\* \* \*

I opened my eyes. My heart jolted like it had just been restarted, and I gasped for breath. I could see him winding his way through the tables back to me. *Act normal.* I desperately brushed the water from my eyes and shoved my phone back into my purse just as my father reached the table.

He didn't seem to notice my distress, casually replacing the napkin on his lap. I bit my cheek. The waitress was just behind him with our cake. *Just a phase*—my reclusiveness? Or something more serious? My father looked up from the cake and frowned at me.

I forced myself to choke down a bite. My whole life I had tried to hide the fact that I wasn't normal from my father, but maybe he had known it all along. I couldn't wait to leave. My dejection would be much easier to bury when I was alone.

My father smiled at me in silence, seemingly oblivious to my heavy emotions. Maybe the distance between us had always been my fault.

**I** fastened my seat belt and touched my purse in the seat next to me. The shape of the tablet inside pacified me momentarily. I couldn't ask my father for answers, but I still had the tablet. Flexing my hand open and closed, I could feel my stitches being tugged apart, but the pain inside consumed me. I was barely aware of the physical world. I let out a long hissing breath.

I pressed my thumbs into my throbbing temples. Whatever I had done in Sigonella to make my father think that I needed help was in there somewhere. I tried to force myself to remember more, but the blackness in my mind was out of my control. His disappointment in me stemmed from something deep. It was my fault. I could feel it.

Once I was safely in my bedroom with the door closed, I pulled the tablet out of my purse. I wasn't sure how long I would have to hold it to allow it to charge. I sat back against my headboard and waited for the green light to begin flashing.

Had I ever felt normal? I tried to remember.

I looked at my phone. After five minutes with nothing happening, I set the tablet down and went back to opening and closing my palm. I finally looked at the texts that had come through at dinner. One from Damien and one from Corey. Damien wanted to know how my hand was doing, and Corey wanted to run with me in the morning. I responded briefly, lifelessly to both.

*Hand feels fine.*

*Sure. A run sounds good. I have some good news.*

I went back to work flexing. I had irritated the stitches. The Band-Aid was wet. Determined to make it work, I continued on. I waited a few minutes, flexing rapidly, before trying again. The screen remained blank. I pressed the button several more times.

In frustration, I threw the tablet toward the end of the bed. I stood up and walked to the bathroom to take off my makeup. Turning on the sink, I waited for the water to warm up. I looked again at the Band-Aid on my palm. It was pretty saturated now. Carefully pulling it off, I threw it in the trash. A few drops of blood collected on the stitches. I opened the medicine cabinet and found my small first-aid kit. Cleaning the area with an alcohol wipe, I unwrapped another Band-Aid. Just before placing it, I had a thought. I shut off the faucet and went back to the bed, picking up the tablet with my bare hand.

I waited a full minute, holding my breath as I watched the light. It began to flash slowly, faintly after about thirty seconds. I waited as the light's intensity grew. Finally, I pressed the button. The Omnibus icon flew into the emptiness above the tablet. I let out my breath with a sigh.

"Jace Vega," I said.

"Voice recognition validated." The three icons appeared.

"Open J file," I said.

"Proceed with password."

"Etna," I said, my pulse racing. The Omnibus icon disappeared and was replaced by two file folders labeled with dates. I read the first date: September 1, 2015. Next Tuesday. The timing was no coincidence.

"Open 'September 1, 2015' file."

"Voice recognition validated," the tablet responded.

A detailed blueprint appeared in the air above the tablet. The long narrow weapon's design looked like a World War II antiaircraft gun. The two images that followed contained tiny pages of schematics and equations. I wondered if Corey would be able to make sense of any of it.

I thought about my overturned bedroom. My entire body tensed.

"Open 'October 18, 2023' file," I said, moving to the next file to try to push away my uneasiness.

"Voice recognition invalid."

I sat up a little taller.

"Open 'October 18, 2023' file," I repeated.

The same response came again. *Strange.* Why had I included a file that I was unable to access? Whose voice would it respond to—Corey's?

I put the tablet down beside me on the bed. The green light continued to flash—even when I wasn't in contact. What was I supposed to do with this blueprint? Where were the detailed instructions I had hoped so desperately to find? My father's voice flooded my thoughts. "Soldiers don't cry. Soldiers don't cry," I repeated over and over. I had no trouble being a soldier under normal circumstances, but I didn't know the protocol in this situation. Soldiers usually have clear-cut orders to follow. They know who their leader is. They know where their loyalty lies, and they trust the other soldiers in their unit. I had no orders, no leader, and no unit—just Corey and his bomb-strapping mentality.

Why couldn't I have inherited more traits from my mom? She wouldn't have put the responsibility of changing the world on anyone's shoulders. She knew how to live in the present and let the future take care of itself.

I pictured her getting ready for that last party. I had watched her so many times as a child. She would turn on a mix of '80s music before sitting down at her vanity. She took her time and made herself breathtaking. The call from my father would have disappointed her—he was delayed at work and would try to join her later at the party. Disappointment wouldn't have lasted long though. I could see her cranking up "Jump" by Van Halen and dancing it away.

She never made it home from the party. She left just after 10:00. My father had spoken to her as she was leaving. At 10:13, a distracted driver ran a red light and plowed right into her door. She hadn't seen it coming. Instant death. No pain. The other driver walked away uninjured.

The pictures from the police report were still burned into my brain. It wasn't her. It couldn't be her. She was a blood-covered mess.

I tried to stop my eyes from filling up, but I couldn't anymore. I let go of my torn-up cheek and the tears fell silently. She had left the world without profound suffering, but she left me suffering profoundly. I don't know how long I cried before sleep overcame me.

* * *

*The coffin appears. I know she is inside, but I want to see her this time. I want to remember what she looks like. I open the lid. The little girl is lying still—alive, her wide blue eyes reflecting flames in the distance behind me. I gasp. I open my mouth to talk to her, but I am mute. She reaches out, softly touching the scar on my palm. Her lips form the word "run."*

*I look behind me and feel it—they are almost able to touch me. I run, but I'm not fast enough. I can never outrun them. They are inside me.*

\* \* \*

I was grateful when my alarm woke me. Hoping the morning air would clear away my somber mood, I rushed to get ready. I started down my familiar path, but something was off. I felt uneasy, unsettled. Looking around behind me, I saw nothing out of the ordinary. I picked up my pace, looking to see if Corey was winding his way through the trees.

I turned on my '80s playlist, hoping it would make me feel normal. I was almost sprinting when I finally saw Corey and Shane in the distance. I felt instant, weird relief. Instead of slowing my pace, I picked it up to a full sprint until I was right on top of them.

Corey slowed down and let me come to him. He didn't take his eyes off me as I came closer. He seemed to sense my mood and looked worried.

"You look like you've seen a ghost," he said.

"No," I said, trying to catch my breath, "but I do feel like I'm being watched or something."

"Did you see someone?"

"*Not* seeing anyone is the problem. Damien has his security company watching my place, but I haven't seen them anywhere. It's unnerving. After what you said about Megan, I'm feeling a little paranoid. Has she seen any more recruiters around campus?" I asked.

He shook his head. "But something is rotten in the state of Denmark," he said with a horrible British accent.

He looked around and motioned for us to start jogging toward McKnight. I took my earbuds out, not sure what I wanted to tell Corey first. As he bounced up and down next to me, I realized what a strong profile he had, with his curly black hair covered by a purple bandana. He was athletic and lean. I pictured him in the suit from the image on the tablet—Doctor Corey Stein was much more attractive than he let himself be in his wrinkled T-shirt and loose shorts.

"Corey, I opened that other file on the tablet, the one with the Omnibus symbol and the J." Corey slowed down and looked over at me, blue eyes penetrating.

"What did you find?"

"Two files. One had a pretty detailed blueprint for a weapon." I hesitated.

"What kind of weapon?" Corey asked.

"I don't know. It was long and narrow, like an antiaircraft gun."

"What else?"

"The other file was password protected, and it wouldn't recognize my voice."

He looked at me, mouth open like he was trying to process what I said. "Was Trent there when you tried to open it?"

"No," I assured him. "The battery had died. I waited until I was alone."

"I wondered how long that was going to take. How did you charge it?"

Still running, I held my bandaged hand out in front of Corey's swinging arms.

"What's that?" he asked, coming to a dead stop and grabbing my hand.

"Omnibus is testing a chip that harvests the body's electricity. Damien immediately thought of it when the tablet died. I had it implanted yesterday."

Corey dropped my hand like a hot potato and immediately covered my mouth with both hands while shaking his head.

"They can hear us," he mouthed before moving his hands. My senses heightened and the world slowed down. I could hear the rustle of individual leaves blowing in the breeze and the creek sounded like Niagra Falls. My hands trembled and knees threatened to buckle.

20

Wow!" he said in an odd tone of voice. "So they put it right in your palm? Did it hurt?"

"Not much. They numbed it with a local." My eyes were wide, my voice was shaky, and I could barely breathe.

"How big is it?"

I showed my palm to him, but he didn't look at it. Instead he walked away and adjusted his bandana before coming back. "Have you told Mr. Trent what you found on the tablet? I imagine he would be pretty interested." He put his finger to his lips and motioned for me to say something, to play along.

"Not yet," I mustered. "It was pretty late when I got it working last night."

"Was this the good news you wanted to tell me about?" His voice had a hint of sarcasm.

I paused for a second, not exactly sure what to say now. "Part of it," I began, "but also, I've been offered a job working as Damien's personal public relations liaison. I'm going to travel with him and help him with PR stuff."

Corey raised his eyebrows. He pulled his phone out of his shorts pocket. He motioned for me to keep talking while he started typing something.

"I'll do some speech writing and research and prep with him on people and companies he meets with. It's an amazing opportunity."

Corey was typing in a notebook app. When he finished, he

handed me his phone, then he picked up the conversation where I left off while I read the note.

"Sounds incredible," he said with a straight tone, rolling his eyes.

His note read:

*Can you cover for what we have said with Trent?*

He started talking about some new responsibilities he had been given by James Lansing as I responded:

*I think so, but I'm worried about your friend Megan.*

"That was quick," I said. "They must like you over there."

*I'll take care of her. I haven't been in contact with her and I won't have her look for anything else,* he typed.

He changed the subject back to the chip. "I read an article a few weeks ago about a chip that Omnibus is developing to power pacemakers. Is that similar to the one they implanted in you?" he asked. He passed the phone back to me as I answered his question.

*Damien wants me to go with him to New York next week,* I wrote.

He paused talking for a second while he read my message. He looked up at me, concern in his eyes.

"When do you start your new job?" he asked aloud.

I told him that I would be in my new office Wednesday. He was busy typing.

*We need to be able to communicate electronically. Was it easy for you to understand my Instagram instructions last week?* he wrote.

I nodded my head. He continued typing.

*I have several active accounts that Megan and I used to send messages. Four of them will follow you in the next few days. Follow them back and watch for messages there. I will alternate which ones I use, so you need to keep an eye on all four.*

I nodded my head again and grabbed the phone away from him.

*How will I communicate back?*

He asked me aloud if I had ever been to New York. I answered his question while he responded to my note. Corey started walking in the direction of the dog park. I stayed right beside him.

*Use your Instagram. Try not to be obvious,* he wrote.

I nodded again. "I had dinner with my father last night," I said aloud. "He's in town on business."

Trying to make my father's visit sound like small talk surprised him. "Where did you eat?" he asked.

He began typing again as I described the restaurant.

*Is it normal for him to visit you like this?* he typed. My spine tingled. The simple answer was no, but his word choice brought back the emotion from my memory. Normal. I bit my cheek and shrugged my shoulders—finally shaking my head.

He watched my reaction to his question with interest. I looked away but not before he read the pain in my eyes. We were both silent. He opened his mouth several times, starting to speak, but stopped himself.

He began typing again. *Did he have any answers for you?*

I shook my head again. He forced the phone into my hands. I looked down at it blankly before finally typing.

*I couldn't ask him yet.*

Corey searched my face, trying to peel away my shroud. I could feel his question. Why not? Why couldn't I trust my own father with something this important?

Finally, he looked down and began typing.

*This trip might be just what we need, Jace. Keep your eyes and ears open.*

I nodded, happy that he was trying to console instead of criticize.

*If you can get evidence of anything shady the company is doing, or find out what the weapon is, I might not have to strap a bomb to my chest after all.*

We had reached the dog park. Shane seemed to know the routine. As soon as we passed into the park, he took off running and left us behind. Corey and I walked in silence for a few minutes. I didn't have much else to say to him. My purpose seemed clear for the first time since I found the tablet—gather incriminating information. Corey would know what to do with it.

"I'd better get home and get ready for work," I told Corey.

"Okay," he said as he typed something on his phone. "This might be good-bye, then. Will I see you before you leave for New York?"

He handed me his phone while I verbally agreed that we would be too busy to see each other before I left.

His note said:

*I know you don't get out much. Be careful. Don't let him implant anything else in you.*

My face fell and my eyes became flamethrowers. His were calm and smiling, even laughing. I whipped around and began to walk away. He grabbed my arm and spun me back toward him.

After mouthing an apology, he said, "Good luck with everything. I'm sure you'll do a great job. Mr. Trent is a lucky guy to have you in his corner." He was still smiling.

I refused to make eye contact. "Thanks," I mumbled. "Good luck to you too."

I tried to yank my arm free, but he didn't loosen his grip. He pulled me closer, forcing me to look at his face. He wasn't going to let me go until I had forgiven him. I wrestled my arm away and stepped back. He began typing something again while holding one finger in the air, commanding me to wait. I have no idea why I complied. I wanted to get as far away from him as possible, but I stood there frozen, waiting for more insults.

He handed me the phone, this time softly touching the arm he had held so firmly.

*Jace, you are beautiful, smart, and strong. You can get what we need. Think with your head, not your heart.*

I jerked the phone away from him.

*Don't blow anything up while I'm gone,* I replied.

M y anger boiled as I ran home. I tried to pretend that I was mad at Corey, but I knew that he had only been pointing out the truth. My weakness and naïveté might as well have been written across the sky. Everything was my fault.

I stood at the closet trying to decide what to wear to work. My father had mentioned that he might like to meet me for lunch. I wouldn't let this opportunity slip by. I had to tell him about the tablet and ask for his help. I reached for my favorite gray suit. When my hand touched the fabric, I realized that I couldn't tell my father anything without risking Damien and Victor Trent hearing it too.

Holly was waiting for me at my desk when I arrived. She rarely came over to talk to me, so I was immediately nervous about what she wanted. She sat on the edge of my desk, looking at the items on my bulletin board. She seemed to be trying to look casual with her arms folded across her chest and her long, skinny legs stretched out. I paused outside of my cubicle and waited for her to say something.

"So I hear that congratulations are in order," she began, looking right at me and flashing a fake smile. "It's funny that you were able to get a position that wasn't posted internally. How did you manage it?"

She had been sharpening her claws, but I wasn't feeling especially catty. I wanted to explain the situation to her. I hated what she must have been thinking about me. I set my purse down and tried to come up with a snappy comeback. I couldn't. I just wanted her to go away.

"I'm honestly as surprised as you are about this promotion. I know that I don't deserve it based on my résumé and experience." I sat down in my chair and turned my computer on. "I just hope I'll be up for the task."

Holly's eyes widened at my humility and honesty. She stood up and straightened out her skirt. "Well, I just came over to wish you well. You've been an asset to the department, even if it was just a speed bump on your way to the top." She began walking away from my cubicle slowly, then she suddenly turned back.

"Just a word of advice, Jace: Be careful with Damien. He's a player."

Her words were like a punch in the throat. It was all I could do to keep from gasping for air. That she had been thinking I had a personal relationship with Damien was bad enough, but warning me about him was mortifying. Was she sharing this information with me based on her own experience with him?

My face flushed. I didn't know how to respond. Holly looked pleased with herself. She watched me for an awkward moment. Then, realizing that I wasn't going to say anything, she shook her head and walked away. My head felt like it was going to explode. I walked to the water cooler while I was waiting for my computer to finish a system update.

On the way back to my desk, I walked past Holly's partially opened office door. Moving quickly, I didn't see who she was talking to, but I heard " . . . wonder how long she'll last. She's pretty, but he loses interest quickly—I give it a few months."

* * *

The day passed slowly. None of the associates came to give me projects, all assuming that I wouldn't be focused on completing them. By noon I finished everything I had been working on the previous week and sat wondering what I would do with myself for the rest of the day. I pulled my phone out of my purse to see if Corey had followed me with any of his fake accounts on Instagram yet. Before I could check, I saw that my father had tried to call me and had left a voice mail. I immediately picked up my purse and walked down to the main floor and out the side door of the building into a courtyard where I could listen to the message. I sat on a bench facing the main building that housed the corporate offices. My new office would be in that building.

As I touched the button to play my father's voice mail, I noticed two men walking out of the corporate building toward the parking garage. The younger of the two was dressed in a full suit, despite the muggy August heat. The other man wore a uniform—an Army general, maybe. I couldn't see how many stars he had on his shoulders, but he had plenty of brass on his chest.

My father's voice mail was apologetic. He explained that he wouldn't have time to see me again before leaving. He had meetings and an early flight and wanted to make sure that he arrived at the airport with plenty of time. A second visit would have been redundant. We had already caught up and taken care of business. I shouldn't have been surprised but I was crushed.

I deleted the message. I ached. I wanted to feel normal. I opened my Instagram and began scrolling through pictures. *Normal people.*

I hadn't posted anything all week. This had been the most eventful week of my life, but my Instagram world was completely in the dark about it. I thought about my conversation with Corey. If I was going to communicate with him via Instagram, I should probably start posting regularly again so it wouldn't seem strange to whoever might be monitoring my electronic activity.

I switched over to the camera and looked up to see if there was anything picture worthy in the area.

The two men had stopped on the way to the garage mid-path. They were deep in discussion. A third man, also in uniform, had left the corporate building and was approaching them. I moved my phone away from the scene, and focused on some flowers planted next to the path near where I was seated. Snapping a picture of two of the larger flowers, I moved over to the filters and began experimenting.

My eyes kept wandering from my screen back to the three men on the path. I was too far away to be noticed or to see many details. The third man now had his back to me. It looked like he was wearing a Class A Navy uniform with admiral stripes. My father. The blood drained from my face. I clicked my phone over to the camera and zoomed in trying to see more details just as a fourth man walked up the path and joined the conversation.

My phone slipped out of my hands into my lap. It was Damien. His profile was clear and unmistakable. He stopped walking as soon as he joined the other men.

I put my phone back inside my purse. Had he really been away on business and come home early, or was everything he told me a lie? Anger and confusion overcame me as I hurried back into the building.

I had just walked into my townhouse that evening when Damien called.

"Hi, Jace," Damien's casual voice greeted me. "How was your last day in PR? I would've called you sooner, but I've been in meetings all day."

I pinched my eyes closed. "No problem," I said evenly.

"Did the chip work to charge the tablet?" He jumped straight to business. I clenched my fist tight until I could feel the stitches. He wasn't even going to tell me where the meetings had been.

"Yes," I smoldered. I had spent the day considering the best way to handle the situation. "There is something on here that I think you're going to want to see as soon as possible."

"What is it?" He sounded excited. I pounded my fist against the bed noiselessly.

"It's some kind of blueprint. It looks like a weapon."

He paused for a moment. I could hear him breathing on the other end. "What kind of weapon? Like a gun or something?"

"I'm not sure on the size, but it looks to me like an antiaircraft gun. If you look at it with one of your people, I'm sure you'll be able to figure it out."

Damien was silent. I continued a bit awkwardly, "There's another file that I wasn't able to open yet. It is password protected, and it doesn't recognize my voice."

"Jace, listen, I'm worried about you. Have you told anyone else about this?"

"I did mention it to Corey this morning," I said. Not sure how to explain myself, I stayed silent.

"Are you sure you can trust him?"

Damien asking if I could trust Corey was laughable. "I think so," I said through gritted teeth.

"Where are you keeping the tablet?"

"In my purse, with me," I answered.

"Good," he said. "Don't go to the office tomorrow. Meet me at my house at 1:30." We said good-bye.

I set my phone down and immediately picked up the tablet. My profession was built on half-truths and so was my relationship with Damien. I had to show him the blueprint, but I didn't have to give him everything.

I left the tablet on my bed, shutting the door behind me. I wasn't hungry at all, but I went to the kitchen and poured myself a bowl of granola. I took my time, opening the fridge several times and clinking the dishes around on purpose. I turned on the faucet to fill a cup of water, pointing my palm toward the source of any sound I made. I sat down at the counter and deliberately, noisily ate my granola.

A few minutes later, I slowly made my way back to my bedroom. I picked up the tablet and my phone and went into the bathroom. I made a few noises with the sink and medicine cabinet. Moving my phone's portable speaker dock to the back of the toilet, I turned on the Bluetooth so I could select the music while still holding my phone. I clicked on my '80s hair band playlist and turned up the volume.

I turned the shower on. Bon Jovi wailed, "Your love is like bad medicine. Bad medicine is what I need." I sang along. "Wo-ho-ho."

With the tablet sitting on my lap, I pushed my left hand through the shower curtain into the stream of water. I pressed the button on the tablet. When the icons appeared, I quietly spoke the prompts to get to the blueprint. Fortunately, the noise from my stereo didn't interfere with the functionality of the tablet.

Setting the tablet on the counter, I opened the camera on my phone. With the use of only one hand, it took a few tries to get the pictures steady enough and at the right angle to be able to read the schematics.

As soon as I had what I needed, I took a deep breath and deleted the images, leaving only the blueprint picture. I navigated to the settings menu and opened the history, completely deleting it, like I had with Corey before showing the tablet to Damien. Satisfied with my handiwork, I powered down the tablet and turned off the shower. Damien would have the blueprint for this weapon from the future, but without the schematics, I hoped it would take him a very long time to understand how to use it.

"Bad Medicine" ended and the intro to "Sweet Child O' Mine" started.

I set the tablet down and picked up my phone, feeling strangely elated. I clicked over to Instagram. I had a notification that @bridger_fa was following me. I followed back and began looking through the images on his profile. @bridger_fa looked like a frat boy at the University of Minnesota. Most of the pictures were of people partying or were taken at sporting events. I couldn't imagine how Corey was going to send me a message using this account.

Axl Rose's strained voice started singing the lyrics I had heard a million times about some girl who had a smile that reminded him of childhood memories. My neck tingled, and my mood became more subdued.

Instagram. I scrolled through picture after picture of my friends girls' nights out, dates, and family vacations—people making memories together. I tried to keep the tears from spilling out of my eyes. None of them really knew who I was. People liked and commented on my pictures, but none of them would call me if they came to town. I clicked over to my profile. Hundreds of pictures with thousands of likes, but they were completely meaningless. My account was as fake as @bridger_fa's. I was so alone.

Axl had moved on to singing about her blue eyes. I blinked away my tears, instantly thinking about my mom and the little girl in the coffin. I hurried out of the bathroom, shut off the light, and then collapsed on my bed. My mom wouldn't be happy with the way I was living my life. She wanted me to build real relationships. She was the one who had talked me into opening the Instagram account in the first place. She had wanted to see pictures of me living, and I had given her them, but I knew I hadn't been fooling her.

The images on the tablet were different. Real. They would have pleased my mom. My life captured in those images was robust and happy. Was my path to that happiness already irreparably altered? I closed my eyes again and pictured the little blonde girl. She belonged at the swimming lessons in the images, not inside the casket.

**23**

I skipped my run the next morning. Instead I took a long shower. It relieved some of my ache. The thought of seeing Damien again made my stomach queasy. I couldn't let him sense my anger. He had to trust me.

I put full energy into getting dressed and ready. I wanted to look professional and irresistible. I finally decided on a knee length, clingy, black-and-white floral wraparound dress. It was professional, summery, feminine, and comfortable. With strappy sandals and straightened hair, I was impossible to ignore.

I tucked the tablet inside my purse and checked my phone one last time before taking off after lunch. No new messages, but two new followers on Instagram. I followed them back without taking time to look at their profiles.

I walked up to Damien's door exactly on time. I rang the bell and took a few deep breaths, waiting for him to answer. I was surprised when the door was opened by a short, balding, middle-aged man. He introduced himself as Peter Watts and invited me inside. He looked familiar, but I couldn't place him. Peter led me through the main hall, past the formal sitting room, and to an office with two antique mahogany desks and six wingback chairs. He invited me to sit down and told me that Damien was on a conference call and would join us shortly.

Peter didn't make any conversation and made no effort to hide his evaluation of me. Looking me over with his beady eyes magnified by his clear-rimmed glasses, he seemed a little amused and perplexed by what he saw. He offered me a drink, and after I politely declined, he poured himself something. He looked over his shoulder several times at me, but never said anything. It almost seemed like he just wanted to make sure I was still there.

We sat awkwardly for about five minutes. I didn't feel any more comfortable asking Peter about his relationship with Damien or his role in the company than he did me. He had just started a strained conversation about the weather, which mercifully lasted only a moment, when Damien made his entrance. Dressed in suit pants and a white shirt, he had taken his tie off and his sleeves were unbuttoned and loosely rolled up to the elbow. I looked away quickly. I could feel my blood warming up.

Greeting us, Damien surveyed the mood of the room briefly before pouring himself a drink. Making his way to the chair behind the desk I was seated in front of, Damien sat down and arranged some papers before saying anything.

"Jace, Dr. Watts is the friend I was telling you about from Chicago." My hair stood on end hearing Damien speak the doctor's name. "He's familiar with the tablet and will help us try to access the other file. I also want him to look at the blueprint you mentioned. He should be able to read it and tell us what exactly we are looking at." I could hear myself breathing. Damien was smooth and calculating.

"Of course," I said, bringing the tablet out of my purse.

"Jace was able to access one of the password-protected files, but the other is not recognizing her voice commands," Damien explained, looking at the doctor.

"With her here, we should be able to ask the right questions to solve the problem," Dr. Watts said confidently.

I held the tablet in my left hand and turned it on. I quickly navigated to the folders in the J file. Damien watched me as I spoke the password. The doctor examined the folders for a moment.

"Show us the blueprint first," Damien said. He had moved his chair around the side of the desk and was sitting close to me now. I opened the "September 1, 2015" file. When the blueprint appeared, both men moved closer, examining the image intently.

"And what happens when you try to access the 2023 file?" Dr. Watts asked.

"Open 'October 18, 2023' file."

"Voice recognition invalid" came the expected response.

"Any idea whose voice it might recognize?" Dr. Watts directed the question to me.

"It could be anyone," I said, "or maybe it's just a glitch."

He took a step toward the tablet. "Take us back to that first screen with the three icons." I commanded the tablet back to the main menu. He asked me to open the Settings. I obeyed, my palms sweating. The options General, Security, Access Points, and Maintenance appeared. He asked me to open Security.

"Open Security settings," I said, sounding surprisingly calm.

"Proceed with password."

"Etna," I said clearly. The Security menu appeared. He saw what he was looking for quickly, telling me to open Users. I complied, bringing up another list of options: Add Users, Set Preferences, and Voice Recognition. Dr. Watts wanted Voice Recognition opened.

"Tell it to show currently recognized voices," he said.

I did as I was told. Three names appeared: Jace Vega, Corey Stein, and Damien Trent. A chill ran down my spine. A list of files each of us could access followed our names. Corey and Damien were only listed on the October 18, 2023 file.

Damien's expression didn't change. "That's convenient." He smiled, but I detected a hint of sarcasm in his tone. "Take us back to the J file, and I'll open it."

I couldn't stop my heart from pounding against my chest as I shakily spoke the prompts to get back to the file. How could I stop him from trying to open it? It was already too late. He was about to access whatever information was in it and there was nothing I could do about it. I suddenly had tunnel vision.

"Open 'October 18, 2023' file," Damien said with confidence.

"Voice recognition validated," the tablet responded. We waited a moment for the image to change, but the voice commanded, "Proceed with second validation."

Damien's forehead and brow wrinkled—a flash of anger or disappointment, but he almost instantly calmed his emotions.

"It looks like we will need to get ahold of Mr. Stein to assist us with this."

**D**amien's phone rang. He answered it and left us sitting alone in the room. It was a relief—I needed time to recover, even if it was just a few seconds. I took a deep breath and let it go silently. I made myself relax my shoulders and neck, and I unclenched my fists.

Corey was going to be dragged back into this. I shouldn't have been relieved, but I was. All three of us must have been involved in sending the tablet back. Maybe my instincts hadn't been wrong to trust Damien.

I glanced at my phone to see if I had any messages from Corey or any new Instagram followers. My notifications were empty. Dr. Watts was looking at the hologram file folders, scratching his chin. He glanced at the door several times, anticipating Damien's return. He was a strange little man, acting like I wasn't in the room, moving his lips as he read something on his enormous phone. I sat quietly, trying not to remind him that I was there.

When Damien came back, his mood had changed. He was no longer smooth and relaxed. He stood at the doorway instead of returning to his chair.

"How do the two of you feel about a little change of venue?" he asked. It appeared from his silence that Dr. Watts didn't know how to respond any more than I did. Damien's pause for comment was purely rhetorical. "I need to leave tonight for New York, and you two are coming with me," he said flashing his perfect teeth. "What I mean is, if you're available, I could use your help with my meetings. The

United Nations committee meeting has been moved up to Monday and I have prep work to do with committee members first."

Opening the last file would have to wait until after New York now, and I would still be on my own. I had to tell Corey somehow. Would he be looking for messages from me already in Instagram? Panic filled me.

I wanted to escape and have time to talk to Corey. I stood up and powered down the tablet, sliding it back into my purse. "What time is our flight? I'll need to go home and pack."

Damien sauntered over to the desk and placed a hand on my purse, preventing me from picking it up. His other hand slid familiarly around to the small of my back.

"Jace," he said softly, "the plane is scheduled to leave in just over an hour. You can take a later commercial flight tonight if you like, but I'd prefer to have you with me. I have a few things you can read on the plane, and then we can get started early tomorrow morning."

"But my things?"

"Can you have your roommate pack what you need? I left a message with Corey asking him to meet us in New York tomorrow. I have a feeling he will be open to the proposition. He can stop by your house and bring your things with him."

Damien's urgent departure for New York was strange enough, but inviting Corey along gave me flu-like symptoms. Damien obviously felt driven to open the second file.

"Okay," I agreed reluctantly.

"I'll go open the gate. Bring your car up the drive and park it in the garage." He gave my back a gentle rub, nudging me toward the door. His hand remained on my purse. I met his eyes, and he gave me another calculating, dimpled smile. I walked with feigned confidence to the door, spinning around when I realized that my keys were inside my purse. Damien was already dangling them from his finger, walking toward me, placing himself between me and the purse. I retrieved them from him as my heart pounded in my head.

The entire scene played out with Dr. Watts sitting quietly in the background. He didn't seem especially interested in anything we said or did, and it was never questioned that he would accompany Damien to New York.

* * *

Ten minutes later we climbed into the back of a limousine for the short trip to the Downtown St. Paul airport. Seated next to Damien on the sleek tan leather seats, I pushed my hands under my knees. I realized that we would be in very close proximity for extended periods of time. My shoulders tensed. Perhaps sensing my fears, Damien lifted the center console that separated us and patted my knee reassuringly, but his action only intensified my emotion. Dr. Watts was engrossed in whatever he was looking at on his phone, and completely oblivious to us, but his presence made me realize how physical Damien was with me. I moved away from him, hugging the door.

Damien reached into his black satchel and brought out a thick file folder, handing it to me. I opened it and glanced at the neatly bound, sheet-protected document titled "Palladium Corporation."

"Can you read over this and pick out the key talking points about this company?" Damien asked. "Everything you need to know should be in that document, but you're welcome to do your own research online too. I need to know a little bit of everything."

I nodded and opened the first page, scanning over the content. I was happy to have a distraction. Damien was busy reading and typing messages on his phone. Focusing my mind on the page in front of me, I began absorbing the details of Palladium Corporation's history.

The limousine delivered us to a hangar where a private jet was ready to board. We climbed the steps as the crew handled Damien and Dr. Watts's baggage. Inside the plane, Damien indicated a seat near the front. The plane was luxurious but not excessive—no sofa beds or minibars, just comfortable black leather chairs with plenty of leg room. I settled in next to the window, facing the tail of the plane. I set my purse in the seat next to me and resumed reading the Palladium brief. Damien was finishing a phone call to someone who must have been arranging our accommodations. He mentioned a specific suite he wanted. I held my breath and looked up casually as he took the seat directly across from me. I relaxed a little. He was at a safe distance. It wouldn't be easy for him to purposely touch me from there, and he wouldn't accidentally brush against me either.

The plane was ready in a matter of moments. I looked out the window as we accelerated down the runway and smoothly took off. The low hum of the engines and lack of conversation made my eyelids heavy. I could see Dr. Watts on the right-hand side of the plane a few rows back. Damien was still busy on his phone. Looking down at the arms of my chair, I found a button that reclined my seat. I let the Palladium brief rest on my legs and closed my eyes, hoping for a few refreshing minutes of sleep. Bright light from the sun struck my face through the window as the plane turned.

\* \* \*

*I am at the window with Herman the stuffed pig, watching the volcano smolder. Smoke has been pouring out of it for several days. My mom wants me to come away and play something, but my father tells her to leave me.*

*"You remember what Dr. Watts said about coping mechanisms. It will pass, Bridget."*

\* \* \*

I was jostled awake by turbulence sometime later. Looking up and around, I quickly remembered where I was. Dr. Watts was sleeping in his seat. Was it coincidence, or was this the same Dr. Watts my parents had been talking about? A chill went through me. Damien looked up from his tablet and grinned when he realized I was awake. I sat my chair up and tried to look normal.

"I see the reading material was fascinating." He laughed. Looking down at the brief and my slightly twisted skirt, I quickly tried to straighten everything out. A glance at my watch revealed that I had been asleep for almost an hour. Outside the window, the sky was turning a deep midnight blue as the sunset faded on the horizon. I tried to suppress my anxiety. *Coping mechanisms.* I shivered.

"You're so quiet, Jace," Damien observed. "You've always been that way, haven't you?" He set his tablet on a little table between the two chairs on his side of the row.

"Yes," I answered. Then, realizing he was fishing for more information, I added, "But when I have something to say, I say it."

"Not necessarily typical of a communications major, especially one who enjoys speech writing." He reached for a small glass on the table and clinked his ice around before taking a drink.

"Talk less, say more?" I said. "I have always been a minimalist."

"I've been meaning to ask you how you figured out the password on the tablet. Is Etna a typical password you use?"

I hesitated. "No," my answer came, "I tried a few of my typical passwords first, but then it was more of a gut feeling—kind of an association between this situation and how I felt in Sigonella." Tingles ran up my spine explaining it to him.

He sat forward a little but didn't say anything. His interest was piqued, but he didn't want to urge me on. I sat back in my seat and looked out the window.

"Sigonella, or the volcano?" he asked. I considered how to word my thoughts.

I took a deep breath. "Both, I guess. The tablet, the future—they both seem volatile, like a volcano."

Damien blinked and looked out his window before commenting. "It does seem to be a big responsibility for one person, but it must help to know that you aren't in this alone. It's obvious that you and Corey and I all had a stake in sending the tablet back. We'll figure out what to do with the information together." His raised brow, dimple, and half smile portrayed sincere kindness. I would have given him an Academy Award.

A flight attendant brought around warm towels just before we began our approach into New York. I appreciated the opportunity to freshen up. I picked up my purse to touch up my makeup. Peeking inside the bag, I looked for the tablet's flashing green light, sighing involuntarily when I saw it. I looked pretty put together considering the long day. My floral dress was a good choice. It could easily go from day to evening and it didn't wrinkle.

On the ground, a limousine waited to take us to the Plaza Hotel. Damien was completely buttoned up and professional when we arrived, including his red-and-gray striped necktie and suit coat. We were ushered by the concierge from the lobby to a private set of elevators, up to the Royal Suite. The contrast between Damien's hotel choice and a place my father would choose to stay was vast. The Royal Suite was enormous and decorated lavishly with an Old World flair. Marble floors, dark-wood paneled walls, and gold trim and chandeliers seemed to be right up Damien's alley—interesting that a man who was changing the future with technology preferred classic comforts over modern design.

Damien, who had obviously stayed in this suite before, made himself comfortable in the spacious living room while Dr. Watts and I were shown to our rooms on the opposite side of the suite. Mine was the larger of the two rooms and had a full sitting area with couches and fireplace. A pair of white silk pajamas was laid out neatly on the bed. I tried to remember the last time I had slept in pajamas.

The concierge introduced us to Oscar, the butler who seemed to go with the suite. He continued the tour of the kitchen, study, dining room, and full private workout facility. The suite was larger than any of the homes I had ever lived in. He led us back through the marble foyer to Damien.

"We have a full day tomorrow. Oscar is putting together a light dinner for us, and then I suggest going to bed early," Damien said. Dr. Watts made himself comfortable on an armchair in the corner near the baby grand piano. I sat down on the sofa next to Damien.

"Corey is going to meet us tomorrow afternoon. I ordered up something for you to wear to meetings tomorrow, and everything you need should be fully stocked in the bathroom." Damien had apparently taken care of everything. I only wished I had my tennis shoes. A run in Central Park would have to wait until Friday.

Oscar called us to the dining room for dinner. Three places had been set at the closest end of a table with space for ten. A spread of sandwiches, soup, and fruit, along with a vegetable tray, was set out on the buffet against the wall. My thoughts kept returning to my flash of memory on the plane. When we were seated with our food, I decided to try to draw out Dr. Watts. In a weird, obsessive way, I was compelled to find out if he had ever lived in Italy.

"You live in Chicago, Dr. Watts?" I asked. Damien looked at me, obviously a little amused that I was finally asking questions.

"Yes."

"Born and raised?" I asked.

"No," he replied. "I was born in Pittsburgh. I studied nuclear physics at MIT. I stayed on doing research there for ten years before moving to Chicago to work for Omnibus."

"Dr. Watts knows more about Omnibus than anyone. He's the one who thought of the chip for charging the tablet." Damien reached for my left hand and turned it over, showing Dr. Watts what was left of the partially dissolved stitches. His touch was electrifying and then embarrassing. Dr. Watts may have seen Damien interacting with any number of women and didn't seem to notice his inappropriate familiarity.

Sliding my hand away from Damien's grasp, I continued asking the doctor questions. I found out that he was a bachelor with no children. His parents had both passed away years ago. He didn't like animals. He didn't seem to mind being asked questions, but he only offered brief answers, and he didn't ask any questions back. When it seemed obvious that my quest was vain, I concentrated on my tomato bisque. If Dr. Watts had lived in Italy and had known my father, he wasn't going to tell me about it.

Damien gave us a rundown of his schedule for the next day. He was meeting with his father's advisor in their New York offices at 7:00 a.m. The rest of the morning would be spent preparing for an afternoon meeting with the CEO of Palladium Corporation. We would come back to the hotel and change in the late afternoon for a black tie reception with the United Nations Department of Political Affairs.

Damien's phone began to buzz as he was eating his last bites of food. He excused himself to answer it and left us to finish alone. A few minutes later, Oscar came in to tell us that Damien had sent his apologies—he would be busy on his call indefinitely. We should go to bed and get ready for the day ahead. Dr. Watts and I said an awkward good night.

Back in my room, I slid into the pajamas and sat in bed holding the tablet with the Palladium brief next to me. In less than twenty-four hours, the last file on the tablet would be opened. I thought about what Damien had said—that I wasn't solely responsible for what happened to the future. I ached to believe it was true.

Turning on the tablet, I opened the personal file. It was the first time I had looked at it on my own. I scrolled slowly through the lovely images of my life. As image after image of the enchanting little blonde girl passed by, a low sinking feeling grew in my stomach. Her world may have already disappeared. If she still existed, would I be the one delivering her to school and swimming lessons? I was starting to care.

I came to the image at the banquet with Corey and Damien shaking hands. I sat up in bed. This image had drawn me in before. I studied it again closely, more interested in the foreground than the focal point of the image. I was only an amateur photographer, and I obviously didn't understand anything about holographic imagery, but something seemed off. The blurry foreground—the entire table, with its long white tablecloth and fine dishes, was unfocused. I zoomed in on the section with my name card. My first name was blurry, but the second half of the card looked like someone had used the smudge tool to make it completely unreadable. I wondered what the future version of Photoshop looked like.

Had I edited the image? Had I also excluded images of my future husband in an attempt to protect him or our future?

I pushed aside the thought, turned off the tablet, and set it down. I switched off the lamp next to my bed and tried to get comfortable in the crisp white covers. Just before closing my eyes, I realized I hadn't set an alarm. I reached for my phone on the bedside table and set the alarm for 5:00 a.m.

As an afterthought, I opened Instagram and scrolled down my feed. I almost turned it off after the first three pictures of a friend's newborn sleeping in three different positions, but when I reached the fourth picture, I sat up in bed. The Minnesota frat boy had posted a picture of a newspaper article. The headline read "Alcohol Use Suspected in the Rollover Accident of a Stanford Student." His caption on the photo said "RIP Megan."

Corey's friend had died. My heart stopped completely before resuming erratically. I couldn't catch my breath for a second. *In through the nose on a three count. Out through the mouth.* I continued scrolling down to see if any of his other accounts had posted pictures. Nothing—until I came to one that had been posted by the St. Paul antique store. I almost missed it. It was one of those low quality drawings with a quote on it. The quote read, "Three things cannot long be hidden: the sun; the moon; and the truth. #buddha."

**26**

Sleep was impossible. The gravity of my situation had come into full focus. I hurt for Corey. I was almost sure that Megan had been, at least at some point, more than just a friend. My throat was dry and my stomach was in knots. I thought about Damien sleeping at the other end of the suite and shuddered. Was sleep easy for him?

I thought about how Damien had manipulated me to get me here. What would he do with me when he had everything he needed from the tablet? What would he do with Corey? I trembled as fear consumed me.

I couldn't just lie still and wait for something to happen to me. If Omnibus would kill Megan for what she had discovered, then their plans were already underway. I needed to find incriminating information that we could take to the FBI or CIA like Corey had suggested in the first place. Why hadn't I listened? I was in so far over my head, I could barely stay at the surface.

Damien's satchel. Electricity buzzed through me. Maybe his resistance to joining the rest of the paperless world would be my advantage. Pushing back the heavy covers, I put my feet firmly on the floor.

I listened at the door before slipping out into the lowly lit hallway. I made my way silently to the kitchen and poured myself a glass of juice from one of the expensive-looking bottles in the fridge. My hand trembled, but my mind was clear. I carried it with me through the oval entry foyer, past the dining room into the living room with the grand piano. Damien's room shared one of the walls with this room, but to get to it, he had to pass through two hallways and a set of double doors. I would hear him coming. It was nearly 1:00 a.m., and Damien hadn't slept on the plane. I hoped he was completely oblivious.

Scanning the room with just the light streaming in from the open curtains, I saw what I was looking for almost immediately. Damien had placed his satchel on the floor next to the coffee table before going in to dinner, and Oscar hadn't disturbed it. I crept noiselessly to the table and set my glass of juice down, lifting the case gently from the floor. It was heavy.

I glanced over my shoulder at the foyer behind me. I began to perspire, considering what might happen if Damien came out to retrieve his case. I turned around and shuffled softly back down the corridor to my room. I held my breath as I passed Dr. Watts's door. Having him between Damien and me suddenly felt like a security blanket. I closed my door quietly, with just a soft click as I released the handle. Once inside, I walked swiftly to the bed and set the case down near the lamp on the table.

Reaching inside, I pulled out a stack of briefs similar to the one Damien had handed me. Ironic that a leader of a technology corporation carried so much paper with him. I thumbed through the titles. Each contained information about a different company. I took out my phone and photographed the title pages. Toward the bottom of the stack, I found several profiles of high ranking military officials. My father's biography was included. I spread out the bios and quickly photographed the title page of as many as I could fit in the frame.

I felt strangely focused as I continued searching through the contents of the case. I had almost finished sifting through the stack of papers when I came to a thin page inside a transparent green sheet protector. The résumé inside was all too familiar. I could feel my pulse in my fingertips as I touched it. I opened the plastic and viewed my name and employment history. Turning the page, I found my Stanford transcripts, followed by a memo that contained all of my vital statistics including age, height, weight, interests, hobbies, and even a history of all of the places I had lived. Anger burned me up. It looked like an outline for a research paper, with categories and bullet points. Had Damien put together the Jace Vega brief after he had offered me the liaison position, or long before that?

I fumbled as I reorganized the stack of papers and placed them as I had found them back in the case. I had to restrain myself from running back down the foyer to the living room. I desperately wanted to run and keep on running. Why didn't I? What was keeping me here? *You have to stop them. They can't continue this way. They can't do this to everyone.*

Walking and breathing as quietly as possible, I passed back down the hallway to the living room. I had only been gone about ten minutes, but I feared I would see Damien waiting for me in the dark living room. I stood still, letting my eyes adjust to the low light. I scanned the room twice, clutching the satchel against my chest, before tiptoeing back to the coffee table. I set the case down just as I had found it and almost immediately turned back toward the foyer.

I was already in front of the passageway to Damien's room when I remembered the glass of juice. "Stupid!" I whispered, mentally punishing myself for the mistake. I spun around and moved quickly back to retrieve it. I passed into the room again and found my first noisy floorboard. My heart stopped. I froze completely and waited for my heart to start again before continuing my journey for the juice.

I picked it up gently and turned around for a final time. Damien's tall, dark shadow filled the doorway. He leaned against the gold trimmed paneling, folding his arms across his chest, the moonlight illuminating his perfect white grin. I jumped, spilling a few drops of the cranberry juice onto my pajama top.

"Trouble sleeping?" he asked in an easy tone.

I couldn't speak. My throat was choked and my mouth full of cotton. I tried to stop my hands from shaking as I raised the juice to my lips and took a small sip. I lowered the glass and walked a few steps away from the table and satchel, hoping that he wasn't coming to find it.

I cleared my throat. "I'm sorry. You startled me."

He moved into the room and turned on the lights. He didn't try to hide how he slowly took in my appearance. The white pajamas weren't revealing, but they were clingy and contrasted my bronze skin and dark hair. I continued moving slowly away from the table and satchel toward the foyer.

"Are you always an insomniac, or just when you're in strange places?" he asked.

145

"I think I'm just a little nervous about tomorrow. This is my first real job, and I don't want to mess it up."

Damien looked pleased and sympathetic. He came toward me, and I instinctively continued my retreat to the door, forcing him to turn his back to the table.

"You don't have to leave because of me," he said. "I couldn't sleep either."

"We should both get to bed," I said. He smiled. I reached out one hand and slid it under his arm, gently guiding him to the doorway. Looking into his eyes, I let my head take over. "Damien, I really need to tell you how much I appreciate you trusting me with this job. My father was so proud when I told him about my promotion. I know it might seem silly, but I still kind of live to please my father. He has so much respect for you and your father and this company."

Mentioning my father had the exact effect I hoped it would. Damien's smile faded. He had to be picturing the imposing admiral. He looked at me again, and this time, his eyes stayed focused on mine.

"You're going to be great, Jace. Don't be nervous about tomorrow. You'll be meeting a lot of important people, but just be yourself." We stopped in front of the hallway to his room.

"Thanks. I'll try." I gave his bicep a little squeeze and then let go of his arm. Taking a step toward my bedroom, Damien reached for my hand, stopping me sharply. I held my breath.

"Jace." *He knows what I'm up to.* I tried to pull my hand away. "You don't have to be afraid of me," he whispered. "I respect you and I would never do anything to hurt you."

He had to feel my erratic heart in my cold clammy hand. I squeezed his angrily. His gaze dropped from my eyes to my chest.

"You should put a little soda water on that so the stain doesn't set in." I looked down at the three large spots of juice on my pajama lapel. "I'm sure we have some." He started walking toward the kitchen, leading me by the hand. My relief grew with each step away from the living room and the satchel.

Turning on the lights, he finally let go of me. He opened the refrigerator and flipped open a can of club soda. I leaned up against the counter opposite the fridge. He opened a few drawers until he found a tea towel. Then he wet the corner of it with the soda. I folded my arms across my chest, half expecting him to try to dab at the juice stain himself, but he kept his distance, handing me the wet towel.

The pajamas cleaned easily with the soda. I steadied my hand and drank the rest of my juice, setting the empty glass next to the sink. Damien took the wet towel from me and turned off the lights in the kitchen. We walked slowly back to the oval foyer. Damien said a casual good night, and I continued down the hall to my room. I felt his eyes on me until I was out of sight in the dark. I heard him turn around and walk back to the living room. I prayed that he would turn off the light without noticing the satchel.

I lay in bed, trying to empty my mind. It would be difficult enough to think straight tomorrow without being completely exhausted. I must have eventually let go because my alarm woke me up just a few hours later. Adrenaline instantly kicked in when I became fully awake.

I found everything I needed to get ready in the bathroom. My head felt clear after a shower. Wrapped in a hotel bathrobe and hair in a towel, I peeked out into the hallway looking for the clothes Damien had promised. A rolling clothes rack was pushed against the wall with a garment bag hanging on it. I held the top of my robe closed with one hand while venturing out onto the cold marble floor to retrieve the bag. Two shoe boxes and a Nike shopping bag sat on the floor next to the rack. I took them all back to my room.

I found running clothes inside the Nike bag. Thinking about Holly's warning, I tossed the bag against the wall. Damien had obviously done this many times before. Disgusted, I opened the garment bag, which was imprinted with a Vivienne Westwood red and gold label. Damien's attention to detail couldn't be denied. He clearly understood my sense of style. Inside I found a grey suit with classic lines. I tried it on, taking a moment to appreciate the exaggerated pockets. They were perfectly placed to accentuate the waistline. Everything about it said elegant professionalism.

I spent a few minutes drying my hair before twisting it into a loose curly bun. I brushed mascara onto my already thick eyelashes, thinking of my father's pre-junior prom lecture. It was one of the few times he had seemed almost sentimental.

"You look like your mom," he'd said with a laugh. "You don't understand the power she has over me, mija. Remember that your beauty is a weapon." He chuckled again. "Use it wisely. Don't let anyone convince you that you are theirs to do with as they please. Use it for good." I hoped I had been doing just that. Damien's attraction to me seemed to be one of the only things I had going for me at the moment.

Damien and Dr. Watts were already eating when I came in for breakfast. Right away, Damien wanted to discuss his agenda for the day. He seemed impressed with the quick rundown I gave him of the Palladium brief.

An hour later, I waited in a small reception area at Omnibus's 5th Avenue office while Damien met with his father's advisor. The simply decorated corner offices on the twentieth floor were modest and functional. I read through a second brief Damien had handed me about a company called Tribunautics.

Damien's meeting would finish soon. I switched quickly over to Instagram and scrolled down my feed, looking for messages from Corey. I found two. The first was one of the most recent accounts that I hadn't taken time to look at closely. @Biyu773 had posted a picture of an airplane wing against a bright blue sky. The caption read, "Flying in for fittings #fashionweek2015."

Clicking over to the profile, I saw pictures of an edgy, attractive Asian girl in her early twenties. She had hundreds of pictures on her account. I wondered why and for how long Corey had been keeping these accounts. Some of the pictures on the account dated back over two years.

The second picture was another ecard posted by the antique dealer, @stpaulvintage. This one was a marginal drawing of Albert Einstein on a purple background. The quote on the photo read, "It gives me great pleasure indeed to see the stubbornness of an incorrigible nonconformist warmly acclaimed." I felt relieved to know that Corey was on a plane to New York, but the second message troubled me a little. I wondered what his stubborn nonconformist plan was. Should I like the pictures or comment to let him know that I had gotten the message? I decided against it.

When Damien came out of his meeting, I was close to the middle of the thick Tribunautics brief. He shook hands with his father's advisor and walked to an office two doors away. Opening it, he motioned for me to follow him.

"Have a seat, Jace. We have a lot to go over in the next few hours." He sorted out several of the briefs and placed them in a pile in front of me. "With a shorter timetable, I need you to help me highlight important information so that I can learn it before tonight."

"If you don't mind my asking, wouldn't this be a lot easier if we had the electronic copies?"

"Maybe you can convert me in the future, but for today, I need you to use my system."

I nodded, immediately going to his desk to find highlighters.

"If you're bent on being technologically useful, you can find pictures of each of the top executives online and print them out. It will help me connect names and faces with information," he said.

We sat together in silence for the next hour, highlighting our respective briefs. He was completely focused and rarely looked up from the page. By the end of the hour, I was stiff and tired of sitting. I set down the page I was looking at and stood up, walking over to his computer.

"Is this where you'd like me to search for the pictures?" I asked.

He looked up from his work and smiled. "Yes. Take breaks and move around when you need to, Jace. Sometimes I forget to act human when I'm working." He ran his hand over his hair.

I opened a project on the computer and started looking up the names and photos. It was much easier than I thought it would be to find what I was looking for. I used my skills to make the presentation simple and professional. When I had finished, I looked around the room for the printer.

"Does the computer print somewhere else in the office area?"

"It's in the empty office behind the receptionist's desk," he replied.

I grabbed my purse, intending to take a full break before returning with the printouts. Damien barely glanced up when I left the room. I passed by the receptionist's desk and into the ladies' room at the far end of the office area.

Once inside a stall, I hung my purse on the door and took out my phone. I didn't have any messages, but the top post on my Instagram feed was from the Minnesota party girl @staciberi90 declaring that she was "Going off the grid for a few days to study for midterms." The picture was a generic stack of textbooks.

Why would Corey be going off the grid? I panicked. He was upset about Megan's death. Maybe he knew something that he wasn't telling me.

I glanced at @staciberi90's profile again. Why had Corey and Megan used these accounts to communicate? What would Damien do if Corey never appeared to open the final file? My stomach dropped.

When I came back into the office with the printouts, Damien pushed his chair back and smiled at me, letting out a deep breath.

"If we can make it through today, I promise that tomorrow will be much more fun," he said. He touched the chair next to him, inviting me to sit. I set the collated, neatly stapled stack of photos in front of him on the desk. He picked it up and started looking at the names and faces. "Are you good with names?" he asked.

I wasn't sure how to answer since "good" didn't adequately describe how I was with names. After enough hesitation that his curiosity was piqued, I finally said, "Yes."

"Yes?" He raised an eyebrow.

"Kind of Rain Man good." I was embarrassed as soon as I said it.

"Really?" Damien smiled. "Do you already know these?" he asked, flipping through the stack.

"Probably."

He stopped flipping near the middle of the stack and covered the name before showing me the picture of the attractive Greek shipping tycoon. His bronze skin and green eyes belonged in Hollywood.

"Pavlos Karalis," I said without hesitation. He uncovered the name and looked at it. His lower lip jutted out. He flipped playfully through the pages again. He closed his eyes, stopping on one that was closer to the bottom of the stack. He showed me the picture. It was a retired American hedge fund billionaire: dark hair, middle aged, receding hairline, and horn-rimmed glasses.

"Fred Peterson," I said with a fake yawn.

Damien laughed. "Rain Man," he conceded. "Yet another reason to keep you close by."

I laughed uncomfortably and went back to highlighting briefs.

I felt increasingly anxious as the afternoon wore on. My mind was consumed, worrying about Corey during Damien's meeting with the Palladium CEO. I wished I knew what Corey's plan was.

Back at the hotel, I found a Givenchy dress hanging on the rack, this time inside my neatly made up room. It looked vintage, Audrey Hepburn inspired—soft black taffeta, form fitting, and ankle length. The front came up above my collarbone and cut off sharply at the shoulders. The back dipped down in a graceful *V*, the point reaching just below the middle of my back. I looked understated and elegant. I added a bit of dramatic eyeliner and a few curls to my hair before piling it up on my head again.

I found Damien in the living room—slick and polished in his tuxedo. He was completely absorbed by his phone and didn't seem to notice that I had come in. He finished typing a message before acknowledging me.

"All ready?" I finally asked.

"Almost," he answered. "I just have a few loose ends to tie up here."

I sat down in an armchair opposite where he was seated on one of the couches. "Anything I can help with?" I asked casually.

He didn't look up from his phone, "No. I'm just trying to finish the arrangements for tomorrow. We'll be meeting with all of the executives that we studied today except Hassan Itamar. He's been delayed on business in Dubai and won't make it in until just before the committee meeting on Monday." His phone chimed, signaling another message.

Almost simultaneously, Dr. Watts came in from the kitchen. He had made himself a sandwich and looked extremely comfortable in a pair of plaid pajamas. He stood in the doorway for a moment, waiting for Damien to look up from typing on his phone.

"Any progress today?" Damien finally asked.

"It looks like it's exactly what you thought." *The blueprint?* I wondered.

"I want to wait to do anything with this until we see what's in that final file," Damien instructed.

Dr. Watts scratched his head and nodded. "What time does he arrive?"

"He must have missed his connection in Charlotte. The driver waited for over an hour after the flight landed and then called to tell me he wasn't on it. When I tried to reach him, it went straight to voice mail, so I'm assuming that he got on the next flight, which lands at 8:15."

"And you'll be at your reception until late?" Dr. Watts asked.

"Yes. I would be surprised if we make it back by midnight."

"Then we'll plan on opening it in the morning," he concluded.

"A few more hours isn't going to kill anyone."

Dr. Watts agreed and wished us both good night. Damien stood up and followed him out into the foyer saying something in a low voice that I couldn't distinguish. I nervously opened my Instagram while he was out of the room to look for new messages. @Biyu773 was the fourth picture down, posted only one hour before. The exotic beauty was enjoying a latté in Soho. The whole thing was so odd. Was Corey asking this girl to post pictures for him, or was he traveling with her? Or maybe she was completely fictitious. Whoever she was, I felt a disturbing burst of dislike for her. Maybe Corey had more resources and fascinating friends than I had given him credit for. I really didn't know who he was. However he was pulling off his fake Instagramming, I could be sure that he was already in New York. I slid the phone into the little black purse that matched my dress and stood up, waiting for Damien to return.

The warm glow of the recessed lighting hit me just as Damien walked through the door. He stopped short, finally seeing me in the dress. His eyes drank in every inch of me. I could feel his admiration. My weapon was loaded.

"You are exquisite," he said, coming toward me and reaching for my hand. I extended it to him and smiled.

"This is only my second time in New York," I said, "but in this dress, I feel like I belong on 5th Avenue."

He didn't respond verbally but leaned in smoothly and brushed his lips against the skin just between my jawline and earlobe. I tried unsuccessfully to contain the shiver that started at my neck and ran down to my toes. I needed to stay in control. I smiled, but I kept my eyes fixed on the floor.

Letting go of my hand, Damien walked away from me. He crossed the room to his satchel on the coffee table. Reaching inside, he pulled out a long black leather box. He opened it and lifted out a double strand of pearls. I met him halfway and turned around so he could fasten them around my neck. The double strand clasped at the nape of my neck, creating a choker in the front. The rest of the pearls draped loosely down my back. After fastening the clasp, Damien slowly traced the pearls against my skin. I held my breath.

His phone chimed, signaling a new message and cutting off the electricity of the moment. He paused, his fingers touching the end of the strand in the middle of my back before walking away to read it. I took a deep breath and tried to walk casually—on my wobbly legs— to the ornate mirror that hung between two crystal candle sconces. I could see Damien responding to the message. I wondered if it had to do with Corey. I casually brought my phone out of the purse and took a quick picture of myself in the soft light of the mirror. After pretending to admire the pearls, I slipped into the hallway, walked past the dining room to the oval foyer, and went around the corner into the powder room.

I felt a little desperate for more solid communication from Corey. What was going to happen when Damien discovered that Corey wasn't on the second plane? What was he expecting me to do? I had the blueprint schematics, but no solid evidence of Omnibus's sinister plans. I hoped to gather more information at the reception, but I couldn't guarantee that I would come up with anything incriminating.

Scrolling down past my old roommate's new puppy, and Jen and Anje's trip to 7-Eleven for 44-ounce Big Gulps, I saw another post by @Biyu773. It was a picture of a large fountain with an angel in the center. Behind it, lush trees surrounded a green pond. I knew the fountain. I had seen it in Central Park on my last visit. I was just about to search Central Park fountains when I noticed another post below @Biyu773's. It was @bridger_fa's new running shoes. Did anyone want to join him for a run at 6:30 a.m. tomorrow?

My hands trembled as I clicked on the camera at the bottom of my screen and selected the picture I had just taken in the mirror. I hadn't meant to, but the face I had made looked overtly seductive. I wished I could retake it, but a bathroom selfie would be even worse. I could imagine how many likes I was going to get from my male followers. I never would have considered posting it if my father was on Instagram.

I thought for a minute before typing a caption: "First day on the new job and already burning the candle at both ends. UN reception tonight and then hit the ground running first thing tomorrow." I only hoped that I would have something useful to tell Corey in the morning.

I clutched the door handle, trying not to press my face against the limousine window as we turned onto 1st Avenue. Manicured hedges and lawns were deep green in the shadow of the city, and the familiar semicircle of flags passed on the left side of the car. The driver slowed and followed a line of cars through a security checkpoint into the driveway surrounding the circular fountain. The fading sun lit up the skyline behind us, and the tall Secretariat building reflected the view.

Damien put his phone in the inner pocket of his jacket, waiting for our driver to reach the doors.

"Just relax and be yourself." He must have sensed my nerves, but the event didn't intimidate me. My mind was consumed with thoughts of Corey and the tablet. I blinked, picturing it secured in the small safe in my bedroom.

"I can handle myself," I assured him.

The driver came around and opened Damien's door. After stepping out, he waited with his hand outstretched for me. I took a deep breath and slid out of the car. Damien tucked my hand in his elbow and began walking toward the entrance of the building.

Inside, we were both asked for identification and sent through a metal detector before joining a group of guests near the elevators. A female guide, dressed in traditional Norwegian garb, conversed sweetly with one of the older men in the group. She was describing some of the unique artwork in the building when the elevator doors opened.

When our small group was comfortably inside, the guide pressed the button for the fourth floor.

"The Conference Building was completed in 1952," she informed us in a singsong voice as she pushed one of her long blonde braids over her shoulder. "Renovations to the building, completed in 2013, returned the Security Council Chamber to its original glory. The room was designed by Norwegian architect Arnstein Arneberg, and the beautiful mural of a phoenix rising from the ashes was painted by Per Krohg, a Norwegian artist." The gray-haired gentlemen she had been talking to before asked another question in a gruff Russian accent.

Damien touched the small of my back lightly when the fourth floor was illuminated. The doors chimed as they opened. We were the last couple to exit the elevator, following a few paces behind the others as we entered the sweeping room. Our guide stood at the door with her hand outstretched.

The room hummed with conversation, and light music played in the background. Floor to-ceiling windows covered the outer edge of the hall, overlooking the East River. The setting sun pulled my attention from the people in the room. Wispy orange and golden clouds hung above a bridge that spanned the river. Against the Persian blue sky, the dark water below the bridge danced with the glow of lights reflected from the suspension cables on the bridge.

We were greeted near the door by a rotund balding man who introduced himself as Zane Brookman, the Under-Secretary-General for Political Affairs. He asked a few questions about me, showing particular interest when Damien mentioned my father. Apparently, Mr. Brookman had met my father on several occasions.

"Your father is a stubborn man," he began. A delegate approached from behind and interrupted the conversation. Damien didn't wait for the Under-Secretary to elaborate on my father's stubbornness; he nodded and led me away.

The low-lit room gradually became more crowded, filled with a variety of international figures. Damien conversed smoothly. I listened for details that might help me understand what the committee meeting on Monday aimed to accomplish.

"Just back from fishing in Ireland?" Damien asked a rusty-blond, bearded man.

"Yes," the man responded, "but not much biting." Damien introduced me to Greg Peterson, who worked as a liaison for Hassan Itamar, the man from the list who was delayed in Dubai. Greg introduced both of us to his date, Camilla. Her long, shapely legs stretched out of her short, black strapless dress. Damien smiled and kissed the back of her hand after shaking it. She awkwardly shook my hand while she looked in the opposite direction.

The two men continued talking about a fishing trip they had taken in Wyoming the year before. Damien didn't seem to be interested in talking shop. His goal seemed to be making personal connections.

We had mingled our way to the center of the room. I watched familiar faces pour in and fill up the iridescent tables. I didn't have much time. I decided to branch out and mingle on my own. Damien threw his head back, laughing at something that a young heiress, who had joined the group, added to the conversation. I wasn't going to learn anything if I was glued to Damien's side. I squeezed his arm and slipped away.

At the outer edge of the room, near one of the floor-lit columns, a familiar salt-and-pepper-haired man sat alone at a table. I approached slowly.

"Mr. King?" I asked.

"Yes?" he said, standing up.

"I thought that was you." I smiled. "I read a piece about you in *World Oil* magazine just this morning."

A large smile covered his face. "I don't believe I've had the pleasure," he drawled.

"Jace Vega," I said, extending my hand. He shook it rapidly. "I work for Damien Trent," I told him.

Randall King was one of the names I had printed out earlier. He pulled out a chair and I sat next to him, brushing my legs under the light green silk tablecloth.

"Ah, Damien Trent," he said. "I'm not surprised. He always manages to monopolize the most attractive employees." Randall sat down, crossing his legs and exposing his shiny black boots.

"Have you known each other long?" I asked, brushing away his flirtatious comment and my twinge of jealousy before my face was completely flushed. Of course Damien came to these events with attractive employees. I knew that already. I just wished that his meaningless touch didn't affect me the way it did.

"Shoot, we go way back," he said. "We're both on the board of directors for Clean Energy Programs for PEWS Charitable Trust. That's where we first met." He took a sip of his wine. "And we haven't stopped collaborating since."

Randall watched me as I brushed a curl that had escaped from my bun behind my ear.

"I knew his mom in college," he mentioned as he took another sip of his drink. "She was a beautiful woman," Randall said, "and brilliant."

I looked toward the center of the room and found Damien still talking animatedly with a group. Was Randall talking about Damien's mother in the past tense because they had known each other so long ago, or because she was gone? I had never asked Damien about her. I had just assumed that she traveled with Victor. The sweet smell of flowers brought me back to the table. Two rectangular brass center-pieces were filled with fragrant fresh-cut pansies and rosemary. I took a deep breath.

"Is this your first time inside the United Nations?" I asked, trying to sound disinterested.

"Hardly," Randall said, laughing. "I'm on everybody's invite list."

The music suddenly halted, bringing all eyes to Under-Secretary-General Brookman, who gave a formal welcome and announced that dinner was ready to be served.

"At any rate, I'm looking forward to seeing Damien's presentation on Monday. You'll be there too?" he asked, touching my hand. I nodded and stood up slowly. A classy woman in a taupe embroidered gown approached the table.

"Monday, then," I said. "It was nice to meet you."

I made my way back to the center of the room where I stood at Damien's side. He pleasantly ended his conversation and led me to a table near the Under-Secretary-General's. We were seated with a diverse group of donors. Several of the men at the table were on Damien's list, but the tables were large and the room was noisy. I had difficulty hearing anyone who wasn't seated right next to me, and, much to my disappointment, Damien's conversation revolved around horse racing.

I glanced at Randall King's table across the room. I thought about his tone when he had mentioned Damien's mother. Why hadn't

Damien told me if she had passed away? His compassion toward my loss and the way he seemed to know what to say began to make more sense.

During dessert, a jazz quartet began playing, and a few couples got up to dance. Damien was deep in conversation with the man seated to his right. They were talking about some important advance in fiber optic cables. The man to my left was Omar Rahal of Tribunautics. I had waited for the opportunity to talk to him as we ate our salmon, but during dinner, he kept up conversation with an older woman to his left.

Finally, his attention turned to me when the music started, a jazzy version of Michael Bolton's "How Am I Supposed to Live Without You."

"How long have you been with Omnibus?" he asked in a thick Middle-Eastern accent.

"Only a few months," I responded.

"What do you think of the company so far?"

"I'm impressed," I said, "and I feel like I've just scratched the surface."

Omar began explaining a current venture that his company and Omnibus's charitable foundation were working on involving wind-powered water purification in Africa.

"Mr. Trent was instrumental in getting the funding that we needed," he said. I smiled.

"Would you like to dance, Ms. Vega?" Omar asked. I set down my glass and straightened my dress, smiling. He took my hand and led me away from the table.

The dance floor was becoming crowded. The recessed lighting between the dropped rectangular blocks on the ceiling created dramatic spotlights and shadows as the dancing couples passed. We made our way to the center of the room. I looked over my shoulder at our table. Damien didn't seem to notice that I was gone. Omar began leading me adeptly around the floor.

He had launched back into conversation about other charitable ventures he was involved in. "I'm impressed that companies like Tribunautics and Omnibus are so socially conscious," I said when Omar paused. "I get the feeling that new money companies find it easier to remember the little guys."

I wondered if the number of charitable interests Omnibus had was typical. They seemed to have a finger in every pie. More accurately, Damien's finger. I changed the subject, not sure how to get Omar talking about Monday's meeting. I mentioned an article I had read about Tribunautics's production of energy efficient vehicles in Malaysia. Omar smiled.

"The plant in Malaysia is part of the reason I am here tonight," he said, "but you probably already know that our facility is operating on 100 percent Omnibus technology."

I shook my head. That tidbit of information was missing from the brief Damien had given me. "The assembly line and computer systems?" I asked.

Omar nodded. "They put together an offer that was almost impossible to refuse," he said, "but it has had even more benefits than I anticipated."

I raised my eyebrows.

"Employee satisfaction," Omar said. "I'm sure that Mr. Trent thinks that we are helping them by offering our employees to test new products, but it has become like an additional benefit in our compensation package."

I swallowed. "New products?"

"I guess I should say more than new products—a completely new network."

I moved my palm across his shoulder, feeling the bump of my chip. Omnibus was implanting chips in Malaysia? Damien had mentioned the network they were working on when he had first suggested implanting the chip in me, but I had been so preoccupied thinking about the tablet, I hadn't asked any questions about it.

The song finished. We applauded and made our way back to the table. Damien stood up before I could sit down and motioned toward the dance floor, silently asking for the next dance. I smiled at Omar, disappointed that I would have to resume my conversation with him later.

Damien's dance skills were, unsurprisingly, very smooth. He directed effortlessly to let me know what was coming. My dancing was mediocre at best, but in his arms, I was graceful and fluid.

"Having a good time?" he asked.

I nodded. "Interesting conversations with interesting people."

"Omar can hardly wait to get his hands on you again," he said, looking back at our table. Omar ran his fingers through his shiny black hair, smiling at us.

My face and hands got hot.

"He seems like a good person," I argued.

Damien tightened his grip a little. "His charitable portfolio impressed you?" he asked. "I suppose that's what it's designed to do."

We danced in silence. Through the windows, I watched the glistening lights of the buildings against the sapphire sky. Were Damien's charities strictly a tool to impress too?

"I noticed you spoke to Randall King earlier," he said. "Did you wow him with your Rain Man skills?"

I laughed a little. "We didn't talk long. Just long enough to find out he went to college with your mother," I said awkwardly. "I realized that I've never asked you about her. Does she travel with your father?"

He tried to look nonchalant, but his palm warmed. He looked blankly at the band playing, over my shoulder.

"I lost her when I was eleven," he said with only a small hint of emotion in his voice. "She was working in our office on the eighty-first floor of the second Trade Center tower."

I looked up just as we danced under one of the lights. I closed my eyes as the flash jabbed me in the temples.

* * *

*I am on a thick rug in the center of a hardwood floor. Crayons cover every inch of the rug. A little blond boy lies on his stomach, scribbling on an oversized coloring book. He looks up at me with his pure blue eyes and grins.*

*I look down at my empty white paper. I have to draw her another picture. My stomach tightens.*

* * *

"Are you okay?" Damien asked. The ballroom came back into focus. I couldn't stop the tears that immediately filled my eyes. Damien pulled me closer and reached my face to brush away a tear that had fallen on my cheek.

I closed my eyes and leaned against his shoulder, trying to catch my breath. His house, his swing set, his mother calling us inside. Why was this all happening now?

"I still miss her," he said softly, "but the foundation makes her life and death more meaningful to me. She made sure her legacy would live on."

"Omnibus's charitable foundation is hers?" I asked, after clearing my voice.

"All of it was hers, but she made some specific stipulations in her will, and the foundation and how it should be administered was one of them."

I thought about how raw my mom's accident had left me—the emptiness, the regrets, the nightmares. I couldn't imagine losing her as a child.

"Jace, you've been exceptional tonight," he said, moving his hand slowly from the small of my back to the point where my dress, skin, and pearls intersected. "You're the whole package. Every Omar Rahal in the room wants to be me."

I shivered. I wanted to pull him closer and push him away at the same time. I let go of Damien's shoulder and brushed away the last of my tears. Was his agenda with the charitable foundation influenced more by his mother's wishes or his father's?

"Don't be embarrassed by your tears," he whispered. I could feel his warm breath in my ear. "They look beautiful on you."

At that moment I felt completely out of control of my weapon.

A pplause. He didn't let go right away. I spent an infuriating moment looking into his eyes—consumed by the electricity. I was shaken when he let me go and led me back to our table. He resumed his conversation. The room, the lights, and the noise became stifling. I waited until Damien had his back to me and then slipped quietly away from the table.

The open doors on the north side of the room led out to a large stone patio. Fresh air. I made a path to the doors that would keep me hidden from Damien's view. As I passed beyond the glass, the breeze encircled and refreshed me. The sounds of city traffic and the river were a welcome change from the chatter and clinking of the dining room.

A few couples and small groups were gathered around the candlelit tables. I made my way to a long buffet table and took a glass of water. The view of the lighted bridge enticed me to the edge of the patio. I leaned against a rail, swallowed by memories. This city. This skyline. Watching the news replay images of the towers collapsing over and over. It was confirmation of what I already felt. I couldn't take my security for granted. I wasn't safe. None of us were. Even before September 11, I had always held my breath watching airplanes approach the city's skyline. But afterward, even looking into the sky in Corpus Christi, where my father was stationed at the time, would bring on a panic attack.

"Jace Vega?" a familiar voice said, touching my shoulder. I turned around and recognized the Russian man from the elevator. How did he know my name? I smiled vacantly.

"Leo Belitrov," he introduced himself. "I know your father," he said. I raised my eyebrows. He stepped toward me, exposing a view of the glistening city lights behind him.

"How do you know my father?"

"We worked together on several occasions before I retired from the Russian navy." Leo smiled. "He is a good man."

I nodded, a lump suddenly forming in my throat. I wished I could easily tell the difference between a good man and a man who did good things for his own purposes.

"Are you enjoying the view?" Leo asked. I turned back toward the water and the bridge.

"It's breathtaking," I said.

"You work for Damien Trent, I understand." He touched the whiskers on his chin.

"Yes," I replied, my stomach tightening at the mention of his name. I tried to pull myself together enough to ask an intelligent question. "Will you be part of the meeting on Monday?"

Leo chuckled. "No," he answered. "My pension did not get me an invitation here tonight either," he said. He must have seen the confusion on my face. "I am on security detail for one of the guests," he said with a wink.

I smiled warmly. It was nice to know that I wasn't the only commoner in attendance. I turned back toward the building's windows and the view of the skyline. "Have you been to New York before?" I asked.

"Oh, yes," he said. "I live here now, but I visited many times before coming."

"It's a beautiful city," I said.

"A beautiful country," he said softly. "Someday, I will be a citizen." In the distance, a faint green light flashed at the top of one of the tall lighted buildings. I wondered how long the process of becoming a citizen took. Would Leo's citizenship be official before the Trents could change everything?

My eyes flashed. "Did you know that Victor Trent was in the navy with my father?" A breeze blew across the patio.

"Yes," Leo said with a serious face. "I understand that they were good friends. I have watched both of their careers with interest."

"Have you met him?" I asked. "Victor, I mean."

"Not yet," Leo said, a strange expression in his eyes, "but perhaps someday. I have a lot of questions for him." He squinted his eyes and reached for my left hand. "Questions that it would be wise for anyone who is close to his company to ask."

Leo squeezed my hand. I could feel the shape of the chip in my palm. "What would you ask?" I almost whispered.

Leo took a few steps toward the wall and the river, pulling me with him. "I would start by asking how an uneducated man like himself was able to triple his wife's fortune in a matter of a few months. I believe in good luck and the American dream, but when I start digging, it doesn't seem to add up." I didn't respond. I watched the people dancing through the windows. Holding my breath, I waited for Leo to continue.

"Someone should be asking why Omnibus is distributing more electronic devices than food and supplies to third world countries. Someone should be asking how these devices work, where no other network provider has availability." His voice had become softer, but more urgent, and his lips were close to my ear.

My father's strange friend's words hit like a hammer. *Thud, thud, thud.* My heart slowed down. Damien passed through the double doors with his phone pressed to his ear. I pulled my hand away from Leo.

Damien didn't notice me. He turned away from the wall where we stood and walked toward the city lights. "And what would you do when you found the answers to your questions?" I asked softly.

Leo laughed low and deep. "That depends on what the answers are, doesn't it?" he said, following my gaze across the patio. "You are in a unique position, Jace. You work very closely with someone who knows those answers."

My spine tingled.

"If you'll excuse me," Leo said suddenly, "I must be getting back inside." He kissed my hand and walked away. Stunned silence. I followed him with my eyes as he passed Damien. He was still talking on the phone with his back turned toward me.

I opened my purse and looked at my phone. 10:13. Damien's man had been expecting to pick Corey up at the airport around 8:30. I hesitated before slowly walking toward the doors and Damien.

Damien's voice was low and hoarse. "Find him!" he said urgently. "We don't know what he's had access to or what he plans to do with it." It was almost as if Damien sensed my presence. He spun around, his expression shifting from stern seriousness to a carefree smile. His tone also changed as he ended his conversation. "Let me know if you need any help with that, and keep me up to date," he said before ending the call.

"Everything okay?" I asked, trying to sound casual.

"Yes, nothing to worry about," he said. "Just a small situation at the plant in Hong Kong. They have it under control."

A lie. His driver must have discovered that Corey wasn't on the second plane. The easy look on his face made my chest burn.

"Have you heard from Corey?" I asked point-blank.

"Nothing yet," he said, tucking his phone into his inner pocket. "I'm sure he was exhausted with his delays and a full day of travel. I left him a message to meet us at the hotel at eight tomorrow morning." He straightened his jacket and wiped his palms on his pants before smoothly tucking one hand inside his pocket.

"He's not staying in the suite?"

"No," he replied slowly, lifting his eyebrows. "He has an aunt who lives on the Upper West Side. He insisted on staying with her." I looked at the wall behind Damien. I wondered if his "aunt" had an Instagram account.

I tried to make my smile casual. "It will be nice to have my things."

Damien lowered his eyebrows and smiled. He seemed relieved that I had shifted the focus from being eager to see Corey to being eager to have my own underwear. "How are you holding up? Can you make it another hour or so?"

"I'm enjoying myself," I said. "I just needed a little break."

He reached his arm around my waist and guided me gently back inside. "Stay with me, Jace. You don't have to work the room alone, you know."

I saw Leo Belitrov sipping a glass of wine on the other side of the room. After hearing his questions, I had no intention of leaving Damien's side.

\* \* \*

I glanced at my phone at 11:20 while Damien wrapped up a final conversation before stepping into the elevator. I had forty-eight likes on my selfie from earlier, but none of the comments were from Corey's accounts. I hoped he was safe, wherever he was. I hastily put the phone back in my purse when Damien turned toward me.

Our guide wore an intricate red kimono and her thick black satin hair was rolled in a loose bun. She didn't speak as we descended and the only other couple in the elevator was also silent. When the door chimed, Damien squeezed my hand and pulled me toward him. The other couple exited the elevator and walked toward the entrance of the building. We stepped out slowly.

"Let's stay a while, Jace. I want to show you something."

Damien asked our guide to take us to the Security Council Chamber. She bowed and smiled, indicating that we should follow her. Each step down the corridor reminded me that I wasn't walking in my own shoes. I pulled back my shoulders and marched forward.

We entered the chamber through a wide set of doors near the opening of the semicircular table in the center of the room. I stepped inside the enormous vaulted theater as our guide turned on the lights and then stepped quietly to the left of the light-colored wood door. I took a slow panoramic view of the muted room. Olive-green textured upholstery covered the walls. I could picture the blue chairs surrounding the table filled with delegates.

Damien watched me but stood silent.

My eyes were drawn to the mural at the front of the room. It was the one that our guide had been talking about earlier with the phoenix rising from the ashes in the center. My eyes started at the bottom and worked upward. The foreground was darker than the background and more monochromatic. A soldier dressed in a World War II uniform stood to the left of the phoenix, setting down his rifle and taking off his cap. People of different nationalities in drab, tattered clothes were in various stages of moving away from and lifting themselves out of the pile of war rubble.

The upper portion of the painting was divided into sections that reminded me of the stained glass windows in my gramita's church. The people inside the panes danced, played music, and held serene blue banners, ribbons, and flags. Many of the figures in the middle of the mural reached down to help pull people out of the darkness. Others waited to celebrate with the new arrivals. The panes at the top and outer edges were back to work. Back to life. Most were in industrial settings, but the upper right-hand pane was a scientist looking through a large telescope.

I stepped farther into the chamber, ignoring Damien and the guide. In the center pane, just above the rising phoenix, a couple knelt facing each other, grasping each other's arms at the elbow. The woman held a bouquet of red flowers, and an angelic blonde baby sat at the couple's knees.

Three other children and a fruit tree framed the couple and their baby. Two boys and a girl. One of the boys hid behind the trunk of the tree and the other hung precariously in the limbs. He reached his arm down, offering the girl a piece of fruit from the tree. I shivered.

"My mother's family is distantly related to the artist." I jumped. Damien was standing behind me—close enough to whisper.

"It's interesting," I said, my eyes still fixed on the couple.

"I come from a long line of peacekeepers and diplomats," he said, genuine pride in his voice.

"Your mother's ancestors or your father's?" I asked without looking at him.

He took a few steps away from me and leaned back against the table. "People always seem to see themselves somewhere in this," he said, ignoring my question. "It really does represent everyone." He stepped toward the left side of the mural and away from the table. "Here I am," he said, pointing to a blond-haired man in dress clothes with his shirtsleeves rolled up to the elbow. The man stood near a woman's back as she opened a blue-paned window, allowing bright sun rays to stream through. The man held a rope firmly, allowing a shapely woman to climb out of the wreckage below.

I couldn't help scanning the mural again. *Who am I?* Damien stepped toward me while I looked. The woman on the other end of Damien's rope? The woman assisting the man with the telescope? The woman reaching down to help the climbers? Or was I the woman in the center holding the flowers in one hand and the man's elbow in the other? I shuddered and closed my eyes. I didn't want to be any of them. I wanted to be the little girl skipping through the streets without a care in the world.

"The more you look, the harder it is to control your imagination. It's no crystal ball or hologram-projecting tablet, but I think it can tell you almost as much," Damien said. He grasped his hands together in front of his chest. "Tomorrow we'll be able to see the whole picture." Could he feel that I knew we wouldn't see it tomorrow? I made myself breathe.

"I wonder which figure is Corey," he said with a meaningful tone. He went toward the right-hand side of the mural, looking up toward the man with the telescope. As he walked toward it, I saw Corey—not with the telescope but directly below. My heart fluttered. Shadowy and shirtless with tattered pants, he lifted both weary arms above his head as he trudged out of the dark, chained to the person above him in the light and the one below him on the war heap.

With the running clothes on the divan at the end of my bed, I forced my eyes closed. Moonlight streamed through the open curtains across my bed. I couldn't help wondering what Damien's people would do when they found Corey. I thought about our last meeting and his disappointment in me for having the chip implanted. Guilt seized my chest. That meeting might have cost Megan everything. I was responsible for her. Did Corey blame my stupidity?

I reached for my phone on the nightstand. 1:16. Seventy-two likes and fourteen comments. I looked at my selfie again before scrolling down the comments. Enticing but empty, this woman wasn't anywhere in the mural. Unless she was the fruit.

Nothing from Corey. Radio silence. He was smart. He had to be okay.

Turning on the light, I opened the blueprint images on my phone. They were all I had to give Corey in the morning. I hoped they would be enough.

\* \* \*

*I watch the explosions from a distance. Not on a television screen. I'm there. First one tower falls, then the other. Flames. I can't stop it. It will happen again and again.*

*The coffin. Blonde hair melting into the satin pillow. I'm running away from something. A woman chasing me. I look back and see her silhouette. I run faster, but she matches my pace almost exactly. I push faster and faster.*

* * *

I woke up, panting, at 5:00 a.m.—before my alarm rang. Shaking away my tension, I used my GPS map to locate Bethesda Fountain from Corey's Instagram picture. I wanted to give myself plenty of time to get there, but the map said it would only take fifteen minutes. When I finished lacing up the shoes Damien had bought me, I drank two little cups of water from the sink in the bathroom. I was anxious to go, but it was still dark outside. I would wait to leave until six.

Looking for a distraction, I turned on the tablet. I went to the personal pictures. I tried not to look at the little girl. I felt deep melancholy for her. Did the dream mean that I was killing her? I came to the selfie of us together. She was innocent and beautiful. I focused on my eyes. I could see what I was thinking, and I could feel what I was feeling: love.

Eventually, I sat staring at the banquet image again. Had all of these images been placed here purposefully? What had I wanted myself to see—that I had a relationship with Corey? That I was interested in his accomplishments? That he was important to Omnibus? Somehow, I didn't think that Omnibus would easily rebuild the bridges that Corey was burning right now. I wanted him to succeed in life. This would have been his future if I hadn't shown him the tablet. I didn't want him to have to fight Omnibus for me. He had lost enough already.

I looked at the name card on the table again. My spine tingled. I felt like a grade school girl playing a game of M.A.S.H., but I didn't care. My future was on the obscured card. If I had included the picture for some other reason, had I obscured the name or had someone else? The more I examined it, the more certain I was that something had been changed. The lighting and focus didn't make sense with the rest of the image.

"Show editing tools."

"Invalid command," the tablet responded.

"Edit image," I tried.

A panel of editing options appeared above the image. I quickly scanned them.

"Show layers," I said. Only two layers. A mask had been placed over the name card, and the name had been blurred using a smudge tool. My heart pushed against my chest.

Closing my eyes, I pictured the image of Corey standing next to me in the lab coat. I wanted it to be him. "Remove layer two in section twelve," I said. Instantly, the blurred section disappeared and I could clearly read the name underneath: Jace Trent.

\* \* \*

My heart pounded in my ears, in my chest, and in my hands. I gripped my phone and crept noiselessly through the hallways and out to the elevator. As soon as I reached the street, I burst out, running at breakneck speed. Nothing made sense. Damien was only pictured in one of the images. Why had I hidden my relationship with him? Was it because I wanted myself to make a different choice? But then what about the little girl? And how could I choose Damien when I planned to betray him?

Following the route I had mapped out, I saw a few runners and dog walkers. The sun was just beginning to warm the horizon as I passed the statue garden that lead to the mall. At the end of it, I would find Bethesda Fountain and, hopefully, Corey waiting for me. I ached to tell him everything, especially about Damien. What would he tell me to do? Who was he in my future? He had been trying to warn me about Damien from the beginning. Would he criticize me for choosing attraction over common sense? *Dating the dictator. Marrying the dictator.*

Looking at my clock, I realized I had made good time. I was ten minutes early. Up ahead, I saw the archways of the terrace near the fountain. I slowed down as I approached the stairs that ascended into the elegant stone structure. A chill ran down my spine.

With no one else around, I could hear the hollow echo of my steps bouncing off the tiles. Inside the darkness of the terrace, the fountain came into view through the middle of the three archways in the dim morning light. The angel's dark wings were frozen at the top of the fountain, but her raised foot and bent arms looked as if she were walking toward me. Suddenly afraid, I ran faster, looking around behind me. No one in sight. I shivered.

Three steps before the edge of the terrace, a shadow moved from behind one of the pillars to my right. Before I could react, the figure darted toward me. Covering my mouth and pushing me into the opposite pillar, he pinned me against it with his body.

Panic surged through me. I struggled, trying to free myself. I couldn't breathe.

Before I fully comprehended what was happening, Corey pushed his face toward mine until I could clearly see his features. I stopped fighting. He moved his hand away from my mouth, his eyes burning with concern. *So familiar.* Relief washed over me. I felt warm everywhere. I had never been happier to see anyone in my life.

With his face only inches from mine, I didn't think. I pushed my lips against his and melted into him, as if I had some right to do it. Corey's eyes opened wide in surprise and then closed tight as he pressed himself even harder against me. His lips moved over mine—heavy and full of emotion. Everything shattered. I didn't feel awkward or inexperienced—I felt like I knew what I was doing and what I wanted.

For a brief moment, I couldn't feel anything except warmth as we exchanged it. But too soon, my mind turned back on and began to reel. What was I doing? I had to pick up the shards. Megan. The banquet table. The little girl—Damien's daughter. I gasped for air and Corey immediately pulled his lips away. He turned his head toward the fountain, breathing hard. Overwhelmed, I wanted to tell him everything. *He doesn't know who I am. I have to tell him about Jace Trent.* I squeezed my palm tight against the chip, trying to keep my whole body from shaking.

Corey turned back toward me and lifted my palm, touching the scar. I didn't need the reminder, but my heart sank. I couldn't tell him everything with the chip in my palm. I silently lifted my phone and turned the screen on. I opened the blueprint images with trembling fingers. He studied the images for a few seconds; then, grabbing the phone away from me, he switched over to the notebook app.

*Let's get out of here*, he typed. His instincts were telling him to run, and he wasn't ignoring them. He wanted me to go with him now. I wanted it too, but I couldn't. Not yet. I took the phone back.

*What about the tablet? What about the chip?* I wrote.

He backed away from me. He had to know I was right. Without me, he had a chance to do something with this information, but with the chip in my hand, neither of us would make it very far. He paced around the pillar. I couldn't leave the tablet behind. If the information in the J file was something that would help Omnibus, I couldn't let them have it.

He came back to the side of the pillar where I still stood frozen, like my feet were cemented in the ground, and took the phone from me.

*Does Trent suspect anything?*

I shook my head slowly. Maybe Damien didn't trust me fully, but he seemed to believe my performance at the UN. I was sure I could convince Damien that I was on his side—that Corey was on his own.

*I need to transfer these images to my phone,* Corey typed. *It will take a few minutes. Keep running up the path past the boathouse. Make a left and follow the path around the pond. You'll come to a bridge that will bring you back to the opposite side of the fountain.*

I nodded. Grabbing Corey's hand, I squeezed it. How could I tell him that I knew what he was sacrificing? That I was keenly aware of everything he had lost because of me? I blinked away tears and brushed my lips against his one more time. His response was raw and unrestrained as he pushed me back against the pillar. I was breathless when he backed away. He took my phone again.

*You're only going back long enough to get the tablet. I'll tell you where to meet me on Instagram. Be careful.*

My skin tingled as I ran away from him past the fountain. I tried to pace myself, hoping to give him plenty of time to transfer the pictures, but I wanted to sprint back to his arms.

The sun flickered above the buildings behind the terrace, lighting the trees on fire across the pond.

With each step away from Corey and the terrace, images of the little girl and the name card crept back into my mind. I tried to calm myself and collect my thoughts. The tablet wasn't telling me everything. I didn't understand the sequence of events that would have led me to choose Damien, but I suspected that my father would have heavily influenced my decision.

I ran faster. The morning felt too quiet—too still. Something felt wrong. It felt like my dreams even though I wasn't being chased. I was alone, and being alone in the expansive park suddenly felt dangerous. I was almost sprinting when I saw the circular carvings on the bridge ahead. Had I been gone ten minutes or an hour? A lone white-haired woman walked her dog past the fountain in the distance, completely unaware of me and the mess I was making of my life.

I forced myself to slow down as I ran back inside the terrace. My eyes scanned the pillars looking for Corey. Blinding sunlight streamed in through the three arches at the far side where I had come down the stairs. Pain stabbed my temples, and I slapped my palms over my eyes.

* * *

*I'm in an unfamiliar light-filled room. A man sits in the corner with his back toward me wearing a large headset. He can't see me. I have to be quiet. I can faintly hear a series of rhythmic beeps. His pencil scratches against the paper as he listens.*

* * *

I uncovered my eyes, but my heart and head pounded. What was happening to me? Was I completely losing it? Kindergarten. What could have happened that my brain had shut it away so deep that I was just now finding it? *In through the nose. Out through the mouth.*

I searched the terrace for Corey, but I didn't see him. I ran all the way to the stairs, praying he would jump out at me again. Nothing. I turned around and rushed back toward the fountain. My stomach dropped and my anxiety soared. Corey was gone.

In a full panic, I sprinted up the stairs on the right side of the fountain to the top of the terrace, where I could see in every direction. Corey's red bandana was nowhere in sight. I couldn't imagine why he would have left with my phone, unless he sensed some kind of danger. I scanned the area again, praying that he would appear on one of the paths. I didn't see a living soul.

I ran down the staircase on the opposite side of the terrace, back through the columns on the inside. I searched the ground, looking to see if he had left any trace behind. I found nothing.

Damien would be expecting me to be ready for the day soon. I couldn't wait here forever. I had no choice. I had to return down the path to the Plaza. I fought with myself as I passed the sculpture garden. Why had I done it? Why had I left him with the phone? Had something happened to Corey, or had he left with what he came for? Left me to fend for myself. Was it safe for me to go back to the hotel? I had no way to communicate with Corey now. I had no idea what Corey was going to do with the information I had given him.

I cut down off the main path onto a narrower trail next to the pond. The light green accents on the roof of the hotel came into view. I was almost there. Suddenly able to hear the traffic and noise of the city, I sped up. Damien and Dr. Watts were probably awake and waiting for me by now. What was I going to say about my missing phone?

I rounded a curve just after passing a footbridge that crossed the pond. Another runner approached me from behind. His swift cadence prompted me to move to the right, allowing space to pass, but when he was within a few steps of me, he slowed down to match my pace. I increased my speed slightly, hoping to put some distance between us, but he kept uncomfortably close.

My instincts told me to sprint to safety. I wasn't far from the busy street where I would be surrounded by people. I picked up my pace a little more and almost instantly felt the runner at my heels. With long strides and arms pumping, I pushed myself forward. Up ahead, a second man jumped from the upper path over the shrubbery and a row of benches onto the center of the path in front of me. He was giant—Polynesian looking, with bronze skin and tribal tattoos on his neck and arms. I knew I didn't have time to slow myself down enough to avoid him. My only options were to plow into him or to hurdle the small fence that protected the flowers next to the path and end up in the pond.

My lungs burned. The guy in front of me squatted down and held his arms out, ready to grab me. The runner behind me sped up enough to shove me hard with both hands into the arms of the man waiting in front of us. I struggled as his tattooed arms pinned me against his chest. I tried to scream, but he pressed my face harder into his meaty shoulder and the sound was muffled.

Irrational survivalist mentality took over, and I bit down hard into the man's shoulder. He groaned through gritted teeth and loosened his grip just long enough for me to twist free. The man who had shoved me looked shocked as I took off running again. Adrenaline coursed through my veins, pushing me faster than I had ever gone before. There wasn't much danger of the bigger man catching up, but the other guy was tall and fast. I could already feel him about to overtake me again.

*Faster.* If I could just outrun him long enough to get to the street I would be safe. I could see my salvation about one hundred yards ahead. I pushed as hard as I could to reach the opening in the trees that would lead to the street and the Plaza, but my assailant was as determined as I was. He dove at me again. This time, instead of shoving me, he threw himself on top of me. I crashed hard against the asphalt path, grazing my right knee and elbow as I fell.

I thrashed wildly, with the runner still partially on top of me. I scratched and tore at his arms, and he struggled to subdue me. I felt the larger man behind us. He lifted my feet into the air, pinning them against his side. The runner punched my jaw hard. Vertigo slowed my thrashing and kicking. Suddenly, I felt a sharp prick in the skin just below my running shorts. Stunned, I stopped thrashing. A warm numbing sensation swept from the prick through the rest of my body until I couldn't feel anything and the world went dark.

*I* am *strapped to a table. I hear beeping behind me. I can't move. A
curtain in front of me blocks my view. Something is covering my mouth
and nose. I can't breathe. I panic. I'm trapped. I'm paralyzed. Something
terrible is about to happen to me.*

\* \* \*

My head pounded, sending bursts of color into the blackness around
me. I had no idea how much time had passed or where I was. Fog.
Nausea. I heard voices before I could open my eyes. I didn't recognize
them, but they were talking about me.

"He's gonna want her back," said a man's low voice.

"I'm not concerned about him," a deeper voice replied.

Slowly opening my eyes, I tried to look around the room. White
sunlight streamed through a window on the opposite wall. I was
lying on a stiff leather sofa. The shadows of two men stood a few feet
away from me. The silhouettes looked the same as the men who had
grabbed me at the park.

With effort, I shifted my head enough to look around the rest
of the room. Black and white décor. I tried to focus my eyes. It was
a large office space, strikingly modern. Shiny black tile floors, white
walls and bookcases. Looking past my feet, I could see the shape of
the door several feet away. I would be at a disadvantage if I tried to
bolt. My legs didn't feel like they were attached. And where would I
run to?

The big man with the tattoos must have seen my eyes open. He spun around on his heels and moved toward the sofa.

"She's awake." His thick voice had an island accent. He unfolded his big arms, prepared to hold me down or silence my screams. My blood pumped faster. My head felt like it was going to explode.

The other man came toward me. I closed my eyes. I remembered the pain and struggle in the park. Fear gripped me. Bright white spots flashed inside my eyelids and then turned into hundreds of small rainbow-colored circles.

"Jace"—his voice grated, elongating the final consonant—"can you sit up?"

I lifted my eyelids. Victor Trent loomed over me. Panic. I sat up quickly to move myself away from him, but whatever they had injected me with was still in my system. My head wobbled and swayed until it fell back against the back of the sofa.

"Take it easy," he warned. "You might be disoriented for a few minutes." He sat down on the sofa next to me on a small section of cushion near my waist. He touched the dried blood on my elbow. My skin crawled.

"What happened?" I croaked in a raspy voice. My throat was burning. "Where am I?"

"Relax, Jace," he said.

I crossed my arms over my chest and tried to turn away.

"My men were instructed to invite you to come see me. Obviously something was lost in translation."

Corey. Did they have him too? Lost in translation. Come see him. Why? *Be careful.*

"I think I was running in the park," I squeaked.

"Yes, you'll excuse me the less-than-friendly invitation," he said. "The struggle they had with your colleague threw them off. Tui has a very sensitive switch, and it was flipped." The Polynesian bodyguard grunted.

"Corey?" I asked before I could stop myself. "Where is he?" I tried to sit up again. Corey had struggled.

"He's fine."

"Where is he?" I pleaded.

"He's close. Don't worry about him now." His voice was calm, like the announcer on an easy listening radio station. Victor signaled to the two men to leave us alone. After they had shut the door, he continued, "Jace, I'm a little concerned about your friend. He had your phone, you know." My phone. I stopped breathing. Victor had my phone.

I looked away and stayed silent. I could smell his musky cologne and feel him breathing on me. He was too close. Smothering me.

"I'm sorry to pry, but when my men found Corey, he was in the process of transferring photographs from your phone to some online dropbox."

The blueprint. What could I say? I was trapped. When I stayed silent, Victor stood up and walked over to a cabinet that opened out into a minibar. Reaching into the refrigerator, he brought me a bottle of water. I wanted to refuse it, but my throat was on fire.

While I was drinking, Victor walked leisurely over to the window, giving me space. Now that my eyes had adjusted to the light, I could see high-rise buildings off in the distance. I couldn't hear the sound of traffic; we had to be several stories up.

"You know that your father and I have been good friends for a long time," he said. "You were so young when we lived in Sigonella, Jace. Do you remember me?" His question baffled me. I closed my eyes.

He continued, undeterred when I didn't answer his question. "My wife had a strange fixation with you. At the time, I thought she just wanted another baby—a little girl." I tried to catch my breath. Why was he telling me all of this? "But that wasn't why, was it, Jace?"

Terrified, I pushed myself up to a seated position. "What do you want from me, Mr. Trent?"

He turned back toward me but stayed at the window. He smiled. It was familiar. He had given Damien his dimples, but Victor's were deep and stretched out—repulsive instead of charming.

"Why did you bring me here?" I asked again.

"I felt safe hiring you because of your father, Jace." His voice was low and deep—almost hypnotic. "I naturally assumed that you would possess his integrity and loyalty. I thought you would be a friend to me and my son, and our company, but I am beginning to have my doubts."

His mention of my father stabbed me with pain. I was disappointing him. My heart jumped into my throat. Would my father want me to tell Victor everything? I wanted to beg for forgiveness and then try to get as far away from New York and the Trents as possible. Would that mean permanently distancing myself from my father too? *Loyal to Victor Trent.*

"I don't know what this is about, Mr. Trent," I said, "but I doubt my father would appreciate the way you have treated me today." My voice cracked.

He came toward me. "I don't have a lot of time for games today, Jace, so let's get to the point: I know that you and your friend have been searching for information on certain aspects of the company that you really shouldn't have any knowledge of. I simply want to know where you are getting your information and what you intend to do with it." He folded his arms sternly across his chest. "You do realize that if you were planning to sell those blueprints, I would have to turn you over to the authorities?"

"Do it," I said, focused on making my voice sound calm. "Turn me over to the authorities. I haven't done anything wrong."

Victor's face changed. He was visibly agitated. "Where did you get the blueprints?" he asked, all charm drained from his tone. A wave of nausea struck me, and the room spun.

His phone began to buzz, rescuing me momentarily. I considered running, even if I didn't know where I was. Would he have any hesitation causing an "accident" like Megan's if I didn't answer his questions? He had enough evidence in my phone to know that I was looking for something—something he didn't want me to know. Victor wasn't going to let me walk away from this office.

He was doing much more listening than talking on his call, and the things he did say sounded generic. He turned his back to me. When he ended the call, he glanced at me with wrinkled brow.

"You'll excuse me for a moment," he said before walking out the door and closing it firmly behind him.

How long would he be gone? I stumbled to my feet and made my way over to the window. My head and heart pounded in unison. I braced myself against the windowpane as I looked down to the street below. I was at least twenty stories in the air, and I could see a river and a bridge in the distance. It looked like the Brooklyn Bridge. I tried to get my bearings. We were somewhere in the financial district. I staggered back over to the sofa and sat down, taking another drink of water.

What were my options? I doubted Victor regularly held people against their will in this office space. There had to be people in the outer office that would be concerned if I made a scene. I got up slowly again and made my way quietly to the door. Pressing my ear against it, I tried to see if I could distinguish how many voices I heard. It was hard to hear anything. The ventilation system in the room created a white noise–type of hum. I reached for the doorknob with weak knees and trembling fingers.

Before I touched it, the knob twisted and the door came flying open, striking my arm and forehead before my body stopped it. I stepped back, thrown off balance and disoriented. Before I completely lost my balance, strong arms wrapped themselves around me. My arms and legs went limp.

"Are you okay?" Damien whispered. He supported my full body weight, walking me back to the sofa.

I didn't know how to answer. I looked into his eyes, trying to think rationally. His entrance was well timed. He had rushed in with his rope, ready to pull me to safety, just like in the mural.

"What happened?" he asked.

"Your father," I whispered, "sent some men to the park this morning. They chased me down and injected me with something before bringing me here."

His response was a look of complete disbelief. He searched the room and then examined me and my running clothes. I wanted to scream. The Trents' tag team efforts to pry information out of me weren't going to work.

"Can you walk?"

I looked at him incredulously. We had just barely sat down, and he had carried me here.

"I'm going to support you, but if you can move your legs at all, that will help."

I was confused, but I nodded. Damien stood up first and then lifted me to my feet. I could feel his heart racing. He wrapped his right arm around my back and under my arm. I felt a little dizzy, but my legs weren't as weak. He guided me to the door and swung it open without hesitating. The outer office was empty except for a receptionist at a desk facing the door. Damien walked casually through the reception area. His dress shoes clicked against the tile. He kept his eyes locked on his destination. He didn't stop when we passed the pretty redheaded receptionist. She was busy typing on her computer. She glanced up.

"Have a good day, Bonnie," he said.

"You too, Mr. Trent," came her squeaky reply. I could feel her eyes following us through the double-glass doors. I couldn't have looked more out of place in my dirty, bloodstained clothes. The throbbing in my head was intensifying, making it harder to process what was happening. Damien couldn't be doing this on his own. The way he had waltzed out of there, I couldn't imagine that his father didn't know that he had taken me.

"The elevators are just around the corner," he said. "I need you to lean against the wall while I press the buttons."

I didn't answer. He leaned me against a wall and then dashed to each of the eight elevators, frantically lighting up their down buttons. My adrenaline kicked in. He believed we were in danger. I let go of the wall and stumbled, with Damien, into the first elevator that opened. He pressed the button for the lobby and then resumed supporting me. I was glad he didn't smell like his father. My stomach couldn't have taken it.

"I have a car waiting in front of the building. We should have plenty of time to get there before anyone notifies security, but be ready to run just in case."

My stomach felt weightless as I watched the digital display above the doors count down to one. The bell chimed, and the doors opened smoothly. We walked into the vast lobby, but my stomach almost stayed behind in the elevator. I spotted the security desk about thirty yards to our right. Damien held me close as we rushed toward the revolving doors.

My whole body tingled. We were both holding our breath. Only eight feet from the door, a voice boomed from the security desk.

"Mr. Trent, I need you to stop right there."

Damien didn't stop; he picked up our pace and pushed me into the revolving door, jumping in behind me. We pushed against the door until I felt the fresh outside air. A black Lincoln Town Car was waiting on the curb. The driver spotted us and threw open the back door. Damien and I were both running when the security guard reached the door.

"Mr. Trent!" he yelled.

Damien loosened his hold on me as we neared the car, nudging me in front of him.

"Get in, Simon!" he ordered, his voice raised in urgency. The driver ran around to the front seat.

I collapsed into the backseat, looking for the security guard behind us. He had drawn his weapon and held a walkie-talkie in his other hand, mumbling something into it as he jogged after us. Damien dove into the car behind me, pulling the door closed.

"Go, go, go!" he shouted.

The tires squealed as we flew away from the building. I watched the security guard shrink into the distance behind us. Victor's henchmen came running out with weapons drawn just before we rounded a corner and lost sight of the building.

"Take the tunnel," Damien directed. "We can change cars as soon as we get to Jersey."

"Where are we going?" I asked.

"Don't worry about it. You're safe."

"Do you have the tablet?" I gasped. I dug my fingernails into Damien's arm.

He didn't answer but picked up his phone. He quickly touched the contact he was looking for. "I found her," he said. "Grab the tablet and get out of there. Take a taxi and call me when you're out of the city." Dr. Watts must have stayed behind at the hotel. Whoever it was agreed to do what Damien asked without question, and the call was over.

I panicked. We were leaving the city. We weren't coming back.

"We can't go!" I cried.

"We have to, Jace. My father knows about the tablet, and he's not going to stop until he gets it."

"But what about Corey?"

Damien looked at me with genuine surprise. "Do you know where he is? We haven't been able to reach him since yesterday. He wasn't on the later flight."

"Your father has him."

Y**ou'd** better start at the beginning and tell me exactly what happened today. What did my father say to you, and how do you know he has Corey?" Damien glared at me.

I took a deep breath, trying to bring my vision into focus. My head pounded, and the seat belt choked me. I had to be careful. Just because Damien had swooped in on his white horse to save me didn't mean that I could trust him. Corey's life was at stake.

Damien spoke again when I hesitated. "Look, Jace, I know you're disoriented and probably scared, but I need you to tell me everything you remember."

My mind raced. How could I possibly tell him everything? Tell him that I had been trying to find a way to destroy Omnibus? Tell him that Corey and I had deleted information from the tablet? Tell him that I had met Corey in the park this morning with the blueprint? Or maybe just tell him that I'm his future wife and the mother of his nonexistent child?

I wished I could ask for another injection that would take me back into oblivion.

I angrily brushed the tears out of my eyes and geared up for another round of half-truths.

"I went for a run in the park this morning. When I stopped to watch the sunrise at Bethesda Fountain, I accidently left my phone sitting on a ledge. I ran halfway around the lake before I realized it, but when I came back for it, it was gone. It was getting late, so I started back toward the hotel. Then I realized that someone was following me. I sprinted to get away, but another man jumped into the path in front of me. I couldn't fight them off. The tall one almost crushed me, and then the other one injected me with something before I knew what was happening."

Damien listened with a serious face and intense eyes. "Go on," he prompted.

"I woke up in your father's office. The three of them were whispering and didn't notice me coming around. One of them said they were going to try to get some answers from me. When they saw me awake, your father sent the other two men away and started asking me questions."

"What did he ask?"

"He wanted to know about some of the pictures on my phone. They must have followed me to the fountain and picked up my phone when I dropped it. He wanted to know why I had a picture of the blueprint and what I was planning to do with it."

"You had a picture of the blueprint?" I couldn't tell if he was surprised or angry.

"Yes," I couldn't think of any logical explanation for my actions, so I didn't give one.

"And where does Corey come into all of this?"

"Your father mentioned 'my colleague' and said something about his goons being rough with me because he had struggled or resisted."

He was quiet for a second. "Do you think Corey was in the park this morning too?"

I gave a little shrug and turned toward the window. Watching the buildings pass on the left brought back the nausea. Damien touched my shoulder softly.

"Jace, if we want to help Corey, we're going to have to trust each other."

I didn't respond.

"Well, he's *your* father," I finally said, still facing the window. "There must be some way for you to find out if he has Corey."

His hand dropped from my shoulder, and he gave up trying to talk to me. I saw his reflection in the window as he returned his focus to his phone. Was he solidifying our escape plan, or was he texting his father about my noncooperation? The situation was impossible. My head screamed for ibuprofen.

I closed my eyes. Flashes from the week played in my head. I thought of Corey's misguided efforts to stop the inevitable. I thought about Megan's death. I thought about my strange relationship with Damien, his protective attitude toward me, and his tingle-inducing touch that I tried to tell myself I was immune to or could at least control. I cringed, thinking of my incessant lies and ulterior motives.

But Corey—I could see his face and feel his lips again. I had brought him into this whole mess. I had ruined his career—his future. I couldn't leave him behind. I had to know he was safe.

I looked up at Damien's reflection again. I couldn't count on his help. He didn't care about Corey. Even if his wide-eyed, altruistic persona was sincere, he had to be bound to his father by some degree of loyalty. I couldn't let Damien control my destiny. Or Corey's. I had to do something.

We turned off a busy street onto a narrow one-way. Scaffolding lined the right side of the street where a building was being remodeled. We passed through an intersection, and I looked down the sidewalk of the cross street. Only a few people were walking on Jay Street. If I wanted to give myself a fighting chance, I needed a crowd. I sat up a little and my heart began beating erratically. Every minute was taking me farther away from Corey. I didn't have time to think this through. I had to act now.

The next two streets we passed were even less populated than the first. Up in the distance, I could see another stoplight. It was red, and a large crowd of pedestrians passed through the crosswalk. Damien was frowning, reading something on his phone. My palms began to sweat. Traffic continued to crawl.

When we were about fifty yards from the intersection, I slowly lifted my hand, touching the door handle. I would have to reach for the lock with my right hand while I opened the handle with my left. I pressed the button, releasing my seat belt buckle, but held it silently in place. I could barely breathe.

The light turned red again and the pedestrians entered the intersection again. We were the fourth car in line. I took one last look at Damien and then watched the hand begin to flash red. I waited until it stopped flashing and then reached for the lock, lifting it swiftly before flinging the door open. The light had just turned green, and the car moved forward. Damien reached for me, but I was already halfway out the door and his grip on my dry-fit shirt was loose. I slid out of his grasp.

"Stop the car!" he yelled.

I took off running, a little off-balance at first. I followed the pedestrians onto Beach Street, dodging and weaving my way through the crowd. The middle of the cobblestone street was blocked off with green tarp-covered chain link fences, congesting the crowd on the sidewalk. I slowed down enough to look back over my shoulder. Damien was several yards behind. In his suit and dress shoes, he wasn't running at full speed. I pushed myself harder as the narrow walkway widened.

I cut sharply to the right onto an even narrower road. Damien was still wading through the pedestrians. Without obstacles, I hit a full sprint, hoping to make another turn before Damien had a view of the street. I was almost to the next intersection when the black Town Car turned onto the one-way street—charging toward me at full speed in the wrong direction. I had no choice but to turn again. I went left, hoping to find another crowd I could disappear into. Damien was gaining on me now that he was free of the human obstacles, and I could hear the car speeding toward the intersection.

The street was empty. I panicked. On my left, a car appeared, coming out of an underground parking garage. The exit was narrow, and I couldn't see the entrance. I turned quickly inside, bumping my arm against the car as it pulled out. Running down the ramp, I was absorbed into the darkness. It would take some time for my eyes to adjust to the dim bulbs. My footsteps echoed off into the distance. I slowed to a walk and moved over to the right until I could touch the cold cement wall. I continued my descent into the garage, but slowly and quietly, listening for Damien's footsteps behind me.

When I reached the bottom of the ramp I rounded the corner and stood with my back against the wall, recovering my breath. For a moment, I didn't hear anything. Damien had probably continued on past the garage but might double back when he realized what had happened. I looked down at my palm as my eyes began to adjust. Even if I was able to escape Damien and Simon, they would be able to track me with the chip. If they weren't already.

Feeling desperate, I ventured farther into the garage. Passing the parked cars, I began to try door handles to see if I could find one that had been left unlocked. Running from car to car, I realized that my search was a waste of time. Even if I could find one that was open, I didn't know how to start a car without a key.

I reached an elevator. Pressing the button, I waited for it to descend. Sweat was beginning to drip from my forehead into my eyes, making them blur and sting. I used the bottom of my shirt to wipe my face. Looking at the elevator button again to make sure it was illuminated, I noticed an ash can just below it. Someone had left a beer bottle sitting in the ashes.

I had to get rid of the chip. My empty stomach tightened in pain when the thought hit me. I couldn't realistically expect to keep running when I would be so easy to find. I had to help Corey.

My breathing turned to a shallow pant as I lifted the bottle out of the tray. I stood holding it out in front of me for what seemed like an eternity before closing my eyes and smashing it against the wall. The noise echoed through the garage. I hesitated, listening for footsteps, before picking up a large, jagged shard of glass.

Squatting down between the elevator door and the ash can, I held my palm open. The scar was tiny, halfway between my thumb and index finger. I touched it firmly and then felt the entire length of the chip. My heart jumped and began beating so fast I thought I might pass out. I couldn't think about it. I just had to do it.

I plunged the sharp end of the glass into my scar, unable to contain a shrill scream.

Burning.

Glass clinked on the ground. Blood erupted from the wound. Pulsing.

At the top of the ramp, heavy footsteps echoed in the darkness. Panic. I dropped to my knees. Trembling fingers felt for the glass a second time. The footsteps pumped in rhythm with my heart. Closer. I bit my cheek, pulling the shard farther down toward the bottom of my hand in one excruciating motion.

*Hold your breath. Don't scream. Keep control.*

The blood-covered chip surfaced. Still trembling, I slowly set the glass down. Touching the chip with my index finger, I dug my thumb beneath it into the sticky, searing mess, tearing it away.

The footsteps reached the bottom of the ramp, and I saw Damien's tall figure coming at me. Pressing my wounded hand hard against my breast, I stood up. I still couldn't hear the elevator descending, but I could see a staircase on the other side of a pillar in front of me. Holding the chip in my right hand, I staggered toward the stairs with the sound of Damien's footsteps right behind me.

I reached the stairs. I grasped for the rail and tried to pull myself up, but his hand jerked me harshly to the ground.

I tried to scramble to my feet again, but Damien threw himself awkwardly on top of my twisted body. My wounded hand lay on the concrete floor, quickly collecting a pool of blood below it.

"What are you doing, Jace?" Damien asked, panting. "I'm trying to help you."

I tried to push him off, but my left arm was numb. My head spun. He rolled off me to his knees, pinning my shoulders back to the ground when I tried to get up. Startled, he looked down at his blood-soaked pant leg.

"What's this?" he demanded. He scanned my body for the source of the blood. His eyes stopped on my palm. He gasped.

Releasing my shoulders, he applied pressure to the wound with his bare hands.

Could I scream? Would anyone hear me? I started to shiver. Dark. Keep fighting. I brought my right knee up sharply, connecting with Damien's ribs. He winced but squeezed my bloody hand tighter.

"You need help!" Damien yelled. He straddled my chest and sat down hard, pushing the wind out of me.

Darker. Can't breathe.

Can't fight.

Darkness enveloped my mind. Reaching my hand up, I pressed the stained chip against his clean white shirt and let go.

**34**

*I am in a comfortable armchair with soft red upholstery. My feet dangle below the chair and I swing them nervously back and forth. I see the doctor's face behind the ink blob cards he is showing me, and I try to read it for approval as I give my answers. He's young—less than thirty—and handsome. I know why I'm here. I look over at the chair next to me. My father smiles at me tenderly. There is some pain in his eyes, but my father trusts Dr. Watts. He's going to help me.*

\* \* \*

"Jace!" Someone was calling my name. At first it was far off in the distance. It grew steadily closer and closer until it was booming in my ear and shaking me.

"Jace! You have to wake up. We need to get you to a hospital." It was Damien. He finished wrapping his necktie around my hand, cinching it tight and tying a knot. He was a mess with his hair out of place and his shirt unbuttoned, untucked, and bloodstained.

I blinked a few times and tried to focus my eyes on the dim fluorescent light bulb above me in the stairwell. The throbbing returned to my head. Damien gently lifted me to a seated position and I prepared myself mentally to try to bolt as soon as he looked away. He didn't break eye contact.

"Can you walk?" he asked softly.

A wave of nausea hit me. Doubling over with gripping diaphragm convulsions, I tried to throw up, but my stomach was empty. Damien put his hand on my back and moved a lock of hair that had fallen from my ponytail away from my face until I stopped retching.

"Jace, Simon is waiting outside in the car. I'm going to carry you out there. Please don't fight me. You can't help Corey if you bleed to death." He was right. He stood up and lifted me easily into his arms. I draped my arms around his neck but couldn't help much with my weak grip.

He carried me through the garage, back up the ramp, and out into the blinding sunlight. My eyes immediately began to tear up, and I had to pinch them shut. The throbbing in my head matched the pulsing pain in my palm, but the warmth of the sun stopped my shivering. I heard Simon opening the door of the car, and Damien set me inside, strapping me firmly in the seat. I opened my eyes as he backed out of the car. He flipped the child lock button before closing the door.

Damien and Simon moved to the far edge of the sidewalk and talked in low voices for a moment. Simon nodded his head several times, and then Damien brought his phone out of his pocket. He seemed to be messaging someone first, and then he lifted the phone to his ear. Simon moved back into the car, looking over the backseat to make sure I was still strapped in.

When Damien had finished his call, he came around the side of the car and sat in the backseat next to me.

"I just got off the phone with your father, Jace. He's going to meet us at Roosevelt Hospital."

"My father's in New York?" I croaked.

"Yes," he said without further explanation. My eyes filled with tears. I bit my cheek and turned away. Irrational desire to tell my father everything that had happened overwhelmed me. His judgment was sound. Whatever lies the Trents had told him could be untold by the tablet. He would help me. He had to.

Simon drove calmly with the traffic. Damien didn't talk to me or look at his phone for the next fifteen minutes. He did look over at my hand several times. I held it against my chest with my fist clenched tight against the necktie. Blood soaked through to the outside of the makeshift bandage.

"We're almost there," Simon told Damien. "I'll pull into the valet entrance on 58th Street. I can wait in the lobby for Admiral Vega."

Damien agreed. "Can you walk now, Jace, or should I get a wheelchair?"

I still felt weak, but I thought I could walk with help. I told him so.

We pulled through the drive of the unimpressive-looking red brick building. Damien jumped out of the car and ran around to my side, helping me out and supporting me as we walked through the sliding doors into the lobby. In the emergency department, Damien said something to the triage people that got us past the line of people waiting and directly into an examination room. An orderly helped me onto the bed and closed the curtain around me, assuring Damien that a doctor would be right with us. As soon as he was gone, Damien moved in close to me and spoke in a low urgent voice.

"Listen, Jace, I know you don't trust me, and I don't blame you. I know what you're thinking—the chip you took out of your hand allowed me to track you and listen to everything you said, and you're right. We've been lying to each other, but it's going to stop. I did it because I wanted to find out why you're so important to my father. We're on the same side. I didn't want to hurt you." His voice was firm.

"Is that how your father tracked me down in the park? With the chip?"

"I don't know how he found you," he told me, "but unless you told him about it, he doesn't know that you had a chip."

"Where is it?" I asked.

He touched his pocket before reaching inside. Looking at the floor as he brought his hand back out, he trembled. Finally, he opened his palm and looked at it momentarily before showing it to me. The silicone wasn't transparent anymore; my blood masked the components of the chip.

"What about my father?" I whispered. "Is he working with you?"

Damien looked surprised. "No."

"I know he met with you on Monday," I said accusingly. "If he's not working with you, why is he in New York?"

"He's working on a project at US Naval Research. I've been trying to get close to him. I'll explain all of that later. Just rest assured that your father is a man of integrity. He's not easily bought or persuaded."

My throat choked as relief swept through me. I wanted nothing more than to believe that my father was innocent of any deception.

Damien watched my eyes fill up. He blinked furiously and looked at the curtain behind us.

Who was Damien? He had easily controlled his emotions talking about his dead mother, but now he was fighting tears for me. I wanted to understand him. How connected was he to his father? He shifted the chip from his right hand to his left. The warmth from his hand had transferred some of the crusty blood to his palm. He wiped it on his pant leg.

"I need to text Simon to tell him where to bring your father," he said. "When he gets here, I'm going to leave you for a little while. My dad is not going to be happy that I brought your father into this. I'm going to have to do some damage control, and I need to get the tablet back from Dr. Watts. When you're released, go with your father to the research center or to his hotel. I'll call him as soon as I can."

"What about Corey? Do you know where he is?"

"He's safe," Damien promised. He looked at the chip before delicately putting his hand back in his pocket. Though it was impossible to know whether I could believe him, I noted the guilt in his eyes.

The next few minutes were a painful buzz as the doctor unwrapped my hand and assessed the damage. I hadn't severed anything important, but the cut was jagged and wide. I would need several stitches. His nurse prepped the area.

"We're going to give you a local anesthetic and a tetanus shot," the nurse informed me as she prepared two needles. I tensed. When he saw me flinch, Damien picked up my right hand. His touch was warm and reassuring. I wanted to believe he was sincere.

I looked away as the doctor expertly stitched my wound closed. When he was about halfway down my palm, my father came through the curtain with Simon. Damien let go of my hand abruptly and walked toward them.

"Admiral," Damien said, "thank you for coming." He glanced down at his bloodstained shirt and brushed his hand over it. My father looked at him with stern, silent mistrust before turning his attention to me.

"Mija, are you okay?" He pushed his way into Damien's place at my bedside. I nodded as he took my dirty hand in his and squeezed it. Damien watched us in silence from the corner he had backed into. My father's eyes moved to my wounded hand. Observing the doctor's skill, he seemed satisfied that I was in no immediate peril. He glared at Damien.

"What happened here?" he demanded.

Damien took a step backward into the curtain. "I'm sure this is all very distressing to you, sir." He glanced at Simon. "I can't explain everything now—I have some urgent business to take care of. Jace will explain, and I'll call you later."

My father looked at me and back to Damien with a stern brow. I was shocked when he nodded his approval. I couldn't fathom that my father was going to let Damien walk away with such an ambiguous excuse. We both watched Damien part the curtains and follow Simon into the hall. He couldn't get away fast enough. My father intimidated him. What had their past interactions been like? How much did he expect me to tell my father?

When the sound of Damien and Simon's footsteps disappeared, I looked back at my father with some trepidation. How was I going to tell him everything, and would he believe me? My father squeezed my hand, silently communicating that my explanation could wait. Then his eyes softened into an expression I didn't expect, but I immediately recognized—the same tender smile he had reassured me with in Dr. Watts's office. I felt like a balloon inflated to capacity. I tried to clear my mind. I wanted to be filled with the same childlike trust I had felt in that memory. I had trusted him to help me then—I only hoped he could help me now.

A n hour later, my father and I made our way across town in a taxi. I held my discharge papers and a prescription for antibiotics on my lap. He had barely spoken to me in the hospital, but I knew that my full explanation was expected when we were alone. The burden of worrying about disappointing him was crushing, but I was too exhausted to plan what I would say.

My father made a phone call, letting someone know that he wouldn't be back to the research center that afternoon. We arrived at his hotel a few minutes later. I realized how horrific I looked in my sweat- and bloodstained running clothes, and I was embarrassed to walk through the lobby with my father. I would have been much more comfortable following at a distance. I felt everyone's eyes on us as he walked slowly beside me, holding my hand like he had when I was a little girl.

When we were safely inside his room, I tensed, preparing for his shower of questions. But he went straight to the closet and opened his suitcase, handing me a Cowboys T-shirt and a pair of pajama bottoms. Still without speaking, he took the plastic bag out of the ice bucket in the kitchenette.

"Give me your hand," he said. Wrapping the plastic around my bandage, he secured it with a tight knot. "Take as long as you need in there to get cleaned up, and I'll order you some food." I swallowed a lump in my throat. I tasted salt. Clutching the clothes he had given me, I went into the bathroom and shut the door.

Stripping off the dirty, unfamiliar running clothes was a relief. The cascading warm water temporarily relieved my aching head and the sore muscles that had plagued me all day. Eventually I began to scrub at the dirt and blood on my right hand. It was hard without the full use of my left. The skin on my hand began to feel raw from rubbing it against the hotel washcloth.

I needed a scrub brush and my nail kit.

*Isn't this kind of excessive, even for you?* Sheila's words echoed in my mind. My shoulders fell forward, and tears began to flow silently. They disappeared as soon as I let them fall, mixing with the water that poured down my body, and then swirled down the drain. *I'm not normal.* My shoulders shook as I tried to control my sobs. *I'll never be normal.* My knees weakened and I hunched down on the shower floor, pulling them into my chest.

Something inside me was broken, and it had been broken for a very long time. My mother must have known it, but it hadn't mattered to her. I had to stop pretending with my father. He had taken me to Dr. Watts, hoping to fix whatever was wrong with me, but it hadn't worked. I had just learned how to hide it from him and other people.

I couldn't hide it anymore. When I had pulled myself together enough, I came out of the bathroom. My father smiled at my improved appearance. Room service must have just brought the tray that he ordered. He was arranging it on the table next to the window. I threw my dirty clothes in a plastic laundry bag from the closet and joined him at the table. Even before opening the lids, I could smell the meat. My stomach growled, and my legs felt weak and crampy.

He had ordered identical meals for us: rib-eye steaks with garlic mashed potatoes and asparagus. I waited anxiously for my father to ask for my explanation, but he just nodded at my food. I picked up the dinner roll and ate it immediately without buttering it. He let me finish it and waited until I was cutting into the steak before asking me anything.

His eyes didn't leave my wounded hand. "Before you tell me what has been going on this week, I need to ask you, Jace, did Damien cut your hand—is he the one that hurt you?" My eyes blurred with water. This protective question wasn't at all what I expected. He didn't want to interrogate me. I considered how to answer him.

"It's so much more complicated than that." I looked into my father's eyes. Everything that had happened from the tablet on the path to the broken bottle in the parking garage spilled out of me. He listened intently as he ate his food. He didn't ask questions. I took my time, eating slowly as I described each of the Omnibus pictures we had deleted. I watched his face when I told him that he was the CNO. He was stoic.

I continued on, telling him about the personal file and the pictures of the little blonde girl. I even told him about the edited banquet image and my discovery of the name card. When I finally finished, he pushed his chair away from the table and stroked his clean-shaven cheek and chin.

"And you have all of the information from the tablet except for the one unopened file." It was a statement—summarizing facts.

I nodded.

"Then we need to get Corey back so we can open the last file before we decide how to proceed," he concluded.

"We need to get Corey back before Victor kills him." My heart sank as I said it.

My father nodded but didn't express any concern for Corey. "I know Victor very well, mija, and I don't think you should worry about him killing your friend."

"I know this all sounds crazy, but I don't think that Victor Trent is the person you think he is," I pleaded. "I never would have embarrassed you like this if I didn't believe he's dangerous." My voice cracked, but I continued on, my tone becoming increasingly frantic. "They killed Corey's friend. Corey's friend from Stanford was helping him dig for information about Omnibus. Omnibus recruiters found her. They knew what she had been looking at. The newspaper said she died in a car crash."

My father continued to frown but didn't say anything.

"Corey doesn't think it was an accident, and neither do I." He looked away. How could I convince him that Victor Trent wasn't what he appeared to be? "You have to believe me. You have to trust me," I begged.

He wiped his mouth with his napkin. "If there's anyone in the world that I trust, it's you, mija. You've never given me any reason to doubt you. In fact, you have far exceeded my expectations, and I expected perfection." I set my fork down. I felt a mixture of relief and pain. *He wants to believe I'm perfect.* My body cramped. *He only wants to believe my façade.* I searched his eyes. They were warm, clear, and a little moist. He was saying what I thought I always wanted to hear, but this wasn't what I wanted to feel anymore. I didn't just want him to be proud of me. I wanted him to know who I really was and still love me.

The dam of tears that I had shut off when I turned off the shower burst. I couldn't control the flood. I looked away from my father and pushed my face into my napkin. My father—I loved him. I idolized him. Everything I had ever done in my life had been to try to become like him or to please him, but it was all pretend. I wasn't perfect. I was a lonely, frightened, friendless mess.

My shoulders shook, and trying to contain my sobs became painful. I pushed my chair away from the table, moving toward the bathroom with my face still covered. I heard my father stand to stop me. He took the napkin away from my face and pulled me against his shoulder. I moaned. I couldn't hold back anymore. He squeezed me tight against him, and I sobbed uncontrollably.

It was ugly and uncomfortable, but strangely freeing. With each wave of emotion, my father responded silently with a gentle pat on my back or stroke of my hair. When I finally regained control, I pulled away from his shoulder, embarrassed about the puddle I had left on his shirt.

His phone began to buzz. He hesitated before reluctantly letting me go. I picked up my napkin and wiped my face as he answered the call.

"Hello, Damien." He listened with low brows. "Yes, I know everything. She's told me everything."

I couldn't hear Damien's side of the conversation, but I could see from my father's frown that something he was hearing didn't please him. He listened without speaking for what seemed like forever. My tension grew.

"Yes," he said, "come here. We're in room 7012."

I panicked. Why was Damien coming here? Had something happened to Corey? The phone call ended.

I looked at my father, begging for information with my eyes. Did Damien have the tablet? Did he know where Corey was and if he was okay?

"Damien is coming here with the tablet," he began tentatively. "Victor is gone. He left New York. He took Corey with him."

"Why?" I asked. "Where?"

"Portland," my father said, "and Damien promised to explain why when he gets here."

What was Victor going to do to Corey? Why Portland? Instead of mounting an operation to rescue Corey from across town, now we would have to travel across the entire country. The familiarity of my stabbing anxiety was a relief after my uncontrolled burst of emotion. I took a deep breath through my nose and released it through my mouth.

My father began cleaning up the table from our dinner, setting our trays outside the door. He put on his shoes and uniform jacket and then placed a chair where he could see the door. He sat waiting for Damien's arrival. I desperately wished I could see inside his mind.

36

Damien came alone. He carried his satchel over his shoulder and dragged a black rolling suitcase behind. I recognized the bright red luggage tag. He must have seen Corey. My heart leapt. But where had my suitcase come from? Corey didn't have it with him at the park. Damien brought the bag to my side. My headache intensified. He frowned and lightly touched the bandage on my hand. Even without making contact with my skin, his electricity surged through the dressing. I shivered.

"How are you feeling?" he asked quietly. I didn't respond. I was a confused mess.

"Sit down," my father ordered. Damien sat on a chair strategically placed directly across from my father. My chair was behind the table and my father, where it wouldn't be easy for Damien to see me or make eye contact. My father didn't prompt Damien to speak, he simply unfolded his arms and held his open palm out, ready for his promised explanation.

"First of all, I'm sure you both want to know that Corey's fine. I saw him myself this afternoon. He hasn't been harmed," he began. My father just nodded, prompting Damien to continue. "He told my father about the tablet and they've been talking about it all afternoon. Corey told him that you deleted some of the images. Some that cast Omnibus in a questionable light. He described them in detail."

Was it possible that Damien was telling the truth? Could this be the first Victor had heard of the tablet? Would Corey have told him about the deleted images without a fight? Damien's assessment that he was "fine" felt hollow.

"Continue," my father said.

"My father was angry about the deleted images. I'm not sure he believed everything Corey told him about them. Without seeing them for himself, he's at a disadvantage. He likes having the upper hand." Damien rubbed his temples. He looked like he had been run over by a truck. He had showered and changed his clothes, but his eyes were dull and tired.

"So what now?" I asked. "Why did he take Corey to Portland?"

"This is where you're going to have to bear with me. They're going to Portland because of the blueprint, and they want me to persuade you to come with me to meet them there."

"What's in Portland?" my father asked.

"One of our research facilities is in the area. Dr. Watts believes that the device on the blueprint is already being tested. He says that the schematics and instructions on your phone will speed the development process." I watched my father for a reaction. Did he recognize Dr. Watts's name?

"What does the device do?" my father pressed, his expression unchanged.

Damien hesitated. "We think it's the device that sent the tablet back in time."

It had never occurred to me that the device could be anything other than a weapon. My spine tingled.

"Why do you need Jace?" my father demanded gruffly.

"My father wants the final file opened. We need all three of us to open it. He assured me that as soon as we see the content of the file, Jace and Corey are free to go."

"What guarantee do we have of that?" My father stood up. He towered over Damien.

"We have no guarantee," Damien said quietly.

My mind raced. I had no choice. I had to go with Damien to Portland. Victor had taken Corey as a hostage to make sure that I would follow. But I couldn't believe that he was going to let us walk away after we opened the file for him. We had too much information. We were a liability.

"You say that you have the tablet?" my father asked. "I'd like to see it." I wasn't sure why I was surprised when he asked. My father was very thorough—of course he'd want to examine all the evidence.

Damien nodded and went over to his satchel to get it. He set it on the table in front of me.

"I don't know how much charge it has, so we should be careful," he said.

My father picked up the tablet and examined it, turning it over a few times. He was deep in thought. He set it down again in front of me.

"I don't like the idea of sending you there without knowing what's in the third file." I was surprised that he would consider sending me there at all after what I had told him about Victor and the tablet and Megan—the man who had methodically trained me to run from and escape danger. My head pounded and my eyes felt swollen.

Damien reached into his pocket. "Corey asked me to give you this," he said, handing me my phone. "He said to remind you of the fight you had at the dog park if you were hesitant to come. He said you still owe him one."

My hair stood on end. Why would Victor have let Damien come here with the tablet and my phone? I opened the camera breathlessly. Nothing had been deleted. The blueprint and schematics were still there.

*Remind me of the fight in the dog park if I was hesitant to come.* My pulse raced. Which fight? The one where he had made me feel stupid for letting Damien implant the chip? *I still owe him one?* I thought about the headline—about Megan's death. That couldn't be what he meant. I bit my cheek. I didn't feel any blame in his kiss in the park. I shook my head, trying to think clearly. Besides, he didn't need to send my phone to remind me that I had killed his friend. The phone had to be part of the message.

Suddenly I realized. The fight had been about the phone. How could I have forgotten? We didn't need Corey to open the file! We only needed a recording of his voice. I had been angry with him for using my voice to look at the files without me. Now he wanted me to do the same. For knowing me so little, he knew me very well.

I opened my phone and found Corey's work number in my contacts. I dialed it and waited. When the voice mail picked up, I held my breath as I listened to the greeting: "Hello, you've reached Corey Stein with Omnibus, please leave a message." I disconnected.

My father and Damien watched me curiously.

"What is it, mija?" my father asked.

"It's a message from Corey. He wants us to look at the file before we follow him to Portland."

"But how?" Damien asked.

I couldn't help grinning. "The tablet will respond to a recording," I said, picking it up and pressing the button to turn it on. My excitement dimmed and then blackened when the tablet didn't respond. *Dead battery.* Before I could stop myself, I threw the tablet down on the bed in frustration.

"I still have the chip," Damien offered meekly.

I looked at him—at first angry and then sympathetic. His eyes were bloodshot and pained.

"You can't possibly be suggesting that my daughter allow you to put that back in her hand," my father said indignantly.

"I can see why you wouldn't want that," Damien said, "but it could be to your advantage."

"What do you mean?" I asked.

"I can give your father access to the system that tracks the chip. If you decide to come with me to Portland, he can track you and hear everything that happens to you."

"What are you suggesting, ripping out her stitches?" My father's voice boomed with rage.

"Admiral, I don't want to hurt Jace any more than you do. I'm just trying to help." Damien's voice matched my father's.

"If you want to help, then give me your palm. I have a pen knife we can cut you open with." He took a threatening step toward Damien.

"Sir"—Damien held his hands out in front of him—"the chip is part of the deal."

"What do you mean?" my father demanded.

"My father intends to bring Jace to Portland one way or another. He doesn't trust me anymore. He was going to send someone else for her. I convinced him that I could do it, but the chip was the only way. He wouldn't agree until I told him he could track her. He wants to know her every move until she joins him there."

My father's face turned red. There was no choice to be made. If I

didn't agree to have the chip implanted—if I didn't go to Portland—
Victor wouldn't hesitate to do to Corey what he had done to Megan.
My heart raced.

"Daddy, I have to do this. We have to find out what's in the J file.
We have to help Corey."

My father locked eyes with me before dropping his to the floor.

He slowly nodded in agreement.

# 37

Damien produced a small medical kit that Dr. Watts had given him. Sitting at the table with my uninjured right palm outstretched, I watched as he sanitized everything. I clenched my jaw as he numbed my hand before cutting a small slit and inserting the chip. This time, instead of closing my eyes, I watched him intently. My father stood over me, observing every move Damien made like a hawk. I could only hope Damien knew what he was doing.

He finished quickly, dabbing the incision with surgical glue. While he cleaned up the instruments, I pressed my bandaged hand against my knee; it throbbed if I let go. My father watched silently until Damien picked up his satchel and walked toward the door.

"Where are you going?" my father asked.

"The chip is activated, but it will take time to harvest enough electricity. I'll be back in the morning. Jace needs some rest."

My father grunted. "Be here early," he ordered. "Six o'clock."

Damien didn't even look at me. He just reached for the door handle and left. We both stood in awkward silence watching the door for a moment before my father quietly walked to one of the beds and pulled down the light green bedspread. He fluffed up the pillows loudly and then motioned for me to climb in, the same way he had when I was little. I took a deep breath and slid between the crisp white sheets gratefully. My body was as tired as my mind.

After switching off the lamp, my father sat on the end of my bed.

"Get some rest," he said. He didn't move, waiting for me to obey him, but I fought it. My temples and hands pulsed in unison. I had so many questions, but I didn't know where to start and I was afraid to ask.

"Can I ask you something?"

"Of course, mija. What is it?" he asked.

"You taught me to run. You pushed me to it. I thought it was your way of keeping me safe from danger—to protect me—so I could outrun it." I paused before blurting out, "Why are you letting me go to Portland? Don't you believe that Victor is dangerous?"

He was thoughtful before answering. "I didn't teach you to run away from danger, mija. I encouraged you to run because I thought you loved it. You were always fast. You were always strong." His eyes shifted in the low light from my face to the painting behind me on the wall. "I trust you. You know how to think. You know how to read people. You will know what to do."

How could he be so confident in me? He opened his mouth to say more but stopped himself. I was fighting tears back again—tears of frustration. He knew that I wasn't normal. He knew something was wrong with me. He had told my mother so, but he had never spoken to me about it. *Why?* Was it some big secret he was trying to keep from the world? I didn't care anymore. I was finished pretending to be what he wanted me to be. I had to know what was wrong with me.

I cleared my throat and broke protocol. "Do you remember taking me to a psychologist in Sigonella?" I could almost feel the question echoing in the silence. I felt uncomfortable, but I couldn't run away from it anymore.

My father patted my knees over the covers. "Yes," he answered simply. Why wouldn't he just tell me what he knew? My heart pounded.

"Why did you take me? What was wrong with me?" I pressed. I didn't care if I was displeasing him. For once.

"Nothing was wrong with you, mija," he assured me "I took you because you asked me to."

His answer was strange. He was acting strange. Why would a five-year-old ask to be taken to a shrink? I shifted, turning on my side toward him.

"Why?" I begged.

He looked into my eyes. *You know the answer*, his expression said.

My neck began to tingle and the feeling spread to every part of my body. I felt the truth of my thought. I did know. It was in there somewhere. I tried to focus my mind. I could see the desk and the ink blobs. I could remember what he had told my mother about coping strategies, but I couldn't remember anything else. My eyes became unbearably heavy, and my soul felt even heavier. I rolled over again— this time away from him. He put his hand on my shoulder, hesitating several seconds before saying anything.

"It will come, mija. Just let it happen. Trust yourself."

His voice was warm—the warmest I had ever heard from him. It covered me like a down quilt. He knew me. He understood something about what was happening to me. There was some purpose—a reason why he didn't tell me everything.

*Trust his silence*, I thought. He didn't blame me for whatever it was, and he was still proud of me in spite of it. I let go. I was asleep within minutes.

\* \* \*

*The twin towers. Explosions. Collapsing. Tumbling into dust and ruin.*

*Another explosion. A volcano. Satin pillow. Blonde hair. I tumble into emotional dust and ruin—deep, crushing pain.*

*But I'm not afraid anymore. I'm not afraid of the pain.*

*Peace. Rest.*

\* \* \*

My father was already awake and dressed when I woke up. I took my suitcase into the bathroom and showered. I dried myself off, then unzipped my suitcase, eager to be in my own clothes. The sight of the disheveled mess Sheila had packed was unpleasant, if unsurprising. I lifted out a few of the lacy items at the top with my thumb and index finger. I hoped that the matching cheetah print panties hadn't come from her collection. Completely revolted, I cringed. They still had the tags on. She had bought them just for this reaction. I could hear my father walking outside the bathroom door. I dropped the lingerie and let the lid fall on the suitcase, stepping away from it.

I took a deep breath and opened the case again. She hadn't followed my instructions at all. I had asked her to pack my conservative suits and a few dresses. She had filled up my bag with every colorful piece of clothing I owned. Nothing coordinated—short skirts, camisoles without tops or jackets to cover. Somewhere near the middle of the jumbled mess, I found a bright red pantsuit that I had bought on clearance at a specialty store in St. Paul a few weeks before. Sheila had pressured me into getting it.

"It would look great on you," she had said, wrinkling up her nose as she looked at my jeans and fitted white T-shirt.

"It's not really my style," I had told her.

"What style?" she had teased. "Just because something isn't black and white doesn't mean you have to run from it and hide in your closet. You need a splash of something bold in your boring life."

"I have color in my life and my closet," I had defended myself.

"Beige isn't a real color," she said, turning away from me.

I had looked at it again, trying to pretend that my ears weren't burning. With a cropped jacket and slightly flared pants, it was well made and tailored. I looked at the tag. *Thirty dollars is a small price to pay to shut her up*, I had thought. I brought it home and hid it behind a silver, sequined Christmas choir dress from high school.

I shoved it back in my suitcase and pulled out a black-belted, floral knee-length dress with flipped sleeves. It was a few years old, but it would have to do.

With full makeup and straightened hair, I looked pretty—a big contrast from the day before. Both my hands were stiff and sore, but I began flexing my right hand. Leaning toward my reflection in the mirror, I wondered how much electricity I had harvested in my sleep.

My father had breakfast waiting when I came out. I savored the eggs and bacon, appreciative that my father had chosen for me. It was a much more satisfying breakfast than the fruit cup I would have ordered for myself.

"Mija, you were crying in your sleep last night. What were you dreaming about?" my father asked softly.

I looked up from my breakfast. I never knew that my father was capable of such tenderness. "It's a reoccurring dream," I said, clearing my throat. "A series of images that plays over and over. I see Mt. Etna erupting. I see the Twin Towers collapsing. I see random explosions. I see Mom in her coffin, and then I see the little girl from the tablet with her blonde curls spread out on a satin pillow, just like the one in Mom's coffin."

"You said that the little girl looks like your mother?" he asked, staring out the window next to us.

"Yes."

"You'll do whatever it takes to save your daughter."

"I know," I whispered. A chill went down my spine. I did know. She was my daughter, not just Damien's. I already loved her. I didn't want her to die.

"I wish I would have been there with your mother that night. I would have been driving," he said softly—tortured. It was the first time I had seen him express any regret. I wanted to reach out and comfort him. I knew all too well how he felt—I wasn't the only one who regretted my choices. He blamed himself too. The lump in my throat began to choke me. It might have been different if he had been driving—he might have saved her, or he might have died alongside her.

I grabbed his hand and squeezed, ready to tell him that I was glad he hadn't been there. I was glad he was still here with me. I needed him. But the sentiment was interrupted by a knock at the door. The tenderness and emotion left his eyes, and he let go of my hand.

My father let Damien in. He looked like himself again—put together and handsome. His concerned eyes were drawn to me. I let myself feel his electricity momentarily before shutting it down with a thought about Corey. What was Victor doing to him right now? Was he as worried about me as I was about him?

Finally, my father broke the silence.

"Let's get to it, Damien," he said. He pulled out a chair for Damien at the table. My father moved our trays aside and pulled his chair close to me. I called Corey's voice mail and recorded his greeting on my phone. I trimmed it down to just his name.

We were ready to proceed. I turned on the tablet, holding it in my unbandaged right hand. The green light began to flash and the icon appeared immediately. My father watched closely as I navigated to the unopened folder.

"Open 'October 18, 2023' file," Damien said without prompting.

"Voice recognition validated," came the familiar reply. "Proceed with second validation."

I pressed play on my recording: "Corey Stein." This wasn't how we had planned it. We wanted all three of us to be here to see this. My spine tingled.

"Voice recognition validated."

The dated file folder faded away as a black image filled the area above the tablet. It took my eyes a second to distinguish faces in the sea of black-clad people. They were facing the camera in a semicircle surrounding a coffin. Brilliant orange, yellow, and red trees laced the background of the picture. My eyes went immediately to the people closest to the casket. Damien's distraught face looked down at the little blonde girl standing next to him. He held her hand. Victor stood to Damien's left, and Corey stood in the background a few paces behind Victor. My father and I were missing from the image. I scanned it several times to make sure.

"It's one of us, mija," he said, quivering. "One of us is in the box, and the other one took the picture."

Damien didn't say anything. I looked up from the image. His eyes were fixed on the little girl. On their hands. One corner of his mouth tilted upward in a half smile that exposed his dimple. He knew now. He was pleased about this discovery, and it was all he could see. He knew he wasn't in the casket. My face burned, and I had to look away.

"Is this it?" my father asked. "Are there other images in the file?"

I didn't want to look at any more images. The most important image on the tablet, the one that had to be seen by everyone at the same time—and I couldn't bear to look at it. I couldn't bear the thought of my father being inside.

"Advance the image, Jace," Damien said stoically.

I ignored him. My father looked at me, gauging my emotions. I couldn't look at him. My eyes shifted back to the casket.

"Someone wanted us to know about this, mija. It's important." He reached out and placed his hand over my bandage. He knew who that someone was. I could feel it.

I took a deep breath. "Next image," my voice cracked as I said it.

I could almost hear the creaking of the casket lid as the first image faded away. Inside the satin-lined casket, my empty shell lay lifeless, eyes closed. Chestnut hair in glossy curls framed my face.

38

None of us spoke for several minutes. My father stared blankly. Damien watched my face. He didn't want to be the first to speak. What would he say? I only felt relief that I was in the casket instead of my father. My fear of being alone was stronger than my fear of death.

They were the only two images in the file. They added to the enigma. Whoever had created the files and sent the tablet might understand the message they were trying to send, but it was unclear to me. Omnibus would dominate the world. I would marry Damien and have a beautiful little girl. Corey would become an important doctor. My father would become the CNO. I would die in my prime. If the purpose of the tablet was to get us to prevent any of these events, it would be difficult to predict the outcome. Stopping Omnibus domination might leave the country in total chaos if the information crisis happened. Staying away from Damien would erase the little girl.

The only clear objective that I could feel was saving Corey. The tablet wasn't telling me to do it. My gut was.

I finally broke the silence. "Well, now we have the whole picture."

My father didn't look at me. "Damien, now that you know what's in the final file, you can tell your father. Jace doesn't need to go to Portland."

"He's going to want to see it for himself," Damien said.

"He'll get over it," my father said firmly.

"What's going to happen to Corey?" I asked.

"I don't know," Damien admitted.

"Your father isn't just going to let him walk away with everything he's told him about the deleted images," I said.

"I think we're focused on the wrong thing here," my father interjected. "Clearly Corey is going to be just fine. He's standing around the casket at the funeral. You're the one in the box, Jace."

"I don't think we can assume that," I said. "We may have already altered the future just by having the tablet. Since I found it, I've made different choices than I would have made without it. My relationships are different than they would have been. *I'm* different. The images on the tablet were the future, but the choices we make become the future."

"She's right," Damien said. "I'm changed too."

My father was quiet again. He walked away from us to the window and stood there, looking out, for several minutes. Damien watched me. What was he thinking about? Who was he really? How was he changed? Changed from a twenty-five-year-old playboy into a husband and father? A change like that couldn't happen so fast.

My father turned around. "Do you think Victor will be changed by seeing the tablet too?" he asked Damien.

Damien shrugged his shoulders. "I don't know."

"Then give it to him," my father said. "Seeing Jace in a casket isn't going to add to his power."

"Yes," I agreed, "give it to him. It's all we have. He already has the information that was on it, but maybe he needs to see it for himself. Maybe seeing the images will change him like it has all of us."

"Seeing his granddaughter?" Damien said almost inaudibly. I couldn't tell if his tone was hopeful or hopeless.

"It's settled," my father said. "You take the tablet to your father in Portland. Jace will stay with me."

"Respectfully, sir, I think we should let Jace decide what to do. She knows Corey, and the tablet is hers." I wasn't sure if Damien was bursting with confidence in me, or if he just wanted to protect himself. It didn't matter. My instincts were screaming to go to Corey. I had to know he was safe. I had to find out what he knew about time travel. I wanted to understand what our kiss in the park had meant to him. I wanted to know who he was in my future.

I had to confront Victor. I wasn't concerned about preventing my death; that would happen eventually no matter what any of us did.

I just wanted to free Corey and the rest of the world from Victor's grasp. I wished that I hadn't erased the images. I wanted Victor to see everything from beginning to end, just as I had. I wanted him to give up his plan. I wanted him to see that his manipulation of and power over people wasn't real. It wouldn't make him happy.

"I have to go," I said, looking at my father's face. "I want to go." He had never looked older. More tired.

He cleared his voice. "Okay, mija," he retreated. Then, turning to Damien, he barked, "You will give me that login information before you go. I want to see that I can track your movements and hear what is happening."

Damien nodded and let out a sigh of relief. He had accomplished his goal. He would go to Portland with everything his father had asked him to bring. He showed my father how to log into the chip's tracking system.

"When will you leave?" my father asked after he was confident that the system was working.

"As soon as Jace is ready," Damien said.

"Can you give us a few minutes to say good-bye?" I asked.

"I'll wait for you downstairs," he said. He left the room without any further interaction. I stood staring at the door for a second before turning around. I was clearheaded but raw. I looked down at the tablet on the table. *My coffin.* The light flashed slowly. My father opened his arms and I came to his embrace. I didn't let go right away. I wanted to let the years of unspoken emotion loose, but I couldn't stop biting of my tattered cheek. I just stood against his rough uniform.

"I not going to let you die, *mi hijita.*" His deep voice almost faltered.

"I'm not afraid," I lied.

\* \* \*

On the way to the airport, Damien was different—distant and awkward. He hadn't touched me since the hand on my bandage. No hand on the lower back. No easing me into the car. No touching my elbow when we walked—for once, he was respectfully distant.

I felt incredibly calm as we approached the airport. This time, Damien was the one that seemed unsure as we boarded his plane. He was nervous as we sat in the same seats we had been in just a few days before, facing each other with the plane preparing to take off. He looked exhausted from lack of sleep. He fidgeted with his phone, then with a magazine, then with a stack of papers from work. We had reversed roles.

"Are you okay?" I finally asked.

He looked up at me, meeting my eyes with a pained smile. He nodded, but he was lying.

"What are you thinking about?" I asked.

He hesitated. "I'm sorry. I don't know what it is. I feel awkward."

"What feels awkward? Honesty?" I asked. "We were comfortable with each other when everything was a lie."

He didn't smile. He looked like he wanted to say something but hesitated. Finally he blurted out, "Something is happening to me, Jace. It started yesterday when you touched me with the chip."

"What do you mean?" I asked, leaning forward and touching his knee. He shifted uncomfortably in his seat. My touch was affecting him. His eyes darted from my eyes, to my lips, to the window, and back again. He couldn't keep eye contact.

"I don't know," he said, looking away from me and down at the *Popular Science* magazine on his lap. I moved my hand off his knee and retreated in my seat. I looked out the window at the bright blue sky. Just a few clouds hung low on the horizon. The city below us was only a checkerboard now. I understood all too well the awkwardness he was feeling. I could be the poster child for awkward, but I didn't feel too sorry for Damien. I imagined that his charm had protected him from most awkward situations. This seemed to be brand new to him.

"I couldn't stop thinking about you last night," his shaky voice said. "I couldn't sleep."

Was I the first girl to keep him awake at night? My heart responded, beating hard in my chest. I looked at him, waiting for him to continue. His eyes were clear and undiluted.

"You aren't like anyone I have ever met, Jace. I knew it before yesterday, but what you did—" He looked at my bandaged hand. "I felt it. I can't comprehend it, but I felt it."

"Because I tore the chip out of my hand?" I asked, heart still sounding in my ears.

"Yes," he said tentatively. "And as if that wasn't enough, when you let me put it back in."

I didn't respond. What could I say?

His eyes flashed. "How long have you and Corey been together?"

My pulse raced. I didn't know how to answer. Did he think that my Victorian style chastity had been an act to avoid him and reject his advances? How could I tell him that I had never *been together* with anyone? I looked away. I had been saving myself for someone—him, I suppose. I wanted him to know the truth, but I was embarrassed.

Damien's tired eyes blinked slowly and his broad shoulders hunched forward. His humility stirred me up inside. Somehow I had done this to him. Confident, arrogant Damien had been transformed into a little child—watching his brother receive the toy that he had asked for at Christmastime. I was what he wanted. It had been apparent before yesterday, but perhaps after seeing the image of himself with the little girl, wanting me had taken on a new meaning.

"Damien," I said, refocusing on his eyes, "the tablet brought Corey to me. I care about him. I can't deny that, but we aren't 'together.' I'm not his. I'm not anyone's."

Moving toward me, his eyes became glossy, almost desperate. "I feel so frustrated and helpless," he said. "I just keep trying to figure out how I'm going to undo the damage I've done. Or is it too late?"

"Too late for what?" I whispered.

"Too late for me . . . for us to be," he stammered, loosening his tie and rubbing the back of his neck. "Too late for you to forgive me," he finally managed.

This wasn't acting. I could see the sincerity in his eyes. I had been fighting my attraction to him—but now that he wasn't sure, now that he didn't believe that he would conquer in the end, his magnetism became overpowering. Humility. Funny, I had expected that finding out he was the girl's father would have the opposite effect on him.

I unbuckled the seat belt that had been restraining me and slid across the aisle into the seat next to him. The electric attraction between us turned to heat now that I was closer. I reached my arm through his and rested my head on his shoulder. He took a deep breath, and I felt him relax. I stayed still for a few minutes listening to him breathe. I had no idea what I was going to say or do next. He would have been my future, but our future was broken—we both felt it. I could feel his pulse with my wrist against his.

"I would have done it for you too, Damien," I heard myself say.

My words revived him like a cool stream. His pulse raced, his shoulders lifted, and his fingers slid through mine. All of my hairs stood on end. Turning slowly toward me, he lifted my chin until his burning eyes met mine. Without fear he slowly moved toward my lips. Our magnetism drew him to me entirely, and our lips met with a spark.

* * *

*I stand in a long, dimly lit hallway. A florescent bulb flickers above me. I see two doors at the end of the corridor. A radio crackles and buzzes before blaring a high-pitched squeal. It begins to beep in long and short intervals as I walk toward the doors. When I reach them, I feel panic—unsure of which I should open. I look down at my short pleated red skirt and Mary Janes.*

*"Trust your instincts," my father's muffled voice in my head reminds me.*

*The one on the right. I know instantly. I slowly reach out my little hand. The handle pulls me to it. My hair stands on end. I am going to see what is behind the door. I connect with the handle and feel an instant jolt of electricity. Searing pain spreads from my hand to the rest of my body. Whatever is behind the door is going to incinerate me.*

* * *

I opened my eyes. With a soft double-armed push, I severed my connection with Damien.

39

Damien had no idea what I had experienced. I had recharged his confidence. He pulled me firmly to his chest, and I heard his heart beating as I recovered my breath.

He held me for a long time. He seemed relaxed and content. I longed to be able to enjoy the moment, but it had all changed. I was reeling. I was losing my grip on reality.

He finally broke the silence. "Jace, I can't lose you."

Was he thinking about losing me to Corey or the coffin? "Don't think about that." I tried to push away the dull ache in my chest. I hadn't even started to live yet. How could I think about dying?

"We have to think about it, Jace."

"We have to live, Damien. We can't let fear of the future control our present."

He sat silent, but I knew conflict was stirring in him. Picking up my right hand, he turned it over and gently rubbed the chip. His fingers tensed. I nudged myself away from his chest. His hand turned cold and sweaty. He stood up and pulled me to my feet, wrapping his arm around my waist.

"Come with me," he whispered in my ear.

"Where?"

"Just trust me," he said.

A bit of turbulence shook us, and he held me tighter until it passed. Letting go of my waist, he led me to the back of the plane. He pushed open the lavatory door and stepped inside. I hesitated. He still didn't understand who I was.

Reaching for my hand, he pulled me in and closed the door awkwardly behind me. I opened my mouth to protest, but Damien startled me by turning on the faucet and plugging the tiny sink. It filled with water quickly. Curiosity paralyzed me. After turning off the sink, he took my hand and plunged it into the cold water.

"What are you doing?" I asked, shocked.

"I need to talk to you," he said, "without our fathers listening."

I looked down at my hand. "It doesn't work in water?"

"Water interferes with the signal," he explained. I smiled involuntarily, thinking about how I'd blared Guns N' Roses when the shower had actually been enough.

"Jace, you've stumbled into something that goes back much farther than last week when you found the tablet. My dad has been looking for the information in those schematics for years."

"What is it?"

"I don't know exactly how he's going to do it, but I know what he's trying to do," he said, pushing his styled hair back from his forehead.

My hand tingled in the water as he continued to hold it there. I looked into his eyes. "Just tell me what it is," I said impatiently.

"He wants my mom back," he said in a low voice. "He wants it almost as much as he wants power and money, but those things are easy for him to get."

I let out a sigh. "Are you serious?" I asked.

"I know it sounds crazy, but he's spent exorbitant amounts of money researching time travel. I never understood his obsession, but this week has started putting together the pieces for me."

"You think he is funding time travel research to get your mom back?" I reiterated. If it was true, I could almost sympathize.

Damien shifted awkwardly.

"Let me try to explain what I've seen from the beginning." He turned on the sink again, refilling what had leaked down the drain. "My father has always been an ambitious man. He grew up poor, but somehow he convinced my grandfather to let him marry my mom. Then he was able to find success through a lot of . . . alternative methods in the Navy. He's good at reading people and building relationships, and he used that to his advantage."

It was hard to imagine Victor coming from humble circumstances. Damien touched the elbow of my bandaged hand before continuing.

"When I was little, my mom and I were happy with him. He knew how to give us what we wanted in order to keep us loyal. But then something changed. It was around the time that we all lived in Italy. I can't pinpoint a specific event, but I just started to notice a change in him. He became distant. He started working late all the time. He wasn't as interested in playing the family man anymore.

"My mom noticed it too, and she blamed herself. I watched her try a bunch of different things to get him interested in being with us again, but nothing seemed to work. In fact, everything we did only made him more distant. She was relieved when he was transferred from Sigonella to San Diego. I think she hoped that a change in environment would bring us back together, but things only got worse between the two of them. I think she told him how she felt, and he turned from cold to ice. He knew just what to say to fuel her insecurities. He destroyed her."

The past was painful to him. His eyes were distant and tense. He squeezed my hand under the water.

"They stayed together but were more like strangers living under the same roof. My mom's beauty started to fade. She gained weight and was being treated for depression. I felt like something needed to change. I was only eight years old, but I wanted her to leave him. I couldn't stand to watch what he was doing to her."

His deep sympathy for his mom touched me. He paused for a moment, like he was trying to think through the sequence of events. I ran my hand down his arm, encouraging him to go on.

"I was honestly shocked and dismayed when he fulfilled his commitment to the Navy and moved us to New York. I couldn't imagine that things were going to get better there, but he surprised me again. Within six months he had started his own company with the money he had made from investing. His ventures earned him a small fortune within a year. I chalked it up to his success and his return to civilian life. And he started to come back to us for a while. He lavished us with gifts and started spending more time at home again. My mom revived.

"She was almost herself again when she went in to check on the progress of the remodel we were doing at Omnibus's World Trade Center office." He paused after his voice cracked a little. "You know the rest of that story," he continued, "but I didn't tell you about my father after the towers collapsed. He became completely reclusive for months, and that's when his obsession started.

"First I noticed the books that he was leaving around the house—everything from thick books about quantum mechanics to H. G. Wells's *The Time Machine*. I ignored it at first, but then he started hiring scientists and funding research projects.

"It has been consistent, Jace—fourteen years of spending every spare moment trying to achieve this, and I didn't realize why until I listened to his conversation with Corey yesterday."

"What did he say?" I asked, completely engrossed in his narrative.

He moved in closer to my left ear, "He was explaining some of the testing that they've been working on in Manila and Portland. My father is convinced that the schematics and the blueprint images are the missing piece of a puzzle he's been putting together. He told Corey that there's some mathematical formula he needs to calibrate the machine he's been testing. He's trying to send something back in time."

I backed up to the door, my arm outstretched to stay in the water. "What does he want to send back?" I asked.

Damien closed his eyes. "I don't know. I didn't hear the beginning of the conversation."

"Why was he telling Corey all of that?"

"It seemed to be a shared passion," Damien said.

"What do you mean?" I asked. "How do you know?"

"Because I don't share the passion, and I couldn't understand what either of them was talking about."

## 40

The water had drained from the sink again, and I waited while Damien refilled it. My head was swimming as I considered everything he had told me. I was stuck on two details: Victor's change in Sigonella and Corey's knowledge about time travel. I thought about my first meeting with Corey. He had been so calm looking at the images. His explanation about the pocket watch had made time travel seem like a logical conclusion, and his interpretation of the code had confirmed it. I had never questioned his easy acceptance of it.

"How much do you know about the research in Manila and Portland?" I asked.

"We have several projects going on, but I haven't been involved at all. I've mostly just seen things on the company's financial reports. As far as I know, both projects are layered. In Portland we have a multi-purpose research facility. One of the things they have been working on is alternative energy sources—something to do with drilling down into volcanic rock and pumping in compressed air on Mount Hood. I think they projected that the stored energy would power up to eighty thousand homes."

"Interesting," I said impatiently, "but what about the time travel?"

"None of that stuff is on the books. I didn't know that the facility in Portland had anything to do with that until yesterday. My father and Corey were talking about mixing magma, magnetic fields, solar flares, and 'geomagnetic excursions.'" He shrugged his shoulders. "Whatever those are. Corey was wide-eyed like a kid in a candy store.

My father didn't force him to go to Portland. He seemed kind of excited about it."

The plane began to shake and jostle again. Damien let go of my hand in the water and steadied me. I suddenly felt claustrophobic. Going to Portland had to be part of Corey's plan to protect me and the tablet. I wanted to talk to him. I needed to hear his side of the story.

"If you knew he wasn't being forced to go, why are you letting me treat this like a rescue mission?"

Damien considered for a moment before answering. "It's just a feeling, Jace. My father has a way of making people think that doing what he wants is their idea. What if he's just going to use Corey to get what he wants? Just because he has these schematics doesn't mean that whatever he is planning to do is good or safe. Corey has no idea what he's gotten himself into."

The sincerity in Damien's voice touched me. "What do you think he wants from us, Damien? Why does he want us all in Portland?" I asked. Damien moved his hand across mine under the water. He touched my left arm with his other hand and leaned forward a few inches to whisper in my ear.

"I don't know what he wants or what he's planning to do, Jace, but I need you to know that I'm not part of it." He backed away again to look into my eyes. They were clear and clean. I believed him. He wasn't his father, and he didn't want to be.

He brushed his lips across my forehead, and I tilted my face up in response. His lips melted on mine again.

The plane bumped and dropped like an old roller coaster. Damien put his arm around my waist and pulled me closer. A tone chimed, and the "fasten seat belt" sign lit up. Still holding me close, Damien lifted the drain and emptied the sink. I didn't want to move yet. I wanted him to tell me more.

"We'd better get back to our seats," he said, giving me a paper towel to dry my hand. Disappointed, I glanced in the mirror, straightening my dress before following Damien back to our seats. The plane continued to shake. I slid into the seat on Damien's side of the row against the window. Through small breaks in the clouds, I could see a mountain range below.

I linked my arm through Damien's again and rested against him.

He was completely relaxed now. After a few minutes of silence, I could feel his steady breathing.

Thick rain clouds filled the sky as we made our descent. Through the mist, I could see the flashing green landing lights guiding us to a small runway. I still held onto Damien's arm as the plane made its way turbulently to the ground. He woke up just as we touched down. He stretched his arms and legs and looked over at me.

"Are you ready?" he asked softly.

I couldn't answer. Suddenly I wasn't thinking about Victor. I was thinking about Damien and Corey being in the same room together. I had spent most of my life avoiding men, and now I was strongly drawn to two of them at the same time—two men who both seemed to care about becoming my future. I looked down at the floor, my cheeks glowing.

When I didn't answer, Damien squeezed my arm.

A car was waiting for us on the runway. It was already getting dark, and a thin mist covered the ground. The car's headlights cut through the fog, illuminating the falling rain, and the windshield wipers squeaked in a steady rhythm. The driver waited with a large umbrella at the bottom of the stairs. I could feel my perfectly straightened hair reverting back to its natural state.

Damien said only a few words to the driver. None of them were directions about where to take us. The man must have had his orders from Victor.

"This doesn't look like Portland," I whispered as we pulled away from the tiny airport.

"Our facility is in Hood River," Damien responded. "We're meeting my father tomorrow morning." My stomach relaxed. I wondered when we would see Corey, but I didn't ask. Damien was frowning. He looked preoccupied.

The drizzle turned into a downpour as our car slowly wound through the sleepy town. Damien's quietness made me nervous. After what seemed like ages, we rounded a curve and slowed down. The lights of a three-story building glowed through the mist and rain. The driver turned onto the stone pathway. My palms got sweaty as I listened to the sound of the wheels bumping over the uneven bricks. Near the end of a tile-roofed Italian stucco building, the driver turned into a dark wooden garage.

My breath fogged up the glass, and I watched two droplets of water chase a third down the car window. The one on the right changed course just before the base of the window and merged with the drop in the middle. The one on the left continued down its path alone.

The driver turned off the motor. We followed him up two flights of stairs, and he unlocked the dark wood door for us. Inside, we were greeted by the smell of Italian seasoning and the warm glow of a fire. I heard dishes clinking in the kitchen. My first thought was of Corey, but Dr. Watts poked his head around the corner before I could get too excited.

"You made it!" he said, smiling broadly. I tried to force my mind to connect him to the Dr. Watts of my strange memories, but there was nothing of the handsome Dr. Watts with the ink blobs in this short, weaselly-looking man.

"Good to see you," Damien said, setting down his satchel and greeting the doctor with a handshake that turned into a hug.

"Why don't you both get settled?" Dr. Watts suggested. "I have dinner almost ready."

Damien nodded, leading me down a short hardwood hallway to a simply decorated bedroom. Green-framed french doors opened out onto a balcony that reflected the shimmering streetlights on a surface of glossy rainwater. Water cascaded from the eaves and clinked against the wrought-iron rail. A cozy fire was lit in the stone fireplace to the left of the doors. I watched the salt-and-pepper-haired driver bring my bag in and set it at the end of my bed. I smiled at him as he left the room.

"Thank you," I said.

"Let me know if you need anything." Damien touched my arm lightly as he left me.

I took a deep breath and zipped open my suitcase. Digging through the random clothes, I wondered what I would wear tomorrow. Sheila would have put together a work of art with the pieces she had packed, but we were polar opposites. I couldn't see anything but chaos. I took off my jacket and hung it in the closet and laid out the red satin Christmas pajama top for later. She could have at least done me the courtesy of packing the bottoms too.

Damien was in the kitchen helping Dr. Watts when I came out.

"—the research results from Manila," I heard Damien say as I came into the room. He stopped talking when he saw me.

"Everything is ready," Dr. Watts said. His eyes were kind and comforting. I followed them to the long, dark wood table, and Damien pulled out one of the high-back red leather chairs for me. I sat down facing the wall of picture windows. It was too dark to see anything except the rain outside, but the room must have looked out at something spectacular.

"Dr. Watts has been getting me up to speed on what he knows about the project in Manila," Damien said as he began dishing some of the seafood alfredo the doctor had prepared. "It's similar to what they are doing here with the compressed air, but we also have several teams studying volcanic activity on Mount Mayon." He paused for a few seconds while he took a drink.

"The studies are irrelevant. He's using volcanic activity to power his machine," Dr. Watts said dryly.

"There's something else going on there, though," Damien said, looking down at the table, his eyes unfocused.

"What is it?" I asked.

"Tell her about the orphanage in Tagaytay," Damien said to Dr. Watts. The doctor set down his fork and scanned my face before speaking. Why did he hesitate? Did he think I was going to sell the company's secrets?

"Omnibus funds an orphanage for mentally challenged children near the research facility there," Dr. Watts finally said, looking at me meaningfully. He raised his eyebrows. I shrugged my shoulder.

"Is that unusual?" I asked.

Damien looked at me. "It wouldn't be unusual for the charitable foundation to fund something like that, but I wasn't aware of this orphanage. It's being funded by the company. My father is funding it."

Dr. Watts ate slowly and continued to watch me.

"Something is happening there that he doesn't want me to know about." Damien's strained intonation seemed to be directed at someone outside the window. I looked at my palm.

"I think I know what it is," Dr. Watts offered quietly. We both looked at him. Damien was as surprised as I was. "He's been testing the machine on them."

"What exactly does the machine do?" I asked through gritted teeth.

"It transports memories through time."

"Memories?" I tried to comprehend what he was saying.

"Yes." Dr. Watts took another bite of pasta and watched me wrestle with my thoughts.

"How?" I finally asked.

"It's a complicated process," he began, "but essentially, a subject with the correct brain chemistry is given a combination of chemicals and hooked up to this machine." Dr. Watts drew a shape above his plate with his fork. "The drugs reverse the electrochemical processes used by the brain to store information as memory. Then the machine transforms the chemical signals into electromagnetic pulses."

Damien leaned forward. "And then he uses the network to transport the memories?" It wasn't exactly a question. He seemed to have heard this before.

"The network?" I was confused.

"Not exactly," Dr. Watts interjected. "Victor's network uses seismic waves to transmit electronic signals. This machine uses seismic waves, but it needs several other factors to create a conduit powerful enough to send a signal back in time."

Damien and I sat silent.

"It needs a volcano?" I finally said.

"Yes," Dr. Watts replied simply.

My head pounded. I didn't need or want to know more. The science behind Victor's machine didn't matter to me. I didn't understand it, but it worked. Or it would work, eventually. The tablet was proof.

Dr. Watts seemed to read my thoughts. "This machine, or one very similar to it, sent back the data on the tablet."

"And who knows what other information has been sent back," Damien added.

It had never occurred to me that other messages might have been sent back successfully—that the tablet wasn't a unique incident. My stomach knotted up. I put my fork down, unable to continue eating.

"How do we destroy the machine?" I thought out loud.

Dr. Watts shook his head. "We have no idea how many of these Victor has built. Destroying one machine will do little more than slow him down."

I felt helpless. Whatever Victor had done with the machine and whatever he was planning to do with it would result in the world on the tablet—the pictures we had deleted. Corey was trying to find a way to stop it. I could feel it.

Dr. Watts leaned forward on his elbow, watching me intently.

"What kind of doctor are you?" I heard myself ask, my heart racing. Dr. Watts's expression didn't change. He met my gaze.

"I am a nuclear physicist," he said with a strange grin.

I cleared a lump from my throat. "You were never a psychologist?" I asked, looking him dead in the eye.

I could feel Damien's eyes on me, but I kept mine locked on Dr. Watts.

"I think you mean my brother." Setting his fork down again, he reached into his pocket and pulled out his wallet. He flipped to a yellowing photograph in a plastic cover. It was unmistakably my Dr. Watts—I could visualize him holding the ink blobs behind the desk. I could hear myself breathing—*in through the nose on a three count, out through the mouth.*

"Where is he now?" I asked, cotton-mouthed. I needed to talk to him. He was the key.

"We lost him fourteen years ago," he said, his eyes dropping to the floor. "He died with Claire Trent in the Trade Center towers." His words shook me. I couldn't blink. I felt light-headed and the room began to reel.

"Can you both excuse me?" I asked, clutching my stomach. "I'm not feeling very well. I think I need to lie down."

They both stood up as I pushed my chair away from the table. Damien looked concerned, and he shot a questioning glance at Dr. Watts. Dr. Watts motioned for Damien to stay as I turned toward the hallway. I heard footsteps behind me. I opened the door to my room.

"I'm here to help you, Jace," Dr. Watts said softly.

"Help me how?" I demanded, looking back at him. "Help me remember what happened to me in kindergarten?" My hands trembled on the doorknob. Fear gripped me. His eyes were steady and he didn't contradict me.

"You obviously remember my brother," he said. "Jason helped you forget." He paused and touched my hand. "Remembering takes time. It must happen naturally. We can't force it."

I looked down the hall toward the table. Damien stood next to his chair, watching us anxiously.

I leaned in and whispered, "Whatever happened must have been terrible. Why would I even want to try to remember?"

"Because it is time," Dr. Watts replied firmly.

I stood frozen for a moment. *Time.* I felt surprisingly calm. My legs carried me through the door, and my arms closed it firmly behind me. *It is time.*

\* \* \*

Exhaustion. I could barely button the pajama top before collapsing into bed. I waited for the cold familiarity of my recurring dream—the coffins, volcanic explosions, and collapsing towers. *In through the nose on a three count, out through the mouth.* I was tired of running from the future. I let go of the fear.

\* \* \*

*Thick fog fills the room. I leave my bed and let it wrap around me completely. I am blind. Pushing the fog away, I begin to walk. I hear branches and twigs snapping under my feet, but I can't see them through the cloud. I have no idea what I am walking toward or away from, yet I feel certain that I am moving in the right direction.*

*As I continue to walk, the fog dissipates. I can see the dense forest around me. Moss and deep green trees create a blanket of color that soothes my soul. I come to a small clearing and stop, drinking in the beauty.*

*The silence is broken by the sound of a newborn screaming in the distance. Panic. The world spins slower. I run toward the sound, but my feet become melted wax. I am confused, disoriented, and lost in the thick trees. The woods close in around me and begin to spin. The crying gets louder.*

*I stagger into another clearing. A strange-looking woman sits on a stump near the far side of the meadow. She rocks a bundle of blankets. Her face is half hidden by a black-hooded coat, but the exposed half is covered with thick purple scars. She looks up at me and holds her finger to her lips before turning her back to me and disappearing into the distant trees.*

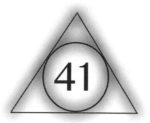

# 41

I woke up tense. The new dream disturbed me more than the reoccurring one had—maybe because it felt just as familiar. Who was the scarred woman, and why did she want to silence me? It was still dark outside, but the steady rain had turned to a drizzle. Damien and Dr. Watts were already awake, talking in the kitchen. I listened at the door for a moment before taking a shower, but their voices were muffled, and I couldn't understand anything.

I turned on the water and stood looking in the mirror for several minutes. I was frozen, fixed on my green eyes. They didn't reflect the turmoil bubbling inside me. My body relaxed slowly. I looked more like my mom today than I ever had—self-assured and strong. *Trust yourself. Stop trying to force it. Let it happen naturally.* She took on problems as they came, and so would I.

After showering, I opened my suitcase and took out the red pantsuit. I tore off the tags and put it on. It fit like a glove. When I came out of my room, I looked and felt irresistible. The sun had burned through the fog, and I could see the spectacular view that had been hidden in the darkness. I walked directly to the windows and looked down. Our hotel was perched on a cliff overlooking a wide, green river. Hills and mountains banked the opposite side. Sunlight warmed the tops of the pine trees and sparkled on the water. It warmed me too.

Damien and Dr. Watts kept their distance, but I could feel Damien's eyes on me. I joined them in the kitchen, eager to eat something and get underway. He watched me quietly throughout the meal, searching my face for answers about the questions I had raised the night before, but I avoided eye contact.

Twenty minutes later, I straightened my lapels as I stepped into the car. The driver shut the door tight behind me. My nervous tension returned momentarily when Dr. Watts didn't follow us down to the garage.

"He's not coming with us?" I asked.

"He and my father don't get along," Damien responded. I swallowed hard.

"Why not? Doesn't he work for your father?"

"Not exactly—he works for Omnibus, but technically he works for my mother." He saw the confusion in my face and explained, "She set up the charitable trust before she died. In her will, she left her half of the company's assets in the charitable trust until I turn thirty. Dr. Watts is the head trustee. My mother also named him my advocate and guardian."

"And what about your father?" I asked. "Does he have any say in the charitable trust?"

Damien shook his head. I could understand why Victor didn't like Dr. Watts. It didn't sound like a conventional thing for a CEO's wife to do with her assets. I wondered when she had set up the trust. Had it been before her relationship with Victor had improved, or had Damien misjudged its improvement?

Damien and I sat next to each other in silence. We stopped at a gas station, and the driver went inside to buy himself some coffee while the car was filled up by an attendant. I watched him chat with the cashier through the window. I wondered if he knew who he was working for, or if this was just an ordinary job to him. When the driver came back, I asked him what his name was.

"Paul Sherman," he told me.

"Are you a native Oregonian?" I asked him.

He smiled. "I've lived in this area my whole life except for a short stint in Seattle."

"How long have you worked for Mr. Trent?" I asked. Damien looked up at me curiously.

"About six months," he said. "But I only met him yesterday," he added.

I turned to Damien. "How long is the drive?" I asked.

"About half an hour."

I touched the tablet in my purse. Giving Victor what he had asked for was our only plan at the moment. I tried to picture him looking at the personal pictures and being affected by the sight of his granddaughter, but my instinct told me otherwise. I was counting on Corey to have a real plan.

The sun rose higher above the trees as we left the center of the small town and got onto a highway going south. Mount Hood rose in the distance, sunlight reflecting off the snowcapped peak. The scene was tangible. It was familiar.

A row of thick shrubs on the right side of the car intermittently blocked out my view of the mountain until we came to an intersection with a flashing green light. The road continued on straight for miles with fruit orchards lining both sides. We had a straight line of sight to the mountain.

My heart was quiet as I reached for my phone.

"Can we pull over here for a second, Paul?"

"Yes, ma'am," he said, pulling through the intersection and off to the side by another row of shrubs.

Damien set his phone down. "Are you all right?" He touched my knee softly.

"I just want to take a picture," I told him, already reaching for the door handle. I stepped out of the car and crossed the road for an unobstructed view of the mountain. Damien opened his door and followed me at a distance. The light was perfect. Brilliant oranges and pinks colored the mountain and clouds. I held my phone steady and began snapping pictures.

Taking a few more paces to my right, I glanced back over my shoulder down the road in the direction we had come from. Another misshapen, snow-covered peak pushed above the green mountains in the distance. My heart began to thump against my chest. I looked back and forth between the two mountains. The dream. It rushed back to the surface—the stream, the rock, and the searing lava flow. I shivered.

Damien had come much closer. He reached for my arm, but I turned away from him and took a few pictures of the second mountain. Without saying anything, I walked briskly back to the car and climbed inside.

"Did you get any good shots?" Damien asked as the car continued down the road. "I bet Paul remembers when it erupted."

"It's a volcano?" I asked.

"Mount St. Helens," Paul interjected. "It erupted in the early eighties, when I was a teenager. Neither of you was even born yet, were you?" He shook his head in answer to his own question.

"I remember reading about it," I said, trying to sound calm. "It was pretty devastating, right?"

"I think around fifty people died, so it could have been worse, but you should've seen the path of destruction. The ash cloud leveled everything in its path."

I watched the mountain through the back window until we rounded a curve and it disappeared behind the tall trees. My heart was barely beating, but each contraction felt painfully heavy. Damien was quiet, pretending not to watch me. The scenery changed from orchards and farms to pine trees and streams as we wound our way up toward the mountain. My anticipation escalated with the altitude.

When I could no longer see the volcano, my mental paralysis wore off. I opened my Instagram and made a collage with the two mountain pictures. I posted it without a caption just before I lost my signal.

Damien reached for my hand when we turned off the main highway into another, smaller town. I wasn't sure if he wanted to comfort me or himself, but his hand was unusually cold. We were getting close. I wanted to let go of him. The electricity was gone. His touch brought anxiety and strange guilt—like enjoying an ice cream cone while other children watched through the window. Helping Corey and stopping Victor were the only objectives that would fit in my mind at that moment.

We drove slowly up a small hill. I looked at my phone when we came over the crest. 8:10. A starkly modern building appeared on the horizon. The dark gray glass-and-metal structure reflected the green meadow surrounding it with eerie, filtered brightness. A steaming stream wound down from the mountains, encircling the building. It seemed to pass below the architecture at some point and then reemerged—continuing its snaking path down the hill. We rolled to a stop in front of the building's tinted glass double doors.

"This is it," Paul said, "the end of the line."

The doors slid open noiselessly, and a blast of air conditioning pushed against us as we entered. A lone security guard sat at a circular, luminescent black desk. The Omnibus logo with the red triangle behind it hung intimidatingly on the matte gray wall behind the guard. My shoes clicked against the slick black granite floor. It was so polished, I could see myself walking upside down.

Damien stopped at the desk. He was nervous. He didn't belong here any more than I did.

"We're here to see Victor Trent," Damien said in a stiff, unnaturally deep voice.

The guard touched his earpiece. "They're here, sir." He listened to a response and then looked up at us. "He's expecting you. Ninth floor. It's the last door on your right, number 34."

We walked around the desk to the elevator. Everything smelled of chemicals—fresh paint, floor polish, air freshener. The bright white light from the open elevator door completed my sensory headache. Damien touched the middle of my back and waited for me to enter before following me. The doors closed behind us, and the lights dimmed. A flat, red number panel lit up on the glass wall. Damien took a deep breath before touching the number nine.

I watched our reflection in the glass. We looked like trapped animals. I closed my palm tight against the chip and pressed my bag against my side. The tablet hit my ribs. The door opened, and Damien stood frozen, waiting for me. His hand on my back was hot and wet. I didn't look at him before stepping out and turning right.

Damien followed a few paces behind me down the long black corridor. Fluorescent tubes lit up the black tile floor. The only other light came from the red numbers on the doors. The doors didn't have handles, just flat number pads on the right-hand side. I listened to our footsteps echo down the hallway and then disappear. This was my dream, only I didn't hear anything behind me. My heart raced. We stopped in front of 34.

"Do we knock?" I asked Damien. He had stopped several feet behind me in the hall.

I looked up at the ceiling.

"Come in," Victor's voice boomed through a speaker above us. Damien jumped. The ground seemed to move slightly, and I lost my footing in my tall heels. I fell forward and caught myself on the doorframe. My temples throbbed. The door slid open, and bright light from the windows blinded me.

\* \* \*

*I am in another hallway. The butterflies in my stomach are trying to break free. I only hope I can hold down my lunch. They are outside waiting for me on the swings. She's pushing him. I know which door the bathroom is, but I pass by it. The wood floor creaks beneath my feet. I look down at my Mary Janes and wish I could take them off.*

*All of the other doors are closed. Which one should I open? I have to find it.*

\* \* \*

Recovering, I walked cautiously inside the bright room. Damien hesitated before crossing the threshold. Victor stood with his back to the door at the far end of an expansive office. The entire wall was thick tinted glass. His arms folded across his chest and his stance wide, Victor peered upward at the mountain.

I walked slowly toward him, sensing a strange familiarity. The room was minimalistic. A black, polished s-shaped desk stood between us and Victor. The desk was completely bare. Not even a computer monitor.

Loud orchestral music filled the room. It felt familiar, but I couldn't identify it or think of where I had heard it before. It reminded me of an Alfred Hitchcock movie. I could almost picture a platinum-blonde actress driving a convertible frantically on a winding mountain road. Strings battled brass in syncopation and dissonant harmonies. I stood still as the music built to a jarring climax. Damien was almost invisible behind me.

Victor turned around slowly. His icy stare sent chills through me. He could look through me after listening to every detail of my life for the past twenty-four hours. Anger boiled in me. I was on unequal footing. I didn't understand Victor or his motivations. My emotions reached a fevered crescendo with the savage pounding of the music. I closed my eyes, wishing I could turn it off.

"Do you enjoy the music?" he finally spoke.

"No," I said simply, opening my eyes again.

"Really?" he asked. "Increase volume ten percent," he said. The music was almost deafening now. "Are you familiar with 'The Rite of Spring'?"

Damien moved forward slowly and stood at my right hand.

"I don't like Stravinsky." I shuddered as the name popped into my head.

"No?" He feigned disappointment. "Perhaps you just haven't learned to appreciate him yet." He continued listening for a few moments. Damien stood lifelessly next to me as the music clashed to a halt and became more subdued. "Pause recording," Victor's deep voice commanded. "Sit down," he told us as he walked around the desk with his hands clasped behind his back.

Victor's eyes never left me. I was like a bug under a microscope. My skin crawled. My mind wanted to run, but my legs carried me around the desk to one of the black leather chairs. Damien touched my arm as he sat in the chair next to me. I looked into his eyes. They were soft and tentative. Was that fear in them? Pain? He looked like a little boy who was waiting to be punished for some misdeed.

"Why are we here?" I demanded, turning my focus back to Victor.

"Why *are* you here?" he smoothly responded.

I couldn't answer. My anger rose.

I closed my eyes and saw the picture window in Sigonella, Mt. Etna in the distance. Why had Herman and I sat for so many hours watching it? We were following orders—standing guard at our post. Doing what my father wanted us to do. I touched both of the scars on my palms with the index fingers of the opposite hand. My father. Was I here because he wanted me to be?

Victor shifted in his chair, watching my face. I opened my purse and lifted the tablet out. I placed it on the table in front of him. He didn't move. He chuckled unnaturally.

"You must already know that I don't want or need that," he said.

"Really?" Damien sounded more angry than confused. "Then why did you insist on me bringing it here?" he asked.

"You brought it so that I could look at the pictures of your happy family." Victor's voice cut with mockery. "My heart is bound to soften when I see your pristine future and the product of your pure puppy love."

The floor trembled and my chair shifted toward Damien slightly. Victor's mouth curled upward, and he glanced up at the window. As his eyes lowered back to my level, he whispered, "Go on, then. Show me your little girl."

Acid hatred swelled in the pit of my stomach. I had to protect her from him. He wasn't human.

"Where is Corey?" I demanded.

Victor laughed, looking at Damien. "After all these years, you still haven't learned how to close a deal."

Damien didn't respond, smoldering in silence next to me. I felt the sting of his words as if they had been directed at me.

"We brought what you asked for. Now give us Corey, and we will go," I said firmly.

"You still don't remember me, do you, Jace?" Victor stood up and walked back to the window. "I could see it in your eyes at your mother's funeral and in my office. You're still lost."

I couldn't breathe. He knew about my memory loss. I wasn't ready to hear what he was going to tell me. Not yet. I thought about the memories that had come back. The hallway. The closed doors. The beeping. Had Victor been behind the door? Had he done something to me in that room? My head throbbed. *Run.*

I stood up. "Take us to him," I demanded.

"Soon enough. I want to show you around a little first."

The floor trembled again—more pronounced this time.

"Is that an earthquake?" Damien asked.

"Follow me," Victor said, reaching for my arm with his right hand and the tablet with the left.

# 43

My hands trembled at his touch, but I followed him almost involuntarily. He led us down the hall to the left of the elevator, where he entered a code at a glass double door. The room faced south toward Mt. Hood with windows just like in Victor's office. Two rows of black computers were set up in semicircles around a large, central flat screen monitor. Seven technicians sat at the computers. The image on the center screen rotated to different close-up views of the mountain. Cameras were zoomed in on areas of rock that emitted smoke or steam at intervals: some more sporadic large amounts, others more constant and gentle.

Victor walked around the computers to the center of the room. I glanced at a worker's monitor as I followed. It displayed a red thermometer on the left half of the screen and temperature readings and charts on the second half. I passed by another screen that was monitoring pressure readings.

"It's dizzying to think of the untapped power of the volcano," Victor said as I reached him. The video on the monitor looked like it was near the summit. Snow surrounded gray rock and the bright blue sky framed the shot. An enormous burst of vapor poured out and turned the sky misty as we watched. "People have universally feared them since the beginning of recorded history. Even now, we have only just begun to realize the power of harnessing geothermal energy." He paced over to the window and looked out. "It is unfortunate that the rest of the world is so pitifully behind when it comes to its potential uses."

The ground rumbled again. I braced myself against one of the desks. A light on one of the computer screens flashed and beeped simultaneously.

* * *

*I feel dizzy. We have been swinging for a long time. He wants to see who can go higher. Blue sky, green grass, blue sky again. The old metal swings screech faster and faster. I look over at the little boy. He's sticking his tongue out and crossing his eyes. We both start laughing.*

*A car horn blares to the right in the driveway. Damien's face drops. He drags his feet on the ground until his swing jerks to a stop.*

*"I have to go in." His voice trembles.*

*Victor steps out of the car and looks at us across the lawn. I can barely keep my grip on the chains as I let my swing slow down.*

*"Are you afraid of him?" I ask.*

*He doesn't answer or look at me. He just runs inside the house without looking back.*

* * *

My spine tingled as I opened my eyes again. How much power was this mountain producing for Victor? Power was what Victor really wanted. Power and control—through fear. I looked around for Damien. He was on the other side of the room near the window.

Victor followed my eyes and moved slowly toward Damien.

"It's unfortunate that you've been so wrapped up in your mother's organization. You never did understand how much more important all of this is, did you?"

Damien didn't answer. He looked out of the window, avoiding eye contact. "We know that you're doing more here than harvesting renewable energy. We know about your experiments in Manila."

I walked away from the center of the room toward Damien. From the corner of my eye, I saw an interior diagram of the mountain on one of the monitors. Two thirds of the shaft in the center was illustrated white. The bottom third of the shaft was red. As I passed by the screen, the monitor beeped and the small red line climbed up a notch.

"Yes, Manila," Victor replied. "I'm glad you brought that up."

"Is everything legal there?" Damien demanded. "How did you get approval to conduct human trials?"

"Legal?" He laughed. "Everything we were doing there was irrelevant."

"You mean dangerous." Damien's volume increased. "You can't just do what you want. You're going to kill someone."

Ignoring Damien, Victor took a step toward me.

"After years of work, my scientists proved a hypothesis that made it all irrelevant." He was talking directly to me. My heart pounded. "It only works with children," he said. Moving the tablet from under his arm, he clasped it in both hands behind his back. "Never more than eight years old." He looked up at the ceiling, shaking his head as if questioning a higher power. "You can see how this roadblock has tormented me, since I know that more is possible. We all know that more is possible, don't we, Jace?"

His menacing stare sent a chill through me. Had he experimented on me like he had the children in Manila? How could he be so casual talking about whatever he had done to me? Why had my parents left me there alone? Had I told Jason Watts what had happened to me in Victor Trent's house? Did my father know?

"I don't understand why you want to do any of this at all," I said, energy surging out of me. "What is the purpose of sending a child's memories back in time? To control and manipulate the past?"

"Well spoken, my darling little hypocrite," he said, lifting the tablet and tapping it against his other hand. "Such conviction and fire in your voice. It would be wrong to try to control and manipulate the past, wouldn't it?" He looked down meaningfully at the tablet. "It is so unfortunate that the loyalty and usefulness of Mr. Stein has been called into question because of this indiscretion. He has given Omnibus so much."

"Where is he?" I demanded, ignoring Victor's intimation. We weren't trying to control and manipulate the past, we were trying to save the future. I shuddered. *Was there a difference between the two?* I tried to repress the anxiety the thought produced.

"He's probably just as anxious to see you," Victor said, touching a lock of my hair. The ground trembled again. This time it was much stronger and lasted for several seconds. "Come along, now," he said, looking over his shoulder at Damien. "I'm sure you'll want to witness this happy reunion." My blood boiled.

We followed Victor into the hallway, walking to a room only a few doors away from his office. I could barely control my breathing. We stopped in front of the door. The heavy metal was the only thing standing between me and Corey. Victor entered a code on the panel, and a red beam passed over his index finger before the door opened.

Corey's dark curls appeared over the top of a high-back leather office chair. My heart leapt. The ventilation in the room masked the quiet door as it opened. Corey didn't stir. He had several white binders spread on the desk in front of him. The desk was identical to Victor's, but a flat glass panel spanned its entire length, following the shape of the curves. It was transparent but tinted, and several Internet windows were projected on it. Corey was reading the one in the center.

"Corey," I called, stepping into the room. He spun around, a look of complete surprise on his face. He looked fine—no visible bruises or scars. A rush of emotion overwhelmed me. He jumped to his feet. My legs carried me to him, and I threw my arms around his neck. Relief.

His eyes never left the doorway. Instead of returning my embrace, he spun me around and stood between me and the Trents.

"You shouldn't have come here," he said, barely moving his lips. The ground shook again. One of the binders that had been perched on the edge of the desk slid to the floor with a thud. A glass of water vibrated against the table, clinking noisily.

"I'm sure that you two would like a few minutes to catch up," Victor said, still standing outside the door. "Come with me, Damien. We can continue the tour and give these youngsters some privacy." Damien's eyes caught fire, but I couldn't say anything before Victor touched the panel again and the metal door slid shut.

Corey watched the door for a moment before turning to me. "Why did you come here?" he asked. "Are you okay?" He didn't wait for a response. He scanned me from head to toe, his eyes stopping at the jagged stitches on my left hand.

"I wasn't going to just leave you," I said. "We have to get away from here."

Corey looked at the door. "I can't leave, Jace." His voice was urgent. He returned to the desk and picked up the binder that had crashed to the floor. "He thinks he has everything he needs," he said.

"For what?" I asked. I followed him.

"Do you know what he's been doing in Manila?" Corey asked,

looking up at the Internet windows on the screen. Pictures of a large volcano. Not a pine-tree-covered, snowcapped mountain—this was a perfectly cone-shaped volcano, completely lush and green, steam pouring out of the top.

"Experimenting on children," I said, "trying to send their memories back in time?"

"These are all of the records of the studies and trials done there." He looked down at the thick binders on the desk.

"He gave you all of that?"

"Because he wants validation," Corey said. Corey opened one of the binders and flipped to a colorful graph. "Look here," he said, "over one hundred unsuccessful attempts in the past eight years. The peak was in 2009."

I looked at the graph. Red and blue lines of varying heights charted the test results from 2007 to 2012; 2009 had the highest lines on the chart.

"Were these adult subjects?" I asked. "Victor told us that they had recorded success with children."

Corey looked surprised. "He told you?"

I nodded.

"Did he tell you what happened to the failed test subjects?" he asked. His voice was trembling like the building.

"No," I said.

"All of the male subjects are in a shallow grave near Tagaytay."

My head pounded and my ears began ringing.

"About fifty men. Dead. All of them." Corey's eyes flashed.

"What about the women?" I asked.

He softened. "About a third of them died too. The rest are in a vegetative state." His voice was heavy, trying to mask his emotion.

"And the children?" I asked, eyes on the floor.

"That's the strangest part." Corey flipped through another binder. He began showing me page after page of pictured profiles. "None of the subjects under the age of eight died, but many suffered some degree of brain damage." He passed a picture of a beautiful, dark-haired little girl with sparkling, empty brown eyes. "Look at this one. Age six. She was unresponsive for three weeks following the injections. Then she had complete memory loss for nine months."

She mesmerized me. Deep sympathy washed over me. Empathy, even. "Why is he doing this?" My head was pounding.

"He wants to send a detailed message back in time," he said, "and he's going to use my machine to do it."

"Your machine?" I repeated.

"Yes," he said without looking at me. "I suspected it before, but Victor has confirmed it. I invented—or will invent—the machine. I am the reason that all of this is happening."

I looked at Corey in silence. His shoulders hunched forward as if he was carrying a heavy load on his back. I could only imagine the responsibility he was feeling for the injured test subjects—for their deaths. The ground trembled again. I was already shaking.

"The mountain is key, remember, Jace?" he said bitterly. "We can't let him continue."

## 44

*Corey has given Omnibus so much.* Victor's words played again in my mind. Corey's machine had sent the images on the tablet through time. Corey had interpreted the message. I longed to understand our relationship in the future.

"What kind of message does he want to send?" I finally asked.

"I don't know," Corey said, pacing away from the table in a small circle. "He has me looking at these test results because he wants to know how to make it work with older subjects. The problem is that I have no idea. It's going to take months of study to even understand the results."

"Why does he need an older subject? If he knows it works with a child, why hasn't he already sent his message back with one of the eight-year-olds?"

"He obviously wants to send the message back farther than eight years." I looked at him blankly. "That's one of the limitations of this form of time travel—the obstacle he's trying to overcome. The signals and memories he's transporting have a homing device: they find the body or technology that originated them. He can't send an eight-year-old's memories back more than eight years, and the images on the tablet couldn't be sent back to a date prior to the assembly of that specific tablet."

"So the tablet already existed, we just sent the memory on it back in time?" I tried to comprehend.

"Yes," Corey said, touching my hand as I tried to let it all sink in.

I thought about what Damien had told me about his mother in the airplane lavatory. My skin chilled.

"Damien thinks Victor wants you to help him save his wife," I said. Corey cringed when I said Damien's name. "She died in the World Trade Center."

He let go of my hand and stepped backward. "I don't know, Jace," Corey said, moving back to the table. "He had pieces of the puzzle long before 9/11. Look at this." He opened a smaller, faded green binder. "He has equations dating clear back to 1995." The binder was a dated journal, written on yellowing lined paper. I shuddered. The equations didn't mean anything to me, but the journal started while we were all in Sigonella.

My hair stood on end. I snapped the binder shut. "Corey, do you think that Victor could have been experimenting on children back then?" I looked out the window. The sky was becoming overcast. "In the early nineties, I mean?"

Corey looked at me. "I don't know," he said softly. "He didn't have the machine assembled back then, but he had most of the calculations for the chemicals needed."

My head began to throb again. I stepped away from the table and the uncomfortable brain fog toward the window. I could see the stream below us, winding away from the building until it disappeared into the horizon. The temperature must have dropped—heavy steam rose above the water.

I opened the binder with the profiles of the Filipino children again. I found the page with the beautiful six-year-old. *Memory loss— six months.* I turned the page. A seven-year-old boy. *Amnesia—three years.* I flipped another. *Permanent brain damage. Loss of motor skills and speech.*

"He did something to me," I said as I continued to look frantically through the pages, "when we lived in Sigonella."

Corey turned his full focus to me. "What do you mean?" His eyes flashed, and his brows came together.

"Did any of these subjects have lasting memory loss?" I asked. I hesitated before adding, "Up until this week, I had a dark spot in my memory—I couldn't remember most of kindergarten." I felt a rush telling him about it. "My parents even took me to a psychologist to try to help me."

Corey stepped toward me and put his hands on my waist, looking into my eyes. "And this was all around the time that you knew the Trents in Italy?"

I nodded.

"You said 'up until this week.' You're starting to remember?"

"I don't know when the first flash happened, but it's been coming back. Slowly," I said. I closed my eyes for a second. I could see the thick wooded path at Battle Creek. The light had come through the trees. The flash had happened just before I found the tablet.

"Are you okay?" Corey's voice was almost pained.

"Yeah, it's just a headache. It seems to go with the flashes of memory I'm having. It gets worse just before I have one."

Corey let go of me and flipped the page over on one of the profiles we had been looking at. "Look," he said. "Headaches, migraines, blurred vision, auras." He turned a few more pages frantically. "All of them," he said.

A robotic female voice eerily like the one on the tablet interrupted us loudly, "Please join Mr. Trent in the observatory on the tenth floor." The door slid open.

"I'm finally starting to understand," Corey said, ignoring the voice, "but why would he send you into the lion's den?"

"Who?"

"Your father," Corey said. "Why would he send you to work for Victor Trent, and how could he let you come here now?"

My eyes misted over. It was the very question that I wanted answered, but I felt irrationally defensive of my father. "Who told you that he sent me to Minnesota? Victor?"

Corey's eyes turned tender. He brushed away a tear that dropped onto my cheek. "Victor didn't tell me anything, Jace. Your father sent me to Minnesota too." His words didn't register. I couldn't speak. "He's been paying me to watch you and keep you safe for six years."

All of the blood rushed out of my head. I couldn't feel anything. Corey had been paid to watch me and keep me safe since freshman year? The ground groaned and shook again. I looked out the window at the angry, cloud-filled sky. It was even darker now. The clouds were moving rapidly. Clouds. I stepped away from Corey, trying to regain my composure. They weren't clouds. They were birds. Hundreds of them filled the sky. Flying north.

The voice came back on the intercom. "Please join Mr. Trent in the observatory on the tenth floor," she repeated.

"We have to get out of here," I breathed.

Corey looked back and forth between the binders on the desk and my desperate eyes. I watched him as he tried to formulate a plan. Had it been easy and natural to rely on Corey since the day I had found the tablet because I had somehow sensed that it was his job to protect me? Why had my father hired him? Was the Corey Stein from the tablet still being paid to protect me in the future? Did he care about me at all, or was I just a paycheck to him? I thought of how I had kissed him in the park. I had completely thrown myself at him. My heart ached.

I pushed those thoughts from my mind. None of that was going to help us now. We needed a plan. The tablet was supposed to tell us what to do. The J file was meant to have the answers. Corey still didn't know what was in it.

"Corey, the J file is images of my funeral," I blurted out. "I'm going to die."

His face became ashen. He stepped toward me and cupped my face softly in his hands. "No," he said firmly. "We can stop it." My eyes filled with tears. I felt the warmth in his gentle touch.

I shook my head. "I'm going to marry Damien," I declared, my eyes filled to overflowing. "I'm supposed to marry him. He's the little girl's father. I'm going to marry him, and I'm going to die." I choked back a sob.

"I know about Damien." Corey's shame-filled baritone struck my heart with a hammer. He cleared his throat and blinked hard. "I shouldn't have done it, but I didn't understand. It didn't seem fair. I couldn't lose you so quickly after finally being allowed to be close to you."

My pulse raced as he touched my shoulders. His eyes begged for forgiveness.

"What do you mean?" My lip quivered.

"The personal pictures. The name card. I . . . I wanted to have a chance. I didn't want you to know." He squeezed my shoulders. He might have expected anger, but I melted. I lifted the back of my hand to his cheek and brushed it across his dark stubble. He cared about me. My heart beat slow and steady. He closed his eyes and pulled me against him.

"Victor's right," I whispered. "We've manipulated our own past. This isn't how any of this was supposed to happen. The tablet is just as dangerous as his machine. We shouldn't have sent it back."

"What if it wasn't us, Jace?" he asked, stroking my hair. I pulled my face away from his shoulder. My heart stopped.

"I thought it had to be us. The code, the pocket watch—who else could it have been?" My confusion was overwhelming.

His eyes were cautious. "I don't know," he said. His eyes told a different story. They seemed to say, *I'm not sure if I should tell you.*

"Jace, I don't believe I could have sent those images in the personal file. Past, present, or future Corey Stein never would have included images that give Damien Trent an advantage." His eyes blazed as he continued, "He already has every advantage: his money, his perfect life, his looks—not that any of that matters to you more than the fact that it's what your father wants for you." I gasped for air. It rang true instantly, but it didn't make sense. My father was paying to protect me, but he sent me to Minnesota—straight into Damien's arms and Victor Trent's grasp.

"I know I'm in a hopeless situation, Jace. Your father has orchestrated and arranged everything. For some reason he wants you to be with Damien. But for what it's worth, I don't think he's best for you no matter what the tablet says. He has no idea who you are. He hasn't watched you kindly accumulate friends, constantly listening to their annoying problems but never discussing your own. He doesn't know and love your routine. Your music. Your runs. He hasn't seen you pore over books for hours on end to make it to the top of the class. He doesn't know your depth, your strong will, your intelligence. If it wasn't for your father, if he hadn't sent you, if Damien had appeared on your path at Stanford, you would have pushed him onto your long list of Instagram followers, just like every other man who ever approached you there."

My head felt like it might explode. I wanted to melt into Corey. The emotion in his voice erased any doubts I had about his feelings for me, but I realized that everything in my relationship with Corey had been orchestrated and manipulated by my father too. Everything was wrong.

"Do you know who dropped the tablet on my path?" I asked quietly, my eyes burning through Corey's.

He looked out the window for a moment before he looked at me again. "We both know who did." His strained apology ripped through me. My routine. My runs. I could suddenly picture Corey there waiting for me. Blinding me, then dropping it and running off in a direction that he knew I wouldn't follow. "But I had no idea what was on it. Your father didn't tell me anything except when and how to give it to you."

The voice called over the intercom again. This time she added "immediately" to the end of her request to join Victor on the tenth floor.

"We have to go," I said, breaking away.

"Do you have your phone?"

I pulled it out of my pocket and gave it to him.

"Do you trust me, Jace?" he begged, caressing my hand as I let go of the phone. My eyes filled again. I didn't understand anything, but I trusted him. I trusted him to get us away from Victor. I nodded.

"We are going to get out of here. I promise," he said. I shivered. "Go to the observatory. Stall Victor until I come. Ten minutes."

I took a deep breath. *In through the nose on a three count, out through the mouth.*

"We are going to stop this, Jace," he said. "I'm not going to let you die, and Victor isn't going to hurt anyone ever again."

45

I let go of Corey's hand and lumbered blindly through the open door into the hallway. The elevator seemed miles away. I listened to my heels click against the tile. I looked at the red-numbered doors as I passed.

I stepped slowly inside the elevator and pressed number ten. The doors slid shut and the lights dimmed. The doors swished open and revealed one enormous room. The wall opposite the elevator was stocked with medical equipment. Two long white gurneys sat in the center of the room, forming an L shape. Both gurneys had attached monitors, tubes, and wires. A pole for IVs stood between the gurneys, ready for use. Large, round adjustable lights hung from the ceiling above the beds.

In stark contrast to the ninth floor, the walls and ceiling were pure white. I walked around the elevator. The entire south wall was lined with tinted windows, providing a full panoramic view of the landscape with the mountain in the center. I walked toward it, wishing I could push through the glass and escape. It all looked too familiar. I could feel Victor's eyes on me from behind.

"Dr. Watts has given you a rough explanation of the memory transfer process." He was standing uncomfortably close to me. I spun around, my heart beating fast. "Tell me what you think of it all."

I didn't hesitate. "I don't think it's a good idea."

He cocked his head to the side and looked at me curiously. "What makes you say that?"

"Just a feeling," I said.

"That's good, Jace. I like that. You should trust your feelings. Go with your *gut*," he said, emphasizing the last word with a vocal punch.

He stepped away from me and touched a control panel near the gurneys. "You must admit that it's a beautiful thing," he said, looking upward. The ceiling buzzed and hummed as the ceiling tiles shifted and pulled away from the center, revealing a skylight that let in the cloud-choked sunlight from above.

"The process has been long and tedious, but in the past few years we've had many successes. The difficulty has always been trying to find candidates with the right brain chemistry. Trial and error." He smiled, taking a step toward the gurney. "We started out with adult subjects—that failed miserably, but it was a necessary step, and we were able to work out some of the dosing bugs." Victor touched a panel next to the gurney. The lights came on above the beds and the control panel lit up. One of the machines began to hum softly.

I gritted my teeth. "How far back were you able to send memories, and how could you tell if you were successful?"

"A very good question," he said, touching more buttons on the control panel. "Most of the subjects were only sent back a few hours or days at best. The scientific method didn't exactly apply. The results had to be measured before the experiment was performed. Otherwise they were invalid." Victor paused, tapping his fingernails on the controls.

"We taught the subjects something new just before sending the memories back. Like rats in a maze. If our attempt was successful, the subject would already know the answer to the maze before we taught it to them."

Victor could see my confusion. He reached into his pocket. "It was always very simple," he said. "Kind of a guessing game. The researcher would retrieve an item from his pocket, like I have just done, and then ask the subject to guess what was in his hand." I looked from his hypnotic blue eyes to his closed fist.

He tilted his head and shrugged his shoulders, waiting for me to play his guessing game.

"A rare coin." I whispered the words before I finished thinking them. Electricity coursed through my body. *Roman. Third century.*

Victor's eyes widened and oozed his pleasure. He opened his fist, revealing a misshapen, tarnished black coin. He held out his hand.

"It's Roman," he said, reaching for my hand and placing the coin in my palm. "Third century."

I turned the coin over and examined the figure and symbols imprinted on it. A heavy cloud formed in my mind. I had been here before. I had held this before. My head was ready to burst. I closed my eyes as hot tears bubbled to the surface. *Not déjà vu. Not Sigonella.* My hands dropped to my sides, and I felt Victor circle around close behind me, his warm breath on my neck. *Now.*

"Do you understand?" he unnervingly hissed softly in my ear.

I shuddered, nodding slowly. Victor hadn't done anything to me as a child. He was going to do it to me now, and it was going to work. "But why?" I asked.

"To give her a message."

I opened my eyes as he completed his circle. Standing uncomfortably close, he held my gaze, forcing a connection that I couldn't break.

"You'll never find her," I said vehemently.

"I already have." He reached up slowly and touched my neck where it met my collarbone. Tracing my arm all the way down to the palm that held the coin, he reached inside and took it from me.

A break in the clouds above us let the sun stream in momentarily, blinding me.

* * *

*I am sitting on a rug in the middle of a wooden floor, surrounded by crayons. My pigtail falls over my shoulder as I reach down to pick up the red one. I hear footsteps behind me, but the light streaming in through the window is blinding when I turn to see who it is.*

*"What an interesting picture, Jace," a lady's sweet voice sings. "What made you think of drawing it?"*

*She looks like an angel with the white light behind her. She touches my shoulder, kneeling down beside me. I finish coloring in the jagged lines while she watches me. "It's for you," I tell her.*

*She takes it from me hesitantly. "Thank you," she manages.*

*The paper flutters in her trembling hands. Painstaking details. The iconic city on an island with two buildings towering above the rest. Flames at the top of the towers. She blinks repeatedly, trying to remove the sting.*

*"Stay away from there," I tell her.*

* * *

Damien's voice brought me back to the present. "Who are you talking about?" He stepped out of the elevator and marched toward us. "What's going on?" He took in the scene—his father still standing unacceptably close to me, the gurney lit up and the equipment humming and beeping around us.

"I don't think Jace is feeling very well," Victor said with feigned concern. "You've lost all of your color. Why don't you lie down? I'll get you a drink." He put an arm around my back and tried to guide me toward the gurney, but I wouldn't move. I couldn't move. I was mentally paralyzed.

Damien reached us and stepped into his father's place, pushing Victor aside. "Are you okay?"

My heart raced and my body trembled as the floor beneath us shook again. My weak knees almost collapsed, but Damien supported me. "You'd better lie down," he said, walking me toward the gurney.

I could remember her fully now. Claire—radiant, soft, and kind. Long honey-colored hair parted in the middle. Sparkling blue eyes. Long, thick eyelashes. Clear skin glowing. No makeup. Pure, natural beauty.

I looked around for Victor.

"We have to leave, Damien. We have to go as soon as Corey comes," I whispered.

Damien looked away from me, and Victor was beside us again with a bottle of water.

"I'm afraid that is unacceptable, Jace," Victor said. "I thought you understood what must happen. I have spent years preparing for today."

I felt nauseated. I began to shiver. Damien put his arm around me. "What are you talking about? What have you done to her?"

"I haven't done anything yet," Victor said, returning to the computer panel near the gurney.

"He's going to send my memory back. Back to kindergarten. Back to Sigonella," I managed. Hearing myself say it cut through the headache momentarily and I felt in control of myself.

Damien's back stiffened. "How?" Damien turned toward his father. "Why?"

"I truly don't know how it works for her. She is an enigma.

255

Unfortunately, we have a very short window of opportunity. We won't have time to prove the answers to these questions."

"What is he talking about?" Damien asked me.

"I'm talking about how Miss Vega has managed to keep her mind as pure as a child," Victor answered, stepping toward the control panels again. He touched a button that dimmed the fluorescent lights in the room. The long panel of windows began to retract, revealing an enormous black circular patio. A rush of cool air hit us.

I breathed it in. My head stopped hurting. In the natural light, I could think. I closed my eyes.

The ground shook for almost twenty seconds. Damien held me tight as instruments and equipment around us clinked and shifted. With the window open, the sound was loud and eerie.

"What have you done?" Damien asked. "These earthquakes are getting stronger."

"The machine doesn't work without conduit," Victor replied. "Dr. Watts explained it sufficiently—it needs an active volcano. An eruption."

A strong breeze blew through the room.

\* \* \*

*A lightning bolt flashes, and I hear the thunder only a few seconds later. Damien sits next to me in the window seat with Herman. The rain begins pouring down. He's worried about her. I feel it. He won't leave the window.*

*"She's coming back," I say. "She would never leave you."*

*He nods his head. "I know that," he says, trying to look tough, but the next bolt of lightning makes him jump. A few seconds later, we see a set of headlights coming slowly around the corner. His face lights up. He jumps off the seat and stands by the door, waiting for her to ring the bell.*

*She won't look at me when my mom opens the door for her. She keeps a distance. She's afraid of me. It was too much—too many pictures.*

**46**

**D**amien stood up between me and his father. "Don't do this," he said. "You can't bring her back. She's gone."

Victor shook his head condescendingly. "Is that what you think I want, boy?" he calmly asked. "I don't want her. I only want what she took from me."

Victor switched on the light above the gurney. Another, shorter quake shook us. They were getting closer together. A jar of Q-tips fell from the shelf behind us onto the tile floor with a crash. The noise brought back the sharp pain in my temple. I pinched my eyes shut. The light started small, but it soon took over every inch of space in my mind.

\* \* \*

*The aura fades, and I am on a swing. He is pushing me, trying to teach me how to pump my legs. I know how to do it, but coordinating my leg and head movement is difficult. My miniature body is awkward.*

*"Jace, Claire Trent was showing me some of the pictures you've drawn for her. She thinks they're very detailed for a little girl your age." My father wants me to tell him about the drawings. This isn't the first time he has asked. I consider jumping off the swing to avoid lying again. "Where did you get the ideas for the pictures, mija?"*

*I don't answer right away. I want to hug him and tell him how much I love him, but he is already worried about me. He knows something is wrong. I wish I could stop Victor without his help. I'll tell him soon, but I want to let him enjoy my childhood as long as possible.*

*"I get the ideas from my dreams," I said quietly. "I know they're scary pictures. I won't draw them anymore."*

\* \* \*

The elevator doors opened again. Corey stumbled out first, pushed by the tattooed bodyguard from the park. I searched his face, trying to determine if he had gotten what he needed with my phone. The second bodyguard came out of the elevator with a gun aimed at Corey's back. My heart sank.

Victor stepped away from the controls toward the elevator. "So glad you could finally join us, Mr. Stein. I didn't want you to miss anything," he said menacingly. "Miss Vega has graciously agreed to test the machine for us."

I shook my head. It didn't matter that I hadn't agreed to it. It would happen. For me it already had.

"You're not going to do this. We're leaving," Damien said, pulling me up next to him.

Victor lifted his arm, signaling to the man with the gun. He came toward us. Damien let go of me, stepping between me and the gun.

"Get on with it," Victor ordered calmly. A deafening shot rang out. My body shook. Damien collapsed to the floor.

I screamed and dropped to Damien's side. Corey took several steps back toward the elevator. Damien was silent and still, and blood was beginning to pool around his left shoulder. I glared at Victor, who had already returned to whatever he was doing at the control panel.

"You are going to deliver my message, Jace, or everyone you care about is going to die," Victor said without looking up.

The room became silent. I couldn't hear the equipment or the wind anymore. "What message?" I asked.

I felt the sharp pain in my head again, accompanied by a ringing in my ears. I covered them and curled into a ball on the floor next to Damien.

\* \* \*

*They are leaving. I look out of the back window of the car as we pull up to their house. Boxes fill the carport. We walk up the path to deliver a basket of goodies my mom has put together and a nice note for Claire. I feel desperate. She has the pictures, but I have to tell her before she leaves. I am never going to see her again.*

*She invites us inside, giving my mom a tight hug and gushing gratitude for the basket. I keep my eyes on the floor until she kneels down and gives me a hug too.*

*"I'm going to miss you, Jace," she says softly, sincerely. I hug her tight. I have to tell her. No matter how crazy she thinks I am.*

*"Don't tell Victor that you know about the signal," I whisper in her ear. "He will kill you."*

I opened my eyes again slowly. Dizzy. The ringing slowly sub-sided. Damien began to moan softly.

*What was the signal?*

"You can't do this, Victor," Corey cried, his voice cracking. "She'll die!"

Victor had moved back to the control panel again. He looked at his watch before opening his mouth. "It hasn't worked on any of our adult subjects yet," Victor said and then coughed loudly, "but I think I finally understand why. We weren't exactly working with the cream of the crop in Manila. Perhaps there is something to the Inca's notion of sacrificing virgins to the Volcano God. Prostitutes certainly weren't getting us what we wanted."

"Why Jace?" Corey asked, frantic. "Why today? What is so important about doing all of this now? Why not give it some time? We can go to Manila. We can study the results. We know this is going to work eventually, so why rush it?"

Victor ignored his questions, turning back to me. "I'm sure you are nervous about what is going to happen and how it's all going to feel, Jace. Let me reassure you that you will feel nothing unpleasant or uncomfortable."

"Where are the adult subjects now, Victor? What happened to all of the failed experiments?" I wanted to hear him say it.

He didn't hesitate with his reply. "Most of them didn't make it. They were expendable."

"And none of them knew the answer to your maze before you annihilated their brains?" I asked, my voice becoming loud and shrill as burning, corroding disgust exploded inside me.

"No," he replied unapologetically.

"Then why continue with the experiment if you knew it was going to be unsuccessful?" I demanded.

"There is always something to be learned, even from a failed experiment." Victor looked up through the skylight at the sun and then down at his watch. Another tremor shook the ground, and I could hear the earth groaning beneath us.

"It's time to start the procedure, Jace. I hope you will be cooperative."

"I still don't understand your confidence," I said. "If I'm going to die or become a vegetable anyway, why should I help you? Why would I help you?"

Victor laughed. I knew his response before it boomed menacingly into the room. "You mean, why *did* you help me?" He took a step toward me, touching my cheek with his cold fingers. "I can only assume that you did it to save your friends, and maybe even to try to save Claire."

"How long have you known that you were going to do this to me? That you did this to me?" I corrected myself.

"My wife talked about you," Victor said. "She wouldn't tell me what you told her, but she said you were a strange child. She thought you had a sixth sense. She became very suspicious of me around that time. I'm sure I have you to thank for that." He moved closer to where Damien and I were still on the floor and crouched down next to me. "I know you're going to try to be clever and come up with your own plan, but I promise you that everything you do to try to sabotage my future will only hurt you and those you love, Jace.

"I am a very powerful man—more powerful than you know. I have been, and always will be, several steps ahead of your weak attempts." He raised his hand, stroking my loose hair as if I was a lap dog.

"Because of the signal?" I asked boldly. His hand tensed and immediately grabbed a handful of my hair, pulling forcefully and jerking my head backward.

"Because I have never been afraid to use the resources available to me to further my ambitions."

The ground rumbled again. He loosened his grip on my hair and looked toward the gurney.

"It's time," he said. He motioned to the tall bodyguard, who grabbed my arm and pulled me to my feet. Corey must have tried to come to my aid too; Tui was holding him with his arms behind his back.

The bodyguard shoved me down on the gurney.

"You will be surprised at how simple and fast this process is. A lifetime full of memories will be copied in just a few short minutes. But before we begin, I want to make you an offer. I am giving you the opportunity to change your past, to change your mistakes. You can use your knowledge and experience to avoid unpleasant things. You can become powerful."

He took a deep breath of the mountain air, flaring his nostrils. "Lie down," he said. I looked at the bodyguard and obeyed. "You have a choice, Jace. You can use all of this to your advantage and deliver my message, or you can die."

I looked back at Corey. My heart pushed so hard against my chest that I thought it would break through. This was it. I was either going to allow Victor to continue like a helpless animal, or I was going to fight him and run for it. The ringing started again and intense shooting pain enveloped my entire skull.

\* \* \*

*My father thumbs through the pictures slowly. She has put them neatly in a three-ring binder. His face is not worried or disappointed. I only see fascination.*

*Looking over his shoulder, I see the crayon drawing of the simple red and black symbol, the circle inside the triangle. He traces his finger over the shapes before turning to the next drawing. The Washington Monument and the Lincoln Memorial with the strange buildings between them is so detailed. I spent hours on it. He doesn't take his eyes off the symbol on the Washington Monument.*

*He turns the page. His brows furrow. It is a volcano with an enormous black cloud above it.*

*"Is this Mount Etna, mija?"*

*I touch both of his cheeks and look in his eyes. "It's Mount Hood." He smiles, confused and a bit uncomfortable. He turns the picture over, revealing the next.*

*My art skills are marginal, but the detail is impressive: A long black helicopter just to the right of an even larger smoke cloud. Flames spewing from the mouth of the volcano lap at the helicopter.*

\* \* \*

The bodyguard began to shake me when I didn't respond to Victor the first time he called my name. I couldn't move. The pain in my head and ringing in my ears crushed me. Trying to focus on the bright light above me, I was slowly able to push the ringing aside. The world came back into focus, and I realized that Victor had taken my incapacitation as an opportunity to have my wrists and ankles strapped to the gurney.

My father knew everything. My eyes filled with blinding tears. He had known everything since I was a child. He had believed me. The running, the training, everything he had taught me was for this. He had made me strong. He would come for me. It was the plan. I could feel it.

I watched Victor for a moment. He had moved back to the control panel. Something he did caused a reflective panel outside the open windows to rotate, optimizing its exposure to the sun. His face was serious but elated. A large section of floor tiles near the window folded in on themselves, and a platform rose up, revealing the machine from the schematics on the tablet.

*Stall,* I thought.

"Did you ever love her?" I asked.

He only smiled. "She gave me more pleasure than anything else, once."

"And what about Damien?"

He threw his hand in the air, waving off my question. He picked up the tablet from the control panel. The glowing green light calmed me momentarily. "You have already changed all of this," he said. "The images you deleted are gone forever. Damien and I will never stand together to save the country or the United Nations now. You have changed everything, and for what purpose?"

"To stop you and your lunacy," Corey answered from across the room. The bodyguard pulled his arms harder until it looked like his shoulders would separate from his body.

"Is this how you planned to stop me?" Victor asked, lifting the tablet above his head. "It seems to be too little too late, doesn't it?" My pulse raced. Victor smashed the tablet hard against the floor. The glass shattered, scattering shards everywhere.

Moving away from the control panel, Victor came toward me. He adjusted the tubes and wires that connected the gurney to the machine. Glass crunched under his shoes with each step. He stopped next to the gurney and reached underneath the head of it. He pulled a metal halo over the top of my head and placed it against my forehead and collarbone. My entire body tingled when the metal touched my skin. He secured the halo with metal bolts, twisting them until they pinched slightly against my temples.

The earth rumbled slow and deep. I looked at the crest of the mountain from the corner of my eye. A large cloud of vapor was forming above it. Victor's breath was hot and sticky against me as he continued to tighten the screws.

"How long do I have?" I pleaded.

"It won't be long now." He plunged an IV needle into a vein in the inside of my right elbow. "You'll begin to relax soon."

Control was slipping away. I couldn't stall Victor forever. Rescue was late. Victor was going to send my memories back. Everything that I had become as a twenty-five-year-old woman would become part of my six-year-old mind. Victor was robbing me of my childhood. Again.

A tear slid out of each eye down the sides of my face and into my ears. The pictures I had shown Claire, my father's plan—all of it had still brought me to this point.

"If this doesn't kill me, what's next, Victor?" I asked, my speech slow and slightly slurred.

"That's the beautiful thing, Jace. If the procedure doesn't kill you, the blast from the volcano certainly will." He stood beside me, looking up at the solar panel. "If you decide to cooperate, I will take you with me. I will take care of you and rehabilitate you."

"Rehabilitate me?" I said, barely able to keep my heavy lids open.

"You will most likely suffer a small stroke. All of the children that we sent back showed varying symptoms, but most recovered fully. Eventually." He scratched his chin, lost in his own thoughts.

My body felt heavy and my mind foggy. Victor's words became garbled. He sounded like he was at the far end of a tunnel. I struggled to stay inside my head. Victor shined a small flashlight into my eyes, bringing me back momentarily.

"You seem to be responding very quickly," he observed. He hung a second bag on the pole above me and hooked it into the line on my arm. Sadness overtook me. Maybe my father wasn't coming. I was alone. I couldn't control the steady stream of tears that poured out of my eyes. I closed them. I was immediately greeted by the sharp mental image of the little girl on the satin pillow, her face hollow and empty amid her silky blonde curls.

Victor stepped back to the control panel and entered a sequence of numbers. The world slowed down. Drip, drip. All I could focus on was the steady drip of the IV from the second bag. I could hear it pouring into my veins. Energy began to seep back into me. As drip after drip fell, my clouds dispersed and floated away. My senses heightened. The sky that shone through the clouds was unearthly blue. It almost burned my eyes. The earthy smell of soil and grass filled the room. Was I really smelling something that was so far away, or were the drugs making me hallucinate? Suddenly, the grassy smell was replaced by the overwhelming scent of sulfuric gases. My heart raced.

I heard another rumble begin before I felt it. The tremor was strong enough to set the gurney and all of its attached wires shaking. The pain in my head returned forcefully, but the ringing in my ears changed. It became a shrill, high-pitched screech. My hands seized upward, trying to cover my ears, but the restraints pinched and bruised my wrists. The bright light, the sharp pain, and the deafening scream in my ears were too much for my stomach. It began convulsing, and its contents pushed their way into my mouth, choking me as I tried to spit them out. I tried to turn my head right and left, but the screws that held the halo in place prevented any motion.

I inhaled some of the bile and began sputtering and choking. The ringing in my ears grew louder. Finally noticing my distress, Victor turned back to me from his control panel. My eyes blurred with water and my body twisted and jerked, fighting against the restraints. Victor came to me calmly and retrieved a suctioning tool from above the head of the gurney. He efficiently suctioned the content of my mouth, and I was able to cough out the rest.

The rumbling continued. Victor hurried back to the controls as I continued coughing. The whining blazed on. I finally squinted my eyes closed, praying that the pain would stop soon. The sun shifted and projected the full warmth of its rays on my face.

\* \* \*

*Brightness envelopes me. I stand in a beautiful room with floor-to-ceiling mirrors in front of and behind me. I am standing on a gray stone pedestal. Dramatic, tall, sheer curtains hang on the windows to both sides of me. Sunlight filters through, catching the crystal chandelier and creating rainbow patterns on my simple white dress.*

*The woman with the scarred, disfigured face comes out from behind the curtains. Love streams out of her eyes as she walks toward me. She steps onto the pedestal and places a crown of white lilies and baby's breath over my soft curls. She doesn't speak; she only nods her head toward my reflection.*

*She places her hand on my right shoulder and her chin on my left. I am overwhelmed as our beauty is repeated infinitely in the angled mirrors. Claire.*

\* \* \*

"Jacc, the process is almost complete. I'll be leaving very soon. It's time for you to decide if you'll help me. Will you deliver my message and take your place in my family? The little girl doesn't have to disappear. You can still give her life."

"You already know that I didn't deliver your message; I won't do it," I said. I felt fully aware and myself again. Adrenaline pumped through my veins. I didn't fully understand what his message or the signal were, but I knew that I hadn't ever considered giving him what he wanted. Only my father knew everything.

Victor stood close, watching my eyes. His brow furrowed as he observed, "You think you understand what it all means, but you are only seeing glimpses," he said. "You started something almost twenty years ago that I am going to finish right now. It doesn't matter that you won't deliver my message. I will find her and you'll both die shortly." He motioned to Tui. I could barely see him pushing Corey forward out of the corner of my eye.

A rush of wind blasted us, and I could hear the rhythmic sound of helicopter blades above us. A tremendous quake began just as the chopper touched down on the roof. The shrill noise returned, but my head didn't ache in response. The chemicals in my system seemed to be blocking the pain while enhancing my senses. The solar panel above us tilted again, allowing the overhead sun to stream down, full-force, into my eyes. I pinched them shut.

\* \* \*

*I am in the empty house again. Claire is still hugging me. She doesn't let go for several seconds. She's trembling a little. She finally pushes me away when she realizes how awkward the moment is for my mom.*

*"Bridget, you have no idea what your friendship has meant to me here," she says softly with tears in her eyes.*

*"Please stay in touch, Claire," responds my mom. "We're going to miss you so much." The two women embrace. I feel desperate. Does she believe me? Will she do what she needs to in order to protect herself?*

*"I have something for you, Jace." She walks around the corner into the kitchen. My mom looks down at me with a sweet smile. Her eyes are misty. When Claire comes back, she's carrying the thick black binder.*

*"These are all of the pictures Jace has drawn for me. I want her to show them to you." She doesn't believe me. She thinks I am crazy. She wants my parents to know. My heart drops.*

*She kneels down to my level again and takes both of my hands, "Jace, you are special. You have a gift. Thank you for sharing it with me. You have changed my life." She squeezes my hands meaningfully three times while keeping intense eye contact. I smile at her. She does believe me. She's going to help me—and herself.*

*I take the binder from her. She hugs my mom again before we walk back to our car. She stands in the doorway, watching until we disappear. Safely in the backseat, with my mom's eyes on the road, I open the binder and turn to the third page.*

*It is drawn with crayons, but I didn't do it. The simple picture of a man sitting at a desk wearing exaggeratedly large headphones has been painstakingly drawn. There's too much detail on the shortwave radio that he is plugged into to be accidental. The brand name, National Panasonic, is written in white crayon in the bottom left-hand corner. All of the buttons and knobs are labeled accurately, and the tuning dial includes all of the lines and numbers. The arrow is pointing to a line directly between 140 and 150.*

49

The noise of the helicopter replaced the ringing in my ears as soon as Victor's bodyguard slapped my cheek. The ground continued to rumble and I could feel Victor's desperation.

"This is your last chance to save yourself, Jace. You're all going to die here unless you can give me compelling evidence that you have delivered my message and that you have what I want."

Corey was standing at the head of the gurney now in an awkward hunched-over position. I could see his face, but the rest of his body was hidden. He was in pain. He must have struggled with Tui. His forehead was bruised, and a little bit of blood was trickling out of his right nostril. He was breathing hard. Damien groaned on the floor.

Victor directed Tui to go to the helicopter. The rumbling got progressively louder. Victor leaned into my ear.

"Tell me where it is," he demanded.

"I don't know. I can't remember," I yelled above the noise of the helicopter. He had to be looking for the shortwave radio Claire had drawn. She must have figured out what he was receiving the signal on. I thought of the green binder and my memories—the room with the radio. The man scratching notes on a paper. I had seen Victor receiving messages from the future. I shivered and my skin stayed prickled with goose bumps. It began to make sense. If he needed the same device in the future and the past to send and receive messages, stealing or destroying the device would stop it. I listened to the crunch of the tablet's glass under Victor's feet as he backed away from me.

The mountain rumbled and moaned again. Another, larger puff of ash and steam billowed above the peak. A red light began to blink on a panel near the light above me. I couldn't give him what he wanted. Maybe my not remembering the details of the plan was to prepare me for this very moment.

Victor looked at the peak of the volcano and retreated toward the helicopter. He turned back one last time.

"You'll be seeing me again very soon, Jace," he yelled. "If you make a better choice, perhaps we won't meet like this the next time around." Without another word, he ran to the helicopter. I watched him close the door as the chopper lifted off the roof and away from the building. It was out of sight in a few seconds.

We were alone with the ground trembling and moaning beneath us. It was coming. *The next time around.* I closed my eyes and saw the crayon picture of Mount Hood in full eruption. The screw by my temple pinched as the crayon melted into a stark mental image of what was coming: Flames. Smoke. Ash. Lava.

"We don't have much time, Corey!" I yelled frantically above the rumbling. "My father is coming for us. He knew all of this was going to happen. He has a plan."

"How could his plan be letting this happen to you?" Corey asked, touching the halo with one hand. I looked up at him. His eyes seemed to bleed confusion and anger.

"I don't know how much of it was his plan and how much was mine. He's been working from crayon drawings and things that I told him when I was in kindergarten. Victor wasn't experimenting on me then—he's sending me back now. It's going to work, Corey."

"Jace, this doesn't make sense. Everything I've looked at, everything he's shown me tells me that what he's doing to you is going to kill you."

"Maybe it is," I said, "but it's going to work. I told Claire and my father about all of this. I told Claire about the World Trade Center. About 9/11."

"If this works, if he is sending your memories back in time, then how do you explain the pictures on the tablet?"

The trembling of the ground increased. I dug my fingernails into my palms as my body trembled too. Corey was right. Light filled my mind. The tablet. The J file. Could its purpose have been to tell me that this wasn't my time to die? *The next time around.* I couldn't comprehend it, but I felt hope. If we had sent ourselves pictures from the future, that meant that my future wasn't supposed to end today.

"We have to get out of here," I said.

He pulled up his right hand until a handcuff clinked against the metal bar. I shifted my eyes to the bag of fluid dripping above me. It was almost empty.

"Both hands?" I asked. He showed me his free left hand.

"Can you reach the control panel?" I demanded.

"I'll try," Corey said, already moving toward it. He moved the cuff along the bed rail and stretched his left side as far as he could toward the panel. He could just reach the edge of it, but couldn't manipulate any of the buttons.

"Give me a second," he said. He walked as far around the left side of the gurney as his cuffed hand would allow. I could hear the glass from the tablet crunching under his feet. With his arms crossed awkwardly, he threw himself into the gurney, moving it forward a few inches. He stepped back and shoved it again.

Each inch of progress toward the control panel dug the screws from the halo deeper into my temples. The pain should have been excruciating, but I didn't cry out. He had to reach the panel. Six pushes and then Corey came back around the head of the bed to the right side of the gurney again, stretching his arm toward the controls. He could just barely touch the buttons on the left side of the panel.

"It has two series of numbers and a timer," he said urgently. "It's counting down, and we have just over five minutes left."

I could hear my heart beating, calm and steady. My stomach was relaxed, and my mind was clear. I smiled. Where was the anxiety that this news should have caused? I looked up at the skylight and waited for the rays to break through the clouds. I didn't have to think about how to breathe. I could feel my shoulders rising and falling against the padded shoulder piece on the halo.

The light came through slowly, but it warmed my face fully after a few seconds. I closed my eyes and focused on the pins in my temples. *Find answer how inside fruitful meadow.* My name was Vega too.

\* \* \*

*I am strapped to a gurney in a bright, white room. The blades of a helicopter deafen me, but the wind they create makes me feel like I am already flying. I can't see Corey behind me, but I know he is there. I turn my head as far as I can and look down at the floor, but Damien is gone. The floor is clean.*

*"Say the numbers again," Corey says calmly. "43 15 13 02."*

*I repeat the numbers back to him slowly, then I begin the second set. "43 03 07 11."*

*He steps away from the panel. His shoes strike against the clean white tile until he is at my side. His bright blue eyes smile reassuringly at me, and he touches my cheek softly. The sleeve of his lab coat brushes against my neck.*

*"You don't have to do this," he says, looking away from me.*

*"I know."*

*"I still love you," he says, pulling my eyes to his. "That's never going to change."*

*I close my eyes. Hearing him say it warms me. He still loves me, even after everything I've put him through. I desperately want to tell him that I still love him too, but I can't. It will hurt too much.*

*"Are you ready, Jace?"*

\* \* \*

"Jace." Corey stood over me and shook me. "Talk to me. Stay with me."

The room came back into focus. Damien was on the floor. The room trembled. I looked up at the mountain. The dome must have blown while I had my eyes closed. An ash cloud was billowing upward, filling the sky. Darkening the sun.

Victor's machine came to life, rotating upward toward the eruption.

"How much time is left?" I asked.

Corey rushed back to the control panel. "Forty-five seconds."

"I need you to change the numbers."

"Why? We have no idea what they mean or what it will do to you." Corey was frantic.

"I don't have time to explain, Corey. Your machine works. I'm remembering the future. You told me what to change the numbers to. That has to mean I'm not going to die. Please trust me." This was more than a feeling or an impression. This was more certain than the coin in Victor's pocket. This wasn't just part of the plan. This *was* the plan.

Corey hesitated. "Even if these numbers send you forward instead of back, it's going to cause damage, Jace. Every case did."

"But I'm going to live."

The rumbling began again. This time I could hear a distant noise along with the squealing in my head—stones rolling and crashing against each other.

"Okay," he yelled in desperation. "What do I change them to?"

He entered both sets of numbers almost as quickly as I gave them to him. The noise increased as the sunlight shifted and the solar panel compensated.

The last drip fell from the bag into my IV. A jolt of electricity coursed through me, pulling me up and away from the bed. My body went numb, but my eyes stayed wide open.

Corey stood with his arm stretched out to the control panel, watching the clock tick down to zero. He looked at me, his dismay visible. The trembling increased and the sound of the landslide was deafening. I felt completely calm.

In one massive explosion, the cap of the mountain blew again. The initial blast moved away from us, but I knew that the pyroclastic flow would devastate everything for miles within a few minutes. I saw the terror in Corey's face.

Victor's machine took on a life of its own, directing the rays of the sun from the solar panel in a narrow beam. The beam disappeared into the volcanic ash. In another pyrotechnic display, the beams made contact with three large explosions, sending the cloud swirling in an almost perfect cylinder straight upward as far as I could see.

"Jace!" Corey yelled, pointing to the trees. The sounds of the exploding volcano camouflaged a second helicopter coming up over the hill. I turned back to the ash cloud. It was still moving down the hill away from us, but I felt the ground rumbling again. Another eruption was coming.

The world slowed down and became dim. The sun was choked out by the ash cloud. The initial upward explosion would come raining down on us soon. The helicopter hovered over the balcony. Three men in uniforms jumped out before it set down completely and they came running toward us, pulling heavy metal cords attached to the helicopter. Leo Belitrov suddenly stood over me.

"I have to detach the halo!" he yelled to the other man, who hoisted Damien over his shoulder and ran back to the balcony, disappearing into the helicopter. The third man picked up the shattered remains of the tablet. Leo began loosening the pins. The halo was the only connection between the gurney and the machine.

"Climb onto the gurney," Leo commanded Corey. "Try to center yourself and hold on tight." Corey jumped onto the gurney, straddling my chest, and held onto the rails on both sides of me. Leo attached the cables from the helicopter to the rails on the head of the gurney as we heard another massive explosion.

I struggled to keep consciousness. The helicopter lifted off, pulling the gurney toward it until the wires connecting the halo to the machine were stretched to capacity. The last pin dug painfully into my skull. Finally, Leo loosened the bolt enough to release the halo. It snapped back toward the machine like a slingshot, and the helicopter continued upward. Corey clung to the rails, and the gurney tilted precariously against the support of the cables.

Leo became a smaller and smaller dot on the balcony as we ascended. Our altitude revealed a red, triangular metal sculpture framing the black circular patio—Omnibus.

"Leo!" I tried to scream his name, but it came as a raspy cry. He looked up at me and saluted. Tears sprang into my eyes. *He'll never become a citizen.* If I knew that his life would end this way, why hadn't I drawn a picture of it so my father could stop it?

The ash cloud expanded—raging toward us. The helicopter was just above the trees now. Full momentum pushed us forward and away from the volcano. The gurney spun and rocked. I lost perspective. Distortion. Fishbowl. The ash cloud was almost on top of us. I couldn't see or feel Corey pressing against me anymore. *Where is he?* I struggled to try to look for him but I couldn't see anything. *Did he fall? I can't breathe.* The helicopter sounded far away.

I took a deep breath and held it, waiting to be enveloped by the searing, burning cloud.

50

He thumbs slowly through all of the pictures again. We have gone over them many times. I've told him everything.

"I have a plan, mija." Daddy looks confident, but he's hesitant to tell me everything. "I have a friend who can help Claire disappear, and if you're right about this, we know exactly when to make it happen. We're going to find a way to get our hands on that radio, and they'll both disappear."

I'm conflicted. How much should my father stop? Should he warn the government about the terrorist attacks? The weight of my responsibility exhausts me. My mind is fully adult, but my six-year-old body and brain still have limitations. My father looks at me sympathetically. It has taken him several days to understand who I really am and see me that way. I wish I could tell him that he would have his little girl back soon, but I know it would be a lie. She is gone forever. I have taken her from him.

"Do you trust me?" he asks quietly. I nod my head without hesitation. "Then let me take care of Claire. Let me take care of everyone." I think about my mom. I haven't told him about what is going to happen to her. Should I tell him? Should he try to stop it?

I think about Victor's invitation to join him, his prompting to change the unpleasant things in my past. As much as I want to save my mom, I know that I can't do it without unimaginable cost. I can't follow Victor down his path to artificial perfection and power. I have to resist. Don't deviate from the plan.

"Daddy, I need your help," I tell him. "I need you to help me find a way to forget all of this. I need to have a normal childhood without these memories."

*He strokes my long, curly hair. "We'll find a way, mija."*

\* \* \*

I gasped for air like I had just come up from a deep dive. A mask covered my face. I couldn't feel anything from the waist down. I opened my eyes, but I only saw a large white drape in front of me. It seemed like I was still on the gurney, but the helicopter had disappeared. I was somewhere inside now. I tried to look around, but a blinding overhead light made it difficult to see anything. I heard a steady beeping in the background and another strange noise. It sounded like two balloons rubbing together repeatedly and in rhythm. The rhythm was much faster than the beeping.

My entire body tensed up, and the rate of both noises increased. *Was I injured on the helicopter? Am I in a hospital? Did I lose my legs?* I panicked, not knowing where I was or what was going to happen next. I felt nauseated. My temples throbbed where the screws had pressed into my skin.

My body relaxed again, and the beeping and rubbing noises returned to a slower rate. I heard muffled voices in the background. I tried to speak. *Where's Corey? Is Damien okay?* My attempts to ask questions were muffled by the oxygen mask that covered my mouth and nose. I needed to let someone know that I was awake.

"Help!" I screamed as loud as I could. I heard the shuffling of feet and felt people swarming around me. Someone below the drape picked up my hand, feeling my wrist for my pulse. Strange, since the beeping monitor seemed to be in rhythm with my heart rate.

I felt someone above my head and to my left. When I looked up, I was greeted by Claire's familiar scarred face. Relief washed over me. *She's alive.* She moved the oxygen mask away from my face.

"Just relax, Jace. You're doing beautifully."

"Where's Corey?" I ask. "Is he okay?"

Claire looked puzzled for a second. "Corey is fine. He's with your father in Washington." Her voice was soothing.

"What about Damien? Did you get to him in time?"

"Damien will be back soon. He's changing his clothes." My anxiety grew as I tried to grasp what was happening.

My body tensed again, and the beeping increased. It was difficult to breathe, and I felt tremendous pressure throughout my numbed torso.

"How long have I been out?" I asked as soon as the seizure subsided.

"Not long," she reassured me.

"Claire?" I asked tearfully.

"Yes, dear?" She gently stroked my brow.

"Where are we?"

She laughed softly. "Shhh," she whispered. "Everything is going to be just fine. Damien will be back soon."

My body seized up again. The beeping sped up, but the scratching noise slowed down.

"Don't hold your breath," Claire directed. I breathed in slowly through my nose and then let the air out with a slow hissing noise.

I heard the door open and the sound of footsteps approach the bed.

"Is she awake?" Damien asked his mother.

"Yes," she replied. "She is a little bit out of it. Whatever they gave her earlier to help her relax must have been strong."

He walked over to the head of the bed. He was wearing a surgical gown and cap. Claire placed the oxygen mask back over my face. I tried to relax, but another seizure hit.

"Are you ready?" Damien asked me softly.

"Is it serious?" I asked through the mask.

He smiled. "It will only take a few minutes. You're going to be fine."

"Will I be completely out?" I asked, realizing how ironic it was to be nervous about anesthesia, considering the strange cocktail Victor had just poured into my veins.

"No," he answered, "but you won't feel anything. They promised me."

My bed lifted up and began rolling toward the door. Damien followed right behind, and Claire's footsteps tapped behind him. The noise in the hallway distracted me. People were talking in the distance, and I heard several monitors humming and beeping. A loud ping alerted the hall that an announcement was beginning on the PA system. A voice rattled off a happy message in a strange French accent. She spoke so quickly that I could only understand a few words. It sounded like she was wishing someone a happy birthday.

I desperately wished I could ask Damien to fill in the details about the eruption and our rescue, but I would have to wait until after the procedure to get answers. How many people were impacted by the eruption? How many died? I could only imagine how Damien felt with his father at the heart of the devastation.

My body tensed again for almost a full minute. Did I suffer a stroke like Victor said? Was that what was causing these seizures? Damien watched the monitors as they sped up. I wished someone would take the mask off of me. I couldn't think. I couldn't breathe. Damien smiled reassuringly at me.

They wheeled the gurney through a set of double doors. One of the nurses covered my hair with a blue hair net. A doctor and a nurse approached the table on either side. I heard the doctor ask for a scalpel. My heart rate increased on the monitor. *What happened to me?* My neck began to tingle as I realized that I had been here before too. I had remembered this scene in Victor's office—the drape in front of me, the mask over my face—all of it.

Damien was standing on my side of the drape, but he couldn't seem to stop himself from peeking around to the doctor's view periodically. Why would they let him come in for the surgery? I couldn't feel anything, but the thought of being awake while they cut me open suddenly became horrifying.

"I want to be put to sleep." My voice was muffled by the oxygen mask.

Damien looked at me and laughed. "Don't you want to be awake for this? Don't be nervous. They've done this thousands of times."

I wanted him to go away. I wanted my father here with me, not Damien.

"Can't we wait until my father gets here?" I asked desperately. Damien wasn't even looking at me. His eyes were fixed on the doctors and whatever they were about to do to me.

"You're just going to feel some pressure," the doctor said. I didn't realize that they had already cut me open. I felt the pressure that he was talking about in my lower abdomen. Why on earth would Damien think that I wanted to be awake for this? The doctor seemed to be pulling out my intestines. I felt light-headed.

"Here she is," the doctor said. A baby began to wail. Damien took a step toward the doctors, his eyes full of tears.

**END BOOK ONE**

# Discussion Questions

1. If you could change one thing in your past, would you do it? What would you change?

2. Jace uses different coping mechanisms including sticking to a routine and breathing techniques to control her stress. How do you cope with stress, disappointment, and tragedy in your life?

3. Have you ever experienced déjà vu? How did it feel? Did you let the scene play out as you "remembered" it, or did you do something different to make the feeling go away?

4. Jace prefers social media to face-to-face interaction because she can portray a life that seems better than what she actually has. In what ways does your social media portray the reality or alternate reality of your life?

5. Jace struggles to understand the difference between chemical attraction and real feelings with Damien and Corey. How have you been able to discern the difference?

6. What makes a person trustworthy? What actions made you trust or distrust Damien, Corey, and Jace's father?

7. Because of her obsession with the tablet and learning about the future, Jace chooses to have the chip implanted. What

are you obsessed with and what do you choose to sacrifice, perhaps unwisely, to feed that obsession?

8.  Do you think Damien is truly on Jace's side? Or is he manipulating her for his father or for some other purpose? What clues in the book led you to that conclusion?

9.  Do you think Jace's time travel and choices at the end changed the future she saw on the tablet? Did she break Omnibus's powerful hold? Why or why not?

# About the Author

Adrienne Quintana is the second of nine children born to professional oil artist John Horejs and his wife and business partner, Elaine. She spent her early years playing on the banks of the Snake River in southern Idaho while her father built a geodesic dome house. When the family wasn't traveling around the country to art shows, Adrienne spent many happy hours reading in her unfinished, tent-like bedroom. The love of reading soon blossomed into a desire to write. If the family's antiquated computer could be resurrected today, a collection of short stories involving local characters and their epic battles with fire-breathing dragons would be sure to entertain.

After completing her high school studies via correspondence, Adrienne studied music education at Mesa Community College. She took an eighteen-month break to serve a church mission in Montreal, Canada, where she gained invaluable life experiences and a few pounds from the local delicacies. After the completion of her mission and a month abroad in Europe, Adrienne moved to Utah with the intention of continuing her education at Brigham Young University, but these plans were short lived when she met her husband-to-be while working at an investment company. Soon after their marriage, the Quintanas packed up and moved to Minnesota, where Adrienne worked while her husband earned a law degree.

After four children and a move to Arizona, Adrienne completed her bachelors of science and communication at the University of Phoenix. In the throes of housekeeping, potty-training, and carpooling, Adrienne discovered that she could find time to accomplish her goals—often in the quiet hours after the children were in bed. Since her graduation in 2012, those quiet moments have been used to fulfill a lifelong dream of becoming a writer.